A
BEGINNER'S
GUIDE TO
FREE FALL

ALSO BY THE AUTHOR

Thank You, Goodnight: A Novel

A BEGINNER'S GUIDE TO FREE FALL

A Novel

ANDY ABRAMOWITZ

LAKE UNION
PUBLISHING

Published by Lake Union Publishing, Seattle

www.apub.com

Amazon, the Amazon logo, and Lake Union Publishing are trademarks of Amazon.com, Inc., or its affiliates.

ISBN-13: 9781542014656 (hardcover)
ISBN-10: 1542014654 (hardcover)

ISBN-13: 9781542014663 (paperback)
ISBN-10: 1542014662 (paperback)

Cover design and illustration by Kimberly Glyder

Printed in the United States of America

This one's for the girls—
for Chloe and Chelsea

and for Caryn, of course

I never thought much of the courage of a lion tamer.
Inside the cage he is at least safe from other men.

—*George Bernard Shaw*

CHAPTER 1

Four months from now, on a secluded beach in Turkey, Davis Winger, who came thousands of miles to start over, will drop his towel and paperback on the sand, wade into the sea, and end up under the tire of a Hyundai that has just come screeching over an embankment. He will be trapped under that car, pinned to the seabed with one final breath crowding his lungs. Time enough to lament that his daughter might now grow up without him; that he might never hear words of forgiveness from the woman he adored, and betrayed; that he might not live to build the roller coaster that his six-year-old had dreamed up from a storybook and that he had spent the summer engineering into reality. Constructing that ride, harnessing his daughter's giddy vision into a set of blueprints, was his best shot at winning back the people he loved and hurt and lost. The promise of redemption was slipping away. All alone and far from home, he'll reach for the surface as the sea encloses.

That autumn day was coming. But today it was still spring, a mild Saturday in May, and when Davis awakened next to his wife in the charmingly overgrown Baltimore neighborhood of Mount Washington, he was still gainfully employed and still welcome in his own home. He planted a kiss on Britt's cheek, then crept out of bed for the weekly bagel run. On the drive, he called Molly.

"Hi, sister," he said.

"Hi, brother," Molly said.

"I've got one."

She paused. Sometimes it took her a minute. "Okay. Let's hear it."

"It's really good."

"I have no doubt."

He cleared his throat. "Here goes. It's a store that sells concert T-shirts, but the twist is that the shirts are only of bands you'd be too embarrassed to see."

"Interesting," Molly reflected. "You buy them, but you can't wear them because it'd be too humiliating."

"Exactly. We're talking about Spin Doctors tees, Culture Club tees. Nobody's wearing Culture Club apparel in public."

"Nor, I would hope, in private," Molly said.

"Yeah. In private is worse," Davis agreed.

"So we'd sell Sheena Easton?"

"Naturally."

"Hanson?"

"Without question. We'd stock The Outfield, Bell Biv DeVoe, Julian Lennon—forgive me, John."

"We wouldn't make a single sale," Molly said.

"Not a one, but what do you expect when your inventory consists of Jack Wagner gear?"

"Ouch," said Molly. "Not Jack."

"Sorry. Business is business."

"So, like, Styx?"

"No, not like Styx," Davis said.

"I see. In other words, you own a Styx shirt."

"I did. Britt may have accidentally tossed it."

"I'm sure it was by accident. Well, brother, this is definitely going nowhere. It's a very bad business idea."

"I know." Davis smiled at the oncoming road. Spring had made a garden path of it, with cherry blossoms weeping like a fall of snow. "Now you," he said.

"Hmm. Okay. I've been saving this one, but I think its time has come. Are you ready?"

"I'm not sure I am."

"It's a store called Closed," Molly said.

Davis paused. "That's the name of the store? Closed?"

"Yup."

"So, just to be clear, hanging in the window is a sign that reads Closed."

"What else would it read?"

He smiled. "That, Molly Winger, is just plain awful."

"Isn't it, though?"

"I'm so proud of you."

"Thanks," she said. "You don't know how much that means to me."

"Oh, I think I do."

"Bye, brother."

"Bye, sister."

CHAPTER 2

His hands reached for the sky, hers gripped the bar for dear life. Higher and higher they climbed, the mechanical crank hoisting them into thin vertigo.

"Are you sure I'm old enough?" Rachel asked, trepidation stiffening her every muscle.

"Doesn't matter. You're tall enough," Davis yelled back over the grinding racket. "And it sure took you long enough. Check out the view!"

Rachel was not checking anything out, least of all the view. The little girl fixed her eyes forward so as not to accidentally glance over the side.

To distract her from the harrowing altitude and the oncoming peak, Davis pointed to the shirtless gentleman in the car directly in front of them. A constellation of freckles and moles dotted the sunburned expanse between his shoulder blades. Leaning into Rachel's ear, he said, "That dude may be tall enough for this ride, but he isn't dressed enough."

How much danger could they be in if he was making jokes? He saw her trying to smile, struggling to love this as he did.

"Want to hold my hand?" he asked.

"No, thank you," she chirped feebly. A nuclear blast couldn't pry her paws off that bar.

Forty-four inches tall, Rachel was legal by a margin of two—a milestone that had prompted a gleeful arm-pump from Davis when the mangy teenager with the measuring stick had allowed his daughter entry. Six long years he'd waited to take her beyond the kiddie rides and into the domain of true adventure, and at long last they were in his province. It was like a chef introducing his child to the kitchen of his bistro, or a trial lawyer bringing her daughter to court. But better, because sizzling pans and pompous judges were no equal to the thrill of a roller coaster.

Davis beheld the assemblage of track below them, an uncoiling reptile of curves, dives, and twists. Science in the service of fun—pure, but by no means simple. "This is going to rock."

To which Rachel asked, "How often do people die on these things?"

Davis laughed. "Rach, when you look at this ride, there are things you can see, like the turns, the drops, the loop—"

"Wait! There's a loop?"

"—but there are also lots of things you can't see, like g-forces and friction and air resistance. You can't see centrifugal and centripetal forces, things that slow you down, that keep your butt in the seat and keep the train on the track. All those things are invisible, but they're there."

Rachel appeared to find no reassurance in abstract concepts or big words, even when spoken by her father, a man who knew of such things, so Davis pointed down to the ground and said, "Hey, look! There's Mommy!" Far below, Britt stood clutching the stuffed bird of indeterminate breed that Rachel had "won" by coming in dead last in a water gun competition. "Wave!" he encouraged.

"You do it," Rachel said. She was still too busy white-knuckling the bar.

At last the train crested the summit, and for the brief moment that separated the climb from the fall, a chip in time fraught with glorious possibility—or needless endangerment, depending on one's orientation—father and daughter teetered over everything: the bumper boats, the carousel canopy, the pony rides. Then Davis hooted an exuberant "Here we go!" and the track beneath them dropped away, sucking them into a steep plummet. They both screamed. The jerks and jolts came upon them like a storm of artillery, g-forces pinning them to their seats one moment, then snapping them up into the restraints the next, heaving them side to side as if the train were trying to rid itself of them. The wind puffed Rachel's feathery hair strands into a fan and Davis's wavy locks into a tight helmet.

"You okay?" he yelled.

"No!" Rachel howled, all pretext of enjoyment vanishing in the face of death.

"It's almost over."

What a curiosity, seeing Rachel afraid. Fear was such an alien emotion on her; she was the fearless one. On her first day of kindergarten, eight months ago now, it had been Davis with the butterflies in his gut, Davis with the lump in his throat when Ms. Janacek, the sturdy young teacher with controlled anger and eyebrows like a Soviet premier, dismissed the parents. *Last hugs, mommies and daddies! We have so much to do today!* (The subtext being, *Get the fuck out, see you in June.*) Unlike Davis, Rachel had been unshakable that morning, striding into the classroom in cocksure pigtails, stowing her Tinkerbell knapsack in the wooden cubby with her name above it, and dispatching Davis and Britt with an economical hug. She was the embodiment of cool in the epicenter of a brouhaha—clingy kids, berserk mothers, dads wearing garish mega-smiles that were supposed to comfort their children but instead just freaked them out more. Davis had stood there waving goodbye to his brave girl, struggling to accept the heartbreaking reality that they were dropping their baby into the wide world. (The wide world being full-day kindergarten.)

It had always been like that: Rachel the lionhearted. She'd been the tough one that day outside the paint-your-own-pottery store when a seemingly rabid German shepherd appeared on the verge of escaping its leash and making a snack of the two of them. "Aww, he's just trying to tell us something," Rachel had cooed about the vicious beast. Nor had she lost her composure that morning in the park when those two delinquents on the swings teased her about the overabundance of pink in her attire. "Mean people are just sad inside," she'd told Davis.

The train thundered down a steep incline that fed into the ride's grand finale: the loop. "Time to get our vertical on!" Davis cheered.

Rachel eyed the imposing circle that lay ahead (technically not a circle but a clothoid—as Davis had often explained—an upside-down teardrop, an invention of physics that tamed the push-and-shove of gravity and acceleration into a more fluid trip around the curve but didn't appear to tame any of Rachel's particular fears at that moment), and she clearly decided the experience would be better if she weren't seeing it. She squeezed her eyes shut and heaved her face into her father's shoulder.

Up and around they went, Davis celebrating the escapade with outstretched arms and a wild whoop of ovation, after which the rusty brakes squealed and the train came to a rude stop at the platform.

"You did it! I'm so proud of you!" Britt exclaimed when Rachel came booking down the ramp and through the exit gate. "How was it?"

Rachel exhaled with relief. "It was medium."

"Just medium? Your very first big-girl roller coaster?"

"It just felt a little unsafe in my opinion."

"I take offense at that, little lady," Davis said, loping down the ramp after her.

"You didn't make this ride, Daddy."

"But the people who did used the same science that I do," Davis argued. "What do I always say about roller coasters? They're made to *feel* dangerous, but they're not *actually* dangerous. It's all very carefully designed and meticulously tested. Do you know what *meticulously* means?"

Rachel turned to Britt. "How many tickets do we have left?"

There were four tickets, but they had time enough for only one ride, since the family had to get home and cleaned up before heading out again to a cocktail party in honor of Davis's father at a local car dealership. Norman Winger had served as the celebrity spokesman for Lenny's Lexus for decades, but at long last, Lenny Baum had decided to retire his old friend's trusted face from his dealership's billboards and commercials.

Rachel, fresh from the trauma of the roller coaster, opted to use her tickets on the fun slide, a colorful cascade of drops so gentle and non-treacherous that the park barely thought to staff it. Davis and Britt stood outside the waist-high fence and watched as the little tyke deliberated needlessly over her mat selection—they were all identical slices of chewed-out foam—then ascended the steps.

Britt's long black hair shimmered almost purple in the warm afternoon sun, and she leaned against Davis as he checked work emails on his phone, which he'd been doing compulsively all weekend. Down in Virginia Beach, High Seas Adventure World was having its inaugural weekend, and one of its key attractions was the Squall, an elaborate log flume designed by Davis's firm, Pavelka & Gates. Davis personally had spent nearly two years, on and off, laboring over the design, monitoring its construction, and observing the standard battery of safety tests. The birthing of a new ride into the amusement park topography always brought on a swell of pride at the accomplishment, but he had to earn that glory by suffering through the launch, which was as anxiety-provoking as things ever got for Davis Winger.

As Britt slouched against his shoulder, he reached out and touched her neck, letting his fingers disorder her fine, satiny strands. A wave of queasiness shot through him. They'd been coming on ever since he'd returned from his most recent (and hopefully last) trip to Virginia Beach. A faint glow of relief followed, the knowledge that he was finally done with the Squall, done with that awful, confusing episode he'd never understand and wanted only to distance himself from. Instinctively, he pulled Britt closer.

"You okay?" she asked.

"Yeah. Why?"

"With the ride and everything?"

"Not a word. No news is good news." He regarded the stuffed monstrosity under Britt's arm. "Is she really going to sleep with this thing?" he asked. With its hostile eyes and belligerently curved beak, the cursed creature resembled a vulture.

"This *thing* has a name, and odds are it's Birdie," Britt deadpanned. Back home on Rachel's overpopulated bed there was already a stuffed rabbit named Bunny and a loopy-eared hound named Puppy.

Up at the summit of the slide, Rachel scooted forward, made sure her parents were watching, and dropped into a smooth, anticlimactic glide that lasted all of five seconds. Britt clapped.

Once his little girl ambled through the gate, Davis scooped her off the ground and hoisted her onto his shoulders. "Let's blow this taco stand and get our party shoes on," he said. "Grandpa Norm is waiting."

The grimy, sun-beat trio moseyed off toward the car. From the high perch above her father's neck, Rachel gazed up at the tiny metallic wink of an airplane and the widening streaks that chased it across the sky. "Daddy," she said, "I liked the roller coaster."

Her parents shared a smirk; Davis had been worrying that Rachel's initiation into his realm had been premature.

"It's okay if you didn't, honey," Britt said. "Daddy's feelings aren't hurt."

"No, I decided I liked it."

Davis reached up and squeezed one of Rachel's knotty knees. "I support your decision, little face."

CHAPTER 3

The wingding was already under way by the time Davis, Britt, and Rachel—all freshly showered—slunk in and stood in the back. Lenny's inventory of shiny, sleek-smelling sedans and SUVs had been parked against the walls and windows, and in their place on the showroom floor was a proliferation of cocktail tables and hors d'oeuvres stations, accessible only if you negotiated a dense jungle of balloons. What was the deal with car dealers and balloons?

A drink in his hand and an unfashionably roomy sport coat flapping at his sides, Lenny Baum alternately thanked and roasted Norman, who had been the wholesome and genial presence in his TV ads since time out of mind. The fifty-odd souls who'd shown up to partake of a light snack before moving on to their proper Saturday night plans laughed perfunctorily at their host's jocular jabs, the hackneyed ribbing as obligatory at these things as the Amstel Light and cheese squares.

It didn't take Rachel thirty seconds to fold her arms and say, "This is boring."

"I know, right?" Davis said. But gigs like this one were a fact of life for him. That's just what happened when your dad spent a quarter century gracing every living room that had a television tuned to WCPK.

"I'm going to go find Aunt Molly," Rachel declared, and rushed headlong into the towering forest of adults.

Britt craned her neck after her. "Is your sister even here?" she asked Davis.

He pointed. "Up front. Near my dad and Tom Petty."

The sound of Lenny's voice, hideous Baltimore dialect and all, was a conjurer of warm memories for Davis. It made him think of afternoons fishing off the back of the Baums' yacht while Norman and Lenny drank beer shirtless, and seasick Molly periodically puked over the side, or all those hours spent in this very showroom, being ten and pretending to drive Lenny's cars and consuming his supply of lollipops and soda. Lenny Baum was a type, Davis thought with a snicker of endearment. The man was well into his sixties, and it had only recently occurred to him to ax the ponytail.

Davis leaned toward his wife and made eyes at the ring of cars encircling the party. "Damn shame to let all those back seats go to waste."

"I think my contortionist days are behind me," Britt told him.

"Ooh. Say that to me again."

"Contortionist?"

"Yeah. And 'behind me.'"

A round of applause rose up as Lenny welcomed the guest of honor to the floor. Norman stepped in front of the crowd and did his thing. He thanked everyone for coming out, appeared flummoxed and humbled at all the attention, and offhandedly engineered a scene of incomprehensible cuteness thanks to the granddaughter who twittered at his side in her rose-colored party dress.

Everyone loved Norman Winger, and the very fact that everyone loved Norman Winger might give rise to the assumption that Norman Winger was, at least behind closed doors, a dick. How could this immaculately coifed, fittingly tanned, tastefully Botoxed article of community property not be insufferable? But as his children, his granddaughter, and his lady friend, Peti, knew, Norman was indeed a different man when he wasn't out in public. He was even better.

Molly had drifted to the rear of the pack and suddenly materialized next to Davis and Britt. They all kissed hello.

"Hiding?" Davis asked his sister. "You think you can avoid Dad's shout-out back here in the cheap seats?"

"I figured it's less rude than standing in the parking lot," Molly replied.

Thank God for Rachel being born and replacing Molly as Norman's ornament. Molly's childhood had been an endless string of painful events where her father was the Honored Guest or Celebrity Presenter or Man of the Hour. Dragged to ArtScape, or Crepes for a Cause at the culinary institute, or the annual Here We Grow Again ruckus at the Discovery Museum, she'd wait tensely for that dreaded moment when Norman would proudly introduce his kids. Davis, who was perfectly comfortable everywhere, was perfectly comfortable sauntering out and charming the masses. Molly, however, tiptoed in the shadows, desperate to go unnoticed. This was the motif of their siblinghood. The high school yearbook was basically Davis's personal photo album, but when Molly graduated three years later, below her photo it read: "Molly Winger—Not Pictured." And the thing is, *she was pictured.* Her photo was right there, above the words "Not Pictured." That was the essence of Molly. Seen yet somehow undetected. There but unaccounted for. Actually, she preferred it that way.

Anchorman Norman was working the crowd. "I'll tell you something, friends. We all know Lenny's a talker. He has said a great many things to me over the years, little of it worth remembering. But a long time ago, he imparted one nugget of wisdom that has always stuck with me. I've shared it with my kids many times, and I'd like to share it with you folks this evening. Lenny said to me, 'Norm, my old friend, we all need to knock hard, because life is deaf.' What a beautiful motto to live by. Knock hard, life is deaf. I know Lenny has lived by those words, and I've tried to, as well."

The guests nodded and mumbled in polite affirmation, but in the back of the room, Davis's hand went up. "Actually, can I get a point of clarification on that?" he called out.

"Oh Jesus," Molly muttered.

"Knock hard, life is deaf," Davis ruminated aloud to the crowd. "I've always kind of struggled with that. If life is deaf, it doesn't matter how hard you knock. It's not going to hear you. Right?"

Norman sighed theatrically. "You've all met my son."

"How about, 'flail wildly, life is deaf'? Doesn't that make more sense? Or 'swing a billy club, life is deaf.'"

The guests laughed; Molly and Britt shook their heads.

"I'm just throwing it out there because this is Lenny's motto," Davis went on. "And if you can't trust your car salesman, who can you trust?"

At that, Norman wound down his remarks. "Enjoy the food and libations, friends. Who else but Lenny Baum could get away with serving alcohol around so many cars?"

As everyone migrated to the refreshment tables, Molly dropped a scowl on her brother. "Someone just can't help but be charming, can he?"

"You call that charming?" Britt asked.

"He's almost as funny as he thinks he is," said Molly.

Davis smirked. "I'm probably funnier than I think I am."

Norman caught up with his family, whereupon he told everyone they were silly to have come, whereupon everyone told him they wouldn't have missed it. Such was the dance. The old man could be scaled back, part-timed, and even retired, but until his bones were in the ground, he would never be permitted to truly go away, never relinquish the civic duty he felt to trot out his face and allow the good people of the city to bask in his toothsome luminosity.

Peti had escorted Rachel to the buffet table, and now the pair was ambling over to the congregation of Wingers. Rachel was holding a plate stacked high with munchies, and Peti was adjusting her old-world

Hungarian shawl, the most prevalent article of clothing in her wardrobe. (Never mind that she was born in Brooklyn, not Budapest.) As they approached, Davis smiled and said, "'Here Comes My Girl.'"

Rachel's plate held a leaning spire of crackers, a scoop of eggplant dip (which Rachel almost certainly mistook for hummus and would not eat once she discovered its true identity), one grilled shrimp, and two sugar cookies the size of hamburger patties. Britt thanked Peti for supervising, but she couldn't have approved of the fact that one cookie hadn't sufficed, especially after a day of cotton candy, caramel popcorn, and Coke.

Peti had been in the picture for more than two decades, practically since the day Kitty Winger up and decided that, you know what, this whole husband-and-kids thing just wasn't her bag. And yet Peti was not, technically speaking, Molly and Davis's stepmother, nor was she Rachel's grandmother, no matter how deserving of those titles she might have been. She was and would always be, at least in the caverns of her own mind, Norman's lady friend. (*Lady friend* was the dignified, if not exactly titillating, term Davis had settled on for the fiftysomething woman who'd cooked for, slept with, and otherwise entertained his old man since their mother split twenty-odd years ago.)

Rachel piled one cracker atop another and inserted them into her mouth. Davis watched uneasily. "Little bites, Rach," he cautioned.

"It's a cracker, Daddy. I can only take little bites." Crumbs puffed in front of her face like sawdust when she spoke.

"But you're eating six of them at once," Davis protested.

"Daddy doesn't want you to choke," Peti said. "He's a bit of a Nervous Nelly about choking, but he's right."

"Come on, Peti. 'Don't Do Me Like That,'" Davis said, barely suppressing a grin.

Davis had been referring to Peti as Tom Petty since middle school, and whenever she was either present or mentioned, he entertained himself by shoehorning a Tom Petty song title into the conversation. The fact that it often went over everyone's head—especially Peti's—hardly diminished the joy of the sport.

A tall woman, gangly of limb, came striding over with a big smile aimed at Davis.

"Heather Baskin," Davis said. "What are you doing here?"

Heather was a colleague, an engineer at IlluMind, a competitor firm. Over the years they'd collided at conferences and in the lobbies of prospective clients when both of their shops were vying for the same projects. Davis liked Heather, found her refreshingly irreverent at a cocktail hour. She could curse a blue streak about clients, coworkers, and her children.

After Davis introduced her to the many members of his family, Heather said, "Lenny's my uncle, so I often get dragged to these things." Then she smiled at Norman. "No offense. Super cool to meet you." She eyed Davis. "And who heckles their own father?"

"Someone needs to remind the old man that he's an ordinary mortal like the rest of us," Davis said.

Molly couldn't let that slide. "Sorry—who needs reminding?"

Heather and Davis had a friendly chat about work. Heather spoke of the projects IlluMind was exploring overseas, parks opening up in Europe and Asia, while Davis mentioned his firm's log flume debuting that very weekend in Virginia.

Heather cocked her head. "Is that the High Seas property?"

"That's the one," said Davis.

"We bid on that."

"You didn't get it."

"Damn you, Winger. I worked my ass off on that proposal."

"It's okay, Baskin. You'll get 'em next time."

"See, that's why my boss hates you."

Davis smiled. "Nobody hates me."

Generally, when their two firms went toe-to-toe, IlluMind won out, not because it offered a better product, but because it was younger and flashier, an upstart that turned heads with its innovation. If Pavelka was Frances McDormand, IlluMind was Gal Gadot. Not that this bothered Davis. He'd worked hard to become Frances McDormand.

Before heading off to mingle, Heather raised her glass at Davis. "Stay out of my way, Winger."

Davis raised his in return. "Let me know when you want to come work for a real firm, Baskin."

The party was beginning to wind down, so Davis invited Molly to come back to his and Britt's house to continue the evening there. Molly seemed to resent the assumption that she didn't have plans on a Saturday night, accurate though that assumption often was.

"I can't. I'm supposed to meet up with Zach and his friends," she said, sounding decidedly not thrilled about it.

"Do their fake IDs work downtown?" Davis joked.

"Ignore him," Britt told Molly. "Davis is jealous. He would kill to be dating a twenty-two-year-old."

Davis squeaked a shoe on the immaculately shellacked floor, then raised an eye to Britt. "I'm all set. Very happy with what I've got."

"Zach's actually twenty-three," said Molly.

"And who cares anyway?" said Britt. "I happen to think he's a really nice guy."

"Really? You do?" Molly asked, sounding genuinely curious. "Why?"

Suddenly Rachel was standing in front of them, tugging impatiently at her parents' sleeves. "I'm still bored," she announced.

"We'll leave soon," Davis said. He snickered in Peti's direction and added, "We'll get out of here—you, Mommy, and me. 'Into the Great Wide Open.'"

"I want to leave sooner than soon," Rachel whined.

"There's no such thing."

"Yes, there is. It's called *now*."

Davis snatched a cracker off his daughter's plate. "Rachel Rose Winger," he said, shaking his head. "'Yer So Bad.'"

CHAPTER 4

Straddling the corner of Molly's desk, Bo, the music critic, clearly thought she'd be the first to get the ax. "The world has no fucks left to give for rock 'n' roll, certainly not in this town," she spat.

"Richard isn't there yet," Molly said, trying to reassure her. "I really wouldn't worry."

"I don't even care, you know? If I'm out, I'm out." Bo's hands dropped with a slap onto her leather pants. It was amazing to Molly how Bo's outrage could so abruptly recede into resignation, then zing right back into fury.

They'd just emerged from an unusually tense staff meeting at which Richard Reinstock, the founder, owner, and emperor of the *Weekly Ramble* and the only editor-in-chief it had ever known, spent a full hour lamenting the paper's financial state and imploring everyone to find new, creative ways to generate revenue. They'd heard it before—this wasn't unique to them; it was the current state of print media—but today the speech had been delivered with an ominous urgency that spiked pentagrams of nervous glances all around the conference table. After the meeting, Bo had followed Molly down the hall to prematurely bitch about being dismissed.

Bo had worked at the *Ramble* for nearly a year now, and Molly still wasn't sure how to talk to her, this unknown animal who moved and spoke with an edgy energy, whose tight-fitting clothes revealed a meth-head physique that cried out for nutrition, who had a pixie cut the color of grape Dimetapp and a resting face of ever-rising annoyance. *Now this?*, her features always seemed to be saying. *Can you just not?*

Bo's journey had been a tempestuous one, and oddly, Molly quietly envied her. In fact, she rather envied all those Bo-like people out there—which, she was beginning to fear, was most of humanity except her. People who heaved themselves into life, damn the consequences, and then simply shook off the damage with world-weary pluck. Bo was a local girl whose punk band had never gotten off the ground. She'd moved to Los Angeles for a boyfriend (either a surfer or an Ultimate Frisbee enthusiast, Molly couldn't recall which), gotten in with some people at *Rolling Stone*, started writing record reviews, then gotten dumped by the boyfriend, suffered a minor to midlevel nervous breakdown, and moved back in with her parents in Baltimore. Richard could only pay her as a contributing writer, but he gave her a desk because she was a colorful character and, bleeding heart that he was, he felt sorry for her.

For Molly, there'd been no punk bands, no surfer dude boyfriends, no flirtations with national magazines, not even the joyride of a mental collapse. There'd been only evenness and predictability. First the college newspaper at the University of Maryland, then the rather apathetic declaration of a journalism major, then some freelance writing for Richard on random local interest matters (often suggested to her by her newscaster father), then a full-time staff assignment here at the Features desk. Most days she welcomed the quiet steadiness of her life and the contrast it posed to the tumult of those early years. Deep down she was still that eight-year-old whose mother shocked them all by running off with another man, never to return; still that tepid child, leery of even slightly disturbing what was stable in the world, what was likely to still be there tomorrow and the day after. There were, however, days when it snuck up on her that you could learn a lesson too well.

It was comfortable living life on the road most traveled, and she could go months without feeling any whispers of professional stagnancy. What troubled her, though, was how her ability to play it safe—to hide, because that's what it sometimes felt like—bled into other aspects of her life. Like her relationship. Molly didn't really know why she was with Zach. Actually, she knew exactly why she was with Zach: he'd asked her out at a point in her life when she lacked other options. (This was most of her life.) What she didn't know was why she was *still* with Zach. Actually, she knew exactly why she was still with Zach: inertia, not only the strongest force in the universe but also a personal favorite of Molly's.

Zach Klinefelter was a nice enough guy who had almost no intersecting interests with Molly's; who could make her laugh; who was both way too young for her and immature for his age; who resided in that curious space between "yeah, he's kind of cute" and "no, I wouldn't say he's cute"; who seemed to genuinely enjoy being with her; who probably did not love her—and thank god, because love, in whatever crude, embryonic form he was capable of, would've only complicated things; who had one or two truly admirable qualities and a whole bunch of weird ones; and who, bizarrely, frustratingly, hadn't ended things with her after all these months of dating. Theirs was a functional, languishing relationship that Molly had long ago figured out was headed nowhere. Why hadn't Zach figured that out too?

For some people, it was their job that prompted them to ask *Is this it?*, and for others, it was the person across the table. Molly had the fortune of having both, a veritable difecta of low-grade malaise that only sporadically spiked to the point where the big questions were begged. Occasionally, her mindset was *I am coasting, and coasting is unhealthy.* Mostly, her mindset was *I am coasting, and it sure feels nice to coast.*

"A job is a job, right?" Bo was saying. "Comes a time we all have to move on. What doesn't kill you—what? Defines you? Makes for a good story?"

Makes you reach for a blanket, Molly thought.

"Besides, do I need this? All day I listen to suck, bands that are doing nothing but kidding themselves. There's a ton of artifice out there and precious little truth."

"Don't stress about it, Bo," Molly told her. "I've been here a long time, and Richard has only fired one person ever. And he threw up right before he did it."

That brought down the rant. "For real?"

Molly nodded, and the two women shared a laugh at their editor's expense, until said editor materialized, eyebrow raised, as if he'd overheard them.

"Am I interrupting?" Richard asked.

"Not at all, boss man," Bo replied, sliding her long, bony fingers into her pockets.

Seemingly comforted to learn of Richard's weak stomach for discharging his soldiers, she winked at Molly—Bo was a winker—and told her she'd swing by later so they could grab lunch together at the falafel joint that Molly would've liked so much more if it didn't have a tattoo parlor in the back.

As though the corner of Molly's desk were a confessional and Molly the priest, Bo slid off and Richard slid on. He folded his arms over his mustard cardigan and dropped a heavy look on Molly.

"I feel compelled, Ms. Winger, to make something very clear to you." He was speaking in low, conspiratorial tones. "Regardless of what went on in that meeting this morning, you do not have my permission to send out your résumé."

His bluntness caught her off guard. "Oh. No. I'm not."

"It's hard times around here, but I'm not giving up without a fight. The end is not yet nigh, but when it is, I promise I will give you plenty of advance notice. You have my word on that."

His eyes drifted nostalgically around the room, taking in the walls and ceiling and floor as though these were to be his final glimpses. The paper occupied a refurbished brick building on the outskirts of Fells

Point and was decorated in a style that Richard sometimes referred to as "contemporary smart," other times as "modern cool," both, in Molly's humble opinion, pretentious and ultimately vacuous pairings of words. But she did share his fondness for the place. How could she not? It had been her professional home for years, this small but enduring local-interest newspaper where week in and week out she quietly ginned up pleasant, eminently readable and unessential pieces about non-news.

Richard tilted his head forward, showing Molly the roof of his accidental pompadour. "You and I. We are going to save the *Ramble* together."

She nodded uncertainly. "How are we going to do that?"

"Well, I don't quite know. But what I do know is nobody cares about this place as much as you or I do. Besides, you have a knack for coming up with just the right idea at just the right time. How can we lose?" He smiled weakly.

Molly, despite a solid tenure at the paper, still didn't think of herself as an insider. She thought of herself as just another staff member bearing helpless witness to the paper's looming irrelevance. Anyone could observe the unhealthy trend: the dwindling of content and simultaneous swelling of cheap ad space. The classifieds and personals, historically tucked in the back, were creeping ever forward, advancing like an army toward the front page. Now those tawdry ads for lord-knows-what (she did not want to know what a "Tokyo escort" or a "Grandma-for-Rent" was) kicked in midway through the issue.

"Richard, if you're depending on me to rescue the *Weekly Ramble*, then the *Weekly Ramble* is in a lot of trouble. My articles are not what the advertisers come for."

"And how would you happen to know that?"

She pointed to her computer screen. "Right now I'm working on a piece about the new exhibit at the Visionary Art Museum. The artist is a homeless man whose drawings were discovered in his mother's attic after he died. This is the kind of thing I do. I think it's cool, but since I personally am not cool, I suspect the appeal is limited."

"Ms. Winger, self-effacement is a nonstarter in this business," Richard said. He'd recently met and fallen in love with the term "nonstarter," and welcomed it into as many sentences as he could. "All I'm asking is that you be on the lookout for that stroke of inspiration that will make this enterprise commercially viable again. I'm counting on you."

"Please don't say that," she fretted. "Don't count on me. It's unwise."

"Look—if this place folds, you're going to be fine," he told her. "You're young, and you've got skills aplenty. You could go anywhere. I'm old and institutionalized. I've been doing this for twenty-five years and haven't a clue how to do anything else. You think I'm going back to med school?"

Richard was a newspaper man in a family of doctors. His sisters, brother, and father were all prominent physicians who had coalesced into a fraternity of sorts from which Richard was often excluded. Drs. Reinstock referred patients to each other, they golfed and brunched together, and they attended fundraisers where Jackson Browne and Jerry Seinfeld performed. Richard himself had dropped out of medical school three decades ago, and to hear him tell it, his mother still hadn't recovered from the blow.

"The question, Ms. Winger, is what do we want, and do we want it badly enough?"

At that, he checked his watch, said, "Oy," and shuffled off to a budget meeting.

Molly prayed that Richard was making the rounds, delivering the same motivational plea to each of his staff members in the faint hope that one might deliver.

The question, Ms. Winger, is what do we want?

What she wanted, she guessed, was to keep doing what she'd been doing—writing about the War of 1812 reenactment at Fort McHenry, or the residential construction project planned for Key Highway. What she wanted was to continue seeing her accessible syntax and carefully chosen adjectives printed in this glorified pamphlet (and online in a slightly updated edition). She didn't need to blow the doors off society with some sensational exposé. She wasn't looking for the story that got everyone's attention. Quite the contrary. What suited her about her line of work was that, at its essence, it entailed shifting the focus away from herself. If she was always conducting the interview, it would never fall to her to be the subject.

And yet everyone assumed Molly wanted more.

"Maybe this is an opportunity," Britt had suggested recently when Molly came to dinner and again mentioned the paper's rocky straits. Her sister-in-law was only trying to be helpful. Job loss, or the threat thereof, always got friends and relatives throwing around the *O* word. *Your inability to pay your rent is going to be very good for you. With any luck, they'll shut off your electricity too.*

"What's the dream, the ultimate assignment, the piece that puts Molly Winger in the same breath as Lesley Stahl or Christiane Amanpour?" Britt had asked that night. "What's your Woodward and Bernstein?"

It embarrassed Molly that all she could offer was a shrug. "Honestly, I don't know."

"You're a terrific writer, Molly. That's why you do features. Features are different from other types of reporting, aren't they? These profiles, these behind-the-scenes stories—it seems like there's more room for color and creativity in the prose, more room for plot, for the characters to come alive. That's your wheelhouse. The question is, does it fulfill you?"

"Yeah," Molly had said, convincing no one, least of all herself. "I'm moderately fulfilled."

"You're adept at getting people to open up," Britt had told her. "People just like talking to you."

"Speak for yourself," Davis weighed in from the kitchen.

Moderately fulfilling probably put her in better stead professionally than most people. But that didn't alter the fact that moderately fulfilling was, definitionally, shy of fulfilling.

Enough fretting, she decided. It didn't solve anything to sit here and stew about the health of the newspaper, or her career, or the inadequacy of her significant other, or her own inadequacy at improving any of the above. She dove back into her profile of the deceased homeless artist. She stared at some of his illustrations on the museum's website. Pursing her lips in thought, she described the artist's colored pencil sketches as "just naive and childlike enough to be haunting." Then she reread her own words and decided they were a pretty fair approximation of childhood itself.

CHAPTER 5

Standing in the elevator bank in an untucked, short-sleeved button-down, Davis slapped a rolled-up newspaper into his palm. By ritual, he began his Mondays by plucking the latest edition of the *Weekly Ramble* from the dispenser outside his office building and flipping to Molly's submission. Her articles were even easier to find now that she'd been awarded her very own column, with a title so whimsical—"Just Winging It"—that there was no shot Molly had come up with it.

"I don't understand exactly what you do," he'd once said to her. "What does *features* mean exactly?"

"It's soft news," Molly had told him.

"And what does that mean exactly?"

"Anything, really. Lifestyle, human interest."

"I'm no closer to understanding," he'd said. "I'm not trying to be difficult."

"Yes, you are. Don't read it if you don't want to."

He did want to. He'd never admit it to her, but it made him proud to read his own sister's prose while sipping the week's first cup of coffee.

He shuffled into the elevator, eager to get upstairs and hear how things had gone over the weekend with the launch of the Squall. Just as the doors began to close, in stepped a man. He was abundantly cologned and bedecked in a pinstripe suit that glistened like a glazed doughnut.

"Hey, buddy."

Davis looked up and saw the man who had sold him and Britt their life insurance policies. "Oh, hey, George."

"How goes it, my man? Everything good? Wife? Daughter? How's work?" George's friendliness always came at you slick and rapid-fire.

It was unfortunate, rather than convenient, that Davis and his life insurance agent shared a building. George's very existence was an intrusion, a reminder of The End. *I am a death in the making to this guy,* Davis always thought. *A hunk of cheese with a hint of mold.* With his feathered blond hair and a sort of pampered, Ken-doll handsomeness, George bore more than a passing resemblance to *Broadcast News*–era William Hurt. Once, Davis had bumped into George at the movies and was flat-out tickled to see that his wife also looked like William Hurt circa 1987. It was anyone's guess whether it was a happy accident for the couple ("You know, sweetie, I've always thought you looked like William Hurt." "Really? Because I've always thought *you* looked like William Hurt.") or a style choice ("Honey, let's always look like William Hurt! What do you say?").

As the elevator ascended and Davis's nostrils fought back the brutal vapors of a bourbon-scented hair product, George said, "I lost one over the weekend." His eyes were alight with event.

"One what?" Davis asked.

"A client. Lawyer. Thirty-eight. Fell down a flight of steps at a restaurant." He snapped his fingers. "Game over. Never woke up."

Davis winced. "That's awful."

"Three kids. Ten, seven, and four. Wife totally devastated."

"I really hate it when you tell me this kind of thing," Davis muttered.

"They got a solid mil and a half coming. That should help."

It seemed unlikely that the widow would see it that way. Then again, it was always a mistake to underestimate the curative properties of a cash payout.

"It's the worst part of my job," said George, shaking his head. Davis wasn't sure if he meant the young man's tragic death or the fat check his company had to fork over.

By the time they'd arrived at the fourteenth floor, Davis was already feeling grave. It was happening again. He could feel it coming on. He lurched off the elevator and through the doors of P&G, scrambling past the unmanned reception desk—Lydia didn't get in until nine—and through the suite to his office, where he closed the door behind him and dropped Molly's paper onto his desk.

As usual, it began with a twitching in the mouth, spasms of facial muscles tugging his lips into a frown. His eyes blinked out droplets that cascaded down the slopes of his cheeks. Air sputtered through his nose and mouth. *Ripken, Palmer.* His chest leaped. *McGregor, Martinez, Martinez.* He mouthed the names of bygone baseball players, Orioles from the team's storied past, conjured up to distract and calm him, to stave off a full-on cry.

He cried. Full-on.

When the grand finale of sniffs subsided, he sat alone in the room, just him and his shame. *Why? Why do you do this? Random crying spells at thirty-five? You're an idiot. What's wrong with you?*

When he quietly opened his door, he noticed one lone office light illuminating a square of carpet at the opposite end of the suite. Hans was in early. Davis gave his face a few minutes to de-redden and un-puff, then made his way down the hall.

He found his boss standing over his desk, hands parked on his hips in a posture that suggested heady thought. Hans mostly stood; he wasn't very good at sitting. A fit fifty-five-year-old with gray hair in full bloom on his head and forearms, he was a serious man with bookish spectacles and the stiff gaze of a Mossad agent.

"Morning," Davis said. "Any word from our friends in Virginia?"

Hans looked up, then beckoned Davis to take a seat on the sofa that flanked the wall. Before Hans closed the door and began caressing the bridge of his nose, Davis felt a tautness in the air.

"It was not a good weekend," Hans began. "There was an incident on our flume."

"An incident? What do you mean?"

"A log flipped over."

"What?"

"A girl nearly drowned, Davis."

The phone call from the CEO of Vantage View Parks and Resorts, Inc., which owned the brand-new park, had come the day before. One of the logs had tipped over and trapped a guest underneath. The log was hollow plastic, not actual lumber like in the old days, but it turned out to be stubbornly heavy and difficult to right in the narrow channel. It took a team of park attendants and spectators a good couple of minutes to lift the thing off the young woman, by which point her chest was flooded with water. An attendant happened to know CPR and soon had her breathing again, but the ride was shut down.

Davis had never heard of such a thing. "Is she okay?"

"Some bruises to the face and head. And a fractured wrist."

Davis pitched back on the sofa, utterly mystified and slightly nauseous. Not once in his career had anything like this happened. He fumbled for causation. "Was she standing up? Leaning too far over the side? Maybe someone was rocking the log."

"I don't know," Hans replied. "But they're saying there was water turbulence between the collection pool and the docking stations."

"Water turbulence? With this design? Impossible."

The Squall, being your basic by-the-book log flume, was so controlled, so drearily unimaginative from a structural standpoint that there was practically no way a wave could boomerang all the way back through the curved channel with enough force to capsize a log. The physics of water currents simply didn't allow for it. But *impossible* wasn't the right word. It was *improbable*, and improbable things happened all the time.

"Vantage View has to submit its preliminary report to the regulators in a few days. We'll know more then," Hans said. With a glance at his watch, he asked Davis to excuse him, as he had to call Keiko, who was currently in Florida to lead a seminar. Keiko was another of the firm's principals, the prickly one, the only person at P&G who was stingy with her affection for Davis.

The hallway back to Davis's office was adorned with sketches, photographs, and pencil renderings of the firm's successes. Gravity-snubbing, structurally beguiling rides erected everywhere from Galveston to Portland, from Vail to the Jersey Shore, his fingerprint on most of them. Even the PowerPoint slides Keiko had taken with her to Miami included diagrams of a coaster in Idaho that Davis had designed.

Back at his desk, he called Britt. His wife was across town in the squat structure that housed the Maryland Domestic Abuse Legal Defense Project, where she had started working as a volunteer lawyer five years ago and was now assistant director.

"Oh god," Britt exclaimed. "Is the girl okay?"

"She doesn't sound seriously hurt," Davis replied. He was staring out the window at the empty-eyed gargoyles perched on the ledges of the opposite building. Peering down on pedestrians like birds of prey from the underworld, these macabre creatures seemed indigenous to the city, as though the fishy tint of the harbor air were essential to their survival.

"How did it happen?" Britt asked.

"We don't know yet."

"Could it have been an engineering thing?"

"I don't know," Davis said. "I can't imagine how it could."

"How's Hans?"

"Freaking out—in the way that Hans does."

"He's not blaming you, is he?" Britt asked.

Davis grunted.

"Davis, you can do no wrong at that place and you know it. You could ride over Hans's mother with your car, and he still wouldn't be mad at you."

It was a weak point. Who would get mad over that?

"It's got to be somebody's fault," Davis reasoned. "If it gets traced back to the engineers, it's my ass in the crosshairs."

"Hans has a right to freak out a little bit since it's his firm," Britt said. "It doesn't mean anyone's ass is in the crosshairs. Don't jump to conclusions."

"How about reasonable conclusions? Can I jump to those?"

They hung up. Davis walked to the bathroom, leaned over the sink, and tried to agree with his wife. It was true that when the game was on the line, it was Davis they called upon. He was the one they counted on to realize the vision, to fix what was broken, to soothe the nerves of a crazed client. And even if a design defect had caused this accident—and he couldn't conceive of how that could be—there was plenty of guilt to go around. Hans himself had signed off on the Squall's every angle, on the selection of every material, every sketch, model, and rendering.

A short while later, Davis was summoned back to his boss's office.

The investigation, Hans told him with a dire sigh, was, as he'd feared, focusing on a structural design flaw. The ride seemed to have been operated by the book, no passengers had engaged in any unsafe shenanigans, and there was no damage to the log that would suggest a manufacturing defect in the plastic. All signs pointed to water turbulence, which could have been avoided with a tweak to the design. Responsibility for the design—and the tweak that evidently did not happen—lay with Pavelka & Gates.

"This happened twenty-four hours ago, and already they've got it figured out?" Davis scoffed.

"They've shut down the ride," Hans said. "It will take years for the park to recover from the reputational harm. And the girl's family is going to sue everyone six ways to Sunday."

Davis pondered the carpet. He stared so deeply into it that soon he wasn't really looking at it at all. Had he missed something? Had he failed to make an adjustment that could've prevented this from happening? His work had never before been implicated in an accident, but that didn't mean his work was perfect. It just meant that an accident hadn't happened.

"I should get down there immediately," he said.

"No, I'm going to go," Hans told him.

"I'm not coming with you?"

"I'm bringing Bob."

"Bob Roman? Bob Roman is a buffoon."

"Davis, Bob has more experience than you."

"At being a buffoon. Clients laugh at that guy. You laugh at that guy. He's been doing this for twenty years and has no skills. He can't pronounce the word *radius*. He has trouble with *triangle*."

"I'll be doing all the talking," Hans said.

"Hans, you know how much time I've spent down there. Everyone at Vantage View knows me. It has to be me. If I don't go, we're basically admitting that it's my fault."

"Davis, if there was a structural design flaw, then the fault lies with all of us."

"And yet it's only me being banned from the Commonwealth of Virginia," Davis said. "What's next? You fire me?"

Instead of scoffing or refusing to even dignify something so patently ludicrous, Hans answered him. "I'm not firing you."

Davis felt the blood drain from his face. "You know when someone says something and you get the impression that what they're really saying is the exact opposite?"

"I'm not firing you," Hans repeated. Then came a heavy breath. "We do, however, have to put you on ice."

"Ice?"

"I don't like it, but having you step back from the firm for the moment is the sensible thing to do."

"Scapegoat your best engineer. That's the sensible thing?"

"Let's not overreact."

"Now, *that's* the first sensible thing you've said."

"We have to listen to our lawyers, Davis. It's not just your reputation and livelihood on the line. That's my name up on the door, and Keiko's. Again, we're just talking temporarily. And you still get paid when you're on administrative leave."

"Administrative leave?" Davis looked with incredulity at the man who for so long had been his colleague and mentor. "Seriously?"

"Everyone around here knows what you contribute, but you were the lead engineer on this project. You must agree that it's wise to have you step back. For now."

Nine years. He'd gotten married, had a kid, bought a house, all of it squeezed between the comfortable intervals of days and weeks spent here.

In his boss's face, Davis detected true struggle, genuine doubt about whether this was really the right thing. For a brief moment Davis almost felt sorry for him.

The moment passed.

"You want me to go?" He stood and glared across the room. "You got it. I'll go. You can deal with this problem on your own."

"Davis, it's our only option. I think you know how I feel about you."

"Well, let me tell you how I feel about *you*," Davis began. But no words came. All he could do was stand there and shake his head—at Hans Pavelka, at Keiko Gates, who wasn't even there, at the lawyers, the investigators, the ride attendants, even at his own damn self.

Then he left.

CHAPTER 6

Just before lunchtime, Zach texted Molly to see if she had a few minutes to come out and say hello. He had taken a walk from his Canton townhouse and was now standing outside her building, which annoyed her and shouldn't have.

"So I have a proposition for you," he said as soon as Molly came squinting into the daylight.

Something in his tone made her wary. "Okay," she said.

"What are you doing the second week of August?"

"I don't know," she replied.

"Two words: Las Vegas." He grinned in enticement.

"What about it?"

"You and me. Together."

"A trip?"

"Uh-huh."

"Why Las Vegas?"

"That's where the American Horror Festival is," he said. Immediately, he rushed in to do damage control. "Now, I know it's not your thing—"

"Yeah, it really isn't."

"But I promise it'll be fun. I swear. Lots of the old-school stuff you grew up with. Wes Craven, John Carpenter. We'll catch a few flicks, we'll partake of the whole Vegas scene. It'll be an awesome getaway for us."

Molly had watched no more than three horror films in her whole life, all on television—network, with commercials and dubbed-out curse words—and only because there'd been absolutely nothing else on. In fact, in her mind, a good premise for a horror movie was getting flown to Nevada for a horror movie festival.

"I don't know, Zach."

"Mol, aren't we always talking about how we should do more stuff together?"

They'd literally never had that conversation. Not once.

"I didn't mean more horror movies," she said. "And I certainly didn't mean more vacations centered around them."

"It's Vegas!" he enthused. "Who doesn't like Vegas?"

"Well, for starters, girls."

"It'll be a blast. We could both use it."

Oh, could we now? How badly did a twenty-three-year-old work-from-home graphic designer who still grocery shopped with his mother need a break from the grind? And he wasn't even really a graphic designer. Proficiency with a few platforms and the bare minimum of artistic ability had landed him a job on a satellite "creative team" for a web-based company that offered low-cost logo designs. If this outfit had a main office, Zach had never visited it. If he had a boss, they'd never met.

Molly hated the meanness that Zach brought out of her, but it was conversations like these that underscored how their nine-year age disparity was the least of their differences.

"Come on, Mol," Zach begged. Then he made jazz hands. "Vegas!"

"I've really got to get back to work," she told him, hoping he wouldn't notice that it was the lunch hour and that, not ten feet away, everyone she worked with was filing out of the building.

"Will you think about it?" he implored.

"Sure," she said, knowing she'd already done all the thinking the subject required.

———

It was only when Britt had endorsed the idea of online dating that Molly had agreed to try it. It seemed so crass: the mug shot, the concise distillation of one's interests and aspirations into a few pithy lines, all with the desperate undertone of *Pick me! Pick me!* It was like putting yourself on a menu and trying to make yourself sound delicious. In the end, the prospect of searching for a date on an app unnerved her only slightly less than the prospect of searching for a date in person. She didn't like dates, and the only way she could get comfortable with the notion of spending an evening one-on-one with a stranger was to imagine she was conducting an interview.

Crafting her dating profile presented a host of challenges. Candor would've compelled her to advertise herself as someone who enjoyed such arresting activities as reading, whipping up a salad, and staying in. She thus embraced the element of harmless distortion, the art of aspirational self-invention. She played up her passion for international travel—which, of late, had taken her to such far-flung outposts as Toronto and Niagara Falls—and the whole journalism thing, whatever that was worth. For body type, since there wasn't a box for "you know, normal," she checked "slender" since it most closely aligned with the image she'd inhabited since high school. (Her male classmates had elected her to the Itty-Bitty Titty Committee, and she'd never psychologically outgrown the designation.) Even choosing the right photo involved some sly strategizing because, although technically a blonde, she had the complexion of a redhead, and redheads were polarizing, like marzipan and universal health care. She felt like a commodity, a product she didn't really believe in. How undignified to be both the game show host and the prize money.

Zach was the very first cyber-connection she agreed to go out with, and her initial thought upon meeting him at the Red Star in Fells Point on that unseasonably snowy evening last fall was that he'd lied about his age. Had he clicked the "between twenty-eight and thirty-five" button by accident? Who would make a claim so easily debunked by producing a driver's license? But he seemed interested in her, even a little impressed that she was a writer. He listened attentively when she described some of her recent articles—even the boring ones, and they were all pretty boring—and she did her best to extend the same courtesy when he went on about his love for science fiction, fantasy, and gothic horror.

"I saw on your profile that you're big into travel," he'd said when the conversation hit a lull. "That's something I wish I did more of. Other than Cancún for spring break, the only time I've been out of the country was a trip to Scotland, and that was with my parents when I was a kid."

Okay, she thought. *We can discuss Scotland.* She told him that she too had been there, as a teen, accompanying her dad to some meeting in Edinburgh.

"Cool town, right?" Zach said. "I remember the Scotch being really friendly."

"They were," Molly said, letting it slide that he'd called Scotland's natives by their signature whisky. Common mistake. No reason to be a snob.

"The Edinburgh Castle was incredible, wasn't it?" she said.

His face went hazy. "I don't really remember a castle. But I was there a long time ago. Maybe it wasn't built yet?"

Possibly, she was tempted to say. *The castle was built in 1280. When were you there?*

But then came the almost offhanded reference to his involvement with foster children, and when she latched on to it and asked him about it, he lit up. He was an only child, and fostering had been a big thing for his parents. They always had a kid living with them. Apparently it was habit-forming, as Zach had been in the Big Brothers Big Sisters program since college. Molly was impressed. It was, in fact, the first time all night she was genuinely interested.

"You'd love the two Little Brothers I have now." Their mention brought a true smile. "Anthony and Gabe. Really great kids."

This hint at even a kiddie pool's worth of depth justified Molly's attention a little longer, even perhaps a second date. But as they walked out together, he asked if she went by Katie or Kate.

Okay—so he called her by the wrong name at the *end* of the date. For most women that would've been it, unless he looked like Matt Damon. Which he didn't. He looked like the guy who hooked up Matt Damon's printer. But Molly had long ago accepted that she was the type of person whose name people either forgot or didn't bother to learn in the first place. The dentist she'd been going to for years still asked *Mary* to open wide, told *Mary* to go ahead and rinse. Instead of correcting him, Molly just sat in the chair feeling bad that her name wasn't Mary.

When the night was over, she concluded that Zach was decent looking (a touch skinny, but nothing she couldn't tolerate), nice enough (hardly magnetic), and somewhat stylish (though perhaps too much of an actual nerd to pull off nerd chic), and the fact of the matter was that the two of them were not an unreasonable pairing, even if her friends and family pretended otherwise. People like Molly dated people like Zach.

Weeks later, she gave in to pressure from her brother and brought Zach out for brick-oven pizza with Davis, Britt, and Rachel. All through dinner, Zach gave off the impression that he was closer in age to Rachel than to the adults at the table, as both he and the six-year-old were oblivious to the smudges of tomato sauce on their chins, and both were conversant in the work of They Might Be Giants.

When the evening ended, Molly braced for a carpet bombing of insults from her brother. But Davis had held back. What really needed to be said? Instead, he went with, "What's his last name again?"

To which Molly had said, "You know it's Klinefelter. You just want to make a joke."

To which Davis had said, "That's the small ball syndrome, isn't it?"

To which Molly had said, "Good night, Davis."

From the outset, Molly had been keenly aware—or periodically reminded by a friend or relative—that she was settling. Every time she was with Zach, every episode of *True Detective* they watched together, every meal they shared, there was at least a moment when she thought to herself, *He's not a bad guy, but I need to end this. Like, now.* Sometimes that moment lasted an hour.

She was walking back into the *Ramble* at the same time that Richard was stepping out for lunch.

"Ah! Ms. Winger," he said, stopping her. "I've got two tickets to Sergei Golotnik tonight at the Meyerhoff, and it appears I won't be able to use them."

She made an apologetic face. "I'm sorry. I don't know who that is."

Golotnik, he told her, was a world-renowned cellist from Moscow whom Richard had been waiting months to hear. However, his husband, Harvey, who was battling myeloma, was having a bad week and wasn't up to it. Harvey's cancer had cost him the occasional night out, but so far not his sense of humor. ("I have multiple myeloma," he was fond of saying, "and yet one would've been more than enough.")

"Take them," Richard bade her. "Go, and bring that boyfriend of yours."

There was no way Molly was letting that boyfriend of hers anywhere near any Muscovite cellist. She'd learned that lesson a few months back when she'd dragged him to community theater, a period drama set in a Dublin pub in the 1880s. Throughout the performance, Zach had sat there throwing shade, criticizing the actors' Irish accents ("None of these people are Irish"), criticizing the set ("About as believable as Sesame Street"), even criticizing the running time ("This thing eventually ends, right?"). Molly had had only herself to blame for that debacle. That's what happened when you took children to the theater.

Skyler, her old friend from her college days, might be game for a night out, so Molly texted her.

Weird question: Any interest in going with me to the Meyerhoff tonight to see some famous cellist? My boss has tickets that he can't use.

Are you inviting me out to listen to the cello? was Skyler's response. When did you turn sixty? Can't do it, little chickie. Dinner with Chad's parents. Sounds like a wild night, though. Be safe!

The only other person who might even be remotely interested was Britt.

I think I can do it, Britt replied. Let me just check with Davis. I'm actually in a cab on my way to meet him. He's having a bit of a meltdown at work.

Molly read the text and laughed. Davis didn't have meltdowns. Meltdown? My brother?

LOL, Britt wrote back. Hissy fit then.

Is he ok? Molly asked.

There was an accident on his new ride, and he's freaking out.

Yikes. Was it serious?

Nobody died, but serious enough for him to leave work and go to a bar.

This just kept getting better. How alcoholic, Molly wrote. Sorry to make light. Please take pictures.

Definitely, Britt replied. I'll call you later.

Molly texted back a smiley face.

CHAPTER 7

Just like that, it became a hard-liquor night. Since it was barely past noon, night would have to arrive a little early. Davis swept picture frames, his coffee mug, and other beloved trinkets off his desk and into his briefcase, then left the office without a word and trudged around the corner to Finnegan's Wake.

Tucked away from civilization down an alley sentried by a dumpster, the Wake was housed in a building that was possibly condemned and certainly unwelcoming. With a long, narrow bar extending into sad oblivion and a smattering of desolate souls hunched around the tap at midday, it was the kind of hole that made you feel drunk even before the first sip. Davis had been inside exactly once before. It was with a college friend, one of those rolling itinerants who spent the first half decade after graduation in contented aimlessness, his only goal being dollar drafts.

Davis sat down at a table and ordered a bourbon. Two lawyer types nearby were going to town on plates of bangers and mash, and Davis was struck with two oppositional notions. The first was: *Who the hell eats at a place like this?* The second was: *In an hour I'll be drunk and hungry, and I'll probably ask these guys if that shit is any good.*

Davis Winger was day drinking on a Monday. The very notion made him laugh. There had been so few opportunities to storm out of the office, to a pub, no less—which, now that he thought about it, might have been a touch melodramatic. Why hadn't he stood his ground and defended his work instead of behaving as though a performance-related rebuke was well-trodden terrain? *Not this again. Oh well. Off to the nearest tap.*

He was on his second bourbon when a diminutive man, no younger than ninety, no taller than five feet, stood on a chair and belted out "Rainy Night in Georgia" in a dusty rasp. The barflies cheered and slobbered with approval.

With the whisky came the burn of a righteous rage. It infuriated Davis that he was here alone in this dive bar, that Hans had pushed the poison on him. They should've all been in a conference room, everyone who worked on the Squall, with blueprints and schematics splayed out on the table, sleeves at half-mast, and everyone trying to figure out if there was something they'd missed. Something they'd *all* missed.

Davis was on his third bourbon when his wife stepped into the bar. Seeing her silhouetted by streams of sunlight as the door creaked open, he was reminded that it was still daytime.

Britt located her pathetic husband in the dimness and strode over. Davis, meanwhile, admired the way her pantsuit hugged the slender curve of her hips, the way her silky black hair reflected the midnight red of the neon Coors Light sign.

"You have fantastic hips, did you know that?" he said to her hips.

In a day of accusations and failings and guilt, Davis felt a sudden, unexpected pang of possessiveness toward his wife. "You're everything to me," he slurred.

She gave him a funny look, wondering, perhaps, where that remark had come from.

She sat down across from him, and the bartender appeared. He was a thick guy, especially about the neck, and any minute now his gut was going to force his stained white shirt out from under his belt. He looked down at Britt. "What can I get you, miss?"

"Could I just get a Diet Coke, please?" she asked.

Davis gazed up at the man. "Are you Finnegan?"

The man winked and said, "We're all Finnegan." Davis wasn't sure whether he meant it as a glib statement about race—all Irish tapsters are Finnegan—or a more philosophical appraisal of humanity, like, *Let's face it, each of us, in some respect, is Finnegan. Am I right or am I right?*

"You want to tell me what went on up there?" Britt asked Davis once the barkeep had left them. She looked bemused, as if the notion that her husband would stomp out of his office and hit the liquor was apparently too surreal to take seriously.

Davis waved his hand. "Pavelka and me, we're done."

"What happened?"

"I told you. A log capsizes and some girl gets banged up, so naturally it's all my fault." His words came out garbled, in a stroke-victim slur.

Britt reached for his glass and slid it to the safety of her side of the table. He didn't appreciate that. "I'm going to need that back soon," he said to the glass.

Britt used to say that one of Davis's most attractive qualities was that he was an eminently reasonable drunk. She'd had two serious relationships before him, and both had been problematic when alcohol was introduced. Bradley, reportedly an otherwise sweet guy, had been quick to belligerence—not necessarily toward her, but toward every other person in sight or imagination. On a dime, he was pissed at his best friend right there in the room, at some kid he grew up with and hadn't laid eyes on in ten years, at the density of traffic on the highway. There had also been Craig, a merry drunk who, Britt frequently recalled, never seemed to realize he was the only person in the bar who was shouting and whose drunken laugh was two octaves higher than his sober one. Britt had always claimed to be ashamed that Craig's high-pitched laugh struck her as effeminate and girlish, but, Davis liked to point out, obviously she was not too ashamed to mention it.

"Did Hans actually blame you?" she asked, staring across the table. "Did he say, 'Davis, this is your fault,' or did he maybe use words to that effect that you might have misinterpreted?"

"The words to that effect were 'we'd like you to leave.' Is there an alternative interpretation of that you'd like to propose?"

"That's not the same thing as being fired," Britt pointed out.

"That, my dear, is a very lawyer thing to say."

Fuck Hans. And double-fuck Keiko. There was no doubt that right at that very moment, somewhere in Miami, Keiko was celebrating the efficiency of a good scapegoating over a pressed Cuban sandwich. God, how he hated her and those stupid lips that always glistened with Aquaphor. Chapped lips all year round? Girlfriend, please.

"He won't even let me go down to Virginia with him," Davis complained further. "He's taking Bob frickin' Roman."

"The bag of hammers?" Britt asked.

"The bag of hammers."

It had gotten too taxing to describe his coworker as "Bob Roman, who is as dumb as a bag of hammers," so years ago, Davis had simply started referring to him as "the bag of hammers." It was just easier.

"I don't get it," Britt said, puckering her non-chapped lips on the straw of the soda that the bartender had just set down. "Hans loves you."

"Love takes many forms," Davis pontificated. "Sometimes we fire the ones we love, blame them for shit they didn't do. A curious emotion, love is."

"Davis."

"You know what? Maybe the old bastard is doing the right thing, after all. Maybe I'm a terrible person and I deserve to be fired."

Britt said, "Okay, number one, we haven't established that you were fired, and frankly, it doesn't sound to me like you were. And two, none of this would make you a terrible person. Weren't you the one who got the firm the Virginia Beach contract in the first place?"

"Indeed I was," Davis replied. "And do you know what that classy broad Keiko said when we won it? 'Cha-ching.' She said, 'Cha-ching.'"

"That's neither here nor there."

"It's both here *and* there."

It was unimaginable that they'd turned on him like this. Had he ever been anything other than a model employee who churned out impeccable work day in and day out? Who else could claim to have kept the customers satisfied for so long without excuses or drama? Not Mary Aguilar, whose ex-husband famously showed up to pitch a fit about child support. Not Jeff whatever-his-name-was, who forced Hans to bust out the sexual harassment policy and explain that there would never, ever be a situation in which it would be appropriate to use the word *lube* in the workplace. Davis chuckled at the memory. "Lube," he said out loud.

"Did you just say *lube*?" Britt asked.

His mood took a sudden plummet, and he gazed desperately across the table. "Britt," he said darkly. "Britt, Britt, Britt."

The diminutive nonagenarian climbed back onto his barstool and gave an encore performance of "Rainy Night in Georgia," belting it out with even greater drunken gusto than before. When it was over, Davis hooted and whistled piercingly with two fingers. "Dude can really sing," he said.

"Yes, he's very talented," Britt said. "Listen, isn't there a possibility that Hans was just feeling under the gun today, and you were feeling a little defensive since you put so much time and energy into this project, and maybe things escalated and you both found yourselves somewhere neither one of you wanted to be? That can happen sometimes, can't it?"

"I suppose it can."

"Do you think maybe that happened here?"

"To be honest, Britt, I don't know anything anymore." Which was as hokey a thing as he'd ever said.

The bartender was standing over them again. "Another round, buddy?"

Davis smiled up at him. "It would be rude to decline."

"Actually, I think we're good," Britt interjected. "Just the check, please."

Davis drained the dregs of his glass down his gullet, capturing every last smoky drop as the jumble of ice cubes crashed into his upper lip.

"Here's what we're going to do," Britt said, shifting to logistics. "We're going to put you in a taxi and send you home to sober up. I'm going to go back to work, and tonight after we put Rachel to bed, we'll talk about how to approach Hans."

Davis leaned toward his wife. "Here's the approach that people generally take when they get fired: they don't go to work anymore."

"Every person at that firm loves you to death, Davis. When cooler heads prevail—"

"This is not a cooler-heads-will-prevail situation. I'm the fall guy." He threw up his hands. "Maybe it's just my turn."

"I'm sure that's how it looks now, but I just can't believe—"

"Call him yourself." Davis plunged his hand into the side pocket of his khakis, extracted his phone, and slid it across the table like a hockey puck. "Seriously. Call the man."

"I'm not going to call him."

"Then I suppose you're just going to have to trust me."

Britt fell silent. Something on Davis's phone had drawn her attention. She studied the display first with something resembling wonder, then with a harrowing motionlessness.

"What?" he asked.

She raised her eyes and held him in her gaze for one endless, forbidding moment. "Who is Jacqueline?"

His lungs emptied of air. "What?"

"Who is Jacqueline?" she asked again. *"And why does she miss you?"*

Britt chucked the phone at his chest. He caught it and regarded the screen. In a show of cosmic indifference to man's dangerous and forgotten secrets, or perhaps in a downdraft of poetic justice, or just random bad timing, a text message had appeared on Davis's phone at the precise moment that he'd unnecessarily, absurdly flung the thing at his wife. It read: I'm back in the States next month. More work in Virginia. Can we see each other? I miss you. Jacqueline. A winking emoji punctuated the message.

Britt looked gored. She waited for the innocuous explanation. Instead, all she saw was her husband struggling to conceal his horrible surprise.

"Britt," he said.

"Oh my god, Davis."

Tears of incomprehension pooled in the whites of her eyes.

"Britt."

Her chair screeched, and before he could form another word, she was out the door.

Even after she'd gone, he could picture her, slicing through the foot traffic, putting a distance between, deep and wide, a frightening space in which they could easily lose each other.

CHAPTER 8

Once the taxi dropped him off, Davis paced in his living room near the front door, his steps teetering and unbalanced, his phone clutched expectantly in his hand. He knew she'd be coming home after taxiing back to the office to retrieve her car. Not even Britt Palandjian could return to work and make like business as usual after so obliterating a surprise.

He waited.

There was one task he could easily take care of, one from which no amount of alcohol could distract him. He opened Jacqueline's text. "I'm sorry," he wrote as a succinct and final reply. Then he blocked her number.

How Davis wished he could shed this bourbon daze, slide out of it like snakeskin and be himself. Not that he'd been himself since that last trip to Virginia Beach. The justice in Britt finally learning the truth was, in some small and confusing way, the very thing he'd been waiting for.

The property owners had hired a Parisian firm to design the layout of the park, engineers whose job it was to position the attractions, food, and games for optimal access and minimal congestion. One day, while Davis was surveying one of the flume channels, she came bounding down the path, unfurled a set of blueprints on a nearby picnic table, and snatched a pencil from behind her ear. Davis took note of how she pouted when she scribbled, how she was messily stylish, how her buoyant mane dropped to her shoulders, then seemed to have second thoughts and curled back up. She was beautiful, but that's all she was, at first. He waved hello. Her name was Jacqueline.

At a planning meeting a few days later, he found himself seated next to her. The way she spoke about foot traffic and shade through the liquid tumble of a French accent, the way she kicked back in her chair and spun her rolled-up blueprints like an airplane propeller—it forced all sorts of French words into Davis's mind. *Nonchalance. Insouciance. Mousse au chocolat.*

That evening, when a dozen or so team members congregated at a fish restaurant down by the beach, and Davis and Jacqueline shared eye contact of an unexpected voltage, Davis entertained for the first time in his life the previously unthinkable notion that, should the perfect storm of motive and opportunity present itself, he could—though not necessarily would, and in all likelihood would not—betray his wife. It horrified him.

Davis Winger was a good guy. Ask anyone. His whole life he'd been known as a good-natured, easygoing, bighearted sport. He was cool, never too cool. He was a practitioner of benevolent sarcasm. He never left anyone out because they were a dork. He didn't think twice about driving someone home when it was out of his way. He paid attention in class not because he found the lectures so absorbing, but because he didn't want the teachers to feel ineffectual; this was their life's work, after all. He stayed late at the office even when that shit wasn't his responsibility. He helped neighbors carry their new claw-foot bathtub out of their minivan and up their stairs, and accepted a beer afterward not as repayment but because, you know, why not hang out for a bit? He couldn't get enough of his daughter and was a constant coconspirator in her efforts to stay up past her bedtime. He had no trouble having sex with his wife thrice weekly, and even after eight years of marriage could do so without needing to picture another woman's body or a tangle of tipsy sorority sisters.

And yet: it was easier than he could've ever imagined, as mindless as swiping a pack of matches off a hostess stand. When the industrial engineer from the second arrondissement subtly reached for his hand after dinner, to his immense amazement, Davis allowed his hand to be taken. When she led him back to her hotel room, he allowed himself to be led. Up until the very second that those things happened, he would've never believed that they actually could.

In no time their clothes were simply off, and she was straddling him and producing a condom from her purse. (Malice aforethought!) It was all so alarmingly unceremonious, just a handful of small steps over the course of a quarter hour, and suddenly he was having sex with a stranger.

It had been so long since he'd felt and smelled the naked body of another woman, and the shock of it sent a rush of panic through his limbs. But she moved so slowly and methodically on him that he couldn't help but fall into her assured, insistent rhythm. She was slightly thicker in the hips and thighs than Britt, but in an almost overpoweringly sexy way, and her soft skin smelled of botanical essences from the hotel lotion. When she placed her hands on his chest, her arms became the flying buttresses of Notre Dame. Her hair swayed as though blown by the winds of Lacoste. Her wine-warm breath whiffed of Bordeaux.

Later that night, when he returned to his room alone, he didn't know quite what to make of his infidelity. There was guilt, shame, even the recognition that from then on, every day for the rest of his life, he'd have to live with the worry that Britt could discover this potentially marriage-ending transgression. But just as powerful, and twice as surprising, was the disappointment. It hadn't been worth it. No one had ever said anything about that.

For the balance of that week, Davis did not avoid Jacqueline's company, but he did resist further hotel room episodes, which seemed to confuse but not upset her. And when at last he steered his car onto the Chesapeake Bay Bridge-Tunnel, the sea swells rolling under him and the raised road pointing him back toward all the happy trappings of his life, Davis exhaled with relief. He had no intention of ever perpetrating that crime again with anyone, no matter how French.

Was it untimely, unfortunate, and unlucky that the very first time Jacqueline ever contacted him his phone happened to be in his wife's hand? Without question. But it was hardly unfair.

Hearing the portentous hum of Britt's Mazda, Davis prepared himself. There was the dull smack of the car door, then the insistent tap of heels coming up the front walk. When she opened the door and saw him, she didn't even pause.

"Is there someone else?" she asked point-blank.

She was standing on the mat, the front door still ajar, the belt of her eggshell jacket still fastened around her waist. She hadn't committed to coming inside.

"Sit down, Britt. Please."

"I just want the truth, Davis. Explanations later. For now, it's just yes or no."

It seemed unimaginable that he actually had something to admit. He still couldn't believe he'd done this. To *her*.

"There was a woman," he said. "I was going to tell you. She worked on the Virginia project. It was one night and it meant absolutely nothing."

She stared at him, wounded, stunned all over again.

"I haven't had any contact with her at all. I know it's hard to believe, but I swear it's the truth."

Britt's face erupted. The edges of her mouth wrenched downward, and she convulsed with such a pained gasp that it almost appeared as though, by coincidence, something physical had overtaken her at that very moment—chest pains or a ruptured appendix. Never had Davis seen her cry like this. In a reflex, he hurried toward her, to hold and comfort her, and she was so demolished that she forgot herself and nearly let him. But then she pushed him away. "Don't touch me."

"You're everything to me, Britt. Everything."

Her face slipped into her hands and she cried, and Davis was forced to watch from across the room, undeserving of the privilege of soothing her.

"Do you remember the last thing you said to me before I saw that text?" she said, wiping her cheeks with her jacket sleeves. "You said I was going to have to trust you."

"Can we just talk? Please?"

But she couldn't even look at him. She rushed past him to the staircase, her black pumps carrying her up the steps in unbreachable strides.

For the longest time, Davis heard nothing. The seconds swelled into minutes and the minutes into hours, and he sat on the couch, head in hands, and waited. At one point he was actually driven to laughter over what a day it had been. An inconceivable day. Had the world forgotten who he was?

From the sofa his eyes wandered into the kitchen and caught Rachel's artwork on the refrigerator door. All her wonderful imaginings detonating from the six colors that spilled out of a Crayola box. What would happen to that imagination of hers if her family fell apart? Those prying little eyes would look at things differently, and her drawings, so unclouded and innocent now, would too soon corrode with nuance and shadow.

After an endless stretch of time, Britt's voice cut the silence from the top of the stairs. "Rachel gets home in an hour. I want you gone by then."

He walked over to the old wooden banister and peered up at her. She was still wearing her jacket. "Britt, I made a horrible, horrible mistake. But I love you. You know that. I don't even know who I am without you."

She looked down at him. "I'm embarrassed for you."

"I was going to tell you, I swear. But in some weird way, telling you felt even more selfish, like hurting you over something meaningless instead of bearing the guilt on my own. I know what a cop-out that sounds like."

"I'm embarrassed for both of us," she said.

The weariness in her voice, the exasperation—this was how she sounded when she spoke of her clients, those poor women who came to her office with their defeated eyebrows and their mute, stricken children. *Your situation never leads anywhere good,* she always told them. *It will not right itself. You have to make decisions. Nothing changes unless you change it.*

"I need some time apart," she said. "You need to leave for a while. Pack your things."

"Britt. Listen." Her words stabbed him into instantaneous sobriety. He was dead straight now, and more afraid than he'd ever been in his life. "You have every right to be angry, but we're going to work through this."

"Maybe, but right now I'm shocked and I'm hurt and I'm really sad. It's going to be a long time before I can look at you."

"People like us, people who really love each other, who have what we have—they don't let something like this tear them apart."

Staring down at him from the top of the steps, her features iced over. "Is that what you were thinking about when you were in Virginia? What we have?"

She marched down the stairs. "I'm going to pick Rachel up before she gets on the bus, then I'm going to take her out for a little while, maybe get her dinner. When we get back, I don't want you here. Do you understand what I'm saying? You're moving out."

He felt the muscles of his heart clench. This was what he deserved. "Please, Britt."

She moved past him, swiftly across the living room. At the front door, she turned and raised her index finger like a warning. "And if you even—" she began, then either abandoned the thought or decided that was enough. Then she pushed through the door and was gone.

Davis remained fixed in the gloom of the empty house, suddenly remembering a night more than twenty years earlier, an argument between his mother and his father. It gave him an icy shudder, like he was a moving part in destiny's scheme.

He looked at the floor and noticed all the nicks and scuff marks that lent the room its worn vitality. *It's a living room,* Britt was fond of saying whenever Davis pointed out a scratch on the wood. *It should feel like it's living, like it has lived.* Now Davis would trade everything just to stay, to be here with his wife and his little girl, scraping and scrawling merry imperfections all over the floor.

He allowed himself a long look around the room, at every piece of furniture, every picture frame, painting, and throw pillow. Then he headed down to the basement to find his suitcase.

CHAPTER 9

A drift of clouds had overtaken the late-afternoon sky. It looked like rain. It had, in fact, felt like rain for weeks now. Everywhere Molly went, a swirl of gloom followed. She couldn't get comfortable anywhere in the world. Not her office, not her house, certainly not her bed, with the lights out and the noises dying down and her brain left alone to spin over and over about how Davis had ruined everything. It wasn't fair. Molly was his sister, not his wife or daughter, and yet she felt just as betrayed, just as entitled to her outrage and this oceanic sense of loss.

She was expected at Britt's for dinner, and since the family home was around the corner from Davis's new apartment, she decided to swing by the mall to buy him some essentials—he'd never had to live alone and thus didn't seem to know how—then drop in on him on the way to dinner. Her one prior visit to her brother's new digs at The Deluxe Apartments—a name that was not so much irony as outright ridicule—was a day or so after he'd moved in almost three weeks ago, and it had set upon her a mood so bleak she thought it might never lift. It was bad enough he'd taken up residence at a sprawling, drab formation of garden apartments slumped on a grassless hill. What was worse, he seemed defiantly opposed to sprucing it up and making it more inviting than some roadside motel. Did he really expect his six-year-old to cozy up on his college sofa, that malarial, mildewy, decomposing corpse that had been *Weekend at Bernie*'ed in and out of tenements before ending up in his basement? And what of the kitchen, which wasn't even its own room so much as the back nine of the living room, which itself was the back nine of the foyer, which itself was just a couple of buckling linoleum checkerboard tiles? Molly knew that Davis didn't care at all about the amenities and that he'd chosen the Deluxe for precisely one reason: it was exactly a mile from the house where his wife and daughter slept. Yet it should still have mattered to him that the toilet only sometimes flushed.

Those first few nights after being kicked out Davis had spent in a hotel, evidently hoping Britt's anger would abate, that he could talk her down from an actual separation before anybody had to sign any leases. But Britt wasn't softening, and Davis couldn't continue to shell out a hundred bucks a night, even if he claimed that the scrambled eggs at the Holiday Inn Express breakfast buffet were out of this world.

"You know, you could always stay with me while you guys work things out," Molly had proposed.

"I can't start crashing on my sister's futon," was Davis's reply. "I'm a grown man with a career. Well, I'm a grown man who used to have a career. And don't even think about suggesting I move in with Dad and Tom Petty. I'd rather be homeless."

Her brother may have been an expert at dreaming up new ways to fling trains down tracks at the speed of a scream, but he was the last person in the universe you'd expect to drive his own mess off the rails.

The mall smelled of penny fountains and scented air, and Molly moved methodically, her first stop a children's store to pick out a bathing suit for Rachel. Summer was approaching, and with it day camp and the daily doubleheader of instructional and free swim. For Davis, she bought a lamp, a table to rest it on, and a bath mat. She also grabbed him some cheap art for his walls: a watercolor of a chili pepper, the mandatory Van Gogh print, and a photo of an aging rock star sloppily consuming nachos in a cantina—which, she guessed, would make Rachel giggle.

Being in the presence of art, even airbrushed, imitative junk holed up between a Kay Jewelers and a Dressbarn, had an oddly stirring effect on Molly. After just a few minutes among the explosion of still lifes, cityscapes, and pastoral scenes, she emerged inspired, hell-bent on finding a cure for her newspaper's ill health. No specific ideas were bubbling yet, but the idea of ideas suddenly seemed attainable.

Driving to her brother's sorry apartment, where he lived shut away from his wife and daughter, Molly couldn't help but smell the burp of history. She wondered if it was preordained that her family would break apart again, if this was the playing out of a curse, a pox on the house of Winger? Down the dark tunnel of her earliest memories she could still see that drive from Columbus. She was six, and they were moving to Baltimore, a larger television market where her father had landed a job at the ABC affiliate. They were happy then. Kitty was warm and playful, full of kisses, brimming with songs, alive with being her children's mother. Molly could still faintly recall the family piling into the wood-panel station wagon, the mountain of jackets on the back seat separating her from Davis, the smell of oak hanging in the autumn chill. She remembered craning her neck for one last look at the brown siding of their house. She remembered the Slurpee machine at the 7-Eleven where they stopped along the way, and how the cherry flavoring stained the rim of her brother's mouth. She remembered the cool window against her forehead and the bracing freshness of her father's aftershave wafting over the seat.

She also remembered her mother's voice. "You're going to love the new house, my littles!" Kitty promised as they traveled the highways between Ohio and Maryland. "And our yard will be perfect for sledding when the snow comes. What do you think about that, Kitten?" Her mother was Kitty, so Molly was Kitten. It wasn't quite logical, but the possessiveness it implied—you belong to me—was safe and seemingly unbreakable. Later, that same voice, delicate as dew, roused Molly from sleep as the station wagon ground up the strange driveway of a strange house. "Wake up, honey, we're here," her mom had said. Or maybe it was "Wake up, honey, we're there." Here, there—what difference did it make? It was the place from which Kitty would eventually abandon them all—her husband, her eleven-year-old son, her eight-year-old daughter—and run off to California with some doctor.

Davis opened his apartment door and peered into the bags that Molly held out. He looked both touched and offended. "I don't need my sister to buy me a bath mat," he said. "I'm not your problem."

"Well, you don't seem to be anyone else's at the moment," Molly said.

She positioned the lime-green side table next to the sofa in the center of the room, then placed the lamp on top of it. She plugged it in and flicked it on. It wasn't enough light. There could never be enough light.

"I still can't believe you live here," she sighed. "Have you talked to Britt?"

"We talk," he said. "Mostly, I talk, and she stands there looking like she'd rather be somewhere else. Which I deserve." He couldn't take his eyes off the new table. "The question is, do I also deserve furniture the color of a Jell-O square?"

Molly had to admit that the table hadn't seemed quite this green at the store.

"Are you guys going to get a divorce?" she asked.

"Let's get this out of the way." Already he seemed to find her exhausting. "I made a horrible mistake, okay? It was a lapse in judgment that still surprises and scares the shit out of me. I've never wanted anyone else, will never want anyone else, and, to be honest, didn't even really want anyone else the night I screwed around on her. I have literally begged her forgiveness. Begged. But Britt is angry, and she has a right to be angry, and nothing I can say will speed up the time line for working through that anger. Do I really have to explain to you how women think?"

Suddenly Molly missed her brother's clipped confidence, his impervious breed of cool. That was the Davis that Molly wanted, the Davis of every yesterday she'd ever known. The one who stood up at a high school pep rally in front of the entire student body, had a mic shoved in front of him, and proceeded to sing "The Greatest Love of All" because that was the song that popped into his head at that moment. Singing Whitney Houston at a pep rally should've been the end of him; it should've conferred permanent pariah status upon him. But, of course, the opposite happened. Every kid started singing along. So did the faculty, the principal, the custodial staff. And then the deliriously amped-up basketball team went out and crushed its opponent. Where was that heroic Davis now? He was right here, replaced by this lesser Davis, one who was lost for explanations, lost for plans, lost for any words except *I don't know, I don't know, I don't know.*

He yanked open the fridge. "You want a beer or wine or something?"

"No," Molly replied.

"Nothing? You sure?"

"Fine. Maybe just a sip of wine."

"I only have beer."

"I don't want a drink, Davis. I want you to fix this."

She eyed the Van Gogh print she'd brought him, blue irises rising up in a field of flowers, and she remembered, with a horror so acute that it actually brought a laugh, that the artist had painted it in the solitude of an asylum. "You need to be back home with your family before they learn not to need you," she said.

"Learn not to need me?" Davis repeated. "Where do you hear shit like that?"

"Things change fast. Get back in that house. Like, tomorrow."

"Stop setting deadlines," he said. "I'm trying, Molly. It might take some time."

"You don't have time. Jesus, Davis, did you not grow up in the same house I did?"

He turned and glared at her. "That's not fair, Molly. I ain't her."

"I hope not," she pleaded.

"Mom walked out and never came back. I was asked to leave, and I've done nothing since but beg to return."

He was wrong if he thought he had time. Did he not see that this was how the end began, that it wouldn't take long for Britt and Rachel to adapt to his absence, to the new space in their house, the new space in their lives? Did he not see that sooner than anyone could anticipate, he would be a satellite circling the planet on which his own family lived?

"I'm just going to ask you this once," she said. "Do you love this woman? This woman from Virginia?"

"What? Lord, no. I barely know her. You can ask me as many times as you want. The answer will never, ever change." He sighed. "It's going to be okay, Mol. I'm just being straight with you about everything. Do you want the truth, or do you want me to lie?"

Why did people ask such obvious questions? "I want you to lie better," she said.

Someone was knocking on the door. When Davis opened it, Molly saw a burly bear of a man. She figured him to be in his late thirties, though dressed for his late teens in athletic shorts and a black Iron Maiden T-shirt. The man raised a plastic cup to his mouth, spit into it, and said, "What's up, D?"

"How's it going, McGuinn?" Davis said.

"It's a stone groove," the man replied. "Yourself?"

"Getting by."

Davis invited him in and introduced him to Molly as his next-door neighbor. Molly attempted a smile while struggling not to look repulsed at the long flows of dark matter that shot through the man's teeth and splashed into his cup.

"McGuinn was the first inmate I met when I moved into this asylum," Davis explained with a smirk. "When he saw my U-Haul, he came down and just started unloading crates. I thought I was being robbed."

"Like there's anything here worth stealing," McGuinn quipped as he deposited his spittoon in a remote corner of the room, lest anyone mistake it for iced tea.

Davis handed McGuinn a beer. "Molly has stopped by to judge me and to freak out a little. Would you please tell her to chill?"

"I just met her. I'm not going to tell her to chill." McGuinn looked at Molly. "You don't have to chill if you don't want to."

To be fair, she had come to judge. But mostly she'd come to worry, because if Davis was in trouble, the balance of the cosmos was in jeopardy. Davis couldn't be in trouble. It was irresponsible of him. Like the time Norman and Peti came home early one Saturday night and caught Davis and his friends smoking pot in the basement. Molly didn't sleep a wink that night, and she charged into her father's bedroom early the next morning to ask if Davis had "a drug problem." Then she cried, so Norman held her for a while and said, "Okay, are we all done crying?"

Molly looked at McGuinn. "How long have you lived here?" she asked, skirting the real question, which was, *Why* do you live here?

"Been here awhile," McGuinn replied vaguely. "I moved in during a period of—let's just call it professional refocusing. I couldn't resist the promise in something called the Deluxe. It's not so bad. And it beats living in a hangar."

Apparently, at one point he'd lived in a hangar.

McGuinn expounded neither on the profession nor on the refocusing it required, but it soon came up, thanks to Davis, that he'd once played professional baseball. Molly's face lit up.

"For real?" she asked.

"I had a cup of coffee in pro ball," McGuinn grumbled to his navel.

"He's being modest," Davis said. "The man was a phenom."

McGuinn had been a highly touted pitching prospect out of Arizona State. Drafted by the San Francisco Giants, he tore through the farm system like a bat out of hell. His career, however, lasted all of four major league innings, derailed in his very first start by a comebacker to the noggin, which got him carried off the field in a stretcher. After that, he found it difficult to bear down on batters. Unable to regain the mental steel that got him there in the first place, he never made it back to the big leagues.

"That's an awful story," Molly said.

He shrugged. "Sometimes turbulence is unexpected." These days he spent his time in the employ of his brother's construction business, swinging a hammer and doing various odd jobs. "Don't feel sorry for me. I still hold the minor league record for ejections. Forty-seven."

There was something outsized—larger-than-life, even—about McGuinn. She liked his gritty voice, which had a smattering of midwestern plains in the broad, slightly overemphasized vowels. He spoke the way an unpaved road looked, and it wasn't hard to imagine this man, with the square jaw, the slightly softening bulk, and the wavy hair shorn down in jock fashion, coming of age in a clubhouse.

"What about you?" he asked her. "Davis tells me you're a journalist."

"I write for a small local paper. The *Weekly Ramble*?"

He nodded with interest. "What do you write about?"

"Anything, really. We don't have a sports section, though."

"Molly's got game," Davis said. "You should read her stuff."

"I do love good writing," McGuinn mused, "or as better minds than mine have described it, 'the bending of desirous eruptions against the wind, electric inspirations into the lightning.'"

Both Wingers blinked.

"My apologies," McGuinn said. "That was Whitman, or Thoreau—I don't remember." He smiled bashfully. "I'm an occasional reader of poetry. And apparently something of a show-off." He cleared his throat. "Where were we? The *Weekly Ramble*. I'll subscribe today."

"No need," said Molly. "It's free."

"Free? You must mean priceless."

"I mean we can't imagine people would pay," she said.

Molly glanced at her watch. Needing to arrive at Britt's in time for dinner, she politely excused herself. Fortunately, Davis didn't ask where she was headed. Not that he would've minded. The last thing he'd want would be to estrange Britt from her sister-in-law and Rachel from her aunt.

Molly gave McGuinn a polite smile. "It was nice meeting you."

McGuinn stood and extended a thick hand. "I get that a lot."

Davis walked her out onto the terrace, which overlooked the parking lot. A light rain had begun to fall. Before heading down the steps, Molly looked hard at her brother.

"I'm not judging you," she said, "but, honestly, I can't believe you're here."

"That's not what not judging means," he said.

"Have you talked to Dad?"

"I will."

"You need to."

"I know. That's why I just said I will. Remember when I said that?"

"He can be cool, you know."

"About some things, sure, but when it comes to playing hell with one's marriage, he's not likely to be cool. That might strike a nerve."

Molly dropped a helpless sigh. "Maybe this is karma."

"Christ Jesus, Molly. Just get in your car-ma and go home. Thank you for all the gifts, but get out of here and take your disillusionment with you."

Davis stood and watched Molly hurry across the parking lot in the soft spring drizzle. The poor girl was wrong. Karma wasn't at fault here. Karma hadn't cheated on Britt. Karma hadn't been seduced by a French accent. Karma was merely the demonstrable truism that bad shit happened to everyone if you waited around long enough. He may have aided and abetted karma by unlatching the door to its cage, but after that, all karma had to do was stand in that nonsmoking hotel room, light a cigarette, and watch Davis drop onto a queen bed and ruin his own life.

The worst part of all of this was not his imprisonment, but Britt's, knowing she had nowhere to run from the sucker punch delivered by her very own husband. How he hated to imagine her turning off that bedside lamp at night and lying there, alone, miles from sleep under the ceiling fan. He knew that each morning brought the cruelty of a wiped memory, a few seconds of forgetfulness before reality pounced and reminded her all over again that the man who'd always been there wasn't there anymore.

Molly was right that at some point Davis would have to come clean with their father. Norman had never let his family down, even with the demands of a highly public, time-consuming job and two kids dealing with the wallop of a runaway mother. Peti may have swept in and been a godsend of operational efficiency, seeing to it that everyone ate their green vegetables and left for school with a lunch in their backpack, but it was Norman who'd worked his ass off to keep the air light, who'd found deep wells of energy and spirit to shower upon his family to fill the strange void. He was the one staging nightly somersault contests in the master bedroom. He was the one making a taco bar of the kitchen counter every Sunday evening. He was the one making the old stereo speakers crackle with Bob Dylan, Jefferson Airplane, and Cream, noising up the house and banishing the sickly gloom that had hung like smoke in the weeks, even months, before Kitty finally left. How exactly did Davis measure up to his old man now?

There had been moments during some of these long days when Davis was tempted to call his father. Like any son, Davis sometimes just needed to hear his old man's voice. But instead, he put on Bob Dylan, Jefferson Airplane, or Cream until the urge passed. Better to piece everything back together before Norman could learn that his son was capable of hurting his family just as Kitty had done decades earlier.

As Molly's Civic cleared the parking lot, Davis noticed a lone female figure down in the parking lot, a young woman with shoulders hunched against the rain. She was taking fitful steps among the cars, holding a set of keys out in various directions and clicking, then searching for the blink of headlights. Davis watched this game of automotive Marco Polo for a few minutes until the girl, perhaps sensing his presence, looked up and spotted him up on the second-floor terrace.

"Hey," she called. Her wet, glimmering hair was matted to her forehead. "Do you see a silver Subaru anywhere?"

He peered out at the cars, clustered unevenly like teeth in a child's mouth. "I see a generic-looking hatchback that looks grayish from here," he said, pointing.

She followed his finger. "Sweet. You're a pal." Then she paused and gazed up at him through the drizzle. "I haven't seen you before."

"I'm new."

She snickered. "Sorry to hear it."

With that, she made for the silver Subaru, and Davis went back inside his apartment.

"Another round?" he asked McGuinn.

"I'm not even going to dignify that with a response."

After he extracted two more beers from the fridge, a thought stopped Davis dead in his tracks, and he looked at his new friend. "Did you really bust out Walt Whitman in front of my sister?"

"I think you're imagining things," McGuinn said, and proceeded to pad his cheek with a wad of tobacco.

CHAPTER 10

Molly hadn't even removed her coat when Rachel began campaigning for a sleepover.

"Don't pressure Aunt Molly," Britt chided her daughter. "She knows she can stay if she wants to."

"She wants to," Rachel insisted. "I'll go get pj's."

"Can we at least let Aunt Molly make it through the door before we ask her to take her clothes off?" Britt asked.

Molly babysat regularly for her niece and acquiesced to an overnight more often than one would expect of a grown woman whose own bed was fifteen minutes away. It just wasn't easy to refuse someone who shivered with excitement over the mere fact that you existed. Each time Molly stayed over, Rachel set up camp for them on her bedroom floor, where they'd ensconce themselves in a sea of blankets and stay up "really late" telling stories, singing songs, and making beaded bracelets by the flashlight's glow. Last time, Rachel had performed every song on the *Annie* soundtrack—twice—and then stated with the utmost earnestness that "those songs got me through kindergarten."

Molly presented Rachel with her new bathing suit, and the little girl immediately began to change into it right where she stood. The adults, meanwhile, drifted into the kitchen.

"How are you holding up?" Molly quietly asked Britt, who was twisting the cap off a bottle of red wine.

Britt shrugged plaintively. "You know."

"I'm actually just coming from my brother's. I stopped by to check on him."

"How's he doing?"

"Well, he's a dope," Molly said.

Rachel twittered into the room, dressed now for a swim, and allowed her aunt and mother to gush.

"You look gorgeous!" Molly crowed.

"Fits you perfectly," Britt said.

"I know," Rachel agreed. "Who's a dope?"

"Oh, just someone at work," said Molly.

"Daddy?"

"No, of course not," said Britt. "Nobody you know."

Britt pulled open the kitchen drawer that housed the pile of take-out menus and solicited opinions from the group. Rachel didn't want to order in. She wanted to make breakfast-for-dinner, another "tradition" she shared with her aunt—although Molly didn't think that something they'd done exactly once before qualified as a tradition. Britt balked at the idea, presumably because life was depressing enough, and eating french toast and Fruity Pebbles on a Friday night didn't ward off depression so much as invite it in and ask it to sit down.

"It's fine, Britt," Molly said. "I'll cook, you drink."

Was it such a crime to allow Rachel to be dictatorial about this one thing when so much else had spun beyond the poor kid's control?

Cabinet doors were pulled open. An extravagance of pots, bowls, plates, and pans were arranged up and down the counter. Eggs were fetched from the fridge. In no time at all Rachel was whisking pancake batter on a stepstool next to Molly, her flimsy limbs looking unbound in her new one-piece swimsuit.

Britt stayed out of the way and let them have their fun. She sat at the table and hovered over her wineglass as if it were a sustaining fire. Molly knew how hard it was for Britt to be here, in this house, without Davis. Britt had already confided that when Rachel was out with her father, she often fled the emptiness and quiet. She took gratuitous Target trips. She brought a paperback to Starbucks and nursed a latte for a few hours.

Reading in a coffee shop: that's how it had all begun, on a cloudless Saturday afternoon in Palo Alto. How many times had Molly heard the tale? Britt, a second-year law student at Stanford, was carrying two coffees out of a café, one for her boyfriend waiting in the car, when she tripped and landed on an innocent patron. That patron, an engineering student who was lost in the oblivion of his headphones (he was listening to Traffic's *Low Spark of High Heeled Boys*), was guiding his highlighter across his textbook when his shoulder was seared by boiling java. This was no mere dribble. It was a splashing of Exxon Valdez proportions that stained his book and swept like a puddle over his Sony Discman. Baristas lurched from behind the counter with paper towels. Strangers selflessly surrendered their napkins. A med student evaluated Davis's forearms for burns.

Britt offered profuse apologies and asked for his number, feeling indebted to this sopping wet stranger to the tune of a disc player, which was also sopping wet and likely destroyed. Davis was far too entranced by the delicate beauty of his assailant to betray any pain.

"Don't worry about it. My chair was sticking out into the aisle. It's my bad," he said.

"No, it really seems like my bad," Britt insisted, and like any law student with a measuring cup's worth of knowledge, she enlightened him as to concepts of proximate causation and comparative negligence.

Long after settling into her boyfriend's car and pulling away, Britt was still thinking about Davis, deciding that she'd literally bumped into the nicest guy she'd ever met. That's all it was for her initially—he was a nice guy. He was cute enough. The quasi-beard smacked of neglect as opposed to style, and she didn't think dreadlocks on a white guy was okay unless you were in the Counting Crows. But there was an accessible sweetness to him, a calm in his eyes and guileless charm in his smile. She just wanted to know him, to have him in her life.

The very next morning, Britt didn't think twice about forking over sixty dollars for a new Discman. When she called Davis, he played it cool and said he'd already forgotten about the incident. Which was the very opposite of the truth. In fact, he'd thought of nothing but. Britt Palandjian was the most alluring person he'd met since arriving in California.

They met later that day at the same coffee shop, and she handed him the replacement CD player in its tight plastic casing with the padded foam headphones.

"I'm sorry it's so yellow," Britt said.

"Yeah, it's pretty yellow," he acknowledged.

"You want me to take it back and see if they have any other colors?"

"I'll take sapphire blue, please," he said. "If they don't have that, kiwi green is fine."

He refused to accept such an expensive portable electronic from her, but she refused his refusal, so he caved, but only on the condition that she let him take her to dinner.

"When?" she asked.

"How about now?" It was three in the afternoon. "The best Thai place in the universe—including Thailand—is a five-minute walk from here."

"Are you proposing Thai food because you think I'm Thai?" she asked, possibly grinning. "I'm not Thai."

"I didn't accuse you of being Thai," he said. "Maybe I'm Thai. Did you ever consider that? And if you're the type of person who engages in racial profiling, maybe dinner isn't such a good idea after all."

They'd been together ever since. Until recently, when they suddenly weren't.

Dinner (breakfast) was almost ready. Under Rachel's supervision, Molly had been spooning pancake batter into the pan, then sliding a spatula under the bubbling puddles in order to flip them. A stack sufficient to feed all three mouths had at last been constructed. Rachel climbed into a chair, and Molly set a plate down in front of her and cut the pancakes into little pieces with the edge of the fork.

Britt cleared her throat. "Thank you, Aunt Molly," she coached her daughter.

"Thank you, Aunt Molecule," Rachel said, upending the syrup bottle over her plate and shaking out a treacly stream.

"Don't thank me—you made them," Molly said.

When Molly placed a stack in front of Britt, Britt too said, "Thank you, Aunt Molecule." Maybe she'd meant to be cute and ironic, but the words landed with a naked vulnerability, and when Molly saw all the gratitude on her sister-in-law's face, it struck her as madly unfair that there was such a thing as marital infidelity, that we built institutions in which so much hurt was possible, and that a night of pancakes and wine couldn't fix everything.

"Oops," said Rachel, as she fumbled a jumbo-size, syrup-soaked piece of pancake that hit the floor with a slap.

Britt ducked under the table to retrieve it, and when she reemerged, there was a small object in the palm of her hand and a stern look on her face.

"Uh, what is this?" she demanded of Rachel.

She was holding a piece of a model, a section of track from one of the miniature roller coasters that Davis kept upstairs in the office.

"Is this Daddy's model?" Britt asked, locking eyes with her daughter.

Rachel shrugged.

"What is this doing down here?"

"Daddy lets me."

"He lets you play with them. He doesn't let you take them apart. Why did you do that?"

"It just came off."

"No, it didn't. Go put it back."

"He doesn't even care," Rachel protested.

"Now. The pancakes will wait."

Rachel slid down off her chair and shuffled petulantly out of the kitchen.

"Put it back where it belongs and don't touch any of those models!" Britt called after her.

"Fine!" Rachel shouted, stomping up the steps. "Christ Jesus!"

"Watch that language, little lady!"

Molly put a hand over her mouth to smother her laughter.

"Common vandal," Britt muttered.

Molly shook her head. She saw only a confused child acting out. "This can't be easy on her," she said, speaking up in her niece's defense. "Poor thing."

Britt disarranged her hair like a madwoman, then sighed. "I know. I guess I'm just not ready to dismantle all things Davis around here."

"It's okay," Molly said.

Anyone who'd ever spent any time in the Winger home knew that those models did, in fact, come down from the shelves and windowsills to be tinkered and toyed with by Davis. He and Rachel would stretch out on the carpet and move the trains along the tracks. He would show her how they worked, explain how the cars gathered just enough speed to crest an incline, how a slight banking of the track kept the cars from flying off into space when they rounded a turn. Molly thought she was seeing the memory of those moments surging within Britt and gripping her with a sharp sadness.

"On second thought, she can do whatever the hell she wants with those stupid things," Britt snapped. "She can take a hammer to them, for all I care."

———

Rachel lobbied and campaigned for a sleepover with her aunt until her persistence became intransigence, and the tenor of negotiations escalated to the point where she flat-out refused to go to bed until her terms were met. With Molly's consent, Britt brokered a compromise: the floor of Rachel's bedroom would be decked out with the standard plenitude of blankets, but Rachel would have to commit herself to them first, and Molly would join her later after the grown-ups had had some time to themselves.

"Are you really going to stay over, or is this a trick?" Rachel asked as Molly tucked her under the afghan with Bunny, the unimaginatively named stuffed rabbit.

"*Moi?*" Molly said. "Have I ever once tricked you?"

"How would I know?"

"I would tell you, of course."

Dicey logic, but apparently not Rachel's beach to die on.

"I'll bet Mommy wants to talk to you about Daddy," the little girl postulated.

"She might," Molly answered. "She can tell me anything. Just like you can tell me anything. Anything in the world, good or bad."

Both Britt and Davis had reported that when they'd sat Rachel down in the living room to tell her about the separation, it had gone exactly as expected—not well. She'd listened, then sprinted up to her room, slammed the door, and started crying. Davis followed her, but Britt stayed back, having started to bawl herself. Sitting next to Rachel on her bed, Davis hit all the standard marks—it was okay to be upset, but everybody still loved each other very much, and Rachel had absolutely nothing to do with any of the adult matters that Mommy and Daddy needed to straighten out. But nothing he could say obscured the fact that the family would now consist of pieces, no longer a whole.

Since then, Rachel had been handling it the way Rachel handled everything. Pragmatic toughness. Minimal negotiating. Even less complaining. There were, however, minor acts of protest and defiance. She'd been a little slower to get out of the house for school. She'd been testing her parents' tolerance for "bad words." She'd even, on occasion, declined the bedtime book-reading, offering a small-voiced and melancholy "That's okay, I'm fine."

Molly made a sarcophagus of Rachel's outline by patting down the afghan, which Peti had knitted six years ago in celebration of the little girl's birth.

"How about you?" Molly asked, hovering over her niece's face. "Is there anything you want to talk about? We're besties, you and I."

"I know," Rachel said.

Molly wanted to tell Rachel that she understood what she was going through, that she'd been there. She wanted to tell her that everything would turn out okay because there were so many different ways for things to turn out okay.

"So?" Molly asked again. "Is there? Anything at all you want to talk about?"

In the soft bedroom light, Rachel pursed her lips in thought. "Aunt Molly?"

"Yeah?"

"Can I ask you something?"

"You know you can."

"Is Miss Hannigan a drunk?"

"What?"

"Miss Hannigan. From *Annie*. Would they really let a drunk take care of all those kids?"

Molly leaned in and kissed Rachel on the cheek. "Let's talk about that in the morning."

Having changed into the pair of gray sweatpants and navy sweatshirt with the words Cape Cod frowning across the chest that Rachel had yanked out of her mother's drawer, Molly descended the stairs. She found Britt burrowed in the couch with the radio tuned to some singer-songwriter purring over the tender pluck of an acoustic guitar.

"I tried to get your daughter to talk about her emotions," Molly said.

"And?"

"She wanted to stage an intervention for Miss Hannigan."

Molly pitched herself into the love seat, and both women emitted simultaneous sighs.

"What's up with Zach?" Britt asked.

"Oh, you know," Molly replied.

Britt laughed at the familiar response, one that highlighted Molly's equivocation and surrender. Hugging her knees in the swaddle of the sofa cushion, Britt said, "Molly, if you're ready to move on, move on. There's no reason to spend these short lives of ours in unfulfilling relationships. You're beautiful and interesting. Don't you want to fall in love and get married?"

"Of course not," Molly said, as though the answer were obvious. "I want to *be* in love and *be* married."

Everyone knew that Zach would never be the object of Molly's love. That didn't mean she wouldn't stay with him and perhaps even marry him, which she could certainly see herself doing out of cowardice or conflict-aversion. If she continued to not break up with him, matrimony was a realistic outcome, was it not?

The misty evening deepened into a rainy night, and the two women became moored to the upholstery. Britt indulged an apparent need for closeness and joined Molly on the love seat, wedging herself into the cushions and slinging a leg over her sister-in-law's waist. A long, comfortable silence ensued.

"Please tell me you're going to forgive him one day," Molly said. "One day soon, if you're taking requests."

Britt was gazing up at the hairline fractures in the ceiling. "I don't know, Mol."

"He's the same person."

"Same as what?" Britt wondered.

Molly stared into her wineglass. "If you don't forgive him, I don't think I'll be able to."

"No," Britt said. "That's sweet, but no. Brothers and sisters should stand by each other."

"Not if they wreck everything," Molly shot back. "Not if they know better. Not if they allow themselves to become the worst of their parents."

Britt looked over at her, full of compassion, as if realizing for the first time that this was about so much more than the three people who lived in this house. This was about Molly and Norman and a woman in California whom Britt had never met. She placed her hand atop Molly's. There they stayed, nestled together in the feathery pillows, letting the minutes pass.

"Maybe you're right," Britt said, sometime later. "Maybe Davis is the same person, and I'm just seeing something new. Or maybe there's this part of him he's managed to keep from me all these years."

"Or maybe he made a mistake," Molly suggested. "The worst mistake, a mistake that carries terrible consequences, but still just a mistake."

"I feel like all the rules have changed," Britt lamented. "It's like when you go canoeing."

Molly couldn't help but laugh.

"No, I'm serious," Britt went on. "When you're in a canoe, you always float downriver. Nothing can change your direction. Something could come along and capsize your boat—rapids, a storm, a fallen tree—but there's no force in the world strong enough to reverse your course. If you're on that river, you're going *down* that river. I feel like my marriage changed directions on me. It decided to swim upstream.

And that feels even more unnatural than if the whole mess just sank altogether. Do you know what I mean?"

She didn't, not really. The only currents Molly had ever known had been unnavigable ones, a surging flow that carried her off against her will, in the direction of who knew where.

"Truth is, Britt, I've only ever felt adrift."

Norman used to take Molly and Davis boating on the river when they were younger, but Molly had never needed to put her faith in the current. She had faith in the man holding the oar. She could still remember her father's boundless bravado as they dipped the bow of the canoe into the Susquehanna. "Don't worry, kids. I know this stretch of river like the back of my hand," he'd assure them. Five minutes later, there'd be a knot in his brow. His neck would be twisting this way and that, and he'd be muttering, "Now where the hell are we?"

Even lost, the men in the family still seemed to know the way.

CHAPTER 11

Davis was an early riser. It was a deeply ingrained habit dating back to the days when his father, needing to get to the station in time for an early broadcast, got moving before daybreak, and Davis would awaken to the sound of his old man blowing his nose, the jarring honk wending its way through the ducts and vents and into his dark bedroom like the bugle call of reveille. It felt like a curse that Davis had never learned how to sleep in, for these days the morning did him no favors by showing up early to remind him that there was no one to make breakfast for, no one doling out parting kisses at the front door, and no one waiting for him in a conference room with printouts of designs.

In those first days of his banishment, he'd been a live wire of revival, a man on a mission. Grief and despair were the heat-seeking missiles of the self-centered, he'd heard Norman say, so Davis Winger, after scarcely being gone, was determined to be the comeback kid. He would return from a morning run, throw on a pot of coffee, and wait for nine o'clock to roll around so he could job hunt. What better way to repay Pavelka's lapse in allegiance than to suit up in another team's uniform? Colleagues and friends at competitor firms had warmly taken his calls, but they chilled noticeably when he steered the conversation toward employment prospects. He was available, he'd told them; they were intrigued. He did good work, he reminded them; they didn't need reminding.

He'd gotten the shaft from Pavelka, he said. *But had he?* they wondered, and they inquired about the precise nature of the shafting, whether he'd actually been asked to clean out his office, whether Hans had truly cut ties with him, and whether any developments in the three-plus weeks since the accident had either incriminated or vindicated him.

"Look, man, there isn't an engineering firm between DC and New York that wouldn't want you on its letterhead," he was repeatedly told.

"But aren't you still on Pavelka's letterhead?"

"Technically, yes. But I don't have to be."

And that's when they'd say, "Sorry, man, we just don't have any openings right now."

He'd heard that a lot—*Sorry, man.* Evidently, the swinging dicks and fuzzy nuts of the engineering mafia weren't going to hire someone who'd been fingered for an accident, no matter how unjust the fingering. It seemed so unfair. What of all the accidents that Davis's handiwork had prevented over the years? Why didn't anybody want to talk about those?

He could do nothing other than wait. Wait out this McCarthyesque blackball, for it could be weeks, if not months, before the regulators issued their report.

On the home front, Britt was still raw, refusing to entertain any of his apologies, appeals for mercy, or calls for a bilateral summit, which he extended almost daily over the phone, via text, or in person when they passed Rachel back and forth. Fortunately, Britt was grasping for normalcy for their daughter and allowed her to sleep at his apartment twice a week, including one weekend night, with additional visits to be considered upon request. Davis had to admit that Britt was being reasonable, which was more than a sinning husband had any right to ask.

When Rachel was with him, he was happy, even if it sometimes felt like an effortful happiness, like he was working to make them both forget that the duo was not a trio. When she wasn't with him, the day was a crawling adagio, the hours dripping by with nothing to fill them.

He understood for the first time in his life why people offed themselves. He wasn't about to do it, of course—not yet, anyway—but the emotional valleys that came with extended solitude and an overbearing sense of uselessness were no longer a mystery. All it would've taken was a particularly gray week and a trip through Tim Buckley's *Blue Afternoon*, and sure, why not chug a bucket of pills and call it a day?

He learned early on to steer clear of the dull, sad tableau of daytime TV. Only the mentally healthiest could hope to survive protracted exposure to that awfulness, with its cut-rate talk show hosts and the remarkable number of stations that found it acceptable to broadcast someone getting a haircut. Even ESPN was like, fuck it, nobody's watching, let's just show a chess match. If only he could motivate himself back into running, a staple of his morning routine that had fallen by the wayside as the days here had worn on and this rudderless funk took hold of him. If only he could bring himself to lace up those ASICS. The exercise would do him good, help him clear his head.

Sometimes he made lemonade—like, literally, not in the figurative sense—because the clink of stirred ice cubes and the citrusy smell of lemons reminded him of the lemonade stand that he and Rachel had launched last summer. It soothed him to think of their supply runs to the grocery store, the signs they drew with Magic Markers, the game table they set up curbside. There was, come to think of it, a fresh crop of thirsty passersby here at the Deluxe, were Rachel inclined to give the venture a second go.

Although mostly they were closed, and only some were opening, in every direction the doors of summer beckoned.

———

Spring's chill was overstaying its welcome, at least today, but Davis knew that once the weather turned, the pool would be an irresistible draw to a splashing six-year-old. So he set out to explore the swimming situation.

Outside his door, he ran into McGuinn lumbering up the steps, a plastic bag swinging from his hand.

"How's it going?" Davis asked.

"It's a stone groove," McGuinn replied. "Your own self?"

Davis suddenly remembered the pair of women in tight dresses he'd seen entering his neighbor's apartment the night before.

"You enjoy yourself last night?" he asked with sly implication.

McGuinn straight-faced him. "I enjoy myself every night, D."

In many respects, McGuinn faithfully obliged the stereotype of the pro athlete. There was the ready availability for an evening of drinking, the locker-room depravity of the bumper sticker on his Chevy truck—MY OTHER RIDE IS YOUR DAUGHTER. Most curious, however, was this otherworldly flow of women who showed up at his door. They were young and foreign and forbiddingly sexy, unsmiling in their fishnet thigh-highs and heels, an almost mail-order misery about them. They outfitted themselves in snug cocktail wear that left little of the chest and even less of the inner thigh to one's imagination. "Say hello to Dagmar," McGuinn would say should Davis happen to knock. "And this over here is Natalya." And with a shot glass in their fingers, Dagmar and Natalya would return the greeting in some Slavic accent where the *r*'s rolled and the consonants stumbled. These women seemed dangerous and feline, conveying heat without warmth. Like characters in a Lou Reed song, they looked strung out, nocturnal, and streaked over with makeup. Davis suspected that sex with Dagmar and Natalya was raw and Siberian, pleasurable but nothing to feel good about, a forum for all involved to work through dark childhood aggressions. But come morning, McGuinn was always downright chipper. He appeared satisfied and exhausted as he stood in his doorway bidding them farewell. "Thanks, ladies. Everyone was delicious!"

Any curiosity Davis felt about these women and the unbound revelry over which they presided was purely intellectual. The only bed Davis had any interest in was the one in which Britt lay. He knew that if you slept with a woman who was not your wife, you earned the privilege of *only* sleeping with women who were not your wife. Such was the karmic spanking, almost poetic in its simplicity. Integrity would continue to edge out biology for Davis (if, perhaps, sometimes only by the skin of its teeth).

"How was your evening with your, uh, friends?" Davis asked as McGuinn poked around in the plastic bag for his morning repast of chewing tobacco and milk.

"Productive," McGuinn replied. "Illuminating. Inspiring."

"I won't ask you to elaborate."

"Then I'll bid you good day." And McGuinn tipped a cap that wasn't there.

Davis trudged along the sidewalk until he came to a fraying aluminum fence that encircled a swimming pool and an adjacent shower house. He stood outside the fence and surveyed the scene. The pool was filled with something green—corrosively green, the color of something that ate through human flesh. Overhead, a heavy panic of clouds swept low. A wind carried all the way from November sent tiny choleric waves rippling in the pool. Davis pictured Rachel here, hypothermic in her bathing suit and water wings, an advertisement for a social services intervention. This could not stand. It wasn't yet summer, but Memorial Day had come and gone, so it was summer enough, and the pool should've been closer to ready than it was. Davis marched himself over to the rental office and entered to the rattle of rusted bells hanging from the doorknob. He saw the assistant manager, a young beanpole of a guy named Guy—the easiest name in the world to remember.

"I was wondering when you expect the pool to open," Davis said to him. "My daughter is going to want to swim."

Guy puffed out a beleaguered breath. "Hopefully soon. We had a lifeguard lined up, but it fell through. I think she was deported or something. We can legally open without someone in the chair, but we need the right signs first, and we're still waiting on those."

"Signs," Davis repeated, hazily.

"No lifeguard on duty. Swim at your own risk. You know—signs."

"You can't just scribble that on a piece of cardboard? I could do that for you right now."

"I wish," Guy said. "We need to shell out for the real ones. My boss is a real stickler for the rules."

Naturally. Who but a perfectionist would permit pool water to turn the color of Shrek?

"Those signs aren't cheap, by the way," Guy went on. "They're like two hundred big ones."

"Two hundred thousand dollars?"

Guy looked confused. "Two hundred bucks."

"Okay, because that's not what a big one is," Davis said. "One big one equals one thousand dollars."

This was going nowhere. Why compound Guy's sense of ineffectualness? Why add to the self-disappointment that seemed to follow him everywhere he went? Clearly, things weren't going according to plan for the young hat rack in the 1974 tie, but they never would so long as he worked here. Every time Davis ran into him, he felt the urge to grab the lad and shake him. *You need to get out of the Deluxe before the Deluxe gets into you! If you think your ticket out is that lame Who cover band you're always talking about—Who Framed Roger Daltrey is a crappy band name, by the way—you will die here! You need better dreams!*

"We should be up and running in a couple of days," Guy told him. "We're also actively looking for a replacement lifeguard, since schools are letting out soon and we have a ton of kids here. Hopefully something will work out."

Nothing in Guy's tone suggested the faintest hope that anything would, in fact, work out. Ever.

Davis considered the morning he'd just spent—the fruitless job hunting, the conscious avoidance of television and exercise, the fact that the most productive thing he'd done all day was make a pitcher of lemonade. That's when something remarkable happened. To his immense surprise, Davis heard his own voice say, "Maybe I'll just do it."

"Do what?" Guy asked. "Interview the candidates?"

"Be your lifeguard. Work the chair."

Guy's features struggled to stay in their proper place. "You want to be the lifeguard? Here?"

"No one else seems to. Is there some sort of conflict of interest since I'm a resident?"

The young manager didn't quite know what to make of the offer. "Are you even certified?"

"It would be difficult to locate my documents," Davis admitted. "But I do have relevant experience."

"And what would that be?"

"Well, it was a little while ago."

In fact, it was in high school, a summer job at a country club. Initially he'd been hired to man the snack bar, and he'd spent a warm June sweating over the deep fryer and distributing popsicles to over-privileged brats. Mostly, though, he'd gazed out the screen window at all those lovely girls lounging on chaises, flipping themselves over like steaks, sizzling around the pool in the juicy largesse of their delicious-ness. One girl in particular captured his fancy, a raven-haired Venus who rocked an indigo bikini and treated him to a tease of a smile each time she came in for a Diet Coke.

She would put the straw to her lips and ask, "Is this really diet?"

"It is," Davis would reply.

"It's just so yummy," she'd remark.

"Thank you," he would say, though he knew she wasn't compli-menting his pour so much as expressing suspicion about whether he'd mistakenly given her regular. After a few weeks of tame flirting, Davis got serious and went to the club manager and begged to be promoted to lifeguard. He took the advanced lifesaving test, got certified, and within a week was twirling a whistle around his finger from the perch of the chair. It was all for naught. The raven-haired Venus continued to lather him with coquettish smiles, but was, in the end, not interested in doing anything more with Davis than drinking calorie-free soda in his presence. Davis retired his whistle, never imagining that the next girl for whom he would engage his lifeguarding skills would be his six-year-old daughter.

"Don't worry, my friend," Davis told Guy. "I know what I'm doing."

Guy just sat there, looking perplexed.

"Look," Davis said. "You want to open your pool, don't you? Well, I'm standing here promising you a clean, danger-free pool area starting today."

"You strike me as a little overqualified," Guy worried.

"Well, if I don't have a certificate, aren't I underqualified? Let's not overthink this."

At war with his limited options—and losing—Guy did what assistant managers at low-rent apartment complexes do.

"Let's give it a try and see what happens," he said.

He rummaged through his desk drawer, produced an overstuffed key chain, and tossed it across the room to his newly minted employee.

"Hold up," Guy said as Davis was showing himself the door. "Don't you want to know what it pays?"

Davis turned and eyed him with undue seriousness. "Are you the man to speak to about such things?"

"Actually, I'm not sure." Guy looked stumped by his own question. "Ten twenty-five an hour, I think. Something like that."

"Okay, then," Davis said. "I sure hope I'm worth it."

CHAPTER 12

As Davis stood on the pool deck and took stock of the daunting task of fixing this place, he had little trouble believing that the previous applicant for this job had bailed, or even opted for deportation. He still wasn't sure why he himself had volunteered, although it was nice to learn that his self-esteem could still withstand the swift plummet from regionally renowned structural engineer to garden apartment lifeguard. Was it self-esteem or desperation?

He certainly wasn't doing it for the money; Pavelka & Gates was still paying him, such being the terms of "administrative leave," a peculiar status that felt like a temporary firing, or a tendered resignation that was still under review. In addition to money, Hans was also sending Davis periodic emails to keep him abreast of the investigation. But because the Virginia Department of Housing and Community Development was still quietly doing its thing, Hans's messages seemed to exist for no other purpose than to tell Davis that a report still hadn't been issued. And, by the way, you know, hello. Davis had no interest in idle greetings from a man who could so easily treat him like a stranger. He was, however, curious about the DHCD's findings, so he read Hans's emails. But he never responded.

A voice suddenly called out from behind him. "Hey, new guy!"

Standing just outside the fence was a young woman, late teens, early twenties. Her face was concealed by sunglasses, those fashionably oversize mirrored ones, and she was holding a leash attached to an ugly brown dog.

"Hi," he called back. "Do I know you?"

"You helped me find my car the other night. It was raining."

"Right," he said. "Subaru girl."

"Subaru girl would be my mom, thank you very little."

She came strutting through the gate, the dog following in a symphony of snorts, and nodded at the potpourri of leaves, insects, and algae colonizing the pool. "Once they clean this place up for the classy clientele, it looks like Tahiti around here," she said.

Davis wasn't amused, seeing as how the *they* in her sentence was now him. "Have you ever been to Tahiti?" he asked.

"No," she said.

"Me neither," Davis said.

They stared at each other a moment. "Okay, then," said the girl. "Hey—you don't happen to have a phone on you, do you?"

"Maybe. Who wants to know?"

"I do."

"What happened to yours?"

"It's currently locked inside my apartment, probably next to my keys."

"You accidentally locked your keys in your apartment?" he asked.

"Do people do it on purpose?"

Scowling at the teen, Davis retrieved his phone from his pocket and held it out to her. "I'm Davis, by the way. In case you were wondering."

"Charlie," said the girl. She pushed her sunglasses up onto her forehead and began to dial. "I can't believe I actually know her number. Who knows anyone's number anymore?"

Davis allowed himself a fleeting audit of the way this Charlie person presented herself. Her thigh-high cutoffs were too short, her fingernails were painted an ostentatious fuchsia, and her toenails were death-black. The effect of this was to make Davis's lips curl with condemnation, for he pined for the days when he could look at a young woman and not see something his daughter might one day become with enough parental mismanagement.

The lucky recipient of Charlie's phone-a-friend was not greased with niceties: "I'm locked out," the girl snapped. Pause. "No." Pause. "No!" Pause. "I borrowed it, from some guy at the pool." Pause. Irritated groan. "Brilliant. How long have you been keeping *that* handy piece of information from me?" Without waiting for an answer, she hung up and handed the phone back to Davis. "Apparently there's a key under the front mat."

"Future reference: you could always swing by the rental office," Davis suggested. "I'm sure the young fellow that works there would be happy to let you in."

"You mean Guy?" Charlie let out a good scoff. "Best I steer clear of that fellow."

"Why is that?"

"Because he's Five-O."

"He's what?"

"He's the po-po. We're not supposed to have pets here, and maybe you haven't noticed, but I have a pet."

"So you do," Davis said. "But maybe *you* haven't noticed that the rental office is about thirty yards away. And it's broad daylight. And there's a squadron of groundskeepers, custodians, and other varieties of law enforcement milling about the property, any of whom could bust you at any time."

Suddenly the girl's eyes narrowed. "Hey," she said, slowly, schemingly.

Davis looked at her with unease. "What?"

"How would you like a dog for a little while?"

"Excuse me?"

"A dog. Just for a few weeks. Couple of months at most."

Davis pointed to the beast at their feet. "That dog?"

"He goes by Tweedy," she informed him.

Davis allowed himself a moment to marvel at this young woman in all her swaggering vanity. "I have a lot of questions," he said. "For starters, why are you trying to give your pet away to someone you don't know? And second, who are you again?"

"Tweedy was an impulse purchase at the mall," she explained, sliding in and out of one of her hot-pink sandals. "He was just too frickin' cute to walk past. One minute I'm innocently petting him; the next minute I'm paying for him. It's when I brought him home that things went south. My mom—Subaru girl to you—wasn't as taken with his good looks."

Davis knelt and stared into the marble-like eyes of the squat little pug, which somehow managed to convey hostility, the persona of a villainess's sidekick. "I'm going to have to pass," he said. "I don't know the first thing about taking care of a dog."

"You could ask one of the four billion people on the planet who have one," Charlie proposed. "I think you'd get the hang of it."

"Why me?"

"Because you're the person I was talking to when this great idea hit me," she said. "And you seem trustworthy. And you live nearby. And I'm short on friends at the moment."

The leashed creature shook its neck with a fluttering spasm, causing its collar to rattle in distress. It was the most horrid-looking animal Davis had ever seen in his life. "Yeah, pass. I'm just not a dog person."

"You'd be surprised how quickly one becomes a dog person."

"I probably would be."

"It won't cost you a penny," she pleaded. "I've got all the kibbles and treats and toys. You'd really be helping me out of a jam."

"I feel like you get into a lot of jams," he mused. "Look, I'd give you directions if you were lost. I'd give you a jump start if you had a dead battery. I'd lend you an extra umbrella if it started to rain. But I'm not going to take on the responsibility of keeping a living thing alive—as much as I love helping total strangers out of jams."

"Do you live alone?" she asked.

"That's both irrelevant and none of your business."

"So, in other words, yes. Doesn't it suck? Being all by yourself?"

"Why don't you just take him back to the store?" Davis suggested.

"He's not a turtleneck."

"Or hand him over to the pound."

Charlie gasped. "You did *not* just say that."

"I didn't?"

"They murder dogs at the pound."

"Really? Murder? Like, in cold blood?"

"Maybe I'll just send him to Korea so he can be somebody's brunch," she snapped.

Davis eyed her ungenerously. "Have you ever been to Korea?"

"No."

"Me neither."

They stared at each other. "Okay, then," Charlie said. She sighed. "Look, I'll be moving out of here soon, and I'll be taking Tweedy with me. Until then, I'll visit all the time, I'll take him for walks, I'll keep you up to your ass in dog food. You'd basically just be boarding him. We're talking six months, tops."

"The period of guardianship keeps getting longer," Davis said. "Don't think I haven't noticed."

Charlie knelt and took Tweedy's face in her hands. His jumpy pink tongue splashed all over her chin and lips.

"You know, Charlie," Davis said, folding his arms, "I haven't compared our leases or anything, but I would imagine that this rule against having pets probably also applies to me. Since, you know, I live here too. That's just a hunch."

"Yeah, but you don't live with a crazy mother who hates dogs, hates you, and would rat you out without blinking." Charlie dipped her head. "Please tell me you don't live with your mother."

Against all rational thought, Davis was now recalling the innumerable occasions on which Rachel had begged him and Britt for a puppy, all her swearing to God that she'd walk it, feed it, clean up after it, let it sleep in her bed. If he took this dog—was he really contemplating this?—he'd officially be the separated dad teasing love out of his child by means of outsized gifts. The other thing was, this Charlie character was not wrong about the suck factor in living alone. Already he was catching himself doing De Niro and Walken impressions to himself in his apartment. How soon before he started doing them in public? Exactly how far was the trip to crazy?

"Tweedy, huh?" he muttered.

Charlie nodded eagerly. Batted her eyelashes for good measure.

"After the Wilco guy or the cartoon bird?" he asked.

"What cartoon bird?"

"Never mind. Okay, fine. I'll do it."

"You will?"

"I guess so."

"You are awesome! Thank you so much!"

"But listen—this is not a long-term arrangement. I'm not going to be living here very long, and when I leave, you're taking him back."

"Duh."

"And if I get busted by that guy Guy, I'm going to sing like a canary. This is all on you. Same story if your mom finds out and comes after me. If anybody gives me trouble, I'm fingering you."

"That's awfully forward. We just met."

"I ain't playin'."

Sometimes, in stern moments, he said that to Rachel.

"You're the best," Charlie purred, and blew him kisses as she strode toward the gate, the leashed varmint ambling miserably after her. "I'll bring him by this afternoon with his crate and toys and whatnot. He doesn't eat much, and he never barks."

Just then, the pug issued a declarative yap.

"That's not what *never* means," Davis said. "And hey—don't you want to know where I live?"

She held up both arms to the sky and maniacally cried, "You live here!"

That shut him up good.

CHAPTER 13

Mail was an erratic visitor at the Deluxe. Some days it showed up by nine, other days after six, and often it avoided the place altogether. Who could blame it? When Davis returned to his apartment and saw a box leaning against his door with his father's home address in the top left-hand corner, his heart sank. It meant the jig was up: Norman had found him. But when he opened the package and beheld a pageantry of culinary majesty courtesy of his old man's lady, his heart took flight.

"You are saving my sad little life, Tom Petty," he brooded. "Davis Winger, 'You Got Lucky.'"

It was almost immediately after Kitty broke out of the Winger home that Petra Kovacs broke in, a young, newly divorced production assistant at WCPK-TV. Norman was a strapping local celebrity and a hail-fellow-well-met, and so it was hardly surprising that Peti was on him in a flash. The kind of flash, in fact, that might cause one to question the chronology. Not that it had ever mattered to Davis. When Mommy Dearest lights out for the territory with some douche bagel, but your house still smells of Salisbury steak and your *Knight Rider* lunchbox is stuffed with homemade brownies, you don't ask questions.

The shy, soft-spoken daughter of Eastern Europeans who'd fled the war, Peti, with her blooming cheeks and heedful eyes, brought kindness and stability to the Winger household, a welcome contrast to the increasingly bitter, ragingly ill-tempered force into which their lovely, loving mother had horrifyingly evolved right before their eyes. Peti taped Molly's stories to the refrigerator. She came solo to Davis's Little League games when Norman couldn't make it. At night, after the kids had been put to bed, instead of raised voices and slamming doors—which had become the soundtrack to every evening in that house—Davis heard the becalming clink of teacups on saucers and the stately opening theme to *Masterpiece Theater*. It had taken Kitty a year to turn the house upside down; Peti had righted it practically overnight.

Still, there was a tiny, almost imperceptible distance that Peti maintained. Their dad's girlfriend stayed and stayed, but she never became their stepmother. She took long weekends with Norman in the Berkshires and the Florida Keys, but made a point of not intruding on family vacations, even though her absence deprived the family of the completeness they enjoyed at home.

"You kids like Peti?" Norman asked one evening in those early goings.

"Yeah, she's nice," Davis had replied. "Doesn't talk much, though."

"Cut her some slack. She's been through a lot," Norman had said, and for whatever reason added, "Her parents are Holocaust survivors."

Regardless of her economy with words, Peti had always spoken most loudly through the sending of care packages. Her confections had pursued Davis to every dorm, apartment, and single-family dwelling he'd ever called home. But now, even as the homey aroma of her delicacies enlivened the Saharan desolation of his room, Davis wondered how this box had tracked him down *here*, to the Deluxe, humanity's loneliest outpost. He'd yet to come clean to Norman about the wreck he'd made of his life, so how had they known?

He saw little choice but to call.

"Okay, old man. You got me. How did you find out?"

"You don't think I speak to my granddaughter and my daughter-in-law?" Norman sighed. "Why didn't you tell me, son?"

"Why didn't you tell me you knew?" Davis countered. "Sending me mail is your way of tipping me off that you're on to me? What are you, in a John le Carré novel?"

"I wanted to call you," Norman told him. "Hell, I wanted to come over there and knock on your goddamn door. But Peti talked me out of it. She said you obviously weren't ready to tell me yet. Maybe you were ashamed, maybe you were planning to fix everything on the quick. Peti insisted that I be patient and respect your privacy."

"Yeah, you didn't really do that."

"I lasted all of a day. You should've called me, Davis. As soon as it happened."

"What were you going to do? Fly back from Barcelona?"

"You don't think I would have?"

The automaticity of his father's love pierced him, struck him silent.

"Tell me what happened, son."

Alone in his apartment, Davis stared out the window. "I made a bad mistake, Dad. Real bad."

On the other end of the line, Norman exhaled, a sigh colliding with the tiny grate of the phone's mic. Even his father's misery Davis found reassuring.

"I left my job too," Davis added. "You hear that part of the story?"

"I couldn't care less about that. Worry about your family. Put right what you did wrong."

"I'm trying, Dad. I promise."

"Are you okay, my boy?"

"I've got strudel and a Bundt cake. I couldn't be better."

Norman let out a soft chuckle. "Well, you know Peti loves her Davey."

Peti was the only person in the universe who called him that, and he'd never forgotten the first occasion. The family was having dinner one night not long after Kitty had left, and Davis excused himself to get his unfinished homework under control. As he sprinted up the stairs, Norman called after him, reminding him that he'd neglected to take his plate and cup to the sink. Davis stomped back down, did as he was told, and completely by accident dropped his plate onto the kitchen floor, shattering it into a thousand pieces. Norman, who rarely got frustrated with his children but who had any number of things to be frustrated about, suffered a momentary loss of composure. "Damnit, Davis!" he hollered. As the boy scrounged for the glittering shards of china, tears surging behind his eyes, Peti knelt next to him. "It's okay, Davey," she said, rubbing his back. "It's all going to be okay, Davey."

Davis now wanted his father to hear that none of this changed the person he was. None of this made him Kitty.

"I'm not Mom, you know," he said into the phone.

"No, you certainly are not."

"She wanted out," Davis said. "I don't want out. I never want out."

"Son, for reasons too numerous to mention, you are not Kitty. Let there be no mistake about that."

It was strange to hear his father speak of his mother so bluntly, to say her name. Kitty had never been the subject of discussion in their home. In fact, her mention was so exactingly avoided in those first weeks and months after her departure that Davis had been unsettled by it, his mother's exit made even more terrible for having been deemed unspeakable. But as the years wore on, his father had seemed even less inclined to bring her up, the passage of time furthering the impression that, as far as Norman was concerned, Kitty was gone and forgotten.

"I honestly don't know why people do what I did," Davis said to him. "I got nothing out of it. Maybe I'm the exception that proves the rule."

"I believe you, and I believe *in* you," Norman told him. "But exceptions don't prove rules, they disprove them."

"I thought all rules have exceptions," said Davis.

"Well, I didn't go to Stanford or anything, but if all rules have exceptions, maybe there just aren't any rules." A dark laugh came from the old man. "I've had that thought more than once in my life."

CHAPTER 14

Part—by no means all—of the disgrace that came with dating someone barely out of college was having to deal with that person's living situation. Recent grads, males in particular, seemed to conduct their migration into the world rather gingerly, barricading themselves behind all the familiar, scuzzy trimmings of campus existence for as long as possible. So it was with Zach. Roommates came and went. Stacks of crusty cereal bowls burgeoned in the sink. Unkempt nerds congregated on the sofa to stare like zombies at video games that celebrated jungle warfare. The front door was always left open, perhaps in eternal hope that a swarm of Chi Omegas might clamor in off the street in yoga pants and bare midriffs. Molly didn't know how many people were actual signatories to Zach's lease, but what she did know was that everyone she encountered in that row home looked upon her and her thirty-two years as something exotic and generationally distinct. Molly was an adult; Zach and his boneheads were something else. Not children, exactly, but certainly children inexactly.

She entered the house and saw three male figures splayed out on the couch, one she could identify as a bona fide rent-paying roommate (Ethan, she thought, although Zach addressed him as "Duker," sometimes "The Duker"), plus two strangers. All six of their eyes were fixed on what was either *Braveheart* or *Gladiator*. The house lights had been dimmed for optimal viewing effect and the surround sound cranked up to the limits of aural tolerance. Molly proceeded up the steps, unnoticed over the sounds of gruesome onscreen carnage. ("Nice!" chortled one of the viewers. "That was cold," said another. "Pause it, I gotta piss," said the third.)

Peeking into the bedroom, Molly found Zach in front of his mirror, trying to decide how many of the three buttons on his polo shirt needed buttoning.

"Hey, you," he said. "Almost ready."

He fidgeted with the positioning of his black-rimmed glasses, which he considered a hipster accessory, though for Molly it brought to mind a scientist in a TV show from the sixties. Turning, he frowned at Molly's attire, the jeans and long-sleeved T-shirt she'd put on for an outing at the park.

"Are you really going to play in that?" he asked.

She blinked back at him. "Play what in what?"

He swung an invisible tennis racquet. "We're taking Gabe and Anthony to play tennis. Remember?"

Zach had made no mention whatsoever of tennis, nor of their being accompanied by his Little Brothers. "I can't remember things I've never been told," she said.

"No worries," Zach said. "I've got an extra racquet."

"No, yes worries. I don't play tennis." She sighed. "It's fine. You guys go and have fun. I'll sit this one out."

"Oh no, you have to come," he insisted. "The guys are dying to meet you."

"I didn't even know you played tennis, Zach."

Checking that his polo was securely tucked into his shorts, he grinned. "Oh, I got game."

Two minutes later, Zach tossed four racquets into the back seat of Molly's car, and off they set for the public park that was within walking distance of his Little Brothers' foster home. Zach used the ride to pitch the Vegas trip again.

"I think we'd have fun," he said. "Rumor has it they're going to premier the first trailer for the new wolfman film. Cool, right? You see the last one?"

Molly shook her head. She was quite certain she'd never in her life watched a wolf movie on purpose.

"They're also reviving the *Wishmaster* franchise. How awesome is that?"

Molly knew exactly how awesome that was.

On Zach went, inventorying all the D-list actors whose empty calendars were allowing them to show up at this convention to sign photographs and be worshipped for their defining roles in such films as *Candyman 2*, *Leprechaun 3*, *Zombie Strippers IV*, and *I Dismember Mama*.

Molly said what she always said when Zach pressed her on the trip: "I'm trying to make it work."

They arrived at the park to find it in full swing. Fathers with baseball mitts heaved pop flies and grounders to their children, preteens in knee pads kicked soccer balls back and forth, and a gaggle of twenty-somethings treated a touch football game as foreplay as they giggled, grabbed, and soft-tackled each other to the ground. As Zach pulled the racquets out of the back seat, he squinted around the park, his eyes eventually landing on two African American boys casually tossing a tennis ball back and forth near the courts. Zach tended not to talk much about his involvement in the Big Brother program, which, Molly had come to believe, spoke not to his interest level but to a respect for his Little Brothers' privacy and, more unexpectedly, his humility. All Molly knew was that every week he met up with these kids and took them to the movies or a baseball game or the comic book store, after which they went for pizza or subs. When Molly inquired about them, Zach generally replied with a repertoire of hazy descriptors. "They've had a rough go" was how he always put their situation. Their mother "wasn't around," and their stepfather was "an addict of some kind." One thing the boys did have going for them was their foster mother, Jenny. Zach, who'd met many foster parents, having worked with many foster kids, thought the world of Jenny.

The shorter, presumably younger brother spied Zach and came running toward them; the taller one, a teenager, lumbered behind, careful not to look too happy or excited about anything.

"What's up, gents?" Zach said, giving each a high five. "Boys, meet Molly. Molly, these are my bros."

The older child, thirteen or fourteen, lanky with sharp eyes, was Anthony. The shorter one, squat, debatably pudgy, and two or so years younger, was Gabe.

"Very nice to meet you guys," Molly said.

"Are you Zach's girlfriend?" Gabe asked.

"I am," she felt compelled to reply, and Zach smiled, pleased to hear his status confirmed seven months in.

Anthony, wearing a zippered jacket and navy athletic pants with white stripes down the sides, looked like he was about to go trick-or-treating as a gym teacher. Gabe was lost under a billowy maroon sweatshirt several sizes too big. His mesh shorts hung down past his knees.

"Molly doesn't think she can keep up with us, so she's just going to watch," Zach told the young men as he distributed the racquets. "You guys haven't played before, right?"

"Maybe once or twice," Gabe said.

"Don't worry. I'll teach you," Zach said, looking mentor-like.

Molly found a nearby bench from which to spectate. The courts had fallen into disrepair, the clay bruised and pockmarked, the nets sagging at the center, but Zach didn't seem to notice. He demonstrated the proper way to hold the racquet, how to stand, how to turn your body and swing through a forehand and a two-handed backhand. The young men seemed to quickly detect that they were not exactly in the presence of Roger Federer, but they humored him. They mirrored Zach's stances and motions, even as they harmlessly mocked his seriousness. Which was really the best Zach could ever hope for in life—that the mockery be good-natured.

Eventually, Zach migrated to the other side of the net and began to hit live balls to his young friends. The first ball was a soft lob to Anthony, who swung hard and rifled it back over the net. Zach watched it whiz by.

"Nice, A-Train," he said. "You're up, Gabe-man."

Zach hit another gentle ball, and Gabe scooted to it and swatted, returning the shot right back to Zach.

Zach looked impressed. "You guys are quick studies."

As they began to rally back and forth, it was immediately apparent to all that Zach, for lack of a better word, sucked, and his mentees, whose collective prior experience in the sport equaled a half hour, could parlay basic athletic ability into a proficiency that blew right past that of their instructor. On one side of the court, Gabe and Anthony motored gracefully over to each ball, set up their shot, and smacked it back over. On the other side, Zach dashed to and fro, whiffing wildly and connecting uncleanly when he connected at all, the balls accumulating on his side of the net or landing on another court entirely.

"You're out of practice, Zacharias!" Gabe hooted.

"Come on, old man!" yelled Anthony.

Zach dragged himself around the paint, gasping. "You guys are giving me a run for my money."

Molly needed to see stuff like this. She needed to be reminded that there were situations in which Zach could connect with other human beings, situations in which his natural cloddishness was, if not inconspicuous, at least unobtrusive. She needed to know that there could be chapters in the oral history of Zach Klinefelter in which he was *not* a tormentor's prey, *not* the daily conferee of noogies, swirlies, and wet willies. (Not that Molly had been prom queen, but it had helped that she had walked under the umbrella of an older brother's popularity and a father's local celebrity.) She sat there wondering if maybe the biggest problem with Zach was that he was immature. That didn't necessarily mean he was worth waiting out, but it did mean there might be more to the story.

Molly watched Zach charge the net, readying a put-away shot and howling, "Here comes Nadal!"

Molly watched Anthony position himself for the return, his eyes narrowed, his forearm muscles as tense as piano strings.

Molly watched the lean teenager explode forward. The racquet whipped around his torso, and the ball sprang like a bullet over the net.

Molly watched something else fly over the net too. An object spinning in tight rotations like a boomerang. It was Anthony's racquet.

Molly watched both the ball and the racquet strike Zach square in the nose. Then she watched Zach crumple to the ground like a sack of potatoes.

"Oh shit," Anthony uttered.

"My man got *plunked*!" Gabe cackled.

Within seconds, Zach's face resembled an Italian dinner.

"Oh shit," Anthony said again, this time with panic. Then the sight of gushing blood sent him leaping over the net.

Molly jumped to her feet and rushed inside the fence to Zach, over whom the boys were standing frozen with alarm.

"Are you okay?" Gabe was asking.

"Fine, totally fine," Zach said. He was pinching the bridge of his nose, vainly trying to stem the red stream pouring out of his nostrils and snaking over his chin.

"I'm so sorry, man," Anthony said. "I don't know what happened."

"It's not your fault, A-Train. I'm okay. I promise." He looked at Molly. "How bad is it?"

Gabe answered for her. "Real bad!"

Molly knelt and cupped the back of his head. "Your nose might be broken. Did you bring a towel?"

Anthony immediately unzipped and removed his jacket. "Here."

"Wait. Use this," Gabe said, pulling his sweatshirt over his head and handing it to Molly. "It's cotton. More absorbent."

Molly hesitated. "You sure? It's going to get ruined." The younger boy nodded fiercely, as though any delay might cost Zach his life, so Molly held the sweatshirt in front of Zach's nose. "Tell me if this hurts."

She'd barely made contact when Zach jerked his head away and screamed.

Gabe's eyes went wide. "He's not going to die, is he?"

"Shut up," Anthony said. "It's just a broken nose."

"The bleeding is going to stop any minute, guys, and then we can keep playing," Zach said, rather heroically. "In fact, I think it's slowing down now."

The wound took that as a dare, and the bloody tide suddenly surged like a breached levee.

"I think a better idea would be to go to the emergency room," Molly said.

"You mean like a hospital?" Gabe looked petrified. "Yeah, I'm not so good with those."

"It's okay," Molly said. "I can drop you guys off at home. It's no problem."

"We're going with Zach," Anthony declared. He threw his little brother a forbidding glower. "Stop being a baby."

"Oh, you're yelling at me?" Gabe shot back. "Am I the one who threw a racquet at somebody's head? No, I don't think so."

"These things happen. It's nobody's fault," Molly said. She was, however, noticing that Zach's speech had become a little warbly and his irises were shivering in the whites of his eyes. Of course Zach would concuss easily. "Let's get him over to my car."

Should this boyfriend of hers be the first person ever to die while volleying with schoolchildren, it would be partially tragic, partially pitiful, and mostly embarrassing.

CHAPTER 15

The gray vinyl of the waiting-room furniture was worn with slashes and craters, wound-like blemishes that suggested the chairs themselves were awaiting medical attention. By the time the foursome was seated—Gabe was rendered arctic and motionless by the gallery of sick and injured, and allowed no space between his left shoulder and his brother's right one—the bleeding had subsided to a harmless trickle, and yet Zach still seemed on the cusp of blacking out. His head kept tipping woozily over his neck like a cantaloupe balanced on a noodle.

On the other side of the room, Molly saw an old man with sagging cheeks seated beside his frail wife, bony hand in bony hand. The sight of these people, who must have trudged together across the years, who'd aged to the point where they couldn't age much more, awakened within Molly an alarming truth that somehow had never before hit her with such inevitability: one day she was going to come to a hospital like this one and her life would end. There would be something wrong with her heart or she'd have cancer of something important, and in one unceremonious moment, in a room so antiseptically bright and sterile that there'd be nowhere for her fear to burrow, she'd be carried out of this world for all of time. A stranger would then draw a sheet over her face and shuffle off to the break room for a snack, leaving the freshly dead Molly Erin Winger, born in Columbus, Ohio, unto Norman and

Katherine Winger, alone among machines and boxes of rubber gloves that were no more alive or less dead than she. Then, a day or two later, some of the people with whom she'd shared the earth would put her in the ground. They'd watch her casket being lowered into the open soil and leave her there, all by herself, on a quiet hill among gravestones. Then those people would drive to someone's house to nibble at turkey wraps and Caesar salad, lament the loss of a life, and ask if there was any barbecue sauce.

It then occurred to Molly that such a thing could happen while her mother was still out there somewhere, very much alive. It was not implausible that Molly could die and Kitty might never learn of it. Molly could imagine nothing more profoundly sad than to lie in some lonesome grave while your own mother carried on blindly with the waltz of life. The pair of ancients on the other side of the room forced her to wonder who would be sitting next to her on that day, who would be holding her hand in the waiting room, unprepared to let go and therefore refusing to do so.

A blunt-looking woman in blue scrubs burst into the room, clipboard in hand, and called out, "Klinefelter." It sounded like a diagnosis.

Zach roused as though from a drugged slumber and got to his feet. He administered valiant fist bumps to his young friends, then looked meaningfully at Molly. "I love you. You know that, right?"

Molly pointed to the nurse. "You have to go back now."

And off Zach went, he and his delicate constitution, staggering through the door like a POW.

Immediately, Gabe slid off his chair and scooted around to the seat next to Molly. He was now wearing Anthony's jacket; the older boy was bearing the hospital's refrigerated air so that his kid brother didn't have to. This was something Davis would've done for her. She remembered a summer long ago when Norman had taken them on a day trip to a water park in the Poconos. He was always shepherding his kids off to amusement parks to bask in the counterfeit dangers and the controlled out-of-control, for it was there, among those trains, swings, pendulums, and drop towers, where the free fall was a ruse and the landings were always safe, that he could let his hair be windblown and delirious. He could be just another dad in the gen pop. "Come on, kids. Let's hit that ski lift and check out the views at the top of the mountain," Norman had suggested that day, whereupon the three Wingers piled onto the chairlift. At some point during the ride, little Molly accidentally kicked off one of her flip-flops, and it dropped into the grass far below, lost forever on the overgrown ski trail. "Oh, Molly-bear," Norman had said, irritated at first, but quickly finding the humor in it. In the ensuing squabble over who would hold on to the remaining flip-flop, it too was fumbled, leaving Molly shoeless. When the family disembarked at the foot of the mountain, Davis turned and knelt, and carried his barefoot sister piggyback all the way to the car.

Molly and Zach's Little Brothers hunkered down for what was sure to be a long wait. Gabe squeaked his sneakers on the shellac shine of the floor, an apparent self-distraction from all the gore and grotesquery surely being perpetrated around every corner. Anthony, meanwhile, slumped in his seat and looked morose.

"This isn't your fault, Anthony," Molly told him.

Gabe spoke up. "Yeah, it is."

"Zach really likes hanging out with you guys," Molly said, "and a little mishap like this is not going to change that."

She proposed that they go looking for a snack. A quick stroll down the main hallway brought them to a coffee stand at the junction of two connected buildings, the spot where the modern wing of the hospital merged into a gothic structure that could have inspired the works of Mary Shelley. Molly ordered three hot chocolates, then surveyed the dwindling selection of pastries in the case.

"I don't see any muffins or cookies, but they have a few scones left," she said. "You guys want a scone?"

Gabe made a face. "A stone?"

"Scone," Molly said. "It's like a muffin, but not quite as sweet, and harder."

"So, like a crappy old muffin," Gabe said.

"Kind of," Molly said.

The scones were a no-go, so Molly paid for the drinks, and they all sat down at a table near the kiosk. The boys removed their lids and blew the steam off the surface of their hot chocolates.

"Are you and Zach going to get married?" Gabe asked.

Molly laughed, not because of the intrusiveness of the question—since when did children abide boundaries?—but because of its sheer ludicrousness. "We haven't discussed it," she said diplomatically.

"You can tell him to shut up, that it's none of your business," Anthony said. "People say that to him all the time."

Molly smiled. "It's okay."

She didn't tell him to shut up, but she did ward off further discourse on the subject by asking about the boys and what their lives were like. It had been nearly two years since they'd moved in with Jenny, a single, childless woman who sounded utterly thrilled to have these two young men in her East Baltimore home. It was a house that seemed to throb with life thanks to the yapping of Jenny's golden retriever and cocker spaniel and the country-and-western golden oldies she was constantly belting out. Each day, when the boys unpacked their lunches at the school cafeteria, they found a napkin on which Jenny had scribbled some fun fact gleaned from the internet. *It requires more brain activity to dream than to do any waking activity.* Or, *the skin recognizes its own touch, which is why you can't tickle yourself.* She always stayed with Gabe until he fell back to sleep after a nightmare. She gave Anthony "the business" whenever he came home after dark without calling. She enforced rules that mattered, like getting homework done on time and wearing a coat when it was cold out, but exercised leniency when it came to rules that didn't seem to matter as much, like making your bed before leaving the house or no snacking after you brushed your teeth. When the boys stepped out of line, she said, "You're good kids. *Be* good kids. Don't be little roughnecks." Something about the word *roughneck* got Gabe laughing even when Jenny was trying to be serious.

"Jenny sounds terrific," Molly said as they all nursed their hot drinks at the table abutting the hallway window. "How did you guys end up with her?"

Gabe shrugged and told her that one day their mother had left the home the three of them shared with Terrance, her live-in boyfriend, and simply never returned. They hadn't seen her in years.

"Terrance was getting on her nerves," Gabe said. "You know, staying out all the time, not being around and stuff."

It was heartbreaking, the naive simplicity of the boy's explanation. "She just went away?" Molly asked.

"She probably thought we'd be fine with Terrance. But after she left, Terrance was like, see ya."

"Are you done running your mouth yet?" Anthony cut in, looking daggers at his younger brother. "She doesn't care about this."

"Of course I do," Molly said. She looked at both boys, then said, "Actually, my mom walked out on us too."

"Really?" said Gabe.

"She fell in love with someone else and just ran off with him. Left us all behind—my dad, my brother, and me."

"She ever come back?" Gabe asked.

Molly shook her head.

Suddenly, Molly found herself wondering why it had never occurred to her to write about foster children, to sit down and talk with them. There were stories here, even ones with uplifting endings. As sunny and well cared for as these young men seemed to be, their childhood was a maelstrom, and this would make it harder for them to do the things that were hard enough to begin with, like chasing good grades, sleeping regular hours, developing the habits that gave you a better chance at merging smoothly into society. Like children raised on a drug corner, it seemed so easy for kids like Anthony and Gabe to veer off course, especially if no one was watching. Why hadn't Molly ever thought to explore that for the *Ramble*?

A voice came shouting down the hall. "There you guys are!" They turned and saw Zach ambling toward them, the center of his face obscured by an ice pack he was holding against it.

They all got up and rushed to him.

"Is it broken?" Gabe asked eagerly. He seemed to want the answer to be yes.

"Nope," Zach answered. Then he glared at Anthony with mock menace. "But I owe you one."

Molly winced at the sight of her boyfriend's face. "What do you have to do for it?"

"Just ice and Advil," he said.

Both boys seemed truly relieved to see Zach alive and lucid and no longer hemorrhaging estuaries of blood, and when they each put an arm around him like one might do with an actual big brother, for the first time in the history of their courtship Molly experienced the urge to do the same.

"I'm starving," Zach said. "Who's feeling tacos? And we need to make a stop for a new sweatshirt. I'm thinking Gabe isn't going to want this one back." He looked over at Molly. "What do you say? You in?"

"Sure," she said, resigned. Apparently, this was what the day was to hold.

"Chin up, everybody," Zach enthused. "This wasn't a total disaster."

"It was pretty close," Molly said. "We were supposed to have a day in the park, not a day at the ER."

"So we had a hospital visit," Zach said with a peppy positivity that was surely drug-induced. "Look on the bright side. At least it was outpatient."

CHAPTER 16

"You think Old Lady Janacek is going to miss you?" Davis asked. This was how he referred to Rachel's twenty-five-year-old kindergarten teacher, because the name somehow worked. "School's over, and you're officially a first grader. She's lost you. You're moving on, never looking back."

"I'll see her in the hall," Rachel said, refusing to see sentimentality where it did not lie. "I'll give her a hug if she needs one."

She tugged a small continent of cheese off her slice of pizza and dropped it into her upturned mouth. The open-jawed box in front of them on the table was now empty of everything except crumbs, grease stains, and smudges of sauce. Summer was on, school already a distant memory. Soon Rachel would begin her third year at Lakeside Camp, a day camp out in the boonies where she and a hundred other hellions spent seven weeks gluing popsicle sticks together, passing around poison ivy, and singing "On Top of Spaghetti."

Tonight, Davis had the rare pleasure of dining with his daughter in the warm embrace of the family home. Prior to this evening Davis had only made it as far as the foyer since moving out, as it was an unspoken but mutually recognized condition of the separation that he wasn't welcome beyond the welcome mat without specific, limited dispensation. Britt had extended such dispensation tonight when her babysitter canceled, thus imperiling her plans to catch a movie with her coworker Arlene. Britt didn't feel right bailing on their evening, as Arlene was going through her own marital unpleasantness, and after all, Britt had a backup babysitter in Davis. She'd sounded leery about letting him back in. They still weren't really talking, at least not about anything that mattered. Nor had she shown any signs of thawing at his apologies.

It was the most heart-wrenching thing he'd ever known, to be *persona non grata* in his own house, a marginally welcome guest in his own caliphate. It was almost surreal, and it made him feel like one of those sitcom characters replaced by a different actor at the start of a new season. The first episode would begin, and here was this stranger pretending to be the patriarch. The same kids were calling him Dad, the same wife chiding him for trying to fix things around the house, but by dint of death or contract dispute, Ted Knight was out and Dick Van Patten or someone else who wasn't Ted Knight was in, slipping into the family and assuming the man's put-upon and endearingly clueless identity. Davis had not yet been replaced, but how long would it be before his character was written out of the show?

Rachel yawned, then immediately stated for the record, "I'm not tired."

"Of course not," Davis said.

The bedtime ritual was one of the things he missed most about this house. (It wasn't the same when Rachel slept over at the apartment.) The mere thought of the nightly routine going on without him could make Davis homesick beyond anything he'd ever felt—his daughter in her soft cotton pajamas, deliberating at her bookshelf, practicing cartwheels on the rug, commanding the performance of a medley of songs before lights out.

"Daddy?" Rachel asked, still toying with the remnants of her slice.

"Yes, little face?"

"What do grown-ups talk about?"

"Well, lots of stuff."

"Politics?"

"Sometimes. We also talk about our kids. Movies, books, restaurants."

"It sounds boring."

"It usually is."

Davis snagged a wedge of crust off Rachel's plate. Fathers not only eat the food their kids have not eaten, but also the food their kids have not yet not eaten.

"Daddy?"

"Yes, little face?"

"When I grow up, am I going to like salad?"

"You might, but you don't have to. I didn't eat a salad until I was like thirty."

"Will I read books with no pictures in them, and have a wobbly butt?"

Davis chuckled. "Probably."

He looked at his daughter's dauntless olive eyes, the fine bubble of her nose, the defiant pucker of her lips; it made his gut sink. Her worries were growing. If everything about adulthood was predestined—right down to a taste for bland vegetables and rancor toward government—maybe the fraying of your family was just another rite of passage. One of your parents pissed off the other, and just like that, somebody gets an apartment.

He leaned toward her. "Listen up. In some ways you'll be just like Mommy and me, and in some ways you'll be totally different. You're going to be you. You're going to read whatever books you want to read, you're going to eat whatever foods you like—but mostly things that are good for you—and your butt is going to be as wobbly or as unwobbly as you want it to be. The important thing is that you're going to be you. That's all Mommy and I want. And you know that no matter what happens between Mommy and me, both of us will always be on your side. You know that, right? No matter what."

How it agonized him to hear himself say *no matter what* to his little girl. The words were like a dark solar system of uncertainty; they implied the need for reassurance. In the no-matter-what world, things hadn't worked out.

She looked up at him, her eyes searching. "Daddy?"

"Yes, little face?"

"Was Miss Hannigan a drunk?"

Davis slumped into the back of his chair. "Well, wouldn't you be?"

They each consumed a chocolate chip cookie, then took the party upstairs, Rachel skipping ahead, her hair twisted behind her ears in Heidi-style braids. Davis imagined that his daughter would spend a good portion of her life barefoot. That was just who she was. She would be indifferent to footwear. A Grateful Dead song would play wherever she went.

Envisioning the many Rachels of the future was one of Davis's favorite pastimes. He cataloged them in his head in an as-yet-unwritten volume he dubbed *The Wondrous Lives of the Fabulous Rachel Winger*. They came upon him at odd times, clear as day. He'd look at her across the Candyland board and see her at nineteen, scooting through the French countryside on a '63 Vespa, stopping to kiss the cheeks of the elderly florist who always slid a daffodil behind her ear and called her by a pet name that meant "fearless orchid" in some exotic language. They'd be upstairs playing school and, boom!, she was twenty-three, the poetess of Soho, holding court amid a dreamscape of lava lamps and incense smoke and never keeping appointments because, well, who knew if time really existed anyway? Sometimes Davis saw her as a lionhearted mountaineer who, one fabled night in Nepal, drank all the locals under the table and became a misty legend, forever remembered, increasingly disbelieved. Other times she was the bookish, bespectacled, bun-haired champion of the downtrodden, a veritable Ruth Bader Winger, striking terror in the hearts of Washington's fat cats as she arrived—still barefoot, of course—to testify on Capitol Hill. Davis never tired of conjuring these wonderfully throbbing future lives of his fabulous daughter. But they didn't hold a candle to right now. These days, right now was everything.

"Brush your teeth and we'll read," he called to her as he stopped outside the office. He flicked on the light and smiled at his model roller coasters that lined the bookcase and windowsill. Some he'd brought home from Pavelka, others he'd bought unassembled at Calhoun's Hobby Shop, a store his father had introduced him to years ago, when those initial engineering impulses had begun to flower. Having these models around him had always soothed Davis. Tonight, however, something was off.

"Rach?" he called.

She couldn't hear him over the gushing faucet and her own operatic alto as she belted out "Maybe" from *Annie*, almost getting the lyrics right.

"Rachel?" he called out louder.

The singing stopped. "What?"

"Can you come here a sec?"

She appeared at the doorway, her chin streaked white with toothpaste.

"Do you know what happened to this roller coaster?" He pointed to the Space Dragon, a savage network of interwoven red-and-yellow tracks with three giant loops. It had been a gift from his old man for making it through the engineering program. So many times he'd set it down on the carpet so that he and Rachel could guide the miniature cars up the track and then, at the very apex, let them go and watch physics work its will on the tiny, invisible thrill seekers. Davis would hold out his thumb and index finger millimeters apart, grin at his daughter, and say, "You have to be *this* tall to ride the Space Dragon."

Rachel wasn't responding to his question, so he asked it again. "Rach, do you know what happened to the Space Dragon?"

"No."

"There used to be a loop here." He pointed to the air between two unconnected segments of track. "You see the problem, right? It's a bit of a safety hazard to have a whole section of track not there. This would never pass inspection." He lowered his eyes at his daughter. "Would you happen to know anything about this?"

She shook her head.

"Did you maybe accidentally remove some of the track?"

Again, a stone-faced denial.

"Look, I'm not mad," Davis said. "I just want to know what happened."

"Well, I'm not mad either," Rachel barked back.

"Hmm. So we're jumping right to the indignation, are we? Okay. Well, tell me this—why would you be mad?"

"Why would *you* be mad? You don't even make roller coasters anymore."

"Yeah, but I made this one, and this is the one we're talking about. Grandpa Norm gave this to me, so it has sentimental value. Do you know what that means?"

"Yes."

"What does it mean?"

"I'm not telling."

"It means it's very special to me. Like every picture you've ever drawn since you were a baby, every birthday and Father's Day card you've ever made me. They all have sentimental value to me."

He dropped onto his back and yanked Rachel down with him. She struggled and yelped, but resistance was futile.

"When I was about your age, Grandpa Norm started taking me on roller coasters. He loved them. He, Aunt Molly, and I would visit all these amusement parks, and we'd go on every roller coaster they had, no matter how big and scary. I was nervous sometimes, but Grandpa Norm always told me there was nothing to be afraid of." He hoisted Rachel over him like an airplane and began to swing her this way and that, rotating her body sideways. She giggled and held out her arms like wings. "Your grandfather always told me that we might get jostled and jiggled and shaken, but in the end, we were going to be okay."

He lowered her down onto his chest and closed his eyes, feeling the carpet strands tickling his neck. He'd helped Britt pick out this carpet, he'd spent hours of his life stretched out upon it. When he opened his eyes again, Rachel was hovering over his face, scrutinizing his every feature.

"Daddy, your eyes aren't smiling," she said.

"Of course they are."

"No, they're not. Your mouth is, but not your eyes. Are you sad?"

"Sad? On a night of pizza and cookies with my best girl? Girlfriend, please. Even my earlobes are smiling."

She continued her meticulous inspection of his face. Never in ten lifetimes would he have followed Jacqueline into her hotel room if he'd thought about the way his daughter smelled right before she went to bed. Then he thought again about the disfigured Space Dragon and how he'd been dismissive of Rachel when she'd insisted she wasn't mad. Who had a stronger claim to anger than she?

"Little face," he said, "are you upset with me?"

"No."

"Are you sure?"

She didn't say anything.

"I know things are weird right now. I so wish they weren't. But if you're upset, talk to me. Yell at me if you feel like it. Just try not to take it out on these poor, defenseless models. They didn't do anything."

"Why don't you just say you're sorry?" Rachel asked.

"I'm sorry."

"No—to Mommy."

He wanted so much to tell her that he'd been apologizing every chance he got, through all available means of communication, but that would only beg the question of what exactly Daddy had done that required Mommy's forgiveness.

"Mommy and I are working some stuff out. It's just like we told you."

"Say you're sorry anyway," Rachel said. "Sometimes I say I'm sorry even when I didn't do anything wrong."

"Why do you do that?"

"Mommy says it makes you a bigger person."

Davis smiled, comforted that his daughter was inheriting his wife's wisdom and awesome magnanimity.

"Rach," he said a short while later, "do you know what the very first word you ever said was?"

"Mommy?" she guessed.

"Nope."

"Daddy?"

"Nope."

"I give up."

"Eczema," Davis said.

"What's that?"

"It's an uncomfortable and often gross skin condition. You see, you had very dry skin as a baby, and Mommy and I were always rubbing lotion on you and talking about whether your eczema was getting better or worse. One day, you pointed to your itchy tummy, made a really sad frown, and said, 'Eczema.' That's when I realized that I had to be very careful around you."

"Why?" Rachel asked. She was now taking stock of the density of hair in her father's nostrils.

"I had to be careful of all the things you knew but didn't tell me you knew."

———

Davis fully expected to be turning the pages of another adventure of Rodney, the titular character in a series about a third grader with a freakishly good jump shot who makes it to the NBA at the age of eight. Rachel was hooked on these books, so thank god the author pumped them out on a quarterly basis, christening them with an if-it-ain't-broke-don't-fix-it economy: *Meet Rodney, Here Comes Rodney, There Goes Rodney,* and the most recent offering, *Rodney Gets Fouled!* So imagine Davis's surprise when Rachel climbed into bed with an old hardcover that had been gathering dust on her shelf for eons.

"*The Magic Carpet?*" Davis said.

Rachel was already too immersed in the illustrations to respond.

"Didn't you tell me a long time ago that this book was for babies?" She shook her head.

"Oh. Maybe it was some other kid who told me that." Davis slid next to her. "Let's do this. I've missed that crazy old rug."

The Magic Carpet was the classic, if uncomfortably sexist tale of a sultan in ancient India whose three sons were all smitten by the same fair maiden. None of the young men would yield the lovely and exquisite Nouronnihar to his brothers, so the Great Sultan was forced to come up with a contest. Each son was to scour the globe for the rarest of treasures, and whoever found the artifact that most enchanted Nouronnihar earned the right to marry her. (At least the girl had some say in the matter, as she got to decide which gift was the one that really blew up her skirt. The fact that the present also came with a husband— well, fairy tales will be fairy tales.)

The three sons struck out in search of something with which to seduce the object of their affection. The eldest, Prince Hussein, journeyed far and wide and ended up in a crowded market in a faraway land, where he encountered a mysterious rug merchant. The merchant told the prince that his were no ordinary carpets, that they were, in fact, a magical means of travel. The possessor of the rug had merely to think of a destination—anywhere in the world—and instantaneously he or she would be whisked away to that very place aboard the magic carpet. Intrigued, the prince paid the merchant, took the rug outside for a test drive, and discovered that it was exactly as advertised. He flew home on it and presented it to the fair Nouronnihar, who was so charmed by the exotic furnishing that she agreed to marry him on the spot. She was rather materialistic, this Nouronnihar, but the best stories have flawed characters.

As he had done on so many nights before, Davis curled up on his daughter's bed and read the story, and Rachel listened, transfixed and transported by every illustration—the domes and minarets of the distant dreamscapes, the braided tassels of the Persian carpet that carried the prince through the clouds, the helix of garments worn by the beautiful Nouronnihar, in whom Rachel may have seen reflections of her Indian American mother.

On the final page, when the happy couple flew off together on their magical tapestry, Rachel looked up at her father, eyes as sharp as midday, and asked, "Is it true?"

"What do you think?" Davis said.

"I know it's fiction, which is when it's a lie—"

"It's a story, not a lie."

"—but could it happen? Are there carpets that fly?"

"Can't say I've ever seen one," Davis said, stroking a nonexistent beard. "Have you?"

"No," Rachel said.

"Maybe we just haven't been looking in the right places."

The little girl sat upright, suddenly aquiver. "We should make one!"

"We totally should," Davis agreed.

"You're good at making rides, so make one that has a carpet that flies."

"Yeah. I'll just figure it out. How hard could that be?"

"You make it, and I can decorate it."

"So don't get me wrong. I'm loving this idea. I'm just a little worried that you're giving yourself the easier job. I design it, I build it, I make it work, and you basically color it in."

Satisfied that a plan was in place, Rachel lay back down and shifted into her father's shoulder. "Let's read it again," she said.

He cracked the front cover and took it from the top.

At the end of the second read-through, Rachel, typically out cold by this point, was still wide awake, and although Davis could've easily been talked into a third reading and a fourth, or into reading her every book on her shelf that night, he knew he needed to be counted on to enforce the rules. "Let's call it a night, little face," he said.

When he'd smoothed out the afghan and tucked it under her chin, Rachel looked up at him. "Daddy, if you had a magic carpet, where would you tell it to go?"

An unexpected hitch caught in his throat, the bluntest yearning. He swallowed it down. "Piece of cake," he replied. "Wherever you and Mommy are."

"That's cheesy," she said.

"Be that as it may, that's my final answer. What about you?"

Her eyes spun. "Hmm. I know! The Great Wall of China!"

"Good call."

"Maybe the Eiffel Tower!"

"*Très* exotic."

"Or Texas!"

"We don't have to decide tonight. Let's sleep on it," he suggested. "Now, then—where's me hug? Where's me kiss?" Davis always went Cockney when saying good night or goodbye.

He secured the night-light in the outlet, flicked off the reading lamp, and closed her door.

———

When Britt came home, she found Davis stretched out on the sofa, feasting on the feel of his own furniture and the scent of the candle that Britt kept lit on the kitchen counter. These candles were so quintessentially Britt. The woman could easily kill a half hour in Bath & Body Works, prying the lids off the candles and sniffing the colored wax. But Davis knew that what really sold her was not the aromas, but the seasonally emblematic names, that she was seduced by the romantic thought of her house smelling like lilac blossom in spring, cottage breeze in summer, apple cupcake in autumn, and maple gingerbread in winter.

"How was the movie?" he asked her.

"It was good," Britt said. "Everything go okay here?"

"Perfect," Davis said.

"How was she?"

"She was great. It was oldies night. She wanted to read *The Magic Carpet*, twice."

"Yeah, for some reason she's back into that one. I've been finding it on her pillow."

Britt set her handbag on the table, which triggered the muted jingle of keys sliding down among the purse's contents. She was showing him all the warmth and intimacy of a bank teller.

"By the way, I think we have a mini-engineer upstairs," Davis said. "Someone's been dismembering my models."

"I hope you gave her hell," Britt said.

"I beat her senseless."

"Just because things are the way they are, that doesn't mean you can't yell at her anymore," Britt said, as if to remind him. "Yesterday she took every article of clothing out of her dresser and said she was reorganizing. When I told her to do it soon because her floor was a mess, she looked me square in the eye and said, 'I'll do it when I get around to it.'"

Davis coughed down a laugh. "The kid's incorrigible. I say military school."

"The kid's acting out," Britt said. Then her features arched with inquest. "Crazy question—did you get a dog?"

"Well, not exactly," Davis replied, looking meek. "I'm kind of watching my neighbor's pug for a little while."

"I thought Rachel had made it up. Since when are you a dog person?"

"I'm not. I'm just vulnerable to favor askers."

"Well, it's your apartment, so you can do what you want, but if Fido is temporary, you need to be careful. According to your daughter, that dog is her soul mate."

Davis's laughter, so sudden and genuine, caused Britt to let down her guard and allow herself a moment of levity in his presence. Standing there in a sweater the color of a monarch butterfly, her laughing lips painted danger red, Britt looked so beautiful it made him weak. He was just about to tell her how terribly he missed her, how painfully, how mortally he wanted her back, when she said, "You should probably go."

He sighed and began an unhurried mosey toward the door. "By the way, thanks for ratting me out to my dad. I'd eaten an entire Hungarian honey cake before I stopped to wonder how Tom Petty knew where to send the care package."

"Peti may have baked for you, but trust me, she and your dad are on my side," Britt said.

"Everybody's on your side, Britt. I'm on your side."

Her eyes tensed. There was bitterness in them, helplessness too. "I honestly don't know how to let you back into this house. I wish I did, but I don't."

"Britt." His shoulders hunched and his head drooped. He stared at the floor a long time before looking up at her. "I'm so sorry, Britt. I was so wrong. It was a dreadful lapse. I lost my mind and took you for granted, and you deserve so much better than that."

She held up her hand. "I'm tired of all the apologies, Davis. They don't matter as much as you think they do."

"What I did is not who I am," he insisted. "You know that. And I think you know how crazy fucking in love with you I've been since the second I saw you."

She shook her head. "All bets are off as to what I know."

How could he convince her that a mistake, even a spectacularly hurtful one, was not necessarily cause to reevaluate everything you thought you knew about the maker of that mistake? Mistake making had to be as deeply encoded in our DNA as everything else, like color vision or bipedalism. If there was an evolutionary purpose behind blushing or carsickness or the hair on our ass, surely the tendency to fuck up was something evolution left in the batter for a reason. He offered this not as an excuse, but as a way forward. If his crimes bled of humanity, were they not, after all the pain and anger, all the dish throwing and disappointment, ultimately forgivable?

"I ran into Nicole Abel the other day at Trader Joe's," Britt said. "Lexi's mom."

"Lexi's the Swede, right?"

"Yeah."

Lexi was a preschool classmate of Rachel's. She was not Swedish, not even partially Swedish, and as far as anyone knew had never visited Sweden. Davis, however, had always seen something Scandinavian in her pale-pink skin, her Arctic eyes, and her white-yellow hair, and had therefore dubbed her "the Swede." Britt had long ago stopped fighting the shorthand.

"Nicole clearly didn't know about us," Britt went on.

"Did you tell her?" Davis asked.

"I didn't know what to say, honestly. But eventually I'm going to have to say something."

Davis felt a flutter of butterflies. "We're not at eventually yet, Britt. I'm not going anywhere. I hope you understand that."

"Actually, you are." And she pulled the door open.

He continued his slow amble to the exit. "We got an extra choco-late chip cookie for you. It's propped up against the coffee maker in a baggie."

"Fantastic," she said. "I'm sure I'll take one bite and forget all about how you fucked a Frenchwoman on a business trip."

"You think so?" He ventured a grin. "Because I sure would appreci-ate that."

The door closed shy of an actual slam but with enough thrust to make a point, and as Davis traversed the dark lawn he ruminated on that dire word. *Eventually.* Forgiveness delayed was forgiveness denied, because if Britt stayed hurt or angry long enough, *eventually* she would move on. That's what people did. When there were gaps in the track, *eventually* they found somewhere else to land.

But for now, what was the party line when encountering acquain-tances, neighbors, or nosy randoms? Which was the lie, that he and Britt were together or that they were apart? Nicole Abel was a bad example because, as everyone knew, she was up-all-night crazy, a good old-fashioned lunatic who hawked over her precious Lexi as if the child were a glass-sculpted hemophiliac. That tyrannical mad-woman had the weird gall to escort her kid to birthday parties but deprive her of the goodies. "I don't believe in cake for children," he'd heard her say. What did that mean, to not believe in cake? Their paths rarely crossed anymore, as Nicole had moved Lexi into private school (perhaps where the sugar, nuts, and wheat couldn't find her), and now the poor kid attended some loopy academy whose website advertised an educational approach grounded in "capital R reality." But it was fair to wonder how long Davis could get away with non-answers when the Nicole Abels of the world inquired about his family at the grocery store or on the soccer sidelines. It was fair to wonder at what point this temporary estrangement would become the new capital R reality.

CHAPTER 17

"Hi, sister."

"Hi, brother."

He cut right to it, his morning voice sounding like crushed rock. "I've got one."

"One what?" Molly asked.

"I'm not going to explain myself," Davis said.

"Ah, okay," she said, after a beat. "Go ahead. By all means, dazzle me."

"Okay. So you know how some stores don't let you walk around with coffee? You step inside some fussy clothing boutique or jewelry store, and they tell you to put your coffee on the counter."

"Yeah," Molly said. "It offends me. I've never spilled anything in my entire life."

"Let's turn it on its head," Davis proposed. "How about a store that *forces* you to drink coffee? You walk through the door and they hand you this huge mug of the darkest, most fiercely caffeinated java, and you have to carry it around with you as you shop, and you can't leave until it's finished."

Molly began to laugh. "That's absurd."

"Totally ridic."

"Horrible idea."

"Horrible. Now you."

He heard the tapping of fingernails on Molly's steering wheel, the rude noises of traffic outside her car window. "Okay," she said. "This too is beverage related, and it's of particular relevance to you. Ready?"

"Bring it," Davis said.

"Cup holders on roller coasters."

He repeated the words slowly, naughtily. "Cup holders on roller coasters."

"You're walking around an amusement park on a hot summer day, you're standing in long lines, baking in the sun. So you buy yourself a cold, refreshing drink."

"A soda," Davis said. "An iced tea."

"Yes, those are examples of cold, refreshing drinks. Now you want to go on a ride, but you don't want to throw away your drink, especially since you probably paid ten bucks for it."

"Plus, you need your hands free so you can wave them in the air when you scream," Davis pointed out.

"Exactly. But with a beverage holder next to each seat, your problems are solved."

"I can't believe no one has ever thought of this before."

"Go pimp it to your engineering buddies," she told him.

"I don't have engineering buddies anymore, but rest assured, that's the only thing stopping me."

"Right," Molly said, and he could almost hear her wince. "Sorry to dredge up the past."

"Well, it's still kind of the present," Davis said. "How about you? You still have a job?"

"Last time I checked. But that could change at any minute, the way things are going."

"And the kid you're babysitting-slash-dating? How're things with Zach?"

"Oh, you know, the usual. He played tennis with schoolchildren and ended up in the ER. He's trying to convince me to go to Vegas for a horror movie convention even though he knows I hate horror movies. Standard relationship stuff."

"You want my advice?" Davis asked.

"No."

"It seems to me you have two options. One, you can start dating men instead of boys. That's probably the fastest remedy. Or two, you can start dating women."

"Even if I were gay, I'd still be me, and that's kind of the problem."

"Hmm. How about transitioning into a man?"

"What will that solve?"

"I don't know. Shake things up. Of course, instead of Aunt Molly, Rachel would have to call you Uncle Molly."

"You're a riot."

"Or Ain't Molly," Davis said. He was cracking himself up.

"Thanks. This has been really helpful."

She waited for his laughter to subside. It didn't.

"Bye, brother," she said.

He caught his breath. "Bye, sister."

CHAPTER 18

It was an ancient fable, innumerable iterations in print, all with varying text and illustrations, but Davis foraged among all the online marketplaces until he located the selfsame edition that resided on his daughter's bookshelf. He even clicked on the sample pages to be absolutely certain. This he did while sipping coffee from his favorite mug, the black porcelain one with the bubble letters that spelled out the word *Boonoonoonoos*, the name of the restaurant in Aruba where he and Britt had supped on the first night of their honeymoon. Both of them were giddily drunk all through the meal of pumpkin soup and macadamia grouper, and Davis could still remember his new bride's hot Bacardi breath when he'd leaned over the table in the middle of dinner and kissed her slow. When he'd moved out, he'd taken that mug with him. It was for the mug's own good, as Britt could no longer be counted on not to smash it to pieces.

Davis ordered the book, even sprang for expedited shipping. Then he looked down at Tweedy. "Don't ask me why I'm doing this, doggie," he said. Tweedy was greedily munching on a bowl of kibble. "I know you get it. You have dreams too." He ruffled the loose flesh on the pug's head and walked out, a whistle clinking around his neck.

Each morning presented a laundry list of custodial tasks for the new lifeguard. Skimming leaves and deceased insects off the water's surface, checking the chlorine and pH levels, plucking debris out of the gutters and filters, making sure the diving board and ladders were secure, shaking Ajax into the toilets in the changing rooms, and collecting abandoned articles of clothing and goggles and depositing them in the "lost and found" (a.k.a. the metastasizing pile of damp stuff under the chair). There was tedium, there was overexposure to the sun, there was the occasional complaint from a tenant—the latticework of a chaise had too many ruptures, there was a feces-colored floater in the shallow end that was, in fact, feces—and there was even a minor peril every now and again, like the garter snake waiting for him one morning in one of the filters. (Davis greeted the reptile with a shriek and a ten-yard retreat.) But there was also a wilderness of time in which to ponder. And to his immense dismay, what Davis seemed to be pondering was flying carpets.

It had been a joke, of course. *Hey, Daddy, build a flying carpet. Sure, honey, no problem. How hard can it be?* But it kept whispering to him, gathering shape in his head the way his projects at Pavelka used to. In one way, Rachel's renaissance of affection for *The Magic Carpet* was innocent and adorable, early-onset nostalgia for the nightly readings of that cherished volume, for the way they would sit cross-legged on the floor, Peti's afghan spread out under them to simulate the magical rug, and pretend to soar over treetops and oceans. At the same time, it devastated Davis to think that his child might be reaching for that book because she couldn't reach for him, that she was carrying it around the house, lugging it along in the car, clinging to it at bedtime, because it offered the comfort that he wasn't there to give.

He didn't fully understand yet why he'd awakened that morning compelled to order that book. It was a children's fable, after all, not a how-to manual. But he was beginning to suspect that, like the winged rug itself, the story would sweep him up and carry him somewhere he desperately wanted to go. Somewhere he needed to go. He just didn't yet know where that was.

As he skirted the pool with skimmer in hand, he heard the gate creak in its hinges. The sound of Charlie's voice followed.

"Business sure is booming," she remarked dryly as she traversed the empty deck. "How's my mutt?"

"He's good," Davis replied. "No looker, that's for sure, but you know what? He's actually an okay guy."

So far, the canine custody arrangement had been agreeable. Tweedy resided with him most of the time, and Charlie had unfettered visitation rights, which she exercised liberally, usually in the evenings when she swung by to cradle, pet, and baby-talk the beast. As advertised, the pug didn't bark much. He napped in a crate, scratched at the door when he needed to go out, didn't soil the floor, and only sporadically launched into vigorous, seemingly unprovoked attacks of growling and sprinting—"the zooms," Charlie called it. When Davis walked Tweedy, he was careful to stay close to his section of the complex, safe from the policing eyes of Guy and any heel-clicking neighbors. And while Davis would confess to having succumbed to a modicum of affection toward the dog, Rachel was flat-out gaga over him, which was reason enough to continue boarding him.

Davis noticed the beefy textbook and spiral notebook under Charlie's arm. "Aren't we looking studious this morning," he said. "Summer school?"

"No, I'm just super curious about"—she read the front cover of the behemoth text—"*Explorations in Conceptual Physics*, the latest page-turner by my favorite author, Prentice Hall."

"Uh-oh. Somebody flunked science."

"And it's a damn shame," she said, "because I'm really going to need to know about light refraction and the atomic nature of matter and Newton's law of motion."

"First of all, Newton has three laws of motion, so already I see where your teacher is coming from," Davis said. "And you never know what you'll end up using. I never thought I'd ever need physics after high school. Then I became a structural engineer, and suddenly I was using physics every day."

"Structural engineer?" Charlie sneered. "Is that what they call guys who pluck dead bugs out of swimming pools? Fine. Knock yourself out. I'm Adele, by the way."

She tossed her schoolwork onto a lounge chair, spread a towel over it, then slipped out of her shirt and shorts, stripping down to a blue one-piece. Merely noticing the color of her bathing suit felt like leering, so Davis kept his eyes on his work, drawing the net across the azure water in smooth, graceful pulls, then tapping his catchings out into the shrubbery.

Other than the snarl of a lawnmower somewhere off in the distance, all was peaceful at the Deluxe. The early-morning diehard, Mickey Hotchkiss, had already come and gone. Mickey was a robust eighty-seven-year-old who strode down to the pool first thing each day with a towel around his neck and cranked out ten laps in slow motion. It was impossible not to know that Mickey was eighty-seven, for he mentioned it within the first thirty seconds of every conversation. It seemed people eventually got so old that they told you their age, then waited for you to be just as astonished as they were. "Come off it, Mickey. Age is all in your head," Davis had said to him. "It sure is," Mickey had agreed, before adding, "Until it ain't, kiddo."

The only other regular was Mrs. Alpert, a cheerful widow in her late fifties who stopped by in the late afternoon mostly to show how comfortable she was parading around without the refuge of a cover-up.

"I was a dancer in my younger days," she'd bragged to Davis.

"I believe it," Davis had replied, eyeing her fascinatingly toned legs, calves so pronounced that it appeared as though her lower leg had swallowed a dinner roll.

"Tried out for the Rockettes, you know. They turned me down."

Davis pretended to scoff. "Big deal, Mrs. Alpert. I could be rejected by the Rockettes, too, if I wanted."

And she'd grinned flirtatiously and told him to call her Diane.

Unfortunately, Diane was the exception. Almost uniformly, the real housewives of the Deluxe were spunkless things that came moping down to the pool with their gloom and their dying dreams, their nicotine spots and low-swinging labias. They lolled miserably under the pitiless sun, paging through gossip magazines they didn't enjoy, until a few hours passed and they sat up realizing, shit, they were still alive, might as well shuffle off and get dinner out of the freezer. Davis sometimes wondered what these women had looked like on the day they moved in, whether the local mood was shaping its inhabitants or the other way around.

After tidying up the changing rooms—glamorous work that included wiping insect carcasses off the mirrors and drenching the showers with mildew combatant—Davis emerged and saw that Charlie had gotten up from her chaise and was inching into the pool. Ten minutes of studying and she'd already rewarded herself with a break. Standing on the steps with one hand on the metal railing, she was kicking water across the pool, her toes spraying arcs of glittering tears toward the deep end. Davis was partly worried—partly hoping, but mostly worried—that she was fixing to talk to him.

"You want to know the truth?" she said.

"The truth?" he repeated. "Have you been lying to me all this time?"

"I got expelled. I have to read that big dumb science book, plus some other boring shit for other classes, because I got thrown out of school."

Davis eyed the young woman. "What did you do?"

"I pushed Lara Buchman down the steps."

"And what did old Lara Buchman do to deserve that?"

"Nothing specific. Just a lifetime of general assholery."

"Was she hurt?"

"It's not like she died or anything. Just knocked unconscious, and only for a few minutes."

Charlie stepped out of the water and moped over to where Davis was reshelving his cleaning supplies.

"Here's the thing," she said. "Lara Buchman is a raging bitch on wheels. We've hated each other since, like, sixth grade, and to be perfectly honest with you, I don't give a giggleberry fuck that she banged her head and spent a night in the hospital. But the truth is—and nobody believes me, but whatever—I didn't mean for her to go tumbling down a flight of steps. All I wanted to do was humiliate her. Just your basic hallway tripping, with lots of flailing into lockers and stuff. Good clean fun. I just happened to pick the wrong spot to do it."

"Well, it sounds like you only had the best of intentions." Davis pulled out a chair and positioned it to face the pool. "I should probably tell you that even if Lara Buchman is the heinous miscreant you claim she is, and even if your animus toward her is justified, you probably should give a giggleberry fuck that you put her in the hospital. Otherwise you sound like a bit of a sociopath."

Charlie seemed to chew on that idea, a brief soul-searching that culminated in a shrug. "Maybe I am a sociopath. I'm not going to beat myself up over it."

She slid her sunglasses up over her forehead and sighed at the world. "Anyway, because of the expulsion, I ended up failing all my classes, so I did not what you might call 'graduate.' And because of that, the University of Maryland did not what you might call 'still want me to attend.'"

Davis grimaced. "They revoked your acceptance?"

"They revoked the fuck out of my acceptance."

Charlie explained that after some groveling by her father, the school board decided to cut the young menace a break. Her expulsion was lifted, but her failing grades stood. She had to retake her classes over the summer, and if by some stroke of luck she passed them, she would be awarded her diploma and—provided she hadn't knocked anyone else down a flight of steps—she would be readmitted to the freshman class at Maryland.

It was with a stab of horror that Davis realized he had a Lara Buchman of his own. Charlie had dispatched someone to the hospital with the sweep of a leg, while he'd done it (if he'd done it at all) through the more elaborate means of a log flume, but both were now doing time for it in the same minimum-security apartment complex that was but one plumbing crisis away from a cold-water flat.

Charlie fixed a probing gaze on him. "What about you?" she asked. "What's your deal?"

"Who says I have a deal?"

"You must. Look where you live. Do you have a thing for shriveled-up grandmas in swimsuits?"

"And what if I do?"

"I mean, you seem like a normal enough guy, but given your situation, you just can't be."

"Yeah, I'm probably not."

"Seriously, I don't get you." Charlie was sizing him up the way one might stare through a snot-flecked sneeze guard at a strip-mall buffet. "There has to be something majorly off about you, but you hide it like a champ. You're nice. You don't have any frightening tics. You're not, like, hideous. You have a semi-decent figure—for an old dude, that is."

"I don't think you're supposed to tell a guy he has a decent figure," Davis said.

"I didn't say you have a decent figure. I said you have a *semi*-decent figure."

"That's something you say to a woman."

"A man can't have a nice figure?"

"You don't say it like that."

"I've lost track of which one of us is being misogynistic."

"You are," Davis said. "You're being misogynistic toward me."

"Do you have a wife?" Charlie asked.

Davis sighed. "Yes, I have a wife."

"How come I've never seen her?"

"We're not going to talk about that."

Charlie crossed her legs and rested her grin in the palm of her hand. "Did you seduce her by talking about Newton's law of motion?"

"Again, there are three laws of motion, so maybe you better get back to work." When he stood, the moist underside of his legs ripped from the chair straps like a Band-Aid. "Run along, now. I need to watch the pool."

"Why? There's no one here," Charlie said. "What are we ordering for lunch?"

Davis patted the budding paunch beneath his T-shirt, the byproduct of prolonged estrangement from his running shoes. "Nothing," he said. "I'm too fat to have lunch."

CHAPTER 19

An old friend was like an old song, or maybe an old song was like an old friend, but either way, it was one of the great sustaining joys of Molly's life that she ended up living in the same neighborhood as Skyler Jones. Now, anytime they wanted, they could hook up for walks or a last-minute glass of wine at one of the nearby bars. Often they bumped into each other at the Morning Dew Café and chatted for twenty minutes.

It was Saturday in Federal Hill, a mild breeze whispering innuendos of summer. All around, people were living life with high-definition vitality. Young mothers fed pieces of muffin to kids in strollers. Bikers in spandex convened curbside, a sheen of sweat on their foreheads. Molly and Skyler walked along these sun-bleached blocks, Molly questioning the future of the *Weekly Ramble*, Skyler lightheartedly lamenting the erosion of her husband's good looks.

"It's the long hours," Skyler complained. "I keep subtly suggesting he make time for the gym, and by subtly, I mean I pack him carrots and yogurt for lunch."

"You're a monster," Molly said. "Chad is so handsome."

"But it's a different kind of handsome now. Less immediate. The kind you have to go looking for, and sometimes you find it, sometimes you don't. Don't you think it's his responsibility to age as well as I am?"

"You're a terrible person," Molly told her.

"What about you?" Skyler inquired. "How's the boy toy? Wait—is it you who's the boy toy or him? A boy's toy? A boy who *is* a toy? I've never been clear who's who in that expression."

Molly was making stomachache face. "Please stop. Nobody is anyone's toy in my relationship. And I'd trade you in a heartbeat, Zach for Chad, straight up."

"Oh man," Skyler said, laughing lasciviously. "I haven't had access to a twenty-two-year-old body in forever."

"Well, first off, he's twenty-three," Molly said. "Do you remember what it means to be twenty-three? It means that every Friday, he and his friends start drinking at four. He won't see a movie with subtitles—unless, of course, the subtitles are translating a space alien speaking in its native tongue. And a classy restaurant is one that has multiple flavors of wings. Still interested?"

Both women limboed under a tree branch that curved down over the sidewalk at neck level.

"I'll say one thing in Zach's favor," Molly added. "He does Big Brothers Big Sisters, and he's very committed to it. It's like his passion. And he's got the nicest Little Brothers. I enjoy their company more than his."

"You've never mentioned that," Skyler noted. "You've always made him sound so vapid."

"That's because his other passion is *Battlestar Galactica*. But I have to give him credit. Those boys really seem to like him. They're old enough to see through him, but they kind of choose not to."

Skyler wanted to hear more about Zach's Little Brothers, so Molly told her what Anthony and Gabe had shared, a narrative that adhered to the typical, depressing trope of a single parent walking out and leaving her kids with a boyfriend who immediately bugs out too. The silver lining, at least from Molly's vantage point, was that these boys, unlike so many others in the system, didn't seem locked onto a path to nowhere.

They had too many good people looking out for them—perhaps most important, each other.

The two women continued their stroll through the neighborhood. They waited in line for doughy bagels at a food truck, then tore pieces off them and ate them while they walked.

After a while, Skyler asked, "Have you ever thought about being a Big Sister?"

Molly shook her head. "Why do you ask?"

"No reason. I was just thinking that you might understand these kids."

"Because my mom walked out on us too?"

"I guess."

"So then it's not no reason, is it?" Molly said. "Look, Zach's Little Brothers have been through a lot, and I can relate to almost none of it."

"I don't know about that," Skyler said.

"I am the daughter of a news anchor. I grew up wanting for nothing."

"Nobody grows up wanting for nothing."

Molly emitted a low growl of frustration. Skyler Jones was the only person in the world at whom Molly growled.

They'd met during the first week of freshman year at College Park, in Geology 101. All first-year students were required to take a science course, and geology seemed to Molly as nonscientific as a science class could get. The professor, a self-consciously undersized man named Zodrov who patrolled the lectern with a puffed-out chest, began the semester by canceling vacation. "Please note, ladies and gentlemen," he intoned importantly, "that October eighth through the eleventh is fall break for the university, but not for us, my young geologists. That is when this class will be taking a trip to the Eastern Shore to get our hands dirty with the study of sedimentation."

What faint appetite Molly had had for a course about rocks vanished under the threat of intrusion into her holiday, a four-day stretch back home where she could sleep in her bedroom and feast on Peti's homey fare. The moment class ended, she marched herself directly to the registrar to switch out.

From behind her in line, a voice called out to her. "Didn't I just see you in Geo?"

The voice belonged to a female student.

"Yeah," Molly replied.

The girl was pretty, with wild blue eyes, dressed to slay in tight jean shorts and a fitted pink tee. She carried herself with an air of overconfidence. They would not have been friends in high school.

"You dropping it?" the girl asked.

Molly nodded. "You?"

"Are you kidding? Instead of fall break I get bussed to the boonies to stare at rocks? Fuck that."

"Right," Molly agreed.

"Plus, that pervy little prof skeeved me out. I'm not leaving campus with that guy."

"Right," Molly said again.

They approached the counter together, and the one who wasn't Molly did all the talking.

"Me and this little chickie here need to get out of Geology 101, stat."

The registrar sized them up through the austere eyewear chained around her neck. "And who might you be?" she asked.

The girl looked at Molly. "Yeah. Who might you be?"

The stern, unsmiling registrar typed in their names—Molly Winger and Skyler Jones—and asked, "Is this Professor Zodrov's class?"

"Is he the short nerd?" Skyler asked.

The registrar stared heavily at Skyler for a moment, then said, "Yes."

When they were asked which class they'd like to switch into, Skyler shrugged at Molly, who was beginning to grasp that the two of them were now a package deal.

"Honestly, I don't care. I just want all my vacation days," Skyler replied. "And if you have any teachers with a little less of a pedo vibe, we'll take one of those, please."

They switched into an introductory psych course and sat next to each other. For Molly this class was a significant upgrade. She found the subject matter far more accessible than the study of sediment, and instead of the dweeby little Zodrov, this class was taught by Professor Brubaker, a scandalously young woman commonly mistaken for a sophomore. Still, Skyler routinely emitted bored sighs that ricocheted around the lecture hall.

"Can you yawn a little more quietly, Ms. Jones?" Professor Brubaker was known to quip.

"Trying my best, Teach," Skyler would reply.

A few weeks later, Molly was dragged to a party that Skyler and her roommates were throwing. Molly went, brought her own roommate (Lin, a Shanghainese, who was even more of an introvert than Molly, although in retrospect, that may have just been the language barrier), and was duped into drinking grain alcohol out of a trash can. She ended up remembering so little about the evening that Skyler later convinced her that Molly had made out with some guy on the lacrosse team, an unlikely incident that to this day she denied but couldn't truly refute.

This Skyler person seemed hell-bent on friendship, and since the making of friends required greater effort for Molly than for the rest of humanity, she simply surrendered to it. Hanging around Skyler and her airy, party-going posse broadened a great many horizons for a wide-eyed innocent like Molly. Doors opened for her.

Other things too. Toward the end of that first semester, Molly allowed herself to be seduced out of a raging Phi Kappa Tau party and back to the apartment of Trent, an exchange student from London who looked the way Drakkar Noir smelled. Having consumed a full beer and a half from the keg, Molly had rendered herself susceptible to the charms of this exotic Brit who referred to friends as "mates," who called everything "brilliant," and whose tales of adventure included a near-death experience with his rugby team aboard "some dodgy Serbian airline." Entranced, Molly went back to Trent's "flat" and rather awkwardly relinquished her virginity.

When morning rolled around, it seemed Trent had relinquished something too: his British accent.

"I could've sworn you were British last night," Molly said, puzzled and massaging her headache.

"Yeah, I just kind of tone it down around my roommates," Trent explained quietly, his English now indistinguishable from hers.

Tone down your natural dialect? "Why would you do that?" she asked.

"Because they don't like it very much."

When Molly reported the incident to Skyler later that day, her friend merely giggled. "You really thought that cheeseball was an exchange student? He's, like, from Minneapolis. Relax—you got the first one out of the way. Now you can start to enjoy it. How was it?"

And Molly said, "Good," because she did not want to say, "I don't see what all the fuss is about."

When December rolled around, Molly and Skyler holed themselves up in an empty classroom with chips and Sprite to prepare for their psych final, and Molly made yet another discovery. Upon seeing Skyler's copious notes and her effortless command of all the exam topics—perception, cognition, states of consciousness, every last page in that glossy text—she realized that her friend's insolence masked an altogether surprising studiousness. "Oh my god, Skyler," Molly said, accusingly. "You're smart!"

Skyler was blasé. "Harvard, this place ain't."

"You didn't even buy the book until last week."

The pair grew closer, and though some of Skyler's other friends tolerated Molly with aloofness bordering on inattention, others, like Sarah and Sara, adopted her as their token wallflower. Sarah conscripted

Molly onto the college newspaper, thus birthing her career in journalism, and Sara got Molly to volunteer with her at the DC-area literacy initiative.

And yet, throughout the four years, Molly retained her outsider status because, fundamentally, an outsider was what she was. She resisted the wanton pull of sorority life, she didn't drink as often as her friends did and never drank as much, and only on the rarest of occasions woke up in someone else's room. But on graduation day, a completely sober Skyler wrapped Molly in a teary embrace, kissed both of her cheeks, and said, "You know, little chickie, I'm going to miss you the most."

A decade later, Skyler Jones was a clinical psychologist living with her husband all of five blocks from Molly's house. And she was still tight with Professor Brubaker.

The winding blocks of Federal Hill led the two friends to the crest of a rise overlooking the southern point of the harbor. Below them, a carousel spun and the bouncing waltz of accordion music drifted up. Across the water among the looming office buildings, Molly spied the utilitarian rectangle that housed her brother's firm—former firm—and was awed anew by what a mess his life had so quickly become.

Skyler brushed bagel crumbs off her sweater. "You know, Mol, it's been a lot of years, but I still think about how I made you drive to California to see your mom."

Molly looked at her.

"Sometimes I'm so sorry that it makes me want to die," Skyler continued. "Other times, I'm not sorry at all."

"That was one of the weirder apologies I've ever gotten in my life," Molly said.

"Well, it's an honest one," Skyler said.

"It seems I can't talk about Zach's Little Brothers without you assuming I'm really talking about myself."

"Give me some credit," Skyler said. "Don't I stay out of your business? I let the little chickie be the little chickie, because I think, by and large, the little chickie is doing just fine. But—"

Molly sighed. "Here we go."

"But—I am a psychologist. Let's not ignore that I spend all day every day listening to people who are trying to work through their shit. And not for nothing, I get a lot of women who went through what you did. That is the very shit they come to work through. My point is, I know it's a sharp wound, and one that tends to stick around."

Molly knelt and touched the grass. The warm blades prickled her palms and fingers. The hillside, musty and herbal, smelled distantly like wine. "I get it, Sky. I'm a deeply damaged individual."

"Molly—you're my number one favorite person on the planet. I don't have a second favorite. I'm just saying it wouldn't kill you to talk about it. Or, seeing as how you happen to write for a living, to write about it."

Molly laughed. "Yeah, I'll just start work on my memoir."

"If you want to pretend not to understand what I'm saying, fine. Knock yourself out. Maybe at thirty-two you're still not ready. But there are tons of motherless daughters out there. If you found some way to write about what happened to you as a kid, how you felt then and how you feel now, I think a lot of good could come of it. For you, for all those women out there who get it, maybe even for your paper too."

Molly gazed up at her. "I thought we were just talking about two inner-city kids in the Big Brother program."

"We're talking about a lot of things," Skyler said. The onetime sorority puma reached down and toyed with the long strands of Molly's hair, and it felt for an instant, as it had on many occasions throughout the years, that they themselves were mother and daughter.

"I'm here when you're ready to talk," Skyler said. "I know you know that. I obviously can't really be your therapist, but I can be your quote-unquote therapist."

Molly stared down the hill and saw knots of children flinging themselves free of the carousel's plastic horses, rushing off to parents outside the circular fence. Beyond them, boats dotted the harbor like shiny metal-backed beetles.

"I think you know me too well to be my therapist," said Molly.

To which Skyler said, "That literally makes no sense."

"I'll keep it in mind."

"I seriously doubt that, but I love you anyway."

CHAPTER 20

Skyler headed off for a baby shower and left Molly on that hill, high atop the muffled city, still feeling the urge to walk. No destination in mind, just the itch to move.

Walking along Charles Street, she came by Hankshaw's, a popular watering hole. Through the open door she heard a band playing, the music an unlikely coupling of psychedelic Pink Floyd–esque soundscapes and jazzy electric piano reminiscent of a Peanuts special. *It's The Dark Side of the Moon, Charlie Brown.* Molly felt temptation's tug to walk in and have a drink, at a bar, by herself, in the middle of the afternoon, something she'd never done before in her entire life, which was shameful considering she lived in the epicenter of one of the city's liveliest drinking districts. But in the end, she forewent alcohol in favor of caffeine.

She sloped into the Morning Dew, and as she waited for her latte, her thoughts kept drifting back to Anthony and Gabe. She knew that no matter how hard she looked in the mirror, she'd never see in herself someone who could lay claim to that degree of loss. Those boys were motherless in a very different way. Strangely, though, on that day in the ER, as she'd sat beside them, the notion of writing about them in her column had actually occurred to her. It wasn't out of any sense of kinship; they had a story—it was as simple as that. Still, there was some loose ligament of common experience hitching her to them. Deep down in the unexplored regions and minor keys in her head, something had stirred within Molly, and maybe it was stirring still, because Skyler sensed it or saw it, or the connection was just so damn obvious that anyone could spot it at a mile's distance.

Latte in hand, Molly meandered down to the harbor, all the way to the aquarium, where she ended up among the throng of tourists flocking around the seal tank. She watched those blissful monsters gliding through the blue-green water like peace-seeking torpedoes, splashing in their Speedo skin and walrus whiskers, indifferent to all the unnecessary evolution around them, changes upon changes that so often seemed to miss the point of everything.

It was strange to learn that Skyler still shouldered regret for having coaxed Molly into that California road trip. The subject had come up so infrequently over the years that Molly might've wondered if Skyler still remembered the trip at all. Sometimes Molly wondered if it had even happened.

It was the end of first semester senior year, graduation mere months away, and Skyler, flying high from the three Long Island iced teas she'd thrown back in celebration of having finished her last exam of the session, popped in on Molly, who was studying for the one remaining final she had the next day. Barreling into the room, Skyler cranked up Molly's stereo, made a microphone of her fist, and began belting out Dave Matthews. "Craaaash into me, crash into me!"

Then, midhowl, she went silent. Something on Molly's computer screen had grabbed her attention. It was a list of search results all bearing one name.

"Who in the wild fuck is Kitty Lowell?" she asked.

"Nobody," Molly replied, hastily closing out.

Skyler's eyes grew wide. "Holy shit. That's Joe, isn't it?"

"Joe?"

"Joe Mama!"

The age of the internet, with its immediate, far-flowing tributaries of information, had breathed new life into Molly's intermittent bouts of curiosity about her mother. For some reason, such fleeting moments had coincided with the turning of the seasons. In early fall, for instance, when accepting a ride home from field hockey practice, Molly would fight back a seeping melancholy as her teammate and her teammate's mom chattered away in the front seat about shopping for new cleats or how long their annoying cousins would be staying with them. In summer, when Norman, Davis, and Molly rented a beach house in Ocean City for a week, Molly would be bombarded by the droves of suntanned women buying fudge for their little ones. They encircled her on Ferris wheels, stepped on her shadows on the boardwalk. These women didn't seem so different from the Kitty Winger who'd inhabited Molly's earliest days, the one who appeared in every single memory she had from before the move. For the first six years of her life, Molly had a mother who cut up her apples into little pieces and sprinkled cinnamon on them because that made it a treat. She had a mother who blew bubbles with her in the driveway on summer days, who climbed into bed with her and read her two books, then flicked off the light and sang "Norwegian Wood" in the yellow glow of the nightlight. Even with all the misery that came later, Molly had to believe that woman was still out there somewhere.

Perhaps it was her looming college graduation—yet another milestone that would sweep through and make Molly Winger one step further from the child she'd been. Whatever the reason, whatever the source, there was a tiny voice inside her, a voice that questioned the sobriety of her mother's desertion. The more Molly learned about human beings, the less plausible it was to her that a mother would simply walk out on her children and never turn around. An image haunted her now: Kitty sitting alone in a house somewhere, staring out a window, her features a web of regret. *She wants me to find her,* the tiny voice was saying. *She doesn't know how to come back.*

"She went to San Francisco with a doctor. That's the last we heard," Molly explained to a drunk Skyler that night in her college room. "I could find only one person matching her name in the Bay Area."

"Are you thinking about going out there?" Skyler asked.

"No. Of course not."

"That sounds like a yes."

"How is 'no, of course not' a yes?"

"You're talking yourself out of it. I can smell it in your voice." Even then, Skyler Jones was a psychoanalyst extraordinaire.

"It's probably not even her," Molly said.

"It probably is," Skyler said. "We're going."

"We most certainly are not."

"We're going tomorrow."

"I have a final tomorrow. Go away. I need to study."

Skyler parked herself firmly on Molly's lap. "You need to do this, little chickie, and you will do it fearlessly."

Molly did nothing fearlessly.

"You will do this fearlessly because I will be with you."

"It's probably not even her," Molly said again.

Oh, but it was.

The doctor with whom her mother had absconded was named Barry Lowell, and a public records search revealed a Katherine Lowell and a Barry Lowell at a matching address in Walnut Creek, California. If it was a coincidence, it was a heartless one.

The tequila, rum, vodka, and triple sec eventually got the best of Skyler, and she conked out on Molly's bed, at which point Molly looked at her unconscious friend and said, "You won't even remember this tomorrow."

Oh, but she did.

The next morning, Molly distractedly sat through a European history final, then phoned Norman with a story about having been invited to a friend's house in DC for a few days. She promised to be home by

Christmas. Then she stuffed some clothes into a bag and climbed into Skyler's Accord. They had nine days until Christmas Eve.

Four days later, on the opposite side of the country, they pulled into the driveway of a split-level with beige wood siding. Unmown grass bowed. Paint on the shutters withdrew.

Skyler reached under the seat and removed a flask. "I have filled this with courage," she announced. Evidently, they were now in a war movie. "Drink it down."

Molly declined. Her brand of fear would not be quelled by chemicals.

Skyler read the torture on her friend's face. "It'll come to you," she said. "You'll know exactly what to say."

All across the continent Skyler had reassured Molly that the right words would be there when the time came, and that in fact there were no right words (though there were likely some wrong ones). This she said in the diners along lost highways where they ate, in the ramshackle motels where Molly lay unsleeping, and in the rest stop parking lots where they stretched their legs and restocked the car with Sour Patch Kids and trail mix. She said it again now as Molly sat stiff in the passenger seat.

"You can do it," Skyler told her. "I'll be right here."

Molly eyed the closed garage door and said, not without some measure of wishful thinking, "Maybe she's not even home."

"She'd fucking better be," uttered Skyler.

She leaned over the bog of wrappers and absorbed Molly into a hug. It was firm and tight, engineered to still the deep, dark trembling. "Remember—the little chickie is lovable. You can't not love the little chickie. Now get out there and talk to Joe."

Molly managed to lift her body out of the car and force herself down the front path. She noticed the dandelions and the blades of grass shooting up in hopeful clusters between the bricks. Life standing up for itself.

She stepped up onto the porch and into the shadow of the overhang. She raised her fist to the door. One knock. A soft knock. Indifferent to being heard.

What would she tell her brother? What would she tell her father?

Somehow it startled Molly when the door was finally drawn open. She'd envisioned every moment of this journey except this one, one set of eyes finding the other.

It was her. The woman from her dreams. Her hair was cropped, and pockets of flesh creased in her cheeks, but it was her. She seemed to be staring at Molly without recognition.

"Mom?" she said, finding her voice. "It's me. Molly."

Kitty's startlingly blue eyes went round with astonishment, with relief years in the making, and in a mad flash she reached for Molly and pulled her close, cupping her daughter's head against her chest. "My Kitten," she whispered. "My Kitten came."

The sound of that pet name spoken through that voice, both of them so long lost, sent an untamable wave of convulsions spilling into Molly's chest. She'd never been one to cry, and this explosion of sobs only made the whole experience farther from this world. She wondered if this was one of the ways things would've been different. Maybe she would've cried more.

As Molly breathed in the almost forgotten but vaguely familiar smell of her mother's skin, her mind raced. She thought of everything that would happen now. The asking of forgiveness, the forgiving, the offering of explanations, the offering of understanding. Talk of all the yesterdays that had fallen away, and the promise of good tomorrows to come. They were the same build, Molly noticed. They could've pillaged each other's wardrobes, borrowed each other's sweaters on chilly Saturdays.

Then Kitty said, "You have to go."

Molly lifted her head.

"I don't think it's right that you're here, honey." There was a sickening tenderness in her voice.

"But I—"

"No." Kitty shook her head. "I left my Kitten behind. I had to. *I had to*. What if Barry finds out?"

"Mom."

Kitty was peering into the driveway. "Who's in the car?"

"Mom—"

"Don't tell them you found me. Please. You won't, will you, Kitten?"

Molly stared back, uncomprehending, her mouth hanging open like a caught fish.

"I'm sorry," Kitty said. "You know I'm sorry, don't you?"

Kitty reached out and glided the palm of her hand over her daughter's wet cheek. She explored the architecture of her nose, the downy strands of her blonde tresses. She smiled with unsettling serenity, then stepped into the house and closed the door.

Molly's chest thumped. Her breath ran away from her. She sprinted off the porch and down the path, then groped for the car door and barricaded herself inside the Honda.

Skyler was white with alarm. "What the fuck just happened?"

"Go," Molly said. "Go!"

Skyler whirled out of the driveway and gunned it to the road that led out of town.

Hours later, as they hummed along Interstate 80, Skyler pulled onto the shoulder and looked at Molly, still slumped in a silent stupor. Neither of them had spoken since the driveway.

"Are you okay?" Skyler asked her.

Molly was staring out at the bright desert sunlight, at the distant jutting skyline of Reno. She sniffed. "Yeah."

"Do you want to stop somewhere and get shitfaced?"

"That was the woman who left us that night," Molly muttered, gazing out the window. "I thought maybe she'd be different. I thought maybe I'd find the other woman, the one from when I was little."

Skyler stared at her. "I'm so sorry I made you do that. Do you hate me?"

"I just don't understand," Molly said. "I don't understand why people change."

An eighteen-wheeler thundered past loud enough to split the highway like a fault line.

After a long, floating silence, Skyler said, "I have an uncle who runs a dim sum restaurant in Reno. All the waitresses are buck naked except for boots and a bolo tie."

Molly turned her head. "For real?"

"No."

Molly never told Davis about California, never even contemplated telling Norman. What she'd been foolish enough to doubt, they'd been wise enough to accept as fact: Kitty Winger was not out there wanting to be found. The embers of the parent-child connection sometimes did go cold, and Davis didn't need to put three thousand miles on his car to certify it. And if he ever missed Kitty, ever longed for the woman, maybe there was a kind of solace to be found in the apparent truth that it was not mutual. Molly finally knew why Norman had never talked about her after she left, why she and Davis never talked about her with each other, not then, not after, not now. It was because there was simply nothing to discuss. Not one thing. She was gone. Everything else was just flapping and flurrying.

From inside the seal tank, two eyes, black and unknowable, were staring out at Molly. The animal had banked off its route and swum over to where she stood. Something about its snout brought to mind a cuddly house pet. Something about its whiskers brought to mind a wise old southern senator. The seal floated on the other side of the glass long enough to imply that he was not there by accident.

Look, I get it, the creature seemed to say. *It looks like one big party. We frolic on the rocks, we clap at each other's wild pinniped antics. But the fact is, we're just like you, Molly. We've all been there.*

Molly was in no mood for advice from yet another mammal. She waved it away. *Goo goo g'joob!*

The seal looked annoyed. *We're not walruses, lady. Listen, each one of us had to learn to swim on our own, which, even for a semiaquatic marine animal, isn't so easy at first—and, if you must know, is a little intimidating. But it's best in the end. I decide when to dive. I decide when to come up for air. It's all up to me.*

Molly couldn't think of a single thing that was up to her.

Room in there for one more? she asked.

The seal flapped its flippers and swam off, and Molly wondered how it felt to live that way, under the waves and free, beyond the constant pulse of echoes.

CHAPTER 21

Guy went ahead and sprang for those signs. He had little choice in the matter, since he had exactly one lifeguard on the payroll, one who occasionally wanted to spend the day with his daughter or skip out for a sandwich. During such times, swimmers needed to be advised of the obvious: The lifeguard was off-duty. They swam at their own risk.

One day in early July, Davis used his lunch hour to drive out to his old haunt, Calhoun's Hobby Shop, vendor of models, action figures, and assorted nostalgia. Housed in a garage-type structure that was unremarkable to the point of being undetectable, the place suffered from a chronic famine of customers. But if that bothered Mr. Calhoun, he never let on. He always greeted Davis with such family-reunion-picnic affection that it was as though he'd been sitting around waiting for him, and only him, to pop in.

Few things brought Davis Winger joy like Calhoun's. He loved milling about the dated merchandise, combing through shelves that were still stocked with nostalgic treasures such as F-16s from the '80s, Chessie System train cars, and model eighteen-wheelers from *Smokey and the Bandit*, *CHiPs*, and other icons of the golden age of interstate kerfuffles. Even the rack of comic books was strictly vintage: the amazing this, the fantastic that, space-age heroes, Cold War–era villains.

"Haven't seen you in a while," Mr. Calhoun said as Davis perused the felt-lined shelving. "How's your old man?"

"He's good," Davis said. "Always asks about you." Which was a nice thing to say and, as it happened, true.

Calhoun was a man of about sixty and had been for as long as Davis had known him. White-headed as a dandelion, he had the physique of a high school football coach.

"Looking to build something with your daughter?" he asked.

"Sort of," Davis said, lifting up the cover of a box that contained a jumble of plastic coaster tracks and trains. "I have this crazy notion of designing something that's part roller coaster, part flying carpet. If that makes any sense."

Mr. Calhoun inspected the shelves and frowned at his merchandise. "I don't think I've got anything like that in the store, but I can always order for you. Want to see a catalog?"

Naturally, Calhoun's catalogs were made of newsprint. You licked your finger to look through them, instead of double-clicking.

"Thanks." Davis smiled. "I'll make do with what you've got."

Mr. Calhoun always allowed Davis to mix and match to his heart's content, to pillage tracks from one box and toss them in with trains from another—à la carte shopping suited to an engineer's sense of invention. And if ever a project called for the misappropriation of model pieces for off-label uses, this magic carpet was it.

In recent days, Davis had finally accepted that a thrill ride inspired by the illustrations in that children's book was something he actually wanted to attempt. The idea having simmered in his imagination for weeks, the project had advanced from the conceptual stage—which consisted mainly of daydreaming—to the beginnings of a design. He was scribbling renderings now, and his sketchbook teemed with etchings and schematics, the fits and starts of a structure. Angles and slopes, parts and paths. How it might look were it actually to exist.

Whoever sits on this carpet is set down at will, be that place near or many a day's journey, the mysterious rug merchant tells the prince. *It once belonged to Solomon, who sailed through the air, caught up by the wind such that he breakfasted in Damascus and supped in Media.*

In his mind's eye, Davis envisioned the riders lying prone, flat on their stomachs as though on a sled. They would board, then be carried off from the embarking station with a swift whoosh, up into the air in a fluid sweep, soaring weightlessly, alternately rising and diving in smooth glides and dizzying corkscrews. They would coast high over the park, the moisture of the clouds tickling their noses. They would drop precipitously in a majestic free fall that swept them over a reflecting pool. The feel of the ride would be one of floating, not rumbling, like sailing upon the woven yak hair of a Persian rug. Davis even had a name for it: *the Sultan of the Indies.* Nothing was set in stone yet, but that's how he'd begun to think of it. The Sultan of the Indies.

He spilled an armload of junk onto the counter, and Mr. Calhoun threw out a price that sounded fair to both of them.

"I hope you got everything you need," Calhoun said, as he swept the mess into a bag with the palm of his hand.

In point of fact, these days Davis lacked most of what he needed.

"Not yet, but I can see it from here," Davis replied with a wink.

And for a moment, Calhoun was the old-world merchant and Davis the humble prince, searching high and low for some spellbinding rarity with which to win a girl's heart.

———

Before heading back to the pool, Davis stopped to pick up lunch. Downtown, the eateries had dignified names. The Graham & Clive Sandwich Shoppe. Pasquale's Since 1950. They served dignified fare, like roasted turkey with brie and honey mustard or chicken salad with apple slices and English cheddar. Suburban options were less inspiring.

Out here, you went to a strip mall pizzeria that sat between a dollar store and a psychic, and you were the one person in line who was there for a sandwich instead of lotto tickets. These joints didn't have names. They didn't even really have menus. Items were spelled out in the grooves of a yellowing lighted board overhead, like a movie theater marquee in miniature—*Now Playing: Eggplant Parmesan*—and everything came with a nice compact boob of coleslaw.

Davis knew that nothing like the Sultan of the Indies existed yet in the amusement world, for it was not to be some Aladdin-themed kiddie ride. He wanted to build an actual magic carpet. The idea was to replicate the experience of gliding, to allow the rider to drift through the air, *on* the air, free of jumps, jolts, and whiplash, free of all friction in fact. He understood that he would need to innovate, to pilot concepts he knew by heart into technology he barely grasped. Far-fetched? Without a doubt. Cost-prohibitive? Almost certainly. But what choice did he have? It was for Rachel. Coaxing such a thing into the world would show Britt that he would abide no limit to realize their daughter's dream. Was there a better way to win his wife's forgiveness?

"Can I help you?" asked the red-faced man behind the lunch counter. He looked exhausted and in no mood to be solicitous.

Davis tried not to look as unhungry as this place made him. "Does your tuna have a lot of mayo in it?"

A bead of sweat slithered down the man's forehead. "Yeah," he replied.

Davis went with a salad, although there was a fair chance that it too would come slathered in mayo. In the suburbs, mayonnaise was implied.

At a nearby booth, a woman was pointing to the grilled cheese that lay picked apart on her young daughter's paper plate. "A few more bites, Professor Pancake."

There was a story there, in the origin of that nickname. What was a family if not a cozy quilt of pet names and inside jokes? If Davis walked up to Britt right now and said, without providing any context, "Remember that thing you bought that time from that idiot?" she'd know he meant the wineglass with the word *MILF* on it that they'd purchased five years ago in the Berkshires just to get the annoying boutique owner to stop telling them his life story. Or if anyone ever mentioned the semicolon—it came up in conversation more often than one might suspect—he and Britt would share a private smirk, remembering how Davis had attempted to cultivate a "summer soul patch" a few years ago, but when it grew in wispy and uneven, Britt had renamed it "summer semicolon," because that's what it had looked like.

Right there in that greasy spoon, Davis became achingly conscious of the volatility of time. It spun everyone around, holding all of humanity together with great centrifugal motion, until the wear of the tracks and the rust of the bolts flung everyone wildly away from each other into outer spaces.

CHAPTER 22

A lumbering army of storm clouds accompanied Davis back to the apartment complex and sent the sunbathers scattering. Alone under the changing house's overhang, he watched the downpour swarm in like irate bees, the drops blistering the surface of the pool, bullets of water ricocheting off the concrete and onto his bare legs.

He retreated into the men's changing room with a rag and a spray gun of Windex, and as he began to wash zit pus and other revolting substances off the mirrors, he heard a man's voice. It was coming from outside, probably right under the awning where Davis had stood moments earlier. Over the beating rain Davis could hear the man talking, presumably, into a phone. Davis listened as the man spoke of having just returned from his sister's funeral in Seattle, how she'd fought the disease longer than anyone had expected, but now that the end had come, her husband and three young children were blown apart. "To be honest with you, Nick, I couldn't wait to get out of there," the man said. "Jesus, she must have been scared."

Suddenly, inside that changing room, Davis was picturing people in Washington State he would never meet. Clear as day he saw a sick woman, pale and skeletal, and her husband, ravaged, unable to make anything better. He saw children waiting for a school bus, stooped under yellow ponchos, feeling unmoored in the world. Davis's eyes flooded. His bottom lip began to quake. *Singleton. Murray.* He implored himself to keep control against another onslaught of tears over faraway grief. *Bumbry. Lowenstein.* He dropped onto the bench in front of the lockers, lowered his head between his knees as if he were aboard a plane going down, and sobbed into the echo of the cavernous room.

You're not a bleeding heart, he scolded himself. *You're just an idiot.*

When he no longer heard the stranger's voice, he collected himself, made sure that the coast was clear, and stepped outside. The rain was easing into a drizzle.

Then, out of nowhere, came another voice, this one female. "Everything okay in there?"

Davis jumped and screamed. "Fucking hell!"

It was Charlie.

"Christ Jesus!" he howled.

Evidently, there was nothing funnier than scaring someone into arrhythmia, and Charlie seized into a long, riotous fit of laughter. "You should've seen your face!" she managed to say between guffaws.

"God, you are so unlikable," Davis hissed.

Eventually, Charlie regained her composure, and Davis returned to a survivable heart rate.

She stood beside him, nominally regarding the weather. "So are you okay?" she asked again.

"I'm fine."

"You sure about that?"

"Yeah. Why?"

"Well, uh, weren't you just crying?"

"No, I wasn't crying," he scoffed. The very notion. He wiped his cheeks.

"Then why is your face wet?" she asked.

"Because it's raining."

"I see. And why are your eyes red?"

He sniffed. "The cleaning solution. It irritates them."

"Okay, cabana boy," she said, toying with the zipper bisecting her sweatshirt. "We don't have to talk about it if you don't want to."

"We're not open for business at the moment," he told her. "You can't swim in a thunderstorm. So, you know, run along now. Shoo."

"I didn't come to take a dip," she said. "Actually, I was kind of hoping to ask you a question." There was a disturbing sheepishness in her voice now. She was twisting her torso, hands in her pockets, elbows locked.

"Is this a question or a favor?" he asked. "Let me guess. You've got a cat you want to pawn off on me. No, wait. A monkey."

"I'm just going to come out and say it," she said. "Will you help me pass my physics class?"

"Will I do what?"

"I'll level with you. I've been reading this textbook, I really have. But I'm grasping almost none of it. Even before my unfortunate expulsion, I was headed for an F. We just don't click, physics and me. But then, guess what? Davis the lifeguard comes into my life, and as luck would have it, he's a doggone physics whiz. He lives for this shit. His whole life is physics. He goes to physics conventions. He reads *Physics Weekly* and *Physics Monthly*. He subscribes to the physics channel on TV."

"Okay, that's enough," Davis said. "There's no such thing as a physics channel."

"This is basically your alphabet," Charlie argued. "So I got to thinking that maybe you'd want to help a girl get her high school diploma."

Davis didn't know where to begin. "I barely know you. And, frankly, what I do know, I don't like. Your dog is living with me. You pop out from behind things and give me a coronary."

"Nobody's looking for an A here," she said. "I just need to squeak by in this one class so I can graduate and throw myself at the mercy of the Maryland admissions committee. Think how good that will make you feel."

"Indifferent. It'll make me feel indifferent."

"That's not the cabana boy I know."

"What about your summer school teacher?" he suggested. "Get some extra help from that poor bastard. That's actually what they get paid for."

Charlie snapped her gum. "Let's just say he's not a fan."

"Shocker."

"I could ask my parents to pay you," she said. "Or I could help you out around the pool. I could do all the grunt work, like collecting bugs and scum with the net, or pouring that shit that makes the water blue. Whatever you want."

"What I want is for you to go away," Davis said. "And why would I need an assistant? No one's ever here."

"What about that morning routine you do? You scurry around looking all serious, checking your readings, shooting your spray bottle. You're like a busy little elf. It's adorable."

"Charlie, you don't need my help to pass high school physics. You just need to apply yourself. You seem like a smart enough cookie."

She wrenched an eyebrow. "Oh, so you're going to go sexist on me. Didn't think you were the type."

"Sexist?"

"When's the last time you called a guy 'a smart cookie'?"

"I was giving you a compliment."

"Benevolent sexism is still sexism."

"Fine, I take it back. You're not a smart cookie. Happy?" He tapped his toe into the puddle under his bare foot. "You're actually a super annoying cookie."

Charlie gazed up at the rolling clouds, the tufts of vapor being pushed westward by some unseen force. With the light of the sky pouring into her eyes, eyes that Davis could now see were not brown but hazel, an earthy hue that brought to mind the smell of burning leaves, he saw something in them he'd yet to see in any of this girl's features:

defeat, the realization that she might actually be destitute of options. Davis almost didn't recognize her, clothed in insecurity as she was.

Then he thought of Rachel. He prayed she would never be on her own like this, turning to a thirty-five-year-old with a fuck-ton of baggage to repair her ruin. But it could happen. Mistakes found their way to everyone, and all the parental love and good intentions in the world couldn't save his daughter from her share of them.

Charlie was still sizing up the elements, thinking perhaps that they had the best of her.

"Okay. I'll help you," Davis said.

"You will? Really?" So great was her relief that she hugged him. "Oh thank god! That is so cool of you."

"Let me be clear: I'm not going to do the work for you. I already passed high school physics. I will not let you waste my time."

"You're seriously saving my ass," she said.

Then, as with the Tweedy transaction, Davis issued some stipulations Charlie almost certainly ignored, and she made promises he surely didn't believe. The upshot was that they would meet for tutoring sessions once a week, or additionally as needed, at his apartment, in the evenings after the pool closed.

"This is it, okay? No more favors," he sternly warned her. "And as I told you before, I don't plan to be here long. When I move back home, you're on your own."

She didn't look worried.

By then the sky had brightened into a tolerant gray. Davis held his palm out past the overhang, and like Noah's dove, it came back dry. A tenant or two would soon filter out of their barely-up-to-code rental for a dip, so Davis needed to tidy up the deck and dry off the chairs.

"Where's home?" Charlie asked.

"What?"

"You said you were going to move back home."

His eyes were instantly drawn in the direction of the old colonial that stood off in the distance, just over the line of trees. He pictured his lawn, wet and strewn with roots, a bike lying on the grass.

"You're divorced?" she asked.

"No."

"Separated?"

"Charlie." He sighed. "I don't give interviews."

"I'm just trying to be a friend."

"We're not friends."

"You know everything about me," she said.

"For your sake, I truly hope there's more."

"Okay, let's recap," she began. "You have a wife but you don't live with her, you have an engineering degree but you're a janitor in charge of this nasty little bathtub, and—deny it all you want—you were bawling your eyes out in the bathroom during a rainstorm. If that's not a run-on sentence of hopelessness, I don't know what is."

Davis stared down at the pavement and brooded over all the ways that teenage girls sucked. He let out a grim huff. "I left my firm because I was blamed for an accident that wasn't my fault, and I didn't appreciate being a scapegoat. Also, I don't actually know that it wasn't my fault, but that's beside the point. In other news, I'm having a bit of a domestic situation, so I'm temporarily separated. It's none of your business and I don't want to talk about it, so seriously, don't ask. My wife and daughter are one mile away, and we see each other all the time. But yes, for the moment, here I am, living at the Deluxe—which is oh so deluxe!—helping you with your homework and caring for your dog." He unfurled a smile of excessive width. "Now you're completely up to date. Happy?"

Charlie gaped unblinking at him, struggling to process the expanse of his misfortune. "No," she said softly. "I'm not. It actually makes me really sad that you were in there crying all by yourself."

"I wasn't crying about my life."

162

"Then what were you crying about?"

"Remember when I said I don't want to talk about it? I know you do. It was nine seconds ago."

"You know," Charlie said, her face budding with a strange fellowship, "we're kind of kindred spirits, you and me."

"We're nothing of the sort."

"Face it—we're in the same boat."

"We're in totally different boats. Now if you'll excuse me, I've got to reckon with this mess." The storm had yielded a bumper crop of twigs, pine needles, and muck, and the air was funky with the stench of bleachy chlorine from the pummeling of rain against the water.

Charlie shook her head at the state of the deck. "They can put a man on the moon, but they can't make a self-cleaning swimming pool."

Davis reached for the skimmer. "NASA put a man on the moon. Around here, we've got Guy getting shit done. Every day this whole place isn't condemned is a win."

CHAPTER 23

Reality came down like a judge's gavel the day Richard fired Bo. Molly should have seen it coming when the editor-in-chief emerged from the men's room with the complexion of an unripe avocado, insisting he was fine and having never looked less so. Molly's mind instantly shot to Harvey, he of the multiple myeloma. But no, Harvey was fine, too, Richard assured her as he slogged on down the hall.

Molly hadn't interpreted Richard's queasiness as an omen of the *Ramble*'s accelerated fiscal doom, especially since he'd promised to give her fair warning if the end was truly nigh. But then she caught the music critic knocking on Richard's office, saying, "You wanted to see me, boss?" When Bo went in and closed the door, Molly's veins chilled. Richard had been puking. He puked before he fired people. It was like his pregame ritual.

Not twenty minutes earlier Bo had been of perfectly good cheer, inviting Molly to catch some band called the Fruit Bats with her later that week. It was a mystery why Bo would want to be accompanied by someone who didn't know any of the band's songs, didn't know most bands' songs, and who was as un–rock 'n' roll as you could get. But Bo was clawing her way back from mental collapse, trying to get to bed at a reasonable hour, trying not to OD on oxy. Was there a safer bet than Molly Winger?

"You know I don't go to a lot of rock concerts," Molly had told her.

"Okay, one, nobody says 'rock concert' anymore, unless you're talking about KISS or REO Speedwagon. And two, they're from Portland. I think you can handle a nice little band from Portland."

A half hour later Bo was stomping down the hall, cursing a blue streak about being "shit-canned" by a "cardigan-loving fucksqueak," and Molly was forced to confront the possibility that Richard was working his way down the hall with his pad of pink slips. If music critics were out, could features writers be far behind?

Instantly the threshold for worthy article pitches dropped precipitously. At the end of the day, equipped with only a shapeless, embryonic idea, Molly tapped on Richard's door.

"Do you have a minute?"

"For you? Always." He sighed. His coloring had revivified from pickle green to its baseline peach.

"I think I have an idea for a piece," she said, lowering herself into a chair whose upholstery was a dark red, the hue of bloodletting. "I don't know if it's really worth pursuing. It's not the type of thing we typically run. Frankly, it's a little off the wall, and to be honest I've given it almost zero thought."

"You sure are selling it, Ms. Winger."

Molly drew in an uneasy breath. "What if we wrote about broken homes? A very specific type of broken home."

"Go on."

"What if we explored what happens to kids when their mother leaves? Not dies or moves out on account of divorce, just leaves."

Richard removed his spectacles and reclined. Bannered by the stately map of turn-of-the-twentieth-century Baltimore that loomed on the wall behind him, the man sometimes had the look of an unlikely conqueror.

"The guy I'm dating is involved in the Big Brother Big Sister program," Molly went on. "He's got these two Little Brothers who ended up in foster care when their mother walked out on them. I was recently talking about them to this psychologist friend of mine, and she starts telling me about all the patients she's had who have experienced this same kind of loss, women who come to her needing to deal with this— this abandonment by their mother. According to her, it shapes them, it remains very much a part of who they are as they move through life. What if we interviewed some of these women and published their stories? We could do it in a series, even a weekly column. My friend assures me that there are legions of these women and that they tend to be eager to share."

Richard's eyes became slits. "So now it's just women?"

"Sorry?"

"You started out talking about boys in foster care, but it sounds like you're proposing to write about only the women, the uniqueness of their experience. No?"

Molly shrugged. "Sure."

"Well, don't let me put words in your mouth," he said.

She was okay with Richard putting words in her mouth. He was welcome to put some ideas in her head while he was at it.

"No, that works," she said.

Richard stared into her. "Hmm," he murmured.

"What's hmm?" she asked.

"Hmm," he murmured again.

"I know it's not earth-shattering," Molly said, feeling herself falter under his meditative mien. "Feel free to say no, obviously."

Richard crossed and uncrossed his legs. "So. You're proposing a weekly column about women whose mothers walked out on them when they were young. We interview them, and because we can't just help ourselves to advanced degrees that we haven't gone to school for, we let the psychology speak for itself. We don't purport to be experts. We just tell their stories. Is that what you had in mind?"

She'd walked in with next to nothing in mind. "Basically," she said.

"Isn't that interesting," Richard said, folding his arms and staring at Molly with such penetrating eyes that it put a flush in her cheeks.

"This isn't autobiography," she said. "The last thing I'd ever want to write about is myself. You know me."

Richard smirked. "Maybe we both thought we knew you, and we were both wrong."

Being the subject of her own writing—or anyone else's, for that matter—filled Molly with horror, and it rather surprised her that she'd guided herself into an assignment that dwelled in such personal territory. Yet here she was.

Skyler's phrase returned to her, and she said it aloud. "Motherless daughters."

"Motherless daughters," Richard repeated.

She saw something like fatherly compassion on him, and it made her bristle. "I'm not blind to the parallels, Richard, but I swear, this is not about me."

"Look," he said with a grand sigh, "my parents are eightysomething Jewish Republicans who love me, love Harvey, love all of our friends, and have never once voiced a single complaint about my life—except they don't seem to be able to get over the fact that I'm not a surgeon. Sometimes we choose our issues, Ms. Winger, but mostly they choose us."

Molly wanted no part of his sympathy. It felt perverse.

She said, "Remember when you asked me what I want? I think what I want is one thing. I'm not certain what that thing is. It's always been kind of formless, but it's a single thing—a topic, maybe a small topic, maybe one that only matters to a small group of people. But I want to dive into it and know it and make it reachable to everyone else. That's what I want out of my career, Richard. This motherless daughters concept—I don't know if this is that one thing that I've been looking for, but it's the best I've got today, so my gut says we should try it. You say that sometimes our issues choose us? Well, my issue right now is this paper. I want to fill it with good content that draws in readers so that you can go out and charge more money for ad space and afford to pay all of us to continue working here."

Once again, Richard said, "Hmm." Then he reached over the stacks of papers festooning his desk and pried open a container of mango spears. He invited Molly to partake, she declined, he overruled her declination, and the two of them sat there taking bites of the wet, fibrous fruit. For Richard, one's office was an extension of one's home. Visitors were offered refreshments and gently bullied into accepting. Over the years, seated in that very chair, Molly had consumed countless pieces of chocolate, every variety of nut, scores of cookies, a lentil samosa, single-malt scotch, baklava, and potato latkes prepared by Richard's sister-in-law.

"I'm intrigued," the man said, and he drew out the word to prove it. As he swiveled toward the window, the late-afternoon sun splintered across his wistful face. "Your idea certainly fires right into my wheelhouse of anxieties. I'm going to be sixty one of these days. *Sixty.* The years are advancing at a brisker clip than ever, and more and more I think about the people who have fallen away, who are lost to me forever. I know this is not what you're proposing to write about, but all the same, loss is loss. Loss is universal. It's as basic to the human condition as these clunky, unperfected bodies of ours." He began to nod, slowly at first, then faster and fuller, as though a motor were revving up somewhere in the back of his head. "Motherless daughters," he purred. "It has potential. It's not the most original idea I've ever heard, but I'd be a fool to reject a pitch of such humanity by someone whose writing has always been so richly leavened with humanity."

This could have only been sarcasm, Molly reasoned, but she saw no reason to debate it.

He gave her the green light. They agreed that she would give some thought to the format, and they'd reconvene in a day or two. In the meantime, Richard would do some research of his own, read up a bit on survivors of abandonment. Was it too much to call them survivors?

"I admire you for coming to me with this," Richard said. "It must be uncomfortable psychic terrain."

The meeting was getting away from her now.

"This is bold for you," he went on, "but I've always suspected that a bonfire of adventurousness burned somewhere inside the deceptively placid Molly Winger."

Most days Molly felt as far from placid as she did from bold, but she knew better than to pursue paths of adventurousness. The very word made her cower. It brought to mind her uncle Tony, the potbellied actuary who divorced his wife and heaved himself into the Alaskan wild for a year of off-the-grid living, who believed he would be embraced by the wild, who believed he would *become* the wild, never mind that his only previous experience *in* the wild had been Disney's Animal Kingdom.

On his first night in Alaska, Uncle Tony was eaten by a bear. Such was the reward of adventurousness.

"Run with it," Richard bade her, snagging another mango slice. "See where it leads."

"I'll try," said Molly. "But in the meantime, you might want to solicit other ideas. I'm not exactly Diane Sawyer."

"Oh, Ms. Winger," he chuckled. "As if you know what you are and what you aren't." Then his skin tone ran pale again. "But if I may be frank, you have to make this work. You just have to. Because I do not have the stomach for firing people."

CHAPTER 24

Molly had impulsively pitched—and Richard had accepted—an under-cooked idea, and now they all had to live with it. Molly called Skyler, not merely because she was the true architect of this problem, but because Molly literally did not know what else to do.

Skyler sounded way too surprised that Molly had listened to her. "People don't usually take my advice," she said.

That was troubling, seeing as how Skyler was in the advice-giving business. "I wish you'd told me that before," said Molly.

"I didn't think I needed to," was Skyler's response.

"I owe my boss, like, ten articles, and I have zero potential interview subjects," Molly complained. "If you're doing the math, that means I'm going to fall short."

"Chill, little chickie," Skyler told her. "Here's where I think I can help."

She volunteered to speak to some of her current and former patients and ask them if they might be willing to violate their own privacy in the name of the greater good. It being a rather confessional demographic, Skyler was optimistic. Then again, this was the same woman who thought driving to California to sneak up on Molly's long-lost mother was a good idea.

Within a few hours, Molly received an email from someone whose name rang an old bell.

Hi Molly,

Skyler told me all about your writing career and the series you're planning at the *Weekly Ramble*. I'd love to help. I wouldn't call my story particularly newsworthy, or even interesting, but it sounds like it's on point. If the goal is to make a few people feel a little less alone in the world, count me in.

Let me know.
Abigail Brubaker

Molly gaped at her screen with abject wonder. *Of course Skyler is Professor Brubaker's therapist,* she thought.

Although Skyler Jones had been the bane of the young academic's existence when she and Molly switched out of that geology class and into Brubaker's psych lecture freshman year, Skyler had ended up convincing the professor to be her adviser when she'd declared a psychology major. Molly knew that the pair had remained friends over the years, but Skyler had never let on—how could she?—that the relationship had evolved in this way, and the revelation put her in awe of her friend. Was there a stronger endorsement of one's professional skills than to have them used by the very person who taught them to you in the first place?

I'm very impressed with you, Molly texted Skyler after receiving Abigail's message.

I owe it all to that weasely little Zodrov guy who scared me right out of his geology class on the first day of school, Skyler wrote back.

Molly and Abigail spoke over the phone the next day. Abigail had no reservations at all about telling her story. People boasted about their cancer battles and their stroke recoveries, she maintained, and yet society still viewed psychological trauma as a lesser affliction, as something you could conquer just by giving yourself a good talking-to. When Molly invited her to pick a pseudonym, Abigail thought for a second, then made her pick: Abigail. "That'll throw the dogs off the scent," the prof said with a snicker.

They scheduled a proper interview for the next morning.

Abigail Brubaker was nine when her mother left her and her younger sister with an abusive alcoholic father.

"The second I say 'abusive alcoholic,' I feel like people picture subsidized housing with upturned bottles of Johnnie Walker Red all over the floor. But my dad was a cardiologist. We had a beach house."

Molly hadn't heard Abigail's voice since the lecture hall freshman year, and speaking with her now produced that old flutter, that knee-jerk reverence toward an authority figure, even though there weren't too many years between them. What a weird, ineradicable strain of shyness that was.

Abigail's mother had bailed on them in the middle of the day while her father was at his office and the girls were in school. "Why not avoid a messy goodbye, right?" she remarked dryly. In the years that followed, Abigail had felt like an oddity because she knew her experience was different from that of her friends, even the ones who only had one parent. She knew kids who were being raised by a father, but none who were in that position on account of a mother simply walking out. The singularity of her loss shivered inside of her like a secret, like a phantom limb.

Then, one day when Abigail had reached high school age, her mother made contact.

"I'd pictured her on the other side of the country, somewhere far away with a whole new family, a totally different life, like the witness protection program. I'd even sort of made peace with that version of reality. Boy, was I wrong. She was in the next town over. She'd moved in with a friend and was literally ten miles away the entire time."

"Did that make it worse?" Molly asked.

"I think it did. I mean, at a minimum, she could've picked me up from choir rehearsal. That was a long walk home in the dead of winter."

As for why a woman would abandon her two little girls with a drunk, a drinker of rum, no less—"Millions of parents out there, and I get the pirate"—Abigail's mother offered only the flimsiest of excuses. She'd come to believe that her husband hated her, but didn't hate their children, and that his cruelty would abate if she removed herself from the equation. It was a hell of a gamble, and as it happened, a misguided one.

"He never hit us or anything, but he could get mean as a rattlesnake. Lots of screaming and cursing, a few wrecked appliances. That was when he was drunk, though. When he was sober, he was merely neglectful. He certainly wasn't the dad who piled ten kids into the station wagon and took everyone to TGI Fridays. He was more like the dad who forgot to pick us up at TGI Fridays. Which happened all the time, by the way. I remember once he promised to come to my all-county track meet, swore on his life he'd be there, and didn't show up. Not only did he miss the competition—no real shocker there, he missed all kinds of things—but he left me stranded on the other side of the county. I'd even promised a few of my teammates a ride home. You know, it's interesting. Even then, I remember blaming myself, knowing it was my fault for trusting him."

Ironically, her father was the parent from whom Abigail continued to be estranged. She hadn't spoken to the man since she was eighteen, although she had heard through the grapevine that he'd cleaned himself up years ago. As for her mother: "I see her occasionally. I keep my distance, which I think is the healthy play, but we do meet for lunch from time to time. She remembers my kids' birthdays. She asks about my career. She doesn't expect an invite to Thanksgiving, but I do get a Merry Christmas call." Abigail paused. "For me, it comes down to this: Am I better off with no mother in my life or a spectacularly imperfect one?"

As the interview concluded, Molly warned her old professor that she didn't know what the article would end up looking like. "I haven't really settled on a format yet," she admitted. "Also, I haven't decided on a narrative or, come to think of it, a purpose for this series." True to her banner in the *Ramble*, Molly was just winging it.

Abigail thought a moment. "Do you really need a narrative?" she wondered. "Look, it's your job to save your paper, not mine, but what's wrong with just having a forum for sharing?"

It wasn't a terrible suggestion. Why should Molly grasp at lofty lessons that were likely to elude her? Wasn't there sufficient drama in the tale itself?

"Years back, one of the student-run newspapers at the university did something like this on date rape," Abigail said. "Every week another young woman's experience appeared in a column. Maybe you should approach it like that. Personally, I think that's powerful enough. But maybe I'm biased, having lived it and all."

When the call ended, Molly felt suddenly hungry for fresh air, so she walked outside to the back of the building and leaned against the shady wall. She stood there a long while, her eyes closed, the bricks cool and scratchy against her neck. Then she went back inside, wrote it all up in the fastest, most free-flowing thousand words that had ever come to her, and sent it off to Richard.

Ten minutes later, her editor slid a marked-up printout of the article onto Molly's desk. "Anchors aweigh," he said.

Which only gave Molly a sinking feeling.

"By the way," Richard added. "I like your concluding observation—that as much weakness as Abigail's mother showed in leaving her family, she showed much more strength in returning."

"I'm not convinced that's true," Molly said, "but I do think there's bravery in coming back. What do you think?"

"Well, I don't know anything about bravery," Richard told her. "But I do know that it's always easier to stay away."

CHAPTER 25

Charlie hadn't moved a muscle. She was right where he'd left her, shielded from the noonday sun by an umbrella and scowling into her physics book. Davis stowed the **Swim at Your Own Risk** sign and snagged his bottle of SPF 50 from the cubby. Squeezing a thick glob onto two fingers, he smeared what resembled melted marshmallow onto his cheeks, nose, forearms, shoulders, and quads. He was ready for action, though as usual, there was no action.

The chronic paucity of swimmers had, from time to time, caused Davis to wonder how he might acquit himself should he ever be called upon to save not just a sunken earring or a five-dollar bill, but an actual human life. He'd earned the job through charm and confidence, as opposed to the arguably more crucial lifesaving training, but had thus far skated by with an immaculate safety record. That was primarily because the pool was about as deep as a mop bucket, and the average swimmer was under ten years old and under a hundred pounds. Yanking waterlogged whelps out of the shallow end hardly required an advanced lifesaving certificate. (That didn't even take into account the kids who weren't worth saving, like the Crockett-Johnson twins, stubby little bastards who showed up daily with video games and supersize smoothies with extra whip, when what they really needed was soccer and portion control. Those ungovernable maniacs persecuted everyone with their nonstop cannonballs and bulldoggish barking, and it would have taken an exceptionally generous mood—not to mention an agreeable water temperature—for Davis to get off his ass and rescue one of them should the need arise.)

"How's that chapter coming?" Davis asked as he lowered himself into a chair across from Charlie.

She blew a bubble with her gum, then snapped it brusquely.

"Want me to quiz you, see if you know it?" he asked.

"I already know if I know it. I don't."

"You know Newton's first law. You can't not know that one at this point."

"Can't I?"

Charlie was no one's idea of a model student. She suffered from an inoperable attitude problem. *She's a pleasure to have in class,* said not one of her teachers at any point ever. But the kid was trying, and it would've been heartless of him to turn his back on her self-reclamation project.

On top of that, there were considerable benefits that inured him to delving into the deep chapters of a physics text. He was, in a way, reclaiming his own expertise, or at least forestalling its atrophy, expertise that he was drawing upon as he pressed forward with his grand project. If tutoring Charlie imbued the summer with purpose, the Sultan of the Indies was imbuing it with meaning. Sure, his dreary living space offered a fraction of the functionality and none of the luxury of his former office at Pavelka. The table tottered when he typed, the soft pop of the leaky kitchen faucet marked the time. But such minutiae could never bother him, and every chance he had, no matter how slim the window of time, Davis bounded back to his apartment to tinker with his renderings on his computer, that beautiful 3-D modeling platform that enabled him to adjust the radius of a loop with a simple click, to refine the angle of a bank by merely highlighting a section of track.

Across the table, the dispirited non-graduate slumped in her seat. "Charlie," Davis said. "You look frustrated. Don't be. I believe in you."

"How does that help me?" she barked.

"Very little, I guess. Give me Newton's first law."

She dropped her highlighter into the crease of the book. "An object at rest stays at rest unless acted upon by an outside force. Inertia."

"All right," Davis enthused. "Say more."

She sighed petulantly.

"Say more without sighing petulantly."

"The velocity of an object in motion also won't change unless acted on by an outside force."

"And that outside force would be?"

"Friction?" she said with a tentative wince.

"Why, Charles, I'm almost impressed. Were you picturing the hockey puck like we discussed? If you picture that hockey puck gliding across the ice, or a soccer ball being kicked in outer space, you'll actually see how these laws operate in the real world. That's a lot easier than memorizing a string of words."

"Oh, I have real-world examples," Charlie said, tucking her legs under her body. "Like for inertia, I think about some geek lifeguard who won't lift his lazy ass out of his chair until an outside force comes along and changes his speed and direction."

"Go with what works," Davis replied. "For me, I think of a girl being thrown down a flight of steps. Her velocity doesn't change until she crashes into a concrete wall." He clicked his tongue. "Friction."

"Is it the same if the girl is thrown from a shittily designed log flume?" Charlie wondered.

"Well, now you're getting into more advanced concepts involving trajectories and projectiles, and those, I'm afraid, are still well beyond your grasp. Like rules about no pushing in school, or no dogs in the apartment."

Before long, they'd made their way through twenty pages, and Charlie demonstrated a firmer understanding of the material than anyone had any right to expect.

Davis handed her a set of practice problems. "Do these for our next session."

Again she sighed petulantly.

"Try doing them without sighing petulantly," he said. "Next time we'll talk about rotational motion, like orbit. I'll show you how satellites work."

"Satellites, huh?" Charlie slammed her book shut. "I guess it takes one to know one."

———

Later that afternoon, while dashing home for another twenty-minute fix of his magic carpet ride, Davis encountered McGuinn reclining under a tree in his portable hammock, a pencil behind his ear, legs crossed at the ankles.

"What's up, McGuinn?"

McGuinn slowly raised his eyes. "It's a stone groove, D. A stone groove indeed."

"You're looking awfully erudite and contemplative," Davis observed. "What's with the pencil? You look like you're composing a sonnet."

"Do you even know what a sonnet is?"

"Not really. I just use it interchangeably with *poem*, like everyone else."

"Actually, I'm sitting here enjoying another insightful exploration of the female experience," McGuinn said, holding up the thin square of newspaper resting on his lap. It was the latest edition of the *Weekly Ramble*, which contained the third entry in Molly's new weekly series titled Maternity Leave: Tales of Deserted Daughters. "Why didn't you tell me your sister was such a big deal?"

Davis looked bemused. "Since when do you read the *Ramble*?"

"Did you know she was interviewed on the radio this morning? The radio, D. When's the last time anyone cared enough about anything you had to say to put a mic in front of you? Never. Exactly."

"Since when do you listen to talk radio?" Davis asked.

McGuinn smacked his thigh with the paper and affected a look of woundedness. "Sometimes I feel like you don't know me at all."

"If only."

"Well, color me dazzled. Your sister's got game."

"We're a family of talent."

Davis was, in fact, just as impressed by Molly's recent output as McGuinn, and more than a little surprised. Having read practically every word Molly had ever published, he couldn't have foreseen his little sister taking on this topic.

"This is really going to be your new thing?" he'd asked when he called her up immediately after reading the first piece in the series. "You're going to write about maternal abandonment?"

"I take it there's an unsolicited opinion you'd like to offer," she'd replied.

"Well, now that you've solicited it."

Naturally, Davis could've produced a wisecrack, but something held him back. It would've required the fingers of no hands to count the number of times he and Molly had talked about—really talked about—what Kitty had done to them. But even if Davis had never seen any profit in burrowing down into that soil, it didn't mean there was nothing growing in it, and it was Molly's constitutional right to weed through it and dig up whatever bones she happened to find. She must've had her reasons.

"My unsolicited opinion," he said, "is that you're really good at your job."

"Thank you," she said. "I didn't see that coming."

All the same, Davis couldn't help but worry about his sister and what had awakened within her here at the dawn of her thirties, urging her to draw out other people's stories, perhaps as a means of making sense of her own, or as a substitute for making sense of her own.

McGuinn rolled into the womb of his hammock and snapped the paper to attention, so Davis scooted off, eager to steal a few minutes with his modeling software. How ironic to feel inspired, here in this drab place, a place of transience and miseries, where everyone's apartments, everyone's clothes, their dreams, their entire lives were so easily stomped clean of inspiration.

CHAPTER 26

Because Molly didn't appreciate receiving unannounced guests, she always tried to avoid being one. But she hadn't seen her brother in weeks, and though he'd assured her over the phone that he was okay— what else would Davis say?—she needed to see for herself. She fired off a warning shot of a text, then a call, and when neither was returned, she simply headed over.

Wending her way through the indistinguishable low-rises, she spied him out by the pool, so she parked. An outdoor visit was more desirable anyway than those gloomy indoors. She didn't know how he'd survived here these few months. Even with the furnishings she'd forced upon him, Davis's apartment felt coldly devoid of an identity. He hadn't gone full-bore bachelor pad, with outsize home theater equipment and buzzing neon beer signs; nor had he reverted to the rebellious teen bedroom, which would've required a guitar he didn't play and a pot stash under his bed. Maybe his was just a lesser known but equally typical identity: the outcast dad.

"Molly." A voice was calling to her as she made her way across the parking lot.

Turning, she saw a man swinging in a hammock. It was that neighbor of Davis's, the one she'd met on her first visit. She couldn't remember his name, only that he went by a one-word handle, like he was Bono or Sting.

The man swung himself out of the elastic netting with well-practiced fluidity, sauntered over, and extended his hand (the hand that wasn't holding a red plastic cup). "McGuinn," he said. "Remember me?"

She did—and his cup too. "Of course. How are you?"

He gestured to the periodical he'd left swaying in the ropes. "Better, now that I've had my weekly fix of quality journalism."

Seeing the front cover of the paper, Molly smiled. "You read the *Ramble*?"

"Why does everybody ask me that? I went to college, you know."

Molly apologized, but laughed nonetheless.

"Where'd you come up with this deserted-daughters thing?" McGuinn wanted to know. "Heady stuff."

"My editor is desperate," Molly told him. "He'll try anything to generate some interest and some advertising. My little column is kind of a Hail Mary."

"Well, Hail Molly," he declared. "This editor of yours must believe you to be the savior, because by my count you've got two columns in this here edition, one of which they're pimping on the cover. They've also got you on the radio—"

"You listen to talk radio?"

McGuinn shook his head dolefully. "Seriously? You too?"

Richard had finagled a brief promotional chat between Molly and a popular morning show personality earlier that day at the prime slot of 6:05. The interview would've produced a lot more anxiety for Molly had it required her to actually drive to the station, to meet the host, and to sit in a booth with a microphone in her face. Instead, she'd dialed in from the safe space of the office conference room while she was the only body in the building. The radio host had lobbed a couple of softballs, enabling Molly to hit all the talking points: the paper's desire to strike a more personal chord with its audience, to give voice to women who'd suffered this unique loss, and so forth. Before she'd even had a chance to hate the sound of her voice and be nauseated by the thinness of her answers, five minutes had come and gone and the interviewer was simultaneously thanking and disconnecting her. McGuinn's mention of it was the only evidence thus far that anyone had actually heard it.

Not so the articles themselves; strangely, people were taking note of those. Almost a month in, it was still just an experiment, but there was no denying the response it had provoked. Emails flooded in from readers who were touched by "Abigail," "Beth," and "LaTonya" and their sad accounts of cars huffing out of driveways in the middle of the night, of stoic mothers trudging off to work and never coming back, of restless divorcées claiming to need a change of scenery. Some of these readers were moved by the sheer power of the stories and the apparent truth that abandoned children sometimes grew up to feel like abandoned adults. Other readers thanked Molly for making them more conscious of their own parenting, or more watchful of those sullen, vulnerable kids down the street who were growing up in a motherless home. Molly was also hearing from other deserted daughters volunteering their own tales. Thanks to them, Molly was flush with material and could pump out pieces for this series for as long as Richard saw fit to publish it. Which figured to be at least a little while, as already the ad sales team was capitalizing on the swell of interest in the columns.

"The attention is well deserved," McGuinn said to her. "Captivating stories you're telling."

Molly swept her hair over her ear. "I'm just the scribe."

"Don't 'aww shucks' me, young lady. You've got a knack for writing about people. There's no pretense, just the story of someone trying to reckon with what life has flung their way. Straight, no chaser. It's human as hell, which is refreshing, because I don't know about you, but I don't always find it easy to feel human."

Feeling herself blush, Molly toed at the buckling tree roots under her feet. "Kind of you to say, but I'm afraid the heavy lifting has fallen to my subjects, not to me."

"Take the compliment," McGuinn said. "We're all good at something. I was good at playing ball, your brother is good at, oh I don't know, measuring stuff with a straight edge, drawing triangles, who knows? And this—this is your thing."

Molly smiled and said, "Thank you." She was trying not to notice the wad of sludge undulating inside his cheek.

"Have you come to check up on your brother?" he asked.

"I guess I have. How's he doing?"

McGuinn gazed toward the pool and located Davis. "Well, if this is what ruin looks like, may our sight be strong and clear. And let no one grieve."

Molly laughed. "If you say so."

This man was a fascination. An exotic species to which she could not relate at all. She had no idea what it was like to be like him, to be a carrier of that gene that made fast friends of everyone, to mosey through the world with a picked-first-in-gym-class mentality.

"I just got a notion about something," he said. The downward curve of the brim of his cap was the mirror image of his smirk. "What if I were to call you up and ask you out for a drink sometime? Don't panic—I'm not asking now. Just floating the idea."

"Oh," Molly said, flummoxed by the proposition. "Thank you. That's a really nice offer, but, uh, I don't think I can."

"Sure, you can," he said. "Live a little."

"Well, the thing is, I have a boyfriend."

"Good golly, Miss Molly. A boyfriend. How about that." He pulled off his cap, caressed his sweaty locks with skeptical meditation, then returned it to his head. "The thing is—I don't really care."

His broad smile exposed a band of teeth stained with gnashed leafy scum, which made Molly laugh, which in turn made him laugh, and for one odd yet oddly pleasant grain of time, the two of them stood there beside the muggy parking lot, laughing into each other's faces. He was a little gross, but gross was not the same thing as repellent.

"It was nice seeing you," she said.

"I get that a lot," he replied, and she continued on to the pool.

Historically speaking, Molly Winger was invisible to the jock demographic. She generally appealed to numbers guys, or midlevel marketing managers, or non–Ivy League English majors. A med student presented himself on occasion. Now she'd been asked out by a former major league pitcher. (A long way gone from his glory days, but still. That counted.)

Live a little, McGuinn had entreated. She'd heard those very words from Zach only the night before. "Live a little," he'd said, beseeching her to join him and his friends at the Vegas horror movie convention. But that wasn't living a little. That was springing for a plane ticket to Nevada to congregate with man-boys who cheered on psychos in hockey masks as they knifed naked women. Yeah, no. That was dying a little.

———

She found Davis scooping debris out of the pool.

"This is a pleasant surprise," he said, the slap of her flats drawing his attention.

He told her he hadn't seen her messages, as he'd been busy. Molly wondered what with.

"You know, I'm a little starstruck," he said. "I was skeptical at first. I see this Maternity Leave piece and I think, what the hell does my sister know about pregnancy? But no. What sly misdirection. You're an overnight success—almost overnight even. You're all over your paper, you're all over the airwaves. You're basically Dad."

Molly hadn't heard a word he'd said. She was hypnotized by the naturalness with which her brother was maneuvering the leaf skimmer through the water.

"Davis," she said.

"Yeah?"

"What are you doing?"

"What am I doing, what?"

"With that net thing in your hand. Why are you cleaning the pool?"

"Oh, this." He flipped the skimmer upright and rested it in front of him like the *American Gothic* pitchfork. "Well. So here's the thing. I'm doing a little lifeguarding."

"As in, you're covering for the lifeguard because he called out sick?"

"Well, no."

"Wait—you work here?" Misery rose up within her as she watched him replace the long aluminum tool on the wall hooks. "Oh no. No, Davis, no."

"Go right ahead, sis. Don't you worry about my feelings."

"A lifeguard?" she lamented. "Are you even qualified to be a lifeguard?"

"It's weird, but I kind of am. I'm, like, almost qualified." He sounded self-congratulatory.

Molly dropped into a chair and heaved a sigh of galactic grief. "Do Britt and Rachel know about this?"

"This being . . . ?"

"That you're thirty-five and have a summer job."

"Can you get out of my cheese?"

"What's next? Hagar's?"

The mere mention of the name sent him off into reverie. "If only," he said.

Hagar's was the popular eatery where Baltimore's teens and twentysomethings had flocked in summers of yore to collect a mindless paycheck as a waiter, busboy, barback, short-order cook, or—if you looked good in a dress and didn't mind your boss regularly commenting on the buoyancy of your breasts—hostess. A hotbed of substance abuse and unreported sexual harassment among the randy and perpetually stoned staff, the place had gone under long ago, but Davis still daydreamed about those glorious days and the hijinks of painless youth, like the humid rendezvous he'd had with a shift manager in a storage closet, which would've been a stainless memory—he could still hear the intensifying clank of wine bottles—had the manager in question not been his second cousin, a fact he sort of knew and had tried to put out of his mind at the time.

Molly, however, remembered the place altogether differently. To her, Hagar's was like The Haight circa 1967 but without the music. Part brothel, part drug den, it was a corruptive force upon her brother. She hadn't expected Davis to seek out the wholesome, educational summer experiences that she'd pursued, like shelving books at the library or volunteering at the zoo, but it had terrified her to watch him behave like a member of Guns N' Roses.

"I don't know why you sentimentalize that place," she said to him now. "Remember your car accident? You drove clean off the road. Into a cornfield."

"In my defense, I was asleep at the time."

"That's not funny," Molly said. "I remember what you became back then. You think that can't happen again? Look at what your life is becoming."

She turned away from him. Peering out over the fence and into the world, she tried to soothe herself with the sounds of the season—the sizzle of the road, the creeping of the lawns, the sleepyheaded drone of insects.

"Can you for once not be so tragic?" Davis asked.

"No. I don't think I can."

"Look, I'm fine. I'm not saying I don't have shit that needs fixing, but I'm going to be okay. And, incidentally, so will you."

"What's that supposed to mean?" she asked.

"I just think if you're trying to work through some childhood issues with these articles of yours, it's cool, you know? It seems totally healthy. We don't have to talk about it if you don't want to, but I support you."

"I'm not working through anything," she snapped. "And I don't have childhood issues."

"Like I said, we don't have to talk about it."

"Don't go looking for dots and then presume to connect them."

He stared at her. "Are you serious? Molly, you're writing about girls whose mommies ran away. There are dots fucking everywhere. I'm not trying to upset you."

Molly folded her arms. "Fine. Why don't we mark our calendars for twenty years from now and see if Rachel is writing about girls whose daddies ran away?"

"Wow. That wasn't nice at all."

"I'm not trying to upset you," she said, her voice acid.

He walked away from her. She watched him as he carried the pool implement across the deck, looking down as if meditating upon his slow, heavy steps.

Molly was hardly obliged to admit anything to her brother, or her boss, or anyone, but she could admit to herself that there were, in fact, dots, and somewhere inside her head, she was connecting them. Kitty Winger had become a tenant in Molly's consciousness in the weeks since she started her new series. Perhaps it was unavoidable. In the middle of an interview, an odd detail would flare up out of nowhere, like the floral robe Kitty used to wear when making breakfast, or the dangly earring Molly toyed with when Kitty held her. Last week, when "LaTonya" spoke of lying in bed as a child and being comforted by the sound of the clothes dryer in the laundry room down the hall, how the churning hum of that machine meant that Mom was there, maintaining order, keeping things clean, a strange memory returned to Molly like a ping of echolocation darting through the decades. Molly had been seven or eight at the time and was racing through the house, eager to share a new story she'd written. Searching every room for her mother, calling out to her and unable to find her, she finally discovered Kitty in the laundry room. The woman was crumpled on the floor, her back against the dryer, her hands cradling a face bloated with tears. Molly had never seen an adult weep before—certainly not one of her parents—and the sight of it chased her from the room. She fled, and pushed the image as far from her mind as it could go. It had stayed gone until LaTonya started talking about clothes dryers.

A man entered the pool area with his young son and daughter and dropped a beach bag onto one of the tables. He removed two sets of deflated water wings and proceeded to puff long, mighty breaths into them.

"I think about Mom too sometimes," Davis said. He was standing over his table now, his lifeguard headquarters. His voice was low, distracted sounding.

"I didn't realize that," she said.

He looked as though he was about to say more, but instead snatched his whistle off the table.

"I'd better go guard some lives," he said. "You're okay, right?"

"Yeah. You?"

"Sure," he said, mustering a smile. "What doesn't kill you makes you stronger, and all that."

"I hate that expression," Molly said. Nothing she'd lived through had killed her, but for the life of her she couldn't see how it had made her any stronger. "That's just another lie people tell themselves."

"Like money can't buy happiness," Davis said, "which I'm pretty sure it can."

"Of course it can. People just shop in all the wrong places."

"Or the truth will set you free," Davis added. "The truth will do nothing of the sort. The truth will incarcerate your ass."

"Or God helps those who help themselves," said Molly.

"Yeah, that's pure bullshit." Davis lumbered off toward the lifeguard chair. "God," he scoffed. "Who knows what that dude's up to?"

CHAPTER 27

Upon entering the bookstore, Davis and Rachel were met head-on by the harsh blow of refrigerated air. It felt good against their skin, the brief walk across the parking lot having put a coat of perspiration on their backs, necks, and brows.

"Can I buy us drinks with my allowance?" Rachel asked, uncoupling her hand from her father's. "It would be my pleasure."

"I think I'll get this round," Davis replied. "But it was lovely of you to offer."

Not that she couldn't have afforded it. The six-year-old had amassed a small fortune—some estimates as high as eighteen dollars—from her weekly disbursements. There'd also been some payments extended to her for not roaming around the house after bedtime. For about a year, Rachel's nightly wanderings had frustrated her parents' attempts at physical intimacy, so Davis began rewarding her with one dollar each time she went to bed and stayed there until morning. He discontinued the program when Britt pointed out that he was, technically speaking, paying for sex.

After procuring a coffee for himself and a warm (but not hot) soy milk for his young companion, Davis found Rachel in the Children's section. She was seated on a bench, narrating a book to a younger boy, who was listening attentively while drooling all over a baby carrot. An image unfolded in Davis's head of a future Rachel, another iteration of the Wondrous Life of the Fabulous Rachel Winger. In this one she was a history professor at a liberal arts college in New England, tenured, though perennially youthful. She flipped chalk in her hand and said things like, "Jason has just told us what *happened* in March of 1941, but can someone take us deeper? There's more to the study of history than recounting facts, people! Someone talk to me about FDR's *motivations*."

Davis parked himself on the far end of the bench and joined the toddler in listening to story hour. The book Rachel had selected was *Are You My Mother?*, the classic P. D. Eastman tale of a hatchling who emerges from the egg only to find himself alone in the nest, his mother having flown off to find food. With the turn of each page, the young bird approaches another prospective parent—boats, planes, and power shovels are among his misfires—and poses the titular question. Rachel read clearly and smoothly, sounding out the words she didn't recognize, holding up the pictures to her audience before turning the page. This scene suddenly had Davis yearning for Britt. How many more of these days did they have left together? Too soon Rachel would wake up on weekends *not* thinking about all the things she wanted to do with her mommy and daddy. Too soon she would be mortified that they existed, that they expected her to spend an hour with them in public, at a restaurant perhaps, where at any minute someone from school might walk in and catch her having parents. *Come on, Britt,* Davis thought, willing her to materialize out of the Fiction and Literature section. *This is our time now. We need to be together.*

When Rachel finished reading, she and Davis went about amassing a pile of books that they would read together over their drinks, as was their custom.

"I just remembered something," Davis said.

"What?" Rachel asked.

"Something we need." His eyebrow twitched enigmatically. "For the Sultan."

Leading her through the labyrinth of stacks to Science and Technology, surely one of the lesser-traveled sections in the store, Davis began to examine the spines of the weighty texts lining the shelves. "There has to be something we can use," he mumbled, his eyes moving methodically across each row. Finally, he homed in on one of the volumes and pinched it over the bookcase's aluminum ridge. It was a thick, sturdy paperback textbook titled *Maglev Fundamentals: The Science of Magnetic Levitation*. He took in the cover, then fingered his way to the table of contents.

"This should do," he hummed.

"Do what?" asked the little girl at his knee.

Davis knelt and placed the pile of books on the carpet, rested his coffee atop the pile, and stared into his daughter's face. "We want to build something special, don't we? Something different. Something the world has never seen before."

Rachel nodded.

"We want a magic carpet ride that *feels* like a magic carpet ride, do we not? We don't want to be knocked around. We don't want to be shaken. We don't want to be stirred."

The kid looked impatient. "Land the plane, Daddy."

"What we want," he said, "is something called magnetic levitation— maglev, to its friends. You know what *levitate* means, right? It means 'to rise.'" He gripped Rachel by the hips and lifted her off the ground. "Through this super cool technology, a train can literally levitate and ride *over* the tracks, as opposed to on them. Only a handful of rides in the entire world use it. And since the cars aren't actually touching the track, there's no friction, which means it's very smooth. It almost feels like floating. See where I'm going with this?"

Rachel was already swept up in her father's enthusiasm. "Can we build this today?" she wanted to know.

"Well, we're not quite at the construction stage. It's going to take some really powerful electromagnetics. And a lot of money."

"More than I have in my allowance?"

"Probably. But the first step is for me to read this book. I need to read it just as carefully as you read that one about that little birdie looking around for his mommy."

Davis secured the stack of books under his arm, picked up his coffee, and began to lead the way to a table.

"Where's yours?" Rachel asked. A quizzical look hung on her face.

"Where's my what?"

"Your mommy."

The question stopped him cold. Rachel knew that Peti was not Davis's mother, but until now she'd never asked about the whys and wherefores.

"Grandpa Norm and Peti raised Aunt Molly and me," he told her. "You know that."

"I know. But where did your mommy go?"

Davis looked his daughter in the eye and, with naked honesty, said, "I don't know, little face. I don't know."

Before the words had even fallen into Rachel's ears, he felt the horror in them. How could someone not know where in the world their parents were?

It had been a long time since Davis had given any real consideration to Kitty's whereabouts. He didn't know where she was, only where she wasn't. Nor had he thought much about the day she left, that confusing afternoon when he and Molly were dispatched to a neighbor's house after school, their uncharacteristically anxious father collecting them at dinnertime. Molly kept asking where Mom was, and Norman kept telling them she'd be home soon, but Davis, who was older and more than tuned in to Kitty's darkening temperament, knew something was up. Norman boiled a box of spaghetti, opened a jar of tomato sauce, and watched his children eat in a tense silence, after which they were permitted a half hour of TV in the living room, then upstairs to brush teeth and get into pajamas.

Soon after bedtime Davis heard Norman shouting into the phone at one of Kitty's friends. He sounded desperate, helpless. "This is the third time in a week! Goddamn it, Judy! You expect me to believe that you have no idea? No idea at all?"

It was late at night when Davis was awakened by slamming doors and raised voices. He shuffled out of bed and into the hall. Molly was already out there, leaning against the railing, listening hollow-eyed to the commotion. Together they ventured down the stairs and sidled into the kitchen. Kitty was slouched against the counter with her jacket still on.

"I've had enough of this, Kitty. I've just had enough." Norman was shaking his head like he was all out of answers. "What happened to us? What happened to you?"

The children gaped uncomprehendingly, as though this were a movie they were too young to see. Davis could still picture Kitty in her crumpled coat, her stringy auburn tresses obscuring her face. He could still see the way she'd buckled into tears when she'd noticed her children standing in the doorway, looking small and terrified in their pajamas.

"I don't know what to do," Norman was saying. "If you want to go with him, you should just go. I don't know how to help you anymore."

At that, Norman shepherded his eleven-year-old son and eight-year-old daughter back up the stairs, put them both in Davis's bed, and covered them under sheet and blanket. "Go to sleep, kids," he said, planting a kiss on each of their foreheads, the sound of his voice sturdy and comforting even then. By morning she was gone. Davis had never seen or heard from Kitty Winger again.

"Here's the deal, Rach," Davis said as they stood between two towering walls of scientific treatises no one would ever read. "When I was your age, my mom was awesome. She was like this big ball of wahoo bursting through the house, always singing, always wanting to snuggle with us, especially with Aunt Molly, because she was little and freckle-faced and cute. My mom made every single one of our Halloween costumes. On snow days she made the absolute best hot chocolate—with marshmallows—then brought down puzzles and made us do them together. 'Family puzzle! Family puzzle!' she would sing."

"I hate puzzles," Rachel said.

"Oh god, they're so damn boring," Davis agreed. "You definitely inherited your hatred of puzzles from me. The point is, my mom loved me and loved Aunt Molly, but she and Grandpa Norm didn't belong together. That happens sometimes, and they both realized they were better apart. But this is all stuff you don't ever need to worry about because Mommy and I don't feel that way about each other. We don't think we're better apart. We just have a few grown-up issues we need to straighten out. But it's not because we don't love each other, and it's not because we don't belong together."

Rachel wasn't buying it. "Then why don't you live together?" she asked. "I think the whole thing's stupid."

"I don't blame you," he said. "Listen up now, because I'm going to tell you something I've never told anybody. You ready?" He leaned closer. "When I was your age, I used to have this dream that I discovered a secret room in my house."

"What was in the secret room?" Rachel asked.

"Secrets, of course. You see, I was little Daddy back then, but in that secret room I saw grown-up Daddy. Mommy was in that room too. You know who else?"

"Tweedy?"

"No, not Tweedy. You."

"You dreamed about me when you were six? I wasn't born then, was I?"

"Not quite."

"Then how can that be?"

"It just be. But since I was only six, I had a lot of waiting to do. I had to wait years upon years to get older so I could meet Mommy. And then we had to wait a few years to meet you. But it all happened just like in the dream. Do you know why?"

"Because you're making this up? Because this is fiction?"

"This is nonfiction," he said. "No, it happened because it was meant to happen. Mommy and I may have some things to work out, but that doesn't change the fact that the three of us were meant to be together. And that, sweet child o' mine, is the truth."

Rachel raised her cup of lukewarm milk to her lips and drank, the wheels behind her eyes spinning. She could've been wondering about the confounding condition of her parents' marriage, or the long gone Kitty Winger, or the unlikely contents of the secret room in her father's unlikely dream. Or she could've been thinking about cupcakes or Tweedy or the lemonade stand. One was just as likely as the next.

"Do you understand all of that?" Davis asked her.

"You said a bad word," she replied. "Before. You said *damn*."

"Did I?"

"You said puzzles are so damn boring."

"Yeah, I stand by that."

Soon they were ready for lunch. The sun-soaked leather seats of his Jetta were like a lit stove against their uncovered legs. Davis fastened Rachel into her booster seat, then went around and started the engine, agitating gusts of warm air through the vents. The Jeep in the adjacent parking spot was the color of army camouflage and was suffering from an outbreak of bumper stickers. Words and images attacked every inch of the grizzled vehicle.

"Daddy?" Rachel said.

"Yeah?"

"Can I ask you a question?"

Davis twisted himself toward the back seat and faced her openly, reassuringly. "Of course you can, little face. You can always ask me anything."

"What does Pussy Riot mean?"

The sticker was giving them a dirty look from the Jeep's door.

"Ask Mommy."

———

A barefoot Britt answered the door, and Rachel wasted no time spilling the beans. "Daddy said the *D* word."

"Thanks, narc," Davis said. That was the takeaway from their day together?

"And we're making a roller coaster," Rachel announced.

"What fun," Britt said. "Did you two go to Mr. Calhoun's store?"

"We're making a real roller coaster, not a model. It's going to be people size, and it's going to be a magic carpet ride, just like in the book."

"That's wonderful," Britt said, throwing Davis a confused glance.

Davis gave Rachel a look. "Dude. I thought this was our little secret."

"Daddy made drawings and bought model trains, and today we got a book from Science and Technology—"

"Okay, I guess it's not our little secret."

"—and I'm going to help, and when it's done, you're going to feel like you're floating on a cloud! And I'll be tall enough to ride it."

Britt absorbed as best she could the sneeze of free-associative details. "Well, all of that sounds pretty cool."

Rachel was anxious to reorganize her bookshelf with her two new acquisitions from the day's visit to the store, and since the front step was as far as Davis would be going, she said her goodbyes. "Bye, Daddy," the little girl chirped.

Davis knelt and spread his arms wide. "Where's me hug? Where's me kiss?"

The requested currencies of affection having been dispensed, Rachel zoomed upstairs.

"Sounds like you two had fun," Britt said, standing in the doorway, a plum-colored V-neck cascading down over her white shorts, her hair pulled back in an unfussy ponytail.

"I know I did."

These brief, insubstantial chats with his wife, the ones that occurred during drop-offs and pickups, were his nourishment, for it was here that Britt looked him in the face, spoke to him, granted him a moment of connection across what often felt like an uncompromising divide. She was still mostly shutting him out, engaging with him only in matters pertinent to the operational do-si-do of co-parenting, like what time he'd have Rachel home or what had she eaten for dinner or who would take her on the days she didn't have camp. But even these little scraps of attachment were attachment nonetheless, and it was during these doorstep chitchats that Davis might tell Britt how their six-year-old had suggested he get rid of his Volkswagen and buy a "Porch," or how she'd asked if her peanut butter–and–jelly sandwich was kosher, or how when her yogurt pack exploded all over her shirt she'd remarked that it was a hard-knock life, which had prompted Davis to point out that, all things considered, it was really kind of a soft-knock life, and then he and Britt might share a mutual eye roll or even a laugh and agree that maybe they should cut back on the *Annie*.

He looked at her. "How are you?"

"I'm fine."

"Do you think you and I could meet one of these days, for lunch or coffee or something?" he asked.

She folded her arms and shifted her weight onto her back leg. Hope hung in the air like a strummed chord.

"I don't think that's a good idea," she said.

"When is communicating ever not a good idea?"

And all at once, Britt looked tired of it all—the disappointment, the aloneness, these new logistical hassles, this whole unremitting summer. "You want my forgiveness, Davis? Is that what you want?"

"This is sounding like a trick question."

"I'm sure I will forgive you at some point, Davis," she sighed. "Where that will leave us, I couldn't tell you. Forgiveness may well be the end, not some new beginning. I hope you understand that."

"Couples get past this," Davis said, his voice climbing toward a plea. "This doesn't have to destroy us."

Britt was staring out onto the lawn, at the big old American elm whose thick trunk sloped like a retired cop. To Davis it seemed like yesterday that three-year-old Rachel had crouched behind that very tree while playing hide-and-seek. How appropriate that we began childhood thirsting for this game. It prepared us for a life lived in search of things we knew were out there but couldn't quite see, hiding from things we knew would eventually find us.

"We were supposed to be different, you and I," she said. "We were the ones who were doing better than just muddling through. We were more than exhausted parents. We still adored each other, we were still attracted to each other. We were better than the others, Davis." She dropped a helpless smile. "Turns out, we're not. We're the same."

"I'm sorry I made you think that," Davis said. "That's not how I feel at all."

A bumblebee flew between them, slow and lazy like a submarine humming through the deep sea.

"What's this about a roller coaster?" Britt asked, changing the subject. "Did you get a job?"

He shook his head. "I would've told you if I got a job."

"So what was Rachel going on about with roller coasters?"

"It's silly," he said, but he told her anyway. He told her about how Rachel's renewed affection for *The Magic Carpet* had got him thinking. He told her about the sketches, about the long hours he'd been spending with models and software and textbooks.

"It's still just an idea, a messy table of tracks and cars," he said. "It's nothing."

But Britt was well acquainted with her husband's rich history of describing things as nothing that were the very opposite.

"So you're going to build your kid an amusement park just to win her affection," she said.

"And here I thought a dog would've done the trick," Davis quipped.

As he watched her face folding into weary gloom, as if to say, *My god, Davis, it would've been so easy for none of this to be happening,* he was desperate to reach for her hand.

"Well, I hope it leads somewhere good," she said, stepping back into the foyer and putting her hand on the door.

"Me too," said Davis. "With any luck, I've got a few surprises left in me yet."

Britt smiled. It was a smile that held exactly zero joy. "A few less surprises would've been just fine."

CHAPTER 28

Molly was reclining against a tree in front of Britt's house when the call came. She was working on an article, her laptop open and propped up against her bent knees as she waited for Rachel's camp bus to arrive.

She did this sometimes, surprising her niece by being the one to greet her as she came off the bus, then whisking her away for ice cream or a smoothie. Molly got such joy out of it that it seemed more like Britt was doing her a favor than the other way around. First there was the look of elation when Rachel saw her, which, if only for an instant, made Molly Winger feel like Miley Cyrus. Then there was the hour or two they spent together, one-on-one, in a ping-pong of conversation that felt both random and deeply consequential. *What would you take with you if you had to move to another planet? What do you think Tweedy would say if he could talk? Did you know that my sandwich sometimes gets soggy when the brown paper bag touches my wet towel?* It was afternoons like those that made Molly think she'd be perfectly happy quitting her job and being a stay-at-home aunt.

It was Richard calling. He had a lilt of mystery in his voice.

"I just had a very interesting conversation," he said. "You'll never guess who called me."

"I probably won't," Molly said. She was not a fan of mystery; she was a fan of the straightforward.

He paused to let the suspense swell. "Jamie Okoye."

The name rang no bells. "And he is?"

"*She* is an editor at *Lotus*."

"*Lotus*? Like *Lotus Magazine*?"

"That's the one," he sang. "And get this: she wants to meet with us."

"She does? Us meaning the paper generally, or us meaning you and me?"

"You and I are the us, Ms. Winger."

"What about?"

"It seems Jamie and her team up there in New York have taken a shine to these tales of deserted daughters of yours."

"Wait. She wants to come down and meet about Maternity Leave?"

"She's already in town," Richard said. "That's why we're meeting with her tomorrow morning."

"Tomorrow morning?" Molly's throat went stone dry. The air rushed from her lungs, and a tremor rippled all through her extremities.

"The best and the worst things in life are sudden, Ms. Winger. Everything else takes too damn long," Richard said.

Molly was sitting upright now, at such a rigid angle that a knot on the tree root upon which she sat felt like it was impaling her coccyx. "What does she want?"

"She didn't say," Richard replied. "She just asked to meet."

Molly knew that Richard had been sending out feelers, putting out word that the *Ramble* would entertain offers for a strategic partnership, any arrangement that might help to keep the lights on. To Molly, that meant being acquired by a publication of similar readership and distribution, a *Ramble*-like paper that was either better capitalized than the *Ramble* or just plain better. *Lotus* was not that. It was a heavyweight women's magazine, published in New York, not Baltimore, and available literally everywhere. *Lotus* was to the *Ramble* what the *Wall Street Journal* was to the student newspaper at your neighborhood middle school. Demographics was also a key difference. Ninety-nine percent of *Lotus*'s subscribers had to have been women. Men only looked at it in the supermarket checkout line, leafing through it not for the fashion tips or "sex secrets bound to get his attention," but for the glossies of angels in negligees, for the close-ups of push-up bras.

"I don't know what's going to happen tomorrow," Richard said, "but it seems your pieces have made quite an impression."

The notion that a single person outside of Baltimore knew that Maternity Leave existed was, to say the least, far-fetched. Who beyond the state line even knew that the *Ramble* existed?

"I'm confused," Molly said. "How did this happen? Why would anyone care?"

"Ms. Winger, false modesty is a nonstarter in this business. We've discussed that."

As it happened, Jamie Okoye's daughter was a photography student at the prestigious Maryland Institute College of Art, and she had read the *Ramble* loyally since moving to the area. Taken by the budding Maternity Leave series, by its heart, by Molly's deft touch, she'd recommended it to Jamie, thinking that, for whatever reason, it would be up her alley. Jamie was an instant fan. She called Richard and said she wanted to talk. She was down visiting her daughter for the night, so tomorrow morning was optimal, if they could make that work. That was as much as Richard knew.

"Dare to dream, my young friend!" Richard told her. "Who knows? Maybe she's thinking syndication. Do you think you could handle that, your articles printed in *Lotus*?"

The very thought knocked the wind out of her. Molly could barely handle Baltimore-scale attention. She couldn't even comprehend New York–scale publicity. She never would've even pitched this series had Richard not implied that the *Ramble* was one ad defection away from becoming a Five Guys. Regardless, why in the world would a major-league operation like *Lotus*, run by people who actually knew what they were doing, have the remotest interest in Molly's small, mildly diverting, perfunctorily rendered stories about broken homes?

"Listen. We don't know what Jamie wants, so there's no reason to whip yourself up into a tizzy," Richard counseled. "But no matter what happens, isn't it nice to be recognized? Today is a good day. I want you to relax. Can you do that?"

"Probably not," she replied.

He laughed. "I thought you were bold now! I thought you were adventurous!"

"Nobody could think that."

"All you need to do at this meeting is be yourself."

Seriously? When had that ever worked?

"This is exciting. Be excited," he said. "*Lotus* was a second-rate hybrid of *Us Weekly* and *Teen Beat* before they brought in all these edgy, energetic minds like Jamie. Now it's mentioned in the same breath as *Cosmo*, *Elle*, and *Marie Claire*."

"I thought you wanted me to relax," she wheezed.

"Ten a.m.," he said. "And no calling in sick."

I'm already sick, she thought.

She gazed up into the sky, wishing to find something placid in it—the soaring of a crow, an early star, anything to hush her nerves. Through the high tree branches, the afternoon sun filtering through them like a Tiffany lamp, she spied a distant airplane at cruising altitude and envied the lucky souls aboard it, each of them bound for somewhere far, far away.

———

When the monstrous yellow camp bus ground to a halt at the curb, Rachel descended the steps in a barely controlled stumble and lit up at the sight of what awaited her. "Aunt Molecule! What a pleasant surprise!"

They drove the short distance into the town center of Mount Washington to their favorite frozen yogurt shop, Molly strenuously fighting off terrorizing thoughts of Jamie Okoye. Rachel was too short to reach the handles of the yogurt dispensers, so she called out flavors and Molly moved the bucket-size cup from tap to tap. Only once was Molly compelled to speak up to prevent her niece from an ill-advised combination. "Mint and orange?" Molly said, making a face. "Let's not."

They settled onto one of the picnic tables that lined the sidewalk, and Rachel immediately eyed the heavy clouds swirling over the sun. She'd become something of a worrier when it came to weather, Molly had noticed in recent weeks. She also worried about being late for things now.

"It's going to rain," the young meteorologist forecasted.

"If it rains, we'll go inside," Molly told her.

"What if we get struck by lightning?"

Molly didn't have that kind of luck. "We won't. That almost never happens."

But almost never was not never, and therefore too often for a six-year-old. "But what if we do?"

"Tell me about Tweedy," Molly said. "I'm dying to meet him."

"He's my soul mate," Rachel declared. "He bit me yesterday, which was very unprofessional, but that was just because he was excited."

Abruptly, as if something critical had just occurred to her, Rachel unzipped the outer compartment of her purple backpack and proceeded to fish around. The open pocket unleashed a mildew stench that almost knocked Molly out cold. After a few moments of rummaging, the little camper extracted an arts and crafts project. Popsicle sticks had been glued onto a sheet of blue construction paper in the shape of a house, or possibly a castle or some other structure, with a single stick rising up on top like a spire. An orange button stood in for the sun in the upper right-hand corner, and pieces of soft, cottony material were affixed as clouds along the top edge. A girl, drawn in crayon, stood next to the house.

Molly beheld the work with the awe and reverence befitting a Rembrandt. "Rachel Rose Winger, this is exquisite. Is there anything in the world you're not good at?"

"Dribbling," Rachel answered. "Mr. Boyd says that if you can't dribble a basketball, you've got problems."

"It sounds to me like Mr. Boyd is the one with problems," Molly said. "Tell me about this masterpiece."

Climbing down from the bench, Rachel carried her cup of melting frozen yogurt around to Molly's side of the table. "It's France," she explained.

"How sophisticated! So that's the Eiffel Tower?"

Rachel nodded. "The clouds are made of felt. I cut them and glued them all by myself. It was a production."

Molly pointed to the long-haired stick figure. "And is this you standing next to the Eiffel Tower?"

Rachel shook her head.

"Is it Mommy?"

Rachel spooned a green gummy bear, one of the few remaining toppings, into her mouth and said, "No, that's Daddy's friend."

"Daddy's friend?"

"From France."

Molly felt a shiver. "I didn't know Daddy had a friend from France," she said delicately.

"He does."

"What's her name?"

Rachel shrugged.

"Have you met her?"

"No. I think they make roller coasters together."

"Who told you that?" Molly asked.

"I heard Mommy and Daddy talking about her."

"Oh."

Molly was thinking that Britt's fridge could do without a portrait of her husband's affair, so she put on an unruffled face and said, "You know what, Rach? I really adore this picture. I'm not sure I can live without it. Do you think maybe I can have it? I'll bet Mommy would understand."

"I don't have a problem with that," Rachel said, stirring the soupy remains of her treat.

"Thank you so much. I'm going to hang it in my office so I can look at it all day long."

"I'll make Mommy another picture tomorrow," Rachel decided. "I'll draw her India, since she's Indian. Did you know I'm half-Indian?"

"I did, sweetie. I knew that before you did."

"Maybe one day I'll live in India."

"Oh, I don't think Mommy and Daddy will go for that," Molly said. "It's too far away. And what would I do without you?"

"But what if I get a promotion?" Rachel asked.

Molly proceeded to fold the artwork into her handbag. "Why don't you just open a satellite office here?"

CHAPTER 29

It was jarring to hear Hans Pavelka's voice. Davis had heard it all day every day for nine years, then abruptly stopped hearing it, hadn't heard it all summer, and then here it was again, that familiar point-blank intonation on his voice mail. Hans had been keeping up with biweekly emails to Davis, and Davis had been keeping up with deleting them, giving the brief messages a cursory scan and sending them to the trash without replying. This voice mail, however, was an invitation. Hans wanted Davis to come in and talk.

Davis didn't see any reason for an audience with Hans, but he also didn't see any harm in it, and through a frugally worded email exchange, a meeting was set up for the following afternoon. Davis felt strangely unrattled by the prospect of returning to his old office. He could hold his head high as he marched back through those doors. Nobody had found fault with any aspect of his work on that flume (as far as he knew). Nobody had tapped a pencil to a spot on his designs and said, "Right here, Davis. This is where you fucked it all up."

As he headed out to the meeting, he found McGuinn leaning on the terrace railing outside his door, elbow-deep in a box of Frosted Mini-Wheats.

"What's up, D?" McGuinn said.

"It's a stone groove, McGuinn. A real stone groove."

McGuinn eyed the clean pair of khakis and neatly pressed button-down in which Davis was clad, a far cry from the laundry-basket dumpster-dive that had governed his dress code since he'd moved in. "Well, aren't you a handsome devil."

"I was hoping you'd notice," Davis said.

His mouth half-full of cereal, McGuinn said, "So, D—there's something I've been meaning to run by you."

"Can you do it quickly? I'm in a bit of a hurry."

"What would you say if I asked your sister out?"

Davis stared at the man. "You want to go out with Molly?"

"You look surprised."

"That's because I'm shocked. She's not really your type."

"And what would you know about my type?"

Davis laughed. "McGuinn, my friend, I've seen the women that come by your place to, quote-unquote, entertain you. I'm not judging anybody here, but they look an awful lot like prostitutes, and if they're not, they're trying really hard to look like prostitutes."

McGuinn appeared amused. "Do they now?"

"They look like they stepped out of some communist bloc nightmare—"

"They're not all Eastern European," McGuinn interjected. "Some are Asian, some are Tex-Mex."

"Tex-Mex is a cuisine, not a nationality. Are you taking them to Qdoba?"

"I don't think you really understand, D," McGuinn said, offering a patient smile.

"But I do understand Molly," Davis said. "Molly doesn't wear the clothes that those women wear, she doesn't apply makeup with the same garish vigor, and while I would have no reason to know firsthand, I'm pretty sure she doesn't do the things those women do. If she does, more power to her."

In fact, it had often occurred to Davis that a McGuinn-like experience or two wouldn't be the worst thing in the world for Molly. Just not with this particular McGuinn.

"There's no cause for concern," McGuinn said. "You trust me, don't you?"

"Trust, in my experience, is a context-specific thing," Davis answered. "Look, I like you, McGuinn. You're an affable cat. But let's be honest—you are a walking red-light district."

"Got me all figured out, do you?"

"Why can't you just find someone else's sister to do with whatever it is you do?"

"There's no reason to be a dick about it."

"Actually, I think there are quite a few reasons to be a dick about it," Davis said. "Here's a quick story. After college I backpacked around Europe with some buddies. I'd never done much traveling before that, and there was a lot of shit I didn't know. When we were in the German-speaking countries, I began to notice that the train stations were all named after someone called Bahnhof. There was Franz Josefs Bahnhof, Spandau Bahnhof, Ulm Bahnhof. And I thought, huh, this Bahnhof family must be of great historical significance to the German people such that they went and named all their train stations after them. And then I realized—"

"You realized *Bahnhof* means 'train station' in German?" McGuinn cut in.

"That's right," Davis said. "The point of this story is that people get exposed to the world in varying measures. Molly's train is moving at its own pace. I'm not sure she could handle a ride on yours."

"I think the point of your story is that there isn't as much grain in your silo as you'd like us all to believe," McGuinn snickered.

"Then I'll be on my way," Davis said. "In the meantime, maybe lay off my sister, if it's not too much trouble."

"I appreciate your input, D. In the meantime, maybe you should lay off the 'stone groove' thing. It's not you."

"Fair enough. And maybe you should stop being so ostentatiously nice to that girl at the pool. I know you think she's got some developmental disability, but she just has a speech impediment."

McGuinn went fishing for more cereal. "I'll be the judge of that."

———

A cloud of disquiet unexpectedly drifted over Davis the moment he stepped into the lobby. Being back in this office building again was like running into an old college buddy you hadn't spoken to in years, then suddenly remembering that the reason you hadn't spoken in years was that he'd decided he didn't like you anymore and had stopped inviting you to his parties. When Davis smelled the medicinal fumes of the cleaning solution on the floor tiles, when he spied the familiar tenants who hadn't seemed to notice his absence these past few months, he felt slightly restored and largely miserable.

He entered the Pavelka & Gates suite, and Lydia, the leggy receptionist who'd manned the door so long she was rumored to have pre-dated both Pavelka and Gates, bolted up out of her chair. "I've been waiting all day for this!" she cried, hugging him madly and squeezing his shoulders until they hurt. "God, we miss you around here. When are you coming back?"

Davis shrugged and inquired about Lydia's husband and kids, and soon a crowd had coalesced by the reception desk, all P&G personnel emerging from their offices and cubicles for a handshake, a hug, or a simple good-to-see-you. Standing in the eye of a storm of people with whom he'd worked day in and day out for years, men and women about whom he knew everything—their children's names and ages, their spouses' professions, their lunch preferences, where they grew up, where they vacationed—Davis suffered the depressing sensation of being an outsider. It was a sensation he should've been getting used to.

Hans materialized at the rear of the herd, looking as stiff and unrelaxed as the pinstripes on his pale blue shirt. "Hello, Davis."

Davis issued a tight smile and acquiesced to a handshake.

"Thanks for coming in," Hans said. "It's good to see you."

To which Davis said, "Okay."

The circle parted, and Davis followed his old boss through the suite, past the framed blueprints of the firm's celebrated achievements that hung on the walls, his own blood, sweat, and tears poured into them all.

"Good summer?" Hans asked as he shut his office door and Davis took a seat opposite the desk. "Britt and Rachel doing well? You guys getting away at all?"

Davis felt unexpectedly affronted by the way Hans helped himself to his wife's Christian name. *It's Ms. Palandjian to you, dickhole.* And did Hans really just look at the man he'd told not to come to work and ask him if he was taking any time off?

"What did you want to talk to me about?" Davis asked.

"There have been some developments on the High Seas incident," Hans told him. "The Virginia Department of Housing and Community Development has concluded its investigation, and the results have been shared with us and the park owner."

Davis stared at the man and said nothing.

"The regulators' conclusions, it turns out, differ somewhat from Vantage View's findings," Hans went on. "I don't know how acquainted you are with the regulatory scheme in Virginia—"

"Let me think for a second," Davis cut in, placing an index finger over his lips. "How acquainted am I with the regulatory scheme? Hmm. I guess I would call myself exceptionally well acquainted. Yup, that's how acquainted I would say I am. Since, you know, it was my job to know all the regulations."

"Of course," Hans said. "So, as you know, Virginia law requires the park operator to conduct an investigation and submit a report to the inspector within twenty-four hours of the incident. To no one's surprise, that hasty investigation pointed the finger at everyone but themselves. They concluded that not only did we design the ride defectively, we specified the wrong materials for construction. DHDC, however, has reached a very different conclusion. They believe the accident was caused by a defect in the operation of the ride, not its design or assembly."

"How about that," Davis said, hoping Hans could see him trying not to smirk.

"The staff apparently didn't adhere to the twenty-second interval between releasing the logs into the channel. There was too much congestion, which led to elevated levels of water turbulence. On top of that, the log that flipped was in excess of its occupancy limit. There was at least one, possibly two, too many people in that log."

Davis tapped the tips of his fingers together. "That's fascinating. Why didn't you just put all that in one of those illuminating emails you've been sending me?"

"Because, Davis, the firm has been cleared. This means you can come back."

Davis reposed against the back of the chair and folded his arms. "Oh, does it now?"

"Davis, you had to know how difficult it was for me to ask you to step back. We had to err on the side of caution, we had to follow our counsel's advice, but I was sick about it."

"That sounds hard," Davis said.

"You know how much we rely on you. We're overloaded with projects. Your absence has not been easy on this place."

Hans was making it sound as if Davis had decided to take a sabbatical or had been out of commission with a herniated disc. Sure, bro, why not a euphemism? Knock yourself out.

"I haven't been absent," Davis said. "I've been fired. You fired me."

"Fired you? When exactly did I do that?"

"Do you want me to get out my calendar?"

"If the firm had fired you, the firm would've stopped paying you. You understand that, right?"

"You hung me out to dry," Davis said. "Without knowing jack shit about what happened down there, you assumed the worst about my work—never mind that I'd only ever given you my best—and you told me to get lost."

"You were the lead engineer," Hans came back, forcefully but calmly. "Did you know for a fact that the firm's work didn't cause the accident?"

"Of course I did."

"Did you know it *for a fact?* I sure didn't."

"I was your scapegoat, Hans. You jumped to conclusions."

Hans placed both hands palms down on his desk and spoke in measured tones. "Davis—my friend—I think it is you who has jumped to conclusions. Nobody fired you, nobody scapegoated you. Our firm was implicated in a high-profile accident, one in which a passenger got hurt, and in fact almost died. Ask yourself: How unreasonable was it of Keiko and me to take action to show the victim, our client, the regulators, and anyone who might do business with us in the future that we were treating this incident with the utmost seriousness? Was it wrong of us to protect the firm's reputation?"

"But you didn't even think about my reputation," Davis shot back. "Word travels fast. After you threw me out, a lot of other firms wouldn't even talk to me. My career could've been done, thanks to you."

Hans's head tilted almost imperceptibly. He seemed insulted by the heretofore unimaginable possibility that Davis might defect to one of

P&G's competitors. Did Hans truly have the gall to appear betrayed by Davis for testing the job market?

A wave of rage rose within him, at the injustice of his dismissal, at Hans's revisionist history, at all those years of loyalty rewarded with— whatever the opposite of loyalty was. Was treason too strong a word? His anger forced him up out of the chair, and he walked over to the window.

He stared out at the steamy haze suffocating the city like a plastic bag and tried to calm himself. The windowsill was lined with picture frames of Hans's family, some of the photos decades out of date, echoing a bygone era when his children, now grown and scattered, wore Halloween costumes and performed in ballet recitals. It was universal, wasn't it, a parent's tenacious longing for the innocent past.

Davis thought of the little girl in his own picture frames, and suddenly it dawned on him that she, Rachel, was the compelling reason to come back to work here. If he returned, surely he could press forward with the magic carpet ride, with the labor of love he and Rachel had devoted their summer to. (It was mostly him doing the laboring; Rachel checked in every week or so to see if it was done yet.) If anyone was going to get behind so risky and expensive a project, it was Hans and Keiko, people to whom Davis's work was a known quantity. Another firm might not be willing to gamble, but Hans would admire the Sultan as a feat of engineering invention. He would want his name on it. His beady little eyes would light up like video poker at the sight of the blueprints, for he would see something innovative and original that might attract an audacious park owner with a healthy budget. This ride was Rachel's dream. It was a grand, spectacular declaration of a father's love and the truest road home. It mattered more than anything. The only question was whether Davis's pride could handle coming back. After everything, could he put those picture frames and coffee mugs back on his desk and go back to work for these people?

"For the record, Davis," Hans said, removing his spectacles and wiping his frames on his immaculately pressed shirt, "even if that report had criticized this firm's work, even if it had concluded that we caused the accident, I still wouldn't have fired you."

Davis's eyes lingered on him a minute, then he turned back to the window and the burning day outside. Britt, like Hans, had warned him against jumping to conclusions. She'd said it that day when everything went to hell. *Don't jump to conclusions—not about the accident, not about Hans.* Yet he'd done exactly that. Convinced that any mistakes could only belong to others, he'd leaped into outrage at the mere suggestion that his work could be flawed, a reaction that made sense only if Davis himself was beyond flaw. And if this summer had proven anything, it was that Davis Winger was not beyond flaw.

The soul of it was, Hans had abandoned him. He'd had his reasons, but justified or not, the man had shut the door and left Davis on the other side wondering why. How could Davis ask Britt to forgive his own betrayal when he wasn't willing to do the same for Hans?

Maybe there was no pride to swallow, after all. Maybe the greatest harm in stepping up and accepting responsibility for one's mistakes was admitting to the world that you were capable of them.

Davis turned. "I forgive you, Hans."

An awkward smile. Hans wasn't getting it, but he clearly saw no reason to argue. "So you'll come back to work?"

"I don't know," Davis replied.

Hans's expression swerved. "Is it a question of money?"

"No," Davis said. "I don't think it is."

"I see. You realize I can no longer pay you unless you're actually working here. You're not on administrative leave anymore."

"I understand," Davis said.

Hans studied his colleague for a long moment, then stood. "Well. It was good to see you, Davis. I'm glad I got the chance to share with you in person the promising news about Virginia Beach, and to let you know how we all feel about you here. I hope I've made that clear. You'll always have a place at this firm."

Davis walked over and took the man's hand. "Thanks, Hans. But here's the thing: a girl nearly drowned, and I fucked around and pissed away my family. So, as far as I'm concerned, I don't think there will ever be anything promising about Virginia Beach."

CHAPTER 30

Molly didn't feel great about being part of the lemonade stand. She was indulging her niece's entrepreneurial spirit, helping Rachel concoct the pitcher of the refreshing beverage and setting up the table upon their return from the frozen yogurt outing. But she knew that this enterprise was a father-daughter joint venture, and a nagging sense of disloyalty to Davis ate at her. When Britt arrived home from work and joined them at the curb, the family affair only magnified her brother's absence.

Then a man and his son came biking up to the stand, where the three women stood in the late-afternoon heat awaiting thirsty customers. The man's name was Gustavo and his son, Jake, was a schoolmate of Rachel's.

"Jake, want to introduce me to your friend?" Gustavo said when they stopped at the Winger home and put their bikes on kickstands.

"We're not really friends," Jake answered.

"Well, you're not *not* friends," Gustavo said. "You just don't really know each other. Isn't that a nicer way of putting it?"

"And you might find yourselves in the same class in the fall," Britt cheerfully offered. "Then you might become first-grade friends."

Molly, who did not take an immediate disliking to many people, took an immediate disliking to this Gustavo person. He was one of those self-serious cyclists, fit and trim in an important sort of way, a topography of toned shoulders and pecs jutting out like a relief map beneath his red spandex racing shirt. Nor did she approve of the instant chemistry between him and Britt, the way they commiserated about the overscheduling of children, how they went on and on together about the feverish calendar of playdates and sports.

"What happened to my little baby who only wanted to be with me all the time?" Britt wondered.

"Tell me about it," Gustavo said. "Feels like only yesterday that I was cool enough to hang out with Jake. Or almost cool enough."

Britt nodded. "Funny how time flies."

"Nothing funny about it," Gustavo said.

When he implied that he too was a single parent, Britt attempted to forge a confederacy with him over the rigors of separation. But then Gustavo's face seemed to tighten, like he was bracing his audience for impact, and he quietly, almost apologetically, told them that he was a widower.

"Oh my god," Britt said. "I'm so sorry."

"Two years ago," Gustavo said, throwing a quick, meaningful glance in the direction of his son to indicate that this wasn't a subject best explored in front of the kids.

"I'm really sorry," Molly said.

Gustavo wanted to sleep with Britt. It was all there in the subtle flirting, the suave grins, the squaring of the shoulders. This was nothing Molly hadn't witnessed before. Most men wanted to sleep with Britt. But Britt had never been as available as she was now, and the realization that this casual exchange at a curbside lemonade stand could have been but was not *necessarily* harmless, that the mother of her niece and wife of her brother was actually "in play," filled Molly with a vast sense of loss.

A brush with a widower should've spooked Britt. It should've reminded her that spouses could die without warning. It should have been the catalyst for an immediate U-turn and sent her doubling back to the man she still loved, the man she hated to hate, the man who would do anything to be back home with her. It should have flung her back to Davis so they could get down to the business of making amends before their brutally short and unpredictable lives became even more so. But Gustavo's situation seemed only to evoke compassion from Britt, not urgency.

"How awful for that guy," Britt said after they'd dismantled the table stand and migrated to the back porch to light the grill and sip sauvignon blanc. "I feel terrible for him and Jake."

Let's not rush to sympathy, Molly thought. *We don't know that Gustavo didn't murder his wife.*

Charcoal hissed at each drop of marinade, and notes of lime and honey wafted into the air. On the lawn, Rachel twittered about under the denim sky, chirping out her favorite showtunes—"You're Never Fully Dressed Without a Smile," then "I Think I'm Gonna Like it Here," then a reprise of "You're Never Fully Dressed Without a Smile."

Leaning down against the porch railing, Britt was now shaking her head. "I'm not past it, Mol." The subject was never far. "God, I wish I were. I know marriages survive infidelity. I just don't know if I can do it. I don't know if I can ever get back what I've lost."

These were the times when Molly felt too ensnared in this war to know what to say. She loved her brother, adored her sister-in-law, and was rooting for both of them.

"He calls Rachel every night at bedtime," Britt went on. "From across the room I can hear him through the phone. The sound of his voice is more familiar to me than anything I've ever known, more soothing than the smell of the house I grew up in."

"Give him another chance," Molly ventured. "Give yourself another chance."

Britt gazed out at the black cherry trees clustered at the far end of the lawn. "We're aiders and abettors, you and I. Everyone, in fact," she said. "We allow Davis to be good old lovable Davis. It's always been enough that he's been him. But after what he did to me, to Rachel, I don't know if that's enough anymore."

Britt opened the grill and proceeded to ply the strips of chicken off the grid.

"Britt, you know I'm just as angry at him as you are, and I'm not trying to trivialize your pain, but what *would* be enough? I know apologies are cheap. Anybody can say I'm sorry. But Davis *is* sorry—not sorry that he got caught. He's sorry that he hurt you, sorry about what his deeds have made him. He's sorry, Britt. You shouldn't question that."

Britt shifted the charred onion and squash slices over the flames. "Look who gets a little notoriety and suddenly thinks she knows everything about everything." Britt was grinning, but she looked sober and unbreakable, and Molly knew, once and for all, that she really could decide that she was done. And if she did, then a lifetime of being good old lovable Davis wouldn't help. There would be nothing he could do about it. All his great powers and invincible charms would, in the end, fail him.

———

That night was a fitful one. Through those dark hours Molly pursued sleep all over the house—to each corner of the bed, to the cool side of the pillow, even out of the room to the shaggy, harvest-gold rug that lay in front of the TV, its tiny fibers upright as if they themselves were watching their favorite show. Sleep never came, so at the strike of five Molly conceded defeat. She showered, slipped on a black pencil skirt and a pink silk blouse, a costume upgrade in honor of their anticipated guest, and stepped out into the breaking day.

All alone for a few hours in the *Ramble*'s office building, Molly sipped tea and read online editions of *Lotus*.

At nine, Richard poked his head in and made a look of mock surprise. "You didn't quit. Who says you're not bold and adventurous?"

At ten, Richard poked his head in and adjusted his cuff links. "Showtime!" he said. Like he was Pat Sajak.

Jamie Okoye was a tall woman in her midfifties with striking features. Her hair had been left to whiten and was shorn into an exactingly windblown style. Clad in a red leather jacket and oil-black jeans, she was snazzily but sophisticatedly fashionable, her appearance within spitting distance of the models who graced the cover of her own magazine.

"I read your latest piece on the train down yesterday, the one about Jodi," Jamie said to Molly as they shook hands. She puffed up her cheeks. "What a story. The essay contest, the deaf sister."

"Jodi" was a twenty-four-year-old English teacher whose mother had split when she was twelve, leaving Jodi and her deaf eight-year-old sister in the care of their father, a real estate developer who, up until that point, hadn't seemed to notice he had kids. Fortunately, their dad was a quick study and administered a perfectly fine upbringing to his daughters in a perfectly acceptable DC suburb. Years later, as an undergrad at Fordham, Jodi entered a creative writing contest and submitted an essay of nakedly autobiographical content that laid bare her family's dirty laundry, changing nary a name nor detail. She won the competition, the prize for which was $200 and publication of the essay in a national magazine. By dint of destiny or fluke, the edition of the magazine containing Jodi's essay was read by a good friend of Jodi's mother. A month after it was published, Jodi received a letter:

Hi Jodi.

I'm not sorry I moved to Myrtle Beach. I don't feel any guilt for trying to better my life. You need to stop thinking about poor Jodi whose mommy moved away. Lots of parents do, like when they get divorced. The hatred you feel for me is unfounded.

Love,
Your mother

"What was your reaction to the letter?" Molly had asked Jodi.

"I was like, oh, I guess Mom moved to Myrtle Beach." And that had been the end of Jodi's bitterness. It was one of the funnier interviews. Darkly funny.

Richard invited Jamie to make herself comfortable, and the three of them settled in around the conference table. An air of vaguely aristocratic affability existed around Jamie Okoye. She seemed given to warm, generous smiles, but at the same time she carried herself like someone accustomed to being heard and not talked over. Molly wasn't surprised when she immediately seized control of the meeting.

"Before anybody says anything, I need to compliment you both on your paper. Richard—you and your team do an amazing job. My daughter reads the *Weekly Ramble* religiously, and having read some issues now myself, I understand why."

"My staff makes me look good," Richard said, throwing a wink at his features writer.

"My daughter started sending me the *Ramble* when Maternity Leave first ran. She knew I'd be interested in it for several reasons, one of which is that she knows that my staff and I try to keep our eyes open. In this age of blogs and webzines and endless channels for written content, every so often we happen upon something that we feel deserves a wider audience but isn't necessarily positioned to reach it. As a women's lifestyle magazine, we're committed to making *Lotus* a fulsome and true reflection of what it means to live as a woman in contemporary American society. So when we come across something that's in sync with our mission, or deepens our readers' experience, we pay attention. I know that so far you've only done a handful of these pieces, Molly, but they're wonderful. Very poignant, but in a stealthy, unobvious way. Just the right dosage of empathy and lack of sentimentality."

She asked how Maternity Leave had come to be, and Molly explained that the idea had taken shape after her psychologist friend mentioned how many of her patients had experienced maternal abandonment at a young age, only to spend their lives struggling to understand it. Her friend thought there might be a story there, and Molly and Richard talked it over and concluded that, no, there were, in fact, many stories there.

Jamie had already been told of the enthusiastic reception that the column had enjoyed from the outset—just ask the swamped ad salespeople—and that it was, in its own limited, local, journalistic way, a hit. But how long could they keep it going? Jamie wanted to know. How long before the well ran dry? In fact, Molly had a backlog of deserted daughters, she told Jamie. She'd been flooded with emails and calls since the first piece ran. Molly still found it so confounding. "You'd think they'd just turn to some online community and Skype with each other," she said.

Jamie lifted the monolithic cup of coffee she'd brought in with her and drew a slow, meditative sip. "Well. It seems to me that you've got an exciting, consequential series that's striking a chord with readers and has the potential to do so for the foreseeable future," she said. "Which is why my magazine is very interested in acquiring the reprint rights."

One of Richard's eyebrows quivered.

"Online and print," she continued. "You'd run them and we'd run them; that way both of our demographics would be served."

Molly looked over at Richard. She could tell he was barely clinging to his composure. The *Ramble* was in desperate need of cash, and while reprint rights for a single column that so far had only appeared in a handful of issues would not a windfall make, money was money, and a top-shelf New York magazine would pay market rate or better for the privilege of running the *Ramble*'s most popular column.

"I'm very pleased you're interested, to say the least," Richard said, "and I certainly think these pieces deserve a wider distribution." He looked at Molly. "What do you think, Ms. Winger? Do you think you could bear the imposition of being published in *Lotus*?"

Molly was still processing what all of this might mean. She knew nothing of syndication arrangements, as none had ever before been extended to their little regional rag. "It sounds like a great opportunity for the paper," she managed to say, and comforted herself with the assumption that these things take time. She'd have weeks, if not months, to adjust to the idea.

But no. Jamie wanted to fast-track everything. The iron was hot, she said. For whatever reason—an oppressive political climate, a public weary for uplifting accounts of female endurance—there was an appetite for these stories right now. Which was why Jamie felt it was critical to get Molly's pieces up on the *Lotus* website as soon as the contracts were signed. It was why they'd optimistically reserved space in the layout for the upcoming edition so that Maternity Leave could appear in print as early as next week.

It was also why Jamie wanted to launch a Maternity Leave podcast.

"Sorry?" Molly said. "A what?"

Jamie swiveled in her chair with her high-voltage smile. "Everyone on my staff thinks this should be a podcast," she said.

Richard's chin shifted thoughtfully. "What a fantastic idea."

"I've done my homework, friends," Jamie said. She was off, her excitement spilling out onto the table. "I listened to a radio interview that you gave, Molly, right after your series debuted. It was just a brief promotional spot, but when I heard you, I thought to myself, *That voice is perfect. These pieces cry out for an audio counterpart.*" Her arms were moving now. Her eyes were wild and piercing. It was as though every part of her body agreed with her and needed to help make the point. "Ten, twelve, no more than fifteen minutes of conversation between you and your subject. Think about it. These tales of deserted daughters are so powerful on the page. Imagine how much more they'd resonate with the added intimacy of actual voices." She rested her chin down onto her fist. "Tell me you love it."

Simultaneously, Richard said, "I love it," and Molly said, "Well, I don't know."

"I think it's a good idea, but I'm definitely not the right person to host a podcast," Molly said. Panic was setting in. It was as good a time as any. "It's really not my thing. But I'm sure we could find someone else."

"Absolutely not. It has to be you," Jamie said. "Molly, I get that you're inexperienced in front of the microphone; that came across in that radio interview I listened to. And I can see that you're a low-key person, the type who tries to stay out of the limelight."

"That's why someone else would be better," Molly said.

"No, that's why you're perfect," Jamie stated. "You know how podcast hosts all have those podcast-hosty voices? They're all theatrical in either a puffy, authoritative way or a quietly brainy way or a laid-back, ironic way. You're none of those. And that's exactly what this needs. We need a voice that's earnest and unrefined, a voice that doesn't always know exactly what to say, a voice that's always on the side of her interviewee."

"The voice of a friend," Richard volunteered.

"Exactly, Richard. The voice of a friend."

"She'll do it," Richard assured Jamie.

"She's not sure she'll do it," Molly said, shooting her boss a helpless look. "She'd really rather not do it."

Jamie urged them to think about it, but to do so quickly. She also urged them to think about the fact that because the podcast landscape was detonating, so too was podcast advertising. There was real money here, and it was only getting hotter. Typically a new show had to ramp up and prove its mettle by attracting a couple hundred thousand subscribers per episode before advertisers got interested, but a Maternity Leave podcast could bypass all that. It wouldn't need runway funding, nor would it require a big distributor right away because they had the *Lotus* website, which provided instantaneous and epidemic exposure.

"We could record it today, post it on our site tomorrow, and sit back and count the clicks," Jamie said. "We'd know pretty quickly how much interest there is in something like this. We can haggle over the specifics, Richard, but I think the advertising dollars from our website traffic alone would make this economically worthwhile for you. You'd get a piece of all that because this would be a joint venture. And if it does well just from the *Lotus* and *Ramble* websites, we can take it further and jump to wider platforms. We've got relationships with all the big distributors, and could easily get this on iTunes, Google, Spotify, Overcast, you name it. Look, do I think this has the potential to be Oprah? No. Of course not. But I know that the success you're having locally can be replicated on a national scale. If I didn't firmly believe that, I wouldn't be here."

Simultaneously, Richard said, "I love it," and Molly said, "Would I have to move to New York?"

Richard laughed; Jamie, trying not to, said, "No, Molly, you would not have to move to New York."

The logistics would be almost too easy. With some basic recording equipment and semidecent software, Molly could record the telephonic interviews right here at the *Ramble*'s offices, then have the files dispatched to the in-house production team at *Lotus*, where they'd be edited, mixed, and adorned with an intro and outro.

"The production values should be extremely unfussy," Jamie said. "Nobody wants this to sound slick."

As Molly sat there feeling faint, the meeting veered off into the foggy realm of contractual details. Jamie and Richard gabbed amicably about the structure of the joint venture—licensure, the payment of royalties, the sharing of ad revenue derived from both the articles and the podcasts, *Lotus*'s citation of the *Ramble* as the original source of the columns, and so forth. It was a discussion, not a negotiation, both parties acting as though they'd already signed on the dotted line.

At the front door, they all said their goodbyes and thank-yous, at which point Jamie put one of her moonglow smiles on Molly and asked if she wouldn't mind walking her out.

They crossed Thames Street and made their way through the midday swelter toward Broadway, where Jamie would catch a taxi to the train station. Molly felt small and insubstantial walking beside this tall woman's imposing strides, even on a day when so much praise had been showered all over her.

"I want you to be on board with all of this, Molly," Jamie said.

Molly didn't really know why she wasn't, other than her default fearfulness. All these plans had the potential to do so much good for so many—for her paper, for all the women out there with stories to tell, for all the women who needed to hear these stories. It was the attention, so sudden and unwarranted, that confused and intimidated her. And for the life of her she didn't understand why a publication like *Lotus* would be interested. And a podcast?

"It's not as if I don't appreciate that there's something special about what my interview subjects have endured. I just don't think there's anything special about the articles themselves," Molly said.

"Most people feel undeserving of success," Jamie said, smirking. "But doesn't it beat the feeling of undeserved failure?"

"I would just hate for everyone to put so much time, effort, and money into something that we all eventually realize is kind of ordinary," Molly said.

For a moment Molly thought she detected disappointment in Jamie's profile, as if she'd believed that she and Molly were both keepers of the same sacred secret and was just now disabused of that fantasy.

"Why are deserted daughters interesting? Why are all these people responding to your column?" Jamie wondered aloud. "Here's one woman's opinion. It's because we're conditioned as a society to believe that women don't leave. It's sort of an article of faith, isn't it? Mommies don't walk out on their babies, and if they do, there must be something wrong with them. A strain of madness, and if not madness, then something deeply broken. But a unique type of brokenness, one that the abandoned child, despite everything, refuses to accept is unfixable. A deserted daughter doesn't just say, 'Mom left, screw the bitch,' as they might about a father. It's something they must make sense of, and it seems to me they never stop trying."

They crossed an intersection, and Jamie waved to the white cab that was about to turn in front of them. The driver stopped, and Jamie pulled open the door. Before getting in, she turned to Molly.

"You want to call your stories simple? Fine. You want to call them straightforward? It doesn't do them any slander to call them that. But ordinary?" She shook her head. "They're not just yours anymore, Molly. They belong to me and everyone else who reads them, and you don't get to call them ordinary." She uncoiled a smile, graceful like the fins of a ray. "I'm going to give you a hug now." And she did. "It was wonderful to meet you."

The taxi sped away and left Molly standing there on the corner under an oppressive sun that had made its daily climb to the top of the sky and left no one the refuge of a shady side of the street. She regarded a nearby trash can and thought she might fill it with the contents of her stomach, but the urge passed. *How did Jamie know?* Talking to Molly about brokenness and madness and the refusal to accept the unfixable, it was as though the woman had read straight from Molly's mind, pages of a book she'd been writing since she was eight years old. Suddenly, Molly felt like a little girl trying to contain a scream.

She walked briskly back to her desk and picked up her phone to call the one voice that might understand, the voice that had never once failed her.

"Molly-bear!" Norman answered brightly. "How's my Jimmy Breslin doing?"

"You're not, by any chance, free for dinner tonight?"

"For you, honey, I'm always free."

"Thanks, Dad."

"Sweetheart, never thank a man for having dinner with his daughter, for surely it is his richest reward."

She spent the balance of the day fighting off the sensation of being buried alive. Or if not alive, then less dead than one should be when buried.

CHAPTER 31

If one took a poll about which Winger child was more likely to find fame, even just the local notoriety enjoyed by their father, it would've been unanimous: Davis's meek little sister would not have gotten a single vote. Even the siblings' ongoing game about conquering the world with the worst business idea was facetious, as the whole point was failure. Molly couldn't even pretend to be famous for real.

That contest, currently in its twelfth year, was born with a death. They had been on their way to their great-aunt's funeral and Davis had wanted to stop for something to eat.

"There's no time," Molly told him, and added absently, "You'll get something there."

"Get something there?" Davis laughed. "Where? At the snack bar? You think they'll have food trucks parked outside the funeral home?" He thought a moment. "It's actually a brilliant idea. Funeral-themed refreshments in the parking lot."

And off they flew into the absurdity, planning a menu that featured "french fries with *grave*-y" and a "good *mourning* breakfast burrito."

"Ice *cremation* for dessert," Molly whispered to Davis as they maneuvered among the bereaved.

"Chocolate, vanilla, and straw-burial," Davis whispered back, just before extending his condolences to his great-uncle.

A few days later, Davis called her up, a rascally gusto in his voice. "Forget about the funeral home treats. I've got something else that'll make us rich. Are you ready?"

"To be rich?" Molly said. "Why, yes, I believe I am."

"Let's open up a store that sells sofas, each one with the flag of a country stitched into the upholstery."

"Go on."

"But here's the thing: the flags belong to countries we're at war with."

"That makes no sense," Molly told him.

"Oh, it's completely asinine," Davis agreed. "You take a country that hates us, and you put its flag on the most prominent piece of furniture in your living room."

"So, like a sofa with the flag of North Korea stitched into it," Molly said.

"Precisely. The Iraqis don't love us either, so we'd carry a lot of Iraqi flag sofas."

"I guess we'd have to think globally and tap into cross-border conflicts on every continent," Molly said with the air of an entrepreneur.

"Indeed," Davis said. "In Pakistan, we'll sell couches with Indian flags. In the imperial outposts of Africa, we'll sell sofas with Union Jacks."

"We could go to Iran and sell sofas with Israeli flags," suggested Molly.

"We could go pretty much anywhere and sell sofas with Israeli flags."

"I love it. It won't make a dime."

"Glad you're on board," Davis said. "Bye, sister."

"Bye, brother."

Since then, every few months Molly's phone would ring with an asinine business proposal, and she was expected to match it with one of equal or greater asininity on the spot.

She wasn't exactly sure why she needed her father's counsel tonight. As difficult as it was to conceive of herself as a syndicated columnist or, even more ludicrously, a podcast personality, she knew this was not her miracle to refuse. People were getting fired.

As she traversed the restaurant parking lot, she spied Norman by the door, shaking hands with a middle-aged couple, doling out friendly how-dos to fawning strangers.

"Zach's not joining us?" he asked as he hugged his daughter. He was wearing his beige sport coat, the stagnant summer heat never enough to put off men of his generation from properly attiring themselves for an evening out.

"Unfortunately, Zach had other plans tonight," Molly lied. "Bummer, right?" Zach's availability was, in fact, irrelevant. He had no role in this conversation, nor would he have had anything to contribute. The sad fact was, if Zach had read any of her Maternity Leave pieces, he hadn't mentioned it.

The restaurant was thronging with the electricity of youth and beauty. The icily stunning woman who showed them to their table was dressed all in black, the only color on her person other than the incisions of turquoise makeup sliced around her eyes. Although Molly was in the mood for a glass of wine, she was bullied into trying the drink special (a spicy cucumber margarita) because the server—also preternaturally, even disconcertingly gorgeous—sold it with such orgasmic zeal that Molly felt any other choice might've caused insult. Norman stood firm on his vodka on the rocks, then invited the server to recommend her favorite menu items. Molly hated when he did that. The menu was written in English, and they were both adults who'd been to plenty of restaurants before and were well acquainted with their own tastes. Why populate the table with dishes favored by someone who wouldn't be eating them? But since her father just couldn't resist being charming and game, Molly sat back and waited for the edamame dumplings,

Szechuan monkfish, and Singapore noodles to arrive simply because they coincided with their waitress's dietary preferences.

A suntan clung to Norman from the Mediterranean cruise from which he and Peti had recently returned. The pair used to be bold, daring travelers, and they had photos of themselves piranha fishing in the Amazon and elephant riding in Thailand to prove it. But lately their trips were beginning to sound like the senior tour, scheduled with increasing levels of supervision and rest so as to accommodate a segment of the population whose spryness was beginning to show its limits, who may or may not have recently broken a hip.

"Your editor must be thrilled at the way these articles of yours have taken off," Norman said.

Molly grimaced and looked put upon. "You want to hear the latest? They want to run my column in *Lotus*."

"You're kidding!" he exclaimed. "And what's *Lotus* now?"

"It's sort of like *Marie Claire*, but a weekly."

"Murray who?"

"You've heard of *Cosmo*, right?"

His eyes bulged. "You're going to be syndicated in a big national magazine like *Cosmopolitan*?"

"It's not a done deal," she said.

"What's it called again? I need to write this down. *Lotus*, did you say?" He took a pen out of his coat pocket and scribbled the word on the back of some receipt from earlier in the day.

"It gets worse," Molly said.

"What do you mean, worse?" he asked, forced to wait while the dictatorial server delivered their drinks and Molly took a sip of the cucumbery concoction she hadn't wanted when she'd ordered it and wanted even less now that she'd tasted it.

"Get this," Molly said. "They want me to do a podcast."

"A podcast! How about that!" He beamed with pride. "Tell me again what a podcast is, exactly."

"A podcast. You know. Like a prerecorded radio broadcast. You remember that thing about the Woodlawn teen who was murdered? *Serial*? That's what they want to do with my interviews."

"Mother of thyme!" He gently banged the table in a stampede of enthusiasm. "You're going to do a radio program? That's wonderful. I'm so proud of you."

"It's just an idea that somebody floated," Molly rushed to say. "It might die on the vine. It's not really my thing."

"Says who?"

"Says every single day of my life, Dad."

Norman looked at her in that fatherly way, supportive yet chiding. "Well, sweetheart, somebody who knows better than you seems to think it is your thing."

And once again, Molly marveled at the vast, limitless ways in which the extroverts failed to grasp the introverts, how the fighters would never understand the fleers. She'd listened to Terry Gross, Sarah Koenig, Howard Stern, and Casey Kasem, and couldn't identify a single trait she had in common with any of them. Which wouldn't have mattered so much if she could just look at her own father, who'd spent his entire adult life before cameras and microphones, and glimpse one iota of that man reflected in herself.

She still remembered that day in fifth grade when he'd come to speak at an assembly in front of her entire school on Take Your Parent to School Day. It had been like escorting the president of the United States through the halls. She would never forget the dizzying glow of standing next to him onstage in an auditorium packed with spellbound kids who couldn't take their eyes off the man from television. They listened to him talk about the hard work that went into every broadcast, about the lighting and the cameras and the teleprompter, about the importance of getting the story right. "I just want to thank everyone for inviting me here to Take Your Parent to School Day," Norman said at the conclusion of his spiel, at which point the principal immediately jumped in on behalf of the feelings of students who had guardians instead of parents. "Or guardian! Or guardian!" the principal cried from the side of the stage with the wild urgency of a 911 call. "Of course. My apologies," Norman said. "Thank you for having me to Take Your Parent *or Guardian* to School Day." That evening at home, Molly and her father kept running up to each other and screaming, "Or guardian! Or guardian!" as though it were the world's best punch line. On so many other occasions through the years, Molly had stood by his side, or off to the side—always within range of his signature aftershave—and watched him with pride, possession, and awe as he owned the masses. To this day, whenever she caught a whiff of that wintery-scented cologne he always wore, she'd look around, expecting him to be there.

Three dishes were dropped off at the table. Norman started in on the noodles, and Molly scooted a dumpling onto her plate. Instead of taking a bite, she looked at her father.

"Dad?"

"Yeah, honey?"

"Do you think it's in me to do what you did?"

"What did I do?"

"You connected with people. You talked effortlessly with them. You made them like you."

Norman twirled long strands of noodle around his fork. "You can make them like you, honey. You'll just do it in a different way. What's not to like?"

When she didn't speak, he looked up into his daughter's troubled face.

She said, "It's just that sometimes I feel like I'm more Mom than you."

"Molly." He set down his fork. "Do you know who I am?"

She didn't have an answer.

"I am a man of rather modest upbringing once destined for a perfectly agreeable future in the family appliance business in Columbus,

Ohio. When I drove up to Television Hill twenty-odd years ago, I felt like a fraud-in-the-making. I was terrified that this city, with its culture and its wonderful babble of ethnicities, was going to see right through me. But your mother had done her homework, and it was she who reassured me. She knew that Baltimore was a small town, too, in the very best sense. Its heroes aren't flashy, its urbanity is unpretentious, and its accent is wonderfully atrocious. She said, 'You just relax, Norm. This place is gritty, down-home, and in its own way graceful, and it's going to take to you and you to it.' That was your mother talking, and, let me tell you, she didn't want to come. But damned if she wasn't right. This town became home. It took me in, it took my children in, and it cared for us. That was a big deal. Especially when your mother, well, lost it."

Molly peered cautiously at him. "She fell out of love with us, Dad."

"She fell out of love with *me*, not you guys, but she took off on you. I call that losing it."

As Norman brought the fork to his mouth, Molly couldn't help but notice age creeping over him. The softness in his cheeks and neck as he chewed, the sunspots flourishing on his hands. Was it strange how little they'd spoken of Kitty in all these years? Right after her stormy exit, Norman had sat between his two children on Molly's bed, an arm around each of their necks. "She's leaving us, kids," he'd said. It was a horrifying thing to hear, but it couldn't have been a complete shock. There were only two ways in which their mother's unhappiness could've resolved itself, and this was one. "These things happen sometimes. We're not the only family, not by a long shot. But we're going to be just fine, the three of us. I promise." Norman pulled them close and kissed the top of each of their heads. And that was pretty much it. He'd promised.

Molly looked across the table at him now, all these years later. "Do you ever hear from her?" she asked.

"No," he said. Then he reached over and put his hand atop hers. "Listen to me, Molly Erin, and listen good. We're all terribly unsure of ourselves, each one of us tunneling toward something strange. But you—you are nobody's shadow. And even if you were, a shadow does not belong to the thing that casts it. Can you do what I did? Of course you can. Probably better. And that's true even if you've got more of Kitty in you than you have of me."

"You don't really believe that, Dad."

"Don't I?" He stabbed at the monkfish. "I'm not perfect—far from it—but I have tried all my life not to be a liar."

CHAPTER 32

It coiled and uncoiled all across his monitor, this gyrating intricacy of lines. Designed, constructed, and stress tested, Prince Hussein's supernatural flight path was complete. Or as complete as it could be. Who really knew? It was, after all, still just a computer file, an organized mess of pixels.

The one thing Davis hadn't yet done was view the whole thing, start to finish, in the high-res virtual reality simulation function. Of course, he'd watched it piecemeal, every inch of every section of track, as many times as was necessary to satisfy himself that it was safe and workable and sensational and entirely original. But not yet the whole, all 163 seconds of it in succession, all the way through. *That*—the true maiden voyage of the Sultan of the Indies—was a treat he was resolved to deny himself until his six-year-old co-visionary was there to share it with him.

Such a thing required a celebration—a themed party, with costumes, with tchotchkes and ornaments that brought to mind a magic carpet ride in ancient India. In terms of cultural signifiers, he knew he might have to paint with a broad brush. Perhaps excessively broad. Perhaps offensively broad. Naturally, he needed a rug: tantalizing, exotic, preferably in the neighborhood of ten bucks. He needed garb: a sari with assorted bling for the lady, maybe a princely headdress for himself. He needed magic lamps and lanterns to hang from the ceiling and some battery-powered candles to scatter on the tables and countertops. He also needed a fitting soundtrack, so he downloaded *Persian Nights Dance Mix Volume 3*, which was the best he could come up with while walking the fine line that separated budget party-planning from outright racism. Fortunately, everything on the list could be purchased at Target, including brownie mix (which had no connection to flying carpets but made the list because Rachel loved brownies).

For whatever reason—Davis had stopped asking—McGuinn joined him on the shopping spree.

They'd barely made it past the security gate of the Deluxe, the car engine huffing against the brume of thick summer air, when McGuinn said, "As a gentleman, I should probably tell you that I did end up asking your sister out."

Davis stretched the muscles in his neck until they cracked.

"Should I take your silence as approval?" McGuinn asked.

"No, you probably shouldn't."

"Well, I probably don't care." McGuinn extended a swashbuckler's smirk. "Relax, my friend. I'm as harmless as they come."

"Yeah, but the thing is, you're not. You see, I'm harmless."

"No, you're boring, and boring is worse than harmless," McGuinn countered. "I've lived, man. I've got stories and scars, and I make no apologies for them. They're me. What's the biggest injury you've ever suffered? Shifting too quickly in your desk chair and smarting your balls?"

"I accept that you and I appeal to very different types of people," Davis said. "If someone needs a recommendation for, say, the best place to contract herpes, they're going to hit you up every time. That's your skill set. My thing is being a safe bet. I exude stability."

"You don't *exyoood* shit. You lost your job and your chick in the span of, what, an hour? And you think that when you're up in that lifeguard chair you make people feel safe? Look at yourself. Don't take all this the wrong way."

"What would be the right way to take all this?"

"You're becoming oblong, my friend. It's distressing. Oblong is the least sexy shape in nature." McGuinn squeezed the loose sag of Davis's triceps. "I can help you with those arms. We can tone those man-boobs of yours."

"I haven't been running as much as I used to." Davis caressed his recently acquired chest flab. "I've had a lot to deal with. And I can't believe I'm being body-shamed by a guy whose diet consists of jalapeño poppers and Apple Jacks."

"Let me set you up with a workout routine. We'll get you on some supplements—aminos, creatine, growth hormone."

"Hard pass," Davis said.

"I use them all the time and I've never had any side effects. No erectile issues, if that's what you're worried about—not that you'd have much of an opportunity to find out. Once in a while my vision goes a little blurry if I vitamin up on an empty stomach, but it goes away."

"Thanks," Davis said. "You had me at macular degeneration."

"Just trying to help."

Three Dog Night came on over the radio and started singing about how easy it was to be hard. It was as if the band had been listening in on their conversation all along.

Inside Target, Davis liberated a cart from the long interlocking train, and the pair began a slow plod up and down the aisles. Soon the cart was populated with a Giant Size box of Froot Loops (McGuinn), three toy genie lamps (Davis), a Princess Jasmine tiara and accompanying jewelry set (Davis), an oriental doormat (Davis; it would have to do as a flying carpet), beef jerky (McGuinn), and brownie mix (Davis).

"Do I want to know why you're buying yourself bracelets and a crown?" McGuinn asked. "Did I miss the invitation to your *quinceañera*?"

"Rachel and I are having a little celebration," Davis told him. "I finally finished that project I've been working on."

"Good for you, buddy." McGuinn was already peeling open the cereal box. "Anybody actually going to build the thing?"

"It would take someone with a lot of money and very poor judgment."

As they turned a corner, Davis saw something that stopped him dead, then sent him tumbling out of view.

McGuinn looked around dumbly. "D?" he called, suddenly alone. "Uh, Davis?"

"Shhh!" whispered Davis from under a nearby rack of maternity dresses. "Don't say my name. Pretend I'm not here." Slowly, Davis raised his head and pointed in the direction of the only other person in proximity, a brunette with the skin tone of a fresh penny guiding her cart toward the laundry products. "That was Britt."

McGuinn's face ignited. "*That* was Britt? Jesus balls, man. How did you land a woman like that?"

"We've got to get out of here," Davis said.

"Or—and this is a nutty thought—you could go and say hello."

"I can't do that. Look at me. It's a weekday afternoon and I'm browsing through the Housewares section of Target with some loaf-about in a Billy Squier T-shirt and tobacco leaves in his teeth."

McGuinn nodded mindfully. "None taken."

"This is a woman I'm trying to win back. I can't look like a jack-wagon with nothing going on."

"You're a half-wit, D, right? I'm not telling you anything you don't know."

"I'll meet you at the register."

McGuinn shook his head. "It's your funeral, man." And he watched as Davis skulked off into Women's Wear.

Davis could safely assume that Britt was working her way around the store in her habitual counterclockwise progression, beginning with the pharmaceuticals and ending up by the random sale items, like the Febreze and the lifetime packs of aluminum foil. Therefore, all General

MacArthur here needed to do to evade detection was double back to the front of the store along the route he'd already traveled. The display of toddler bathing suits just ahead would be his jumping-off point. From there, he'd hightail it down to the Wall of the Vacuum Cleaners, then sneak to the front. Home free. Bullet dodged.

Ten seconds in, Davis imperiled the mission. While crawling through a thicket of leotards and tutus, he paused to inspect a lavender dance camisole. Rachel's ballet class kicked in again after Labor Day, and this would be perfect for her. The image of his daughter twittering around onstage, weightless and tinted with makeup, landed heavy. He hadn't expected it to be this hard to walk through Target without his family. But they'd spent so much time here together. It was here that they used to roam their way through the midafternoon lag of a weekend, requiring not so much the merchandise of a superstore but its spaciousness, its hospitality, its Starbucks kiosk. Rachel would try out a dozen little pink tricycles, Britt would buy facial cream, and Davis would test-sniff every deodorant.

"Davis Winger?" A woman's voice startled him.

Slowly lifting his face out of the crotch of a rainbow-ruffle one-piece, Davis found himself under the gaze of Heather Baskin, she of IlluMind Design & Consulting, chief competitor of Pavelka & Gates.

"I thought that was you," she said.

"Oh. Hey, Heather."

She squinted at him. "I saw you somewhere recently, didn't I?"

Davis thought a moment. "Lenny's Lexus."

"Right. My uncle's dealership. You were obnoxious to your dad."

"Yeah, that sounds like me," Davis said.

"I heard you left P&G," she said, looking straight at him, evidently keen to ignore that she'd discovered him nose-deep in a romper.

"It's complicated," Davis replied. "That's my relationship status with Pavelka at the moment—and, as it happens, with the entire world." He was glancing around like a jittery drug dealer, fearing Britt's sudden appearance.

"You mean because of the accident?" Heather asked.

"Yeah," Davis replied vaguely. The safest course of action for all parties right now was to keep his mouth shut.

"But you're not back with Hans yet."

He shook his head. "Not yet. Things good with you?"

Heather rolled her eyes to convey what a tiresome frenzy her life was. "Nutso at work. And we leave for the Outer Banks tomorrow, hence the obligatory Target trip to stock up on sunscreen and pretzels and Goldfish and games and every conceivable distraction for the car ride. I'm hoping not to have to murder my children on the drive."

"That would be unfortunate," Davis said.

"Yes and no."

A gawky ostrich of a woman, she had the air of the middle school teacher who was once known as the hard-ass, but who'd been worn down over the years and had stopped grading homework and started shooting the shit with her students. Davis had always found her raspy voice oddly amusing; she always sounded like she'd been screaming her head off.

"So, Davis." She appeared to be measuring him in some very specific way. "What are your plans? Work-wise."

"Not sure yet."

"But you're going back to Pavelka when the Virginia Beach thing blows over."

"Right now my plans are simply to do a little shopping," he said serenely. "We'll see how that goes. One thing at a time."

Way down at the end of Heather's reedy leg, her toes were tapping. "We all just assumed your leave of absence was a temporary thing, like for PR. Nobody actually thinks Hans would let you go."

Davis's tongue poked around in his cheek. "Like I said, it's complicated, Heather."

A football field away, McGuinn was waiting by the checkout lines. There was still no trace of Britt, which was worrisome, because it meant she could be anywhere. Never again would Davis underestimate what a social hub Target could be.

"Well, it was nice running into you, Heather. Have fun on your vacation."

Heather's eyes narrowed in calculation. "You should come by," she said.

"The Outer Banks?"

"The office. Stop in and chat with Brian Ong. Not to talk out of school, but he would hire you in a heartbeat."

Davis reverse sniffed. "Brian Ong has no idea who I am."

"Brian Ong knows exactly who the fuck you are. He knows your work." Then, with a grin that shouldered an unsettling coefficient of menace, she said, "And the chance to klepto Hans Pavelka's right-hand man, I assure you, would be irresistible to Brian."

Davis drifted off into the sunbeam of an intriguing proposition. He hadn't thought seriously about other job prospects since those desperate phone calls earlier in the summer. His stock hadn't been trading at its summit at the time, and he hadn't even bothered to call a princely outfit like IlluMind, a shop slightly higher of profile than Pavelka and significantly swankier of office. Since that time, when he wasn't guarding lives at the pool or squireling himself away on the Sultan, he'd only contemplated going back to work for other types of jobs, fantasy jobs, drop-everything-and-change-yourself-entirely jobs. There had to be a high school in Oregon that needed a track coach. Or he could go to law school, then find some small town in Indiana that needed a country lawyer, a quaint burg where the legal representation consisted mainly of folksiness. *Now, Your Honor, you and I have known Bobby since he was yea high, and we both know he didn't mean to hurt anybody. He just had one too many at the Tipsy Cow that night, and he's awfully sorry. Aren't ya, Bobby?* Surely, there were easier lives out there waiting to be found. There just had to be.

"IlluMind is the bomb, Davis," Heather said.

"Da bomb, huh?"

"It's a great environment. We have a constant flow of super groovy projects. And you should see our toys! The tech is all state-of-the-art. Brian gives us plenty of independence and creative leeway, always pushing us to come up with our own crazy ideas to pitch." She interrupted herself. "I'm starting to sound like a car salesman."

"I was beginning to get a bit of a Lenny Baum vibe," Davis joked.

She laughed obligingly, whereupon Davis wished her a good trip and promised to give her proposal some thought.

"Oh, and Davis," Heather said before walking away, "apropos of nothing, where *I* work, we stand behind our people."

"Apropos of nothing, huh?" Davis said, smirking.

"Nothing," Heather said, smirking right back at him.

Once she was gone, he executed a series of furtive glances in panorama, saw neither hide nor hair of his wife, then scooted toward the cashier. Finally, he reached McGuinn.

"Sorry for the holdup," he said. "There was an ambush."

"You get busted?"

"Actually, I got a job offer. Sort of."

"Right on," McGuinn cheered. "Patio Furniture or Electronics?"

They paid quickly, and the doors slid open to allow their escape. Davis ignited the Jetta and scrambled out of the lot, his rushed turns felling the plastic bags in the back seat.

By the time they reached the first red light, Davis had a new text. He read it.

"Fuckbiscuits!" he uttered.

McGuinn looked over at him.

"She saw me," Davis said, and read Britt's missive aloud. "Reconsider the tutu. You might've had the legs for it at twenty-five, not so much at thirty-five."

"I was right," McGuinn said, laughing. "It was your funeral."

His funeral indeed.

"Fuckbiscuits," Davis said again.

"That's the thing about funerals, D. Either you're hearing about theirs or they're hearing about yours."

"Thing about funerals," Davis said, with a bleak sigh, "is that someone's always dead."

CHAPTER 33

The *Weekly Ramble*'s tech epicenter was in the basement. It was a musty subterranean dungeon where peninsulas of desks shouldered outdated monitors and uncoupled keyboards, where modems blinked nervously in the half light and cables to nowhere disappeared into the drywall. It was also where Wyatt, the in-house computer Merlin, hid from the world, alone, doing God-knows-what on the internet while listening to Devo and Weezer amid the stench of fermenting apple juice.

Wyatt was the paper's webmaster, IT director, electrician, handyman, plumber, craftsman for minor woodworking projects, parking lot auto mechanic, and once when someone left an egg salad sandwich out all weekend, cockroach exterminator. He was also a highly skilled naysayer. Nothing was feasible, the impossibility of everything due not to any limitations on his own ingenuity but to inexcusably poor resources. He was known to begin sentences with, "If this were a *real* newspaper . . ." or "I've been telling these guys for years that they need to [insert gripe], but do they listen to me?" Richard did not particularly like Wyatt but could not fire him because, for starters, Richard disliked firing people more than he disliked Wyatt. But more important, the arrogant oddball was the only person who knew how stuff worked around here.

Earlier that morning Richard and Molly had met with Wyatt. He'd walked into the meeting late—still buckling his belt after a protracted men's room event—and had to be cajoled and flattered into agreeing to help out with the *Maternity Leave* podcast.

"So basically you want me to produce it," he'd said.

Richard seemed to see no profit in fighting. "Sure. If that's what you want to call it."

Wyatt had then launched into a Gettysburg Address about how, given his underfunded resources, the *Ramble's* ability to record a broadcast of legit audio quality, something they wouldn't be embarrassed to send to "the head honchos in New York," rested exclusively on his heroism.

"Maybe I don't understand," Richard had said, taking the bait. "All we're doing is capturing a phone conversation. Won't any old recording device do?"

Wyatt lowered his head to share a private chuckle with his flannel shirt and baggy jeans. "The short answer is no, any old recording device won't do. There's still a lot of variance in the quality of phone mics, so depending on the other person's device, you could get a lot of snap, crackle, and pop. We've got *some* equipment downstairs, but it ain't great, I'll tell you that. I still have my old Audio-Technica—good mic, used it when I ran sound at the Cat's Eye Pub. What I can do is plug it directly into the jack, then download some software to get a decent enough DAW going—digital audio workstation. I've messed around with enough editing applications and mixing features that I can probably raise the levels and filter out a lot of the hiss. Look, I'm not making any promises, but I think I'll be able to slap something together." He'd then showed Molly and Richard a look engineered to appear both weary and valiant.

Richard, as usual, seemed to find Wyatt's condescension and quicksand of detail insufferable. (The "short answer" was never that.) Molly was about to ask a few questions of her own, but the meeting came to an abrupt end when Wyatt announced he needed to "take a whiz." Richard, either annoyed or confused, asked him if he hadn't just "whizzed" a few minutes earlier, which led to an awkward standoff in which nobody knew if Richard was denying his employee permission to pee or merely expressing concern for the man's renal function.

"Does that poor boy really need to consume a jug of apple juice every day?" Richard had wondered aloud to Molly after Wyatt had walked out.

When Molly came down the basement stairs, Wyatt silenced his Oingo Boingo and directed her to a chair. After wading through the broil of A/V equipment, she lowered herself onto the primitive wooden chair—something out of a nineteenth-century schoolhouse—and slid on the ungainly set of headphones resting on the table before her. Languishing in the beam of an industrial spotlight, she splayed out the notes she'd typed up about "Harper," with whom she was about to speak. Meanwhile, Wyatt bobbed like a hobbit between his computer and the mic stand, making absurdly fine adjustments until the boom hung over Molly like a sword.

At the strike of three o'clock, she dialed the number.

Harper was cheerful from the get-go, friendly and forthcoming, a true gift of a draw for Molly's very first broadcast experience. She went over the ground rules with her guest, which weren't so much rules as an insultingly obvious rundown of telephonic interview basics: Molly would ask questions calculated to elicit Harper's story, Harper would tell said story, they would both strive for a conversational tone, and the whole thing would be recorded.

The housekeeping matters dispensed with, Molly glanced over to her engineer, and Wyatt, hunched in front of his monitor with enormous headphones riding his bulbous head, gave Molly a thumbs-up. She let out a shaky breath that hit the mic like a winter wind, then calmly read the introduction that she'd drafted and which would be the lead-in to every episode.

"I'm Molly Winger, and you're listening to *Maternity Leave: Tales of Deserted Daughters*, a weekly podcast that explores the unique experience of girls whose mothers walk out and leave them behind. What kinds of women do these girls become? The answer is, of course, all kinds. But they share a bond. For some, this experience is something they spend their lives running away from. For others, it's something they run toward. And for still others, it's another kind of presence, riding quietly in the back seat. We are brought to you by the *Weekly Ramble* in Baltimore, in association with *Lotus Magazine*, and we're here to tell stories. My guest today is Harper. That's not her real name, but this is her real story. Welcome, Harper. Thank you for joining us today."

"Happy to be talking to you, Molly," said the self-assured voice on the other end.

First, the innocuous basics. Harper was twenty-seven, in a relationship that had just marked its five-year anniversary, and currently working in the catering industry in New Jersey. She'd only been at her job a year but liked it enough that she was considering enrolling in culinary school.

Seconds in, Molly was overcome with remorse for having allowed herself to be put in front of a microphone. She'd conducted countless interviews throughout her career, but now that they were being recorded, committed to tape so that they could be cast indelibly into the world—posted, no less, on the website of one of the most popular magazines in America—she became fixated on how inept she was at navigating the flow of conversation, how her sentences stumbled forth and seemed to abate midthought, words and fragments limping along in search of a period. Things that weren't questions came out like questions. She cleared her throat for no reason. The sound of her own voice felt like an unbreakable prison.

"So, Harper, you were twelve years old when your mother left home," Molly said. "Do you remember how it happened?"

"I don't think I'll ever forget it," Harper replied, and with an air of detachment that sounded like the hard work of therapy, she spoke of the day her mother informed the family that she was moving out of the house and into a nearby apartment with a woman.

"My mom was pretty up-front about it. She was like, 'I love this woman and I want to be with her. You'll understand one day.' The thing is, I understood then. Understanding wasn't the problem. Sure, I would've preferred that she stay, but it wasn't the end of the world. I knew I'd be just fine living with my dad and my brother. And my mom and I fought a good bit, so I probably thought a little distance might do our relationship some good. But then she went a little overboard with the distance thing. She and her partner decided to move from that apartment seven minutes away all the way out to Oregon. We were in York, Pennsylvania, and she was moving to Portland, Oregon. Hard not to take that as a fuck-you." She paused. "Can I say 'fuck' on the radio? I hope I can because I've now said it twice."

"It's a podcast. Say whatever you want," Molly told her.

"Cool. 'Cause I've got a bitch of a potty mouth."

While Harper and her mother fell out of touch after that, Harper always remained close with her maternal grandparents. "Sweet, wonderful people. So good to me. When I turned eighteen, they threw me a party and got me drunk on Irish whiskey." She chuckled. "I don't think they realized the drinking age was twenty-one. My friends and I sure as hell weren't going to enlighten them."

Harper's grandfather had died last year, and at the funeral, she ran into her mother for the first time in years.

"She came over to me, crying her eyes out," Harper said, the lightness in her voice falling away for the first time. "She tried to hug me, and you know what I did? I walked away. I totally rejected her."

"I think most of us would've done something similar," Molly said. "That was certainly an understandable response."

"Well, it may be understandable, but that doesn't make it right. I felt really guilty about having acted that way, so much so that I wrote her a letter. I told her I was sorry that her father was gone and that I know she must be hurting. I apologized for walking away from her at her own dad's funeral, which was a very cruel thing to do. Nothing she'd done to me excused that."

"Did she ever write you back?" Molly asked.

"No. But that's probably because I never sent the letter." Harper's laugh sounded like self-spite. "This is going to sound trite and lame—you're probably going to edit it out—but after I wrote that letter, I realized that if you want to be the bigger person, all you have to do is act like the bigger person. You don't have to actually *be* that person. People make it so hard. They wage war on themselves, they have these little battles in their head. But it really is easy. You just fucking act the part. Oops. Sorry. Did it again."

"That's okay," Molly said. "You're forgiven."

"Am I?" Harper said. Now her laugh was lighter. "God, it's good to hear someone say that."

To which Molly, for some reason, replied, "I know."

Truth was, Molly did know. This warped force that got an abandoned child feeling remorse toward an abandoning parent—this was not beyond Molly's experience. Often she'd imagined her own mother's feelings, feelings she knew nothing of, feelings that could only be a figment of her own imagination, and presumed to grieve for them. Sometimes it was in waking hours, other times in some lawless dream, but Molly could see Kitty, could picture her coiled up in a dark room far away, aching for the little boy and girl she'd left behind. It seemed an absolute certainty to Molly that, wherever Kitty was, she was tormented by her crimes, was awakened by them in the middle of the night, fleetingly haunted by them at dinner parties, in movie theaters, at the pharmacy. Even after everything Kitty had done, Molly still sometimes felt as though it were within her power to fix it all, and the fact that she hadn't was her own crime.

After twelve minutes of recording, Molly thanked Harper for sharing her story, plugged the column, now available in both the *Ramble* and *Lotus*, and assured any lonely souls who might actually be listening that another episode would be available soon. Then she removed her headset and breathed out the last of her angst.

"Was that terrible?" she asked Wyatt with a pained expression.

"Not really." He shrugged. "You sound a little nasal. Do you have a cold?"

"No," Molly said.

Wyatt patted his cheeks like he was bearing down for an all-nighter. "I might be able to fix it by modulating the EQ. I'll see what I can do."

———

Using her emails, notes, and a transcription of the interview that had been spit out in real time by the recording software, Molly drafted the article and sent it to Richard at the end of the day. Then she headed out to meet Zach and his Little Brothers at Broadway Square.

As she walked past the squadron of tugboats at Recreation Pier, her eyes drifting out over the peaceful diamond bay, it occurred to her that the podcast hadn't gone nearly as poorly as she'd feared. Once Harper got to talking, Molly had forgotten to fret about the mic, the headphones, the caliber of her questions, the very unradio cadence of her speech, and the terrifying number of subscribers *Lotus* had. Perhaps it didn't matter who was doing the hosting. Maybe you got these women on the phone and just rolled tape. But it felt like more than that to Molly. It felt oddly right for her. Just so long as no one was paying attention.

Out of nowhere, Gabe came flying down the cobblestone street and grabbed Molly's arm. "Come on," the boy said. "We're over here."

He led her to the bench where Anthony and Zach were taking the final bites of dinner, their hot dogs oozing with copiously applied condiments, their shirts—the boys' tees, Zach's Izod—bearing the stains of unwieldy, table-free eating.

"There she is!" Zach cheered as Molly and Gabe approached.

Anthony, the tall teenager, offered a smile. "Hey, Molly. How's it going?"

"Honored to be included in boys' night out," she replied with a smile.

Zach licked his fingers clean. The facial injury he'd suffered earlier in the summer was now nearly healed, the swelling on his nose completely gone and only a faint purple shadow under one eye. "I was just telling the fellas about what awaits me in Vegas," he said, grinning in a way Molly hoped the boys didn't fully grasp.

Zach was to leave for the convention the following day, and Molly couldn't wait until it was over so that he would stop talking about obscure B-movies and imploring her to buy a last-minute plane ticket.

"It's not too late to come," Zach sang, putting on an unfortunate puppy-dog expression.

"It's not a great time," Molly told him.

She had mentioned to Zach that today was her first taping. To say that he'd apparently forgotten would suggest that he'd actually been conscious of it at one point, that he'd shown some degree of curiosity about *Lotus* or the syndication deal or any of the goings-on with her job. He had, in all fairness, poured them both a celebratory glass of cheap champagne when Maternity Leave was first published, which was nice. But it wasn't the same as showing interest.

"Aren't you hungry?" Gabe said to Molly. "Zacharias, get your girlfriend some dinner."

Molly bought a soft pretzel from a nearby vender, and as dusk descended upon the city, the foursome lounged on one of the benches in the middle of the square. Jenny was taking the boys to Ocean City in a few weeks, and they were both intent on finishing their summer reading assignments beforehand so that their vacation wouldn't be marred by anything educational. Anthony's book was *To Kill a Mockingbird*. Gabe's was "something stupid about the Revolutionary War."

"You're going to love *Mockingbird*," Molly told Anthony. "One of my all-time favorites."

Anthony shuffled guardedly, the way a thirteen-year-old boy does in the presence of an older woman. "I don't know. I'll give it a shot."

"I hate reading," Gabe declared. "It's boring."

"Yeah, I didn't like it much either when I was your age," Zach said. "All the stuff I had to read for school was a drag."

Disdain for the written word was ironic from someone who could not have more closely resembled the caricature of a bookworm. Zach did read, but his literary tastes were in perfect alignment with his cinematic tastes. In both cases there needed to be superheroes or psychos or futuristic scenarios involving small pockets of plague survivors. Once, he'd handed Molly *The Stand*, a chunky Stephen King tome, and said, "You'll appreciate this." As if he had any appreciation for what she might or might not appreciate. She gave it a try one night in bed, but conked out on page four and woke up at three in the morning with the paperback resting facedown on her chest.

A game of tag broke out among Zach and his Little Brothers, and Molly watched the three boys zooming and yelping all over the square, leaping over benches and around parking meters in the carefree summer evening. Then her phone rang.

"I hope it's okay that I bullied Richard into giving me your cell number," said Jamie Okoye. "I did that right after I bullied him into sending me a rough cut of today's taping."

Molly plugged her free ear with her index finger and drifted away from the noisemakers. "Of course. Happy to hear from you," she said.

"I won't keep you," Jamie promised. "I just felt the urge to gloat."

"Gloat?"

"Well, the podcast was my idea, wasn't it?" Jamie said. "The production team tells me there's some editing to be done, but I have to tell you, this is exactly what we had in mind."

"Really?"

"You're kind of a natural. I think these are going to work."

"Really?" Molly said again, her incredulity deepening.

Jamie laughed. "You're going to need to work on camouflaging your self-doubt. The rest of us do a much better job."

"I'm glad you're happy," Molly said.

Jamie paused. "Remember when I mentioned that there were several reasons my daughter brought your pieces to my attention? I won't bore you with the details—you get your fill of such things these days—but let's just say that maybe one day I'll be a guest on your podcast."

Molly felt foolish for not having suspected. "Oh," she said.

"Yup. Raised by my grandmother. She got me through the most turbulent years of my life, and she didn't draw upon any great wisdom to do it. So there you go. A kind, understanding voice edges out wisdom any day."

"Thank you for telling me that, Jamie," Molly said.

"So we have something in common, Mol?"

To Jamie Okoye, Molly Winger was Mol. "I guess we do," she replied.

They hung up, and Molly gazed across the square at her companions. Anthony and Zach were easily evading Gabe's swatting. He was "it," and his shorter legs seemed destined to keep it that way until one of the others took pity or ran out of steam. A street musician was strumming an acoustic guitar and singing that old Rod Stewart song, "Maggie May," and as Zach zigged and zagged out of Gabe's wingspan, he sang along, substituting his girlfriend's name into the lyrics so that the song became "Molly May." She chuckled at Zach's silly vocal stylings and recognized that everything happening to her was happening because of him. It was because of his Little Brothers that she was being published in *Lotus*, was recording podcasts, was receiving cell phone calls from editors of major national magazines. These deserted sons, Anthony and Gabe, had been on Molly's mind the day she took that long walk with Skyler, and just mentioning them had planted ideas in Skyler's head, ideas that Molly had kicked and screamed against, but were, in the end, the reason all of this was happening. And more incredibly than any of it, Molly was happy about it.

CHAPTER 34

It wasn't that the room looked hokey. What child-oriented activity wasn't hokey? It was the whiff of racial misclassification that bothered him: the disco music with singing in Farsi, the genie lamps from a North African folktale, the oriental rug from a story supposedly set in India. It was a crude conflating of cultures that were related only in the sense that the men in each one sometimes wore turbans.

As Davis whisked the brownie mix and prepared for his exclusive party, for which only Rachel had made the guest list, his phone burped in receipt of an email. He wiped his chocolate-stained fingers on a towel and read the new message from Hans. He was, again, gently following up on their discussion. Had Davis made any decisions about returning to work? Did they need to discuss terms? Did he want to hear about the new roller coaster in South Florida that P&G had just been hired to design? Hans was still keeping things low-pressure, perhaps allowing the economic squeeze from the discontinued paycheck to do his dirty work.

"Thanks, Hans. Still figuring things out," Davis wrote back. Which was true, even if it misleadingly implied that he was giving this rigorous thought, that he was up late making lists of pros and cons over buckets of coffee. In fact, Davis was preoccupied with higher things. He'd make his decisions about the future soon, since the Sultan was nearly ready to be shopped. But soon wasn't now. Soon was later. Now he was planning a party for his daughter, who was to be dropped off soon.

Then Charlie showed up.

"I'm wigging out," she declared.

"Okay," Davis said, staring at her on his front mat but not letting her in. "Does that have to happen here?"

She knelt and caressed Tweedy, who had galloped to the door at the sound of the knock and was frothing with saliva and throbbing for affection. "I had a weird day," she said. "I really needed to see my doggie. My exams are in, like, a week, you know."

"I know," Davis said.

"I'm probably going to fail them."

"I know."

As Davis retreated into the kitchen, Charlie waded uncomfortably into the apartment, taking a gander at the ornate welcome mat that had been dropped in the center of the room, as well as the cheap party favors stationed on every available surface.

"The fuck's going on here?" she asked.

"I'm getting some things together for a little party that my daughter and I are going to have this evening," Davis explained as he stirred the batter that had assumed the color and consistency of ash.

"Are you celebrating some cult holiday?" Charlie asked.

"You know that roller coaster I've been working on? I think it's done."

"Really? Wow." She seemed truly happy for him. "That's badass. Congrats." Then she dropped into a chair with the pulsating pile of dog flesh in her lap. "Now what?"

"Probably nothing," he said, matter-of-factly. "I've designed a ride that is both ridiculously cool and far too expensive to build."

"Then what was the point?"

"The point," Davis said, "is that this is the ride Rachel and I dreamed up. It's for her. Maybe someone will share that dream and build it, but if not, we live with the satisfaction of having chased the ideal and achieved it. We didn't settle for the cheap knockoff. We refused to compromise."

"You're a diva," Charlie noted. "I respect that."

"I'm not a diva. I'm just a guy who knows that sometimes in life you have to settle for the moral victory. Those tend to come along more often than actual victories."

"Yeah," Charlie sighed. "I think these exams are going to have to be moral victories for me. It's not looking like they'll be actual ones."

"Not on my watch, sister. Get out of here and hit the books."

"I don't know if I can concentrate after what happened to me today. Want to hear what I did?"

"Sure. It's not like I'm busy or anything," Davis said, pouring the thick molten mush into a pan and sliding it into the oven's gaping maw.

Charlie proceeded to tell him anyway. "I babysat my father's girl-friend's five-year-old."

"Father's girlfriend's five-year-old," Davis repeated with concentra-tion, pointing into the air at each successive branch on an invisible family tree. "That was nice of you, since such a person is basically a total stranger."

"Money changed hands, believe me," Charlie confided. "So I show up, and Gloria heads off to work. Gloria is my dad's current fuck buddy. Why anyone would want to fuck someone named Gloria is beyond me. Gloria changes your transmission with a cigarette pinched in her lips. Gloria misses work because her kid has a court date. This is beside the point. Anyway, first thing Lucas does—Lucas is the tyke, by the way, and, not for nothing, a total asshole—the first thing he does is he takes me to his room to show me his hamster. Do I give a shit about a hamster? Of course not, but here we go, into his room to see the stupid hamster. And when we get there—you ready for this?—the hamster is dead."

Davis's eyebrows shot into the air. "*Dead* dead or, like, playing dead?"

"It's a hamster, not a possum. Hamsters don't know shit about playing dead. This hamster is graveyard dead, and the kid knows it."

"Let me stop you right there," Davis said. "If a dead hamster is the traumatic event that has you all tizzied out, I'm going to be really short on sympathy."

"If I may continue," Charlie said. "So the kid sees the dead fur-ball and bursts into tears. Sobbing, wailing, totally inconsolable. I just want to grab him and yell, 'It's a fucking hamster, man! Pull yourself together!' But I don't. Instead I call Gloria and tell her about our tragic situation. Gloria, I should tell you, has been trying super hard to like me, but she just doesn't, and she's like, 'I'm not coming home for some stupid hamster,' and I'm like, 'Dude, I totally hear you. I wouldn't either.' She tells me to figure it out, maybe give him a pudding packet to distract him. So I give him a pudding packet, he goes to town on the pudding packet, and as soon as he's done, what does he do? He goes right back to wailing. So I sit the little pain in the ass down, I put my arm around him, and I tell him, look, your hamster will always be with you. That's how death works. You won't be able to see him, but he'll be with you in spirit, every day, him and all your wonderful memories."

"Nice move," said Davis.

"You would think so. But it turns out that when you tell a little kid that their dead pet will always be with them, apparently what they hear is that some ghost rodent will be lurking around their room in the middle of the night. I basically scared the shit out of him. Now he's crying even harder."

Davis pulled out a chair and joined Charlie at the table. "I have to admit, I'm a little involved in your story. So what did you do?"

"What everybody does: I staged a funeral. We put the gross carcass in a shoebox and buried it out back—which was a good distraction, if I say so myself. I also turned him loose on the rest of the pudding packets—also a good distraction."

Davis folded his arms and nodded admiringly. "Charles, if the whole college thing doesn't pan out, and I have no expectation that it will, go be a parent. You will make a nearly adequate one."

"Yeah, it's great fun. Sign me up," Charlie said. "So Gloria eventually comes home and pours us both a soda like we're going to bond. She sits down, tries to like me a little more, doesn't, so I go home and hit the books. And that, cabana boy, is when it hits me: I'm going to get pantsed by these exams. There's so much to know, and I don't know nearly enough of it. Look, I may one day finagle a high school diploma out of the Board of Ed, but there's no way any college will ever take me. I will end up alone in some apartment that's even nastier than this place, and it'll just be me and Tweedy. And then one day Tweedy will bite the dust, and it'll just be me." She ran her hands through her hair and sighed majestically. "Me and a fuck-ton of pudding packets, 'cause those things are delicious."

Davis stared at his young pupil. She'd taken a surprising and accelerated turn for the dark. "When did you become such a bummer?" he asked. "I thought I'm supposed to be Lennon and you're McCartney, not the other way around."

She crinkled her forehead. "And that means . . . ?"

"Never mind. Look—it's perfectly natural to stress out before an exam. It doesn't mean you're going to die alone in some three-story walk-up with a fire escape. Honestly, I don't know if you're a loser or not. What I do know is that you're not a loser *yet*. You can't be. You're only eighteen. That's not how loserdom works."

The sugary scent of baking chocolate overtook the room's baseline odor of dog food—equal parts cardboard and barf—but Davis didn't notice. He was busy noticing Charlie and how all that arrogance and sarcasm, her two most prominent personality traits, concealed an abounding sense of aloneness. That was Charlie's hidden truth: she was alone. Davis didn't know why he hadn't bothered to recognize that before today.

He hunched forward, forearms on his knees, the pose of a guidance counselor. "You have a confidence problem," he said. "I know that's hard to stomach, since I would imagine that for most of your life you've had an *over*confidence problem. But the thing about confidence is that it comes and goes—over the course of a day, over the course of a week, over the course of your life. Take me, for instance. Everyone I've ever known would tell you that I'm the dude who's got it all together."

Charlie snorted. "Yeah, that's certainly been my impression of you, cabana boy."

"I'm not saying it's terribly apparent these days, but for most of my life, things have come very easy to me. Some days I feel exactly like the person everyone thinks I am, and some days I feel so distant from that guy that I have no clue who everyone is looking at."

Somewhere in the apartment, Davis's phone rang.

"Hold that thought," he said.

"Will do, 'cause I'm totally riveted," Charlie muttered, her attention already redirected to the petting of her dog.

Davis located his phone next to a Jasmine action figure, squinted at the number he didn't recognize, and picked up. It was Guy from the rental office.

"I just wanted you to know that I'm leaving," Guy said.

"Okay," Davis said. "You don't have to check in with me. You can just go. You're my boss, I'm not yours."

"No, not I'm leaving for the day. I'm leaving, like, forever. I've resigned."

"Resigned? You mean quit?"

Guy was leaving his job and, as it happened, the state. His girlfriend, Amber, had a cancer-stricken father in Detroit who had taken a turn for the worse. Not only did she want to move back there and spend what time she could with her old man, but once the inevitable came—as, definitionally, it always did—she couldn't envision leaving her mother alone and companionless in Michigan. Guy wasn't sure what he would end up doing out there, although working in an apartment complex rental office had dropped off the list. All he knew was that Amber wanted him to go with her, and that was good enough for him.

Leaving Charlie at the table, Davis slipped outside for some privacy. "Jeez. I'm really sorry, Guy. Sounds like a tough situation."

"Yeah," Guy said, somewhat absently, as though still grasping this drastic realignment of his plans.

"I feel awful for your girlfriend."

"Yeah," Guy mused again. "Oh, hey—don't let anyone catch you with that dog."

Davis snickered guiltily. "I'll try. He's really a well-behaved pug. And his name is Tweedy, after the Wilco guy, not the cartoon bird."

"What cartoon bird?" Guy asked.

"Never mind."

Davis wished him luck and hung up. But his mind refused to move off Amber and her gravely ill father and widow-in-the-making mother. Inside his head these strangers took form, sharpening in clarity until the grim scene unfolded before his eyes. An American-made sedan pulling up a driveway. A weakened man with a ghostly complexion being helped out of the passenger seat by his wife, his eyes sunken from a lifetime of bracing against the Great Lakes chill. Tears came upon Davis and warped everything in view—cars in the parking lot, trees rising up behind the buildings. He rested his forehead against the railing and cried for the suffering of people he would never meet. He snorted and panted. He wiped streaks of snot all down his forearm. He considered sending a card to Amber's family, but how would he sign it? *With prayers and good wishes, Davis Winger, tenant at the apartment complex in Baltimore where your daughter's boyfriend (whom you've perhaps not yet met) worked until his recent resignation.*

He squeezed his eyes shut and tried to force it back.

Dauer. Dempsey.

He'd already had one near-miss with Charlie on that stormy day outside the shower house. If she saw his face now in yet another post-cry bloat, she would have serious concerns about his emotional stability. Maybe rightly so.

Roenicke. Sakata.

The roster of the 1983 Orioles was what had always saved him. His father had taught him the names, positions, batting averages, and ERAs of everyone on that World Series team, and in moments like these, he called upon those hometown heroes to distract him, to parachute him out of the embarrassment of a public weeping. There was no crying in baseball—Tom Hanks had taught him that. And you certainly couldn't cry if you were thinking about a World Series victory over the Phillies in five games. Well, tears of joy, perhaps.

But here was the thing about his little coping mechanism, this handy sports-themed diversion: it never really seemed to work.

Thanks just the same, Tito Landrum and T-Bone Shelby. I think I'll just take my lumps today.

When he stepped back inside the apartment, Charlie, who was down on the floor with Tweedy, looked up at him and immediately went stiff. "Oh shit. What's going on?"

"Nothing," Davis sniffed. "Everything's fine."

"Who was on the phone?"

"It was just Guy."

"Guy? Is he dead or something?"

"No. Guy wasn't calling to tell me he's dead." He wiped the last of his tears onto his sleeves. "He was calling to tell me that he's moving to Detroit. His girlfriend's father is the one who's dead. Or almost dead."

Charlie, who didn't seem to know what to say, said, "Oh."

"Guy's girlfriend's dad has cancer."

"In Detroit?" Charlie said.

"In Detroit," Davis said.

Charlie gazed at Davis's red eyes and damp cheeks. "Okay, so I actually don't know what's going on right now."

"What's going on is"—Davis blew out a breath—"sometimes I cry over things I shouldn't cry over."

Charlie stared at him.

"Remember that day at the pool when I came out of the changing room and you were standing there? You thought I'd been crying, and I denied it? Well, you were right. I'd just overheard some guy talking about his dead sister in Seattle."

Charlie remained knee-to-linoleum, her pink cami stained with canine slobber. "Wait—are you crying because Guy is moving?"

"No."

"Okay. Because that would be really weird. Are you crying because his girlfriend's dad has cancer?"

"Sort of."

"Okay. That's weirder."

"Mostly I'm crying because random bawling is just something I do. It's this quirk, this highly inconvenient quirk I've somehow managed to conceal from everyone my entire life."

Bewilderment reigned on Charlie's face. "I'm not sure what you want me to do. I can get you a tissue . . ."

"No, I don't need a tissue," Davis said. "And I don't want you to *do* anything. I'm telling you this for a reason. This was kind of what I was getting at before Guy called. Nobody in the world—not my wife, my daughter, my sister—no one knows that on a fairly regular basis I'm driven to sobs by events that have virtually nothing to do with me, which is not, as you've already pointed out, normal behavior, and it's also not anything anyone would expect of Davis Winger. But I'm sharing this with you so you can see that things are complicated for everyone. I know you think you're more fucked than the rest of humanity. You're eighteen, so it's kind of your job to believe that. But at eighteen, you're also too dumb to see that that's not how things really are."

He yanked a dish towel off the counter and wiped his nose with it; it felt like a McGuinn thing to do.

"Look, if you fail your exams, it will suck and it will create some problems for you, but it's not likely to alter the long-term course of your life. You don't know this yet, Charlie, but you're going to be okay."

Draping his hand in the snot-strewn towel, he opened the oven and slid the pan of brownies off the rack. This was the first time in his life he'd unburdened himself and told another person about this private glitch that he'd been shouldering solo for so long. It felt strangely good. And a glitch was precisely what it was, for it had always made him feel defective in some constitutional way. He hadn't cried when his mother left, nor when Britt ejected him from the house. He reserved his weeping for things that couldn't actually hurt him, sometimes even for things appallingly undeserving of his tears. Like the West Texas Butcher, the serial killer whose execution he'd read about. This monster, this abominable shit-scrape on the curb of humanity, raped and murdered half a dozen women in ways so unpardonably gruesome that death seemed far too light a punishment. Davis hadn't cried for the victims—no, that would have made sense. Instead, what had upset him was the part of the article that pointed out that not a single friend or family member of the condemned man had shown up at the execution. This man was the West Texas Butcher, but he was also Timothy Heath Carr Jr., and before that he was someone's innocent infant, then someone's bright-eyed crack-up of a boy who loved his superhero action figures and his toy dump trucks and was proud of himself for doing well on a math test and got his feelings hurt when he wasn't invited to a classmate's birthday party, and he died all alone on a table, without a mother or a brother or a friend to watch him go. Ushered out of the world forever while a flock of people looked on and were happy about it. Only Davis Winger cried for him. Two thousand miles away and a week after he was put under the dirt.

"Not for nothing," Charlie offered, "but moving to Detroit is a perfectly reasonable thing to cry about. Don't beat yourself up over it."

Davis went to the fridge and took out a soda for his guest and a beer for himself. He sat down at the table and swigged loudly. Except for the hum of the air-conditioning unit, the world had gone silent.

"I always thought that having one thing that set me off into a disturbance wasn't so bad," he said. "Until I realized that most people don't have any."

"Oh, please," Charlie snorted. "I have, like, ten. I'm expelled, I'm a bully, I'm unprepared for my finals, I'm well on my way to a pot dependency, I'm a child of an ugly divorce, I'm Canadian, I'm Canadian but I'm also unlikable—who ever heard of that?—my vocabulary sucks, no colleges love me, very few people love me, and I use the expression 'Nobody puts baby in a corner' but I've never actually seen *Dirty Dancing*. None of this is okay. So I may not be a crybaby like you, but I've got issues, cabana man."

Davis laughed, then slurped. "I've heard your symptoms, and I'm diagnosing you as being a teenager. Don't worry. It's treatable."

"Well, I've heard your symptoms, and I'm diagnosing you as being the sensitive type," Charlie said. "Stage four."

But that wasn't exactly it, though, was it? Davis wasn't the sensitive type. He was something else. The sensitive type found a piano in the middle of a party and played "Against All Odds." The sensitive type stewed all weekend after some jerk made fun of his shirt. Davis's emotional disturbances weren't personal to him. They were a reaction to the immutable drift of pain, the sorrow that shrouded all lives. Bad things happened in his life—that was sad, but generally solvable. But bad things were constantly happening in everyone's lives all the time—that was sadness, and it was here to stay.

"You know, you and I might be more alike than you want to think," Charlie said.

"If we're alike at all, it's more than I want to think," Davis replied. "Now go hit the books, Hawking. Hydrostatics isn't going to study itself."

She let out a grievous groan.

"Relax," he told her. "You'll be ready."

"You really think I'm going to pass?"

"I didn't say that. I said you'll be ready."

Out came her middle finger. "You're all blasé now, but if I fail, you're going to blubber like a punk-ass baby."

"If it means you end up sticking around here, yeah, I'll be devastated," he said. "No doubt about that."

CHAPTER 35

We are animals. Animals form attachments to things, especially to other animals. That, Davis told himself, was why he felt his heart muscles clench when Britt appeared at his apartment to drop off Rachel. She'd been inside so few times that it was jarring to have her there, his own wife a guest in this space where he lived and she did not.

"Interesting decorating flourishes," Britt observed, not quite sure what to make of the profusion of otherworldly trinkets and adornments, her elegance overwhelming the dismal room.

Davis stuffed his hands into the pockets of his shorts and attempted a mysterious grin. "Rach and I are having a party. It's an exclusive guest list, but I might know someone who could get you an invite."

Rachel was down on the floor trying to coax Tweedy into conversation by looking him dead in the eye and repeating the word *woof* over and over. Occasionally, she tried *bark*.

"What are you celebrating?" Britt asked him.

"Why, the Sultan of the Indies, of course. It's complete. I mentioned our little project, didn't I?"

Britt nodded. "Right. The roller coaster."

"Rach and I would really prefer that you not call it a roller coaster," he said. "It's more of a feat of engineering exotica. If you need a shorthand, you can call it a flying carpet. Magic carpet is also acceptable."

"Forgive me," Britt said, moseying over to his work table and eyeing the model with measured appreciation. It resembled a dinosaur skeleton in miniature. "It's quite beautiful. Rach, did you really help Daddy build this?"

"I was the big-picture girl," Rachel replied.

"Which is the most important role in any project," Davis added.

Britt smiled with just enough warmth that Davis dared hope she might be seduced into staying. "How about a brownie?" he offered. "Fresh from the oven. You know I make a mean brownie."

"Since when?" Britt chuckled. "The last time you attempted to bake anything, you gashed your finger opening the mix, used salt instead of sugar, and then forgot to turn the oven on."

"That's nitpicking, isn't it," he said, doing his best *Spinal Tap* Christopher Guest.

"Thanks for the offer, but I can't stay," she said. Then she changed the subject. "It's nice that you're helping that high school student."

Britt and Rachel had arrived just as Charlie was getting ready to leave. When his wife walked in on them, he felt like he'd been busted, as if this attractive young woman's presence in his apartment were illegal, inappropriate, or just otherwise wrong. But when he made introductions, Britt had smiled and said, "Oh sure. Davis has mentioned you. You're the physics student," and Charlie had looked astonished and remarked, "Never thought I'd hear anyone call me that." Rachel had wanted to know why Charlie appeared to be a girl but had a boy's name, so Charlie explained that it was only a nickname. "What's your real name?" Rachel had asked.

"Franklin," Charlie had deadpanned. Then she'd thanked Rachel for taking such good care of her pug. "He really likes you," she'd said.

"He does? How do you know?" Rachel had asked.

"He told me," Charlie had replied.

That encounter could've been awkward all over the place. The wife could've felt threatened by the eighteen-year-old hottie in the bloom of her comeliness, or the teenager could've felt overpowered by the self-possessed adult striding in awhirl with purpose and clamoring with keys. But Britt made people feel uncomfortable only when she wanted to, and she didn't seem to want to. Which was a relief. It was also a tad depressing. Britt had discovered her husband behind closed doors with a fetching girl in a tight camisole (an article of clothing not always diligent about concealing its wearer's navel), and had evidently thought nothing of it. Davis had hoped to cling to sexual relevance longer than this.

Strolling about the room, Britt paused to consider a painting on the wall, a framed print Molly had brought over during one of her decorating interventions. The painting was of a remote lake nestled in a forest of sickly trees. As the milky dawn was just beginning to pour itself into the thick night sky, a lone cottage could be seen at the lake's edge. It was a scene of lonely, desolate beauty and almost unbearable stillness.

"Molly got me that," Davis said. "You like it?"

"No," Britt said, turning away from it.

She readjusted her pocketbook strap on her shoulder and knelt down to Rachel for a goodbye kiss. "Well, looks like you two are in for quite a celebration. Congratulations on your model. I'll see you tomorrow, baby love."

Davis found himself compelled to speak up. "Uh, Rach. Does Mommy think that all we've built is a model?"

Rachel lifted herself up off the floor and straightened her dress, which was the yellow of a runny omelet. The three of them exchanged pregnant looks.

"She doesn't know," Davis said, grinning collusively with his six-year-old.

"What don't I know?" Britt asked.

"You see, Mommy," Davis began, with a ringmaster's showmanship, "when Rachel came up with this mind-blowing idea for a magic carpet, we both knew right off the bat that this was a concept that couldn't be contained on the puny scale of a model. It wasn't meant to be constructed with tiny plastic pieces and set out on some sad table, admired like some dust-gathering artifact. The Sultan of the Indies was a dream—oh yes, a most magnificent dream—but it was never meant to remain a dream. Rachel, please tell your mother what the Sultan was truly meant for."

With the seriousness of a supernova, the little girl parked her eyes on Britt and said, "It was meant to be rode."

"You heard the lady," Davis said. "It was meant to be rode."

"I'm confused," Britt said, looking confused. "So it's not a model?"

"It's not *just* a model," Davis clarified.

"Oh! Somebody actually built it?"

"Well, no, not yet."

"So right now it's still just a model."

"Will you just let us do our thing here? You're killing the moment."

"Sorry."

Davis cleared his throat. "Now then. Look around the room. Feast your eyes on the relics of ancient India! Feel yourselves transported, and prepare . . . to fly!"

Rachel and Britt shared an eye roll, and Davis turned on *Persian Nights Dance Mix Volume 3* (which was essentially *Brooklyn Nights Dance Mix Volume 3* with singers sounding native to Greater Iran) and flicked off the lights. The room glowed gold from the tiny bulbs inside the plastic lamps.

"Welcome to the Middle East in the Middle Ages," Davis intoned somewhat nonspecifically, his face half-lit by the domes of a toy palace.

Britt said, "Ooh."

Davis said, "Ooh."

Rachel said, "Why do you have a sword? There's no sword in the story."

"I think it came with the vase," Davis said.

"What vase?"

"I mean the lamp. Should I just start over?"

"No!" they said in unison.

Davis exhaled. "Maybe we should just watch the video."

The oriental rug had barely the expanse of a bathmat, but the three of them managed to scrunch on it together like passengers in a canoe. Rachel took the bow, Britt sat in the middle, and Davis slid behind them at the stern. They faced the large rectangular computer monitor Davis had lowered onto a crate so that it was eye level for viewers seated on the floor. In full-screen mode, the monitor showed the passengers' point of view, like a YouTube video posted by a thrill rider wearing a GoPro.

Davis instructed the women to keep all hands and feet inside the vehicle at all times; then he clicked the arrow in the center of the screen, and the video commenced.

Off they went. From the moment of departure, there was an uncommon fluidity and finesse to the way they moved through space. The software rendered everything in amazingly realistic definition: virtual tracks, virtual loops, virtual sky and trees, virtual people on the ground. And while it required leaps of imagination to meet the promise of a truly immersive experience, all three riders were game for latching on to the fantasy. When the animation zoomed them up and away, they oohed and aahed as if they were actually shooting up into thin air. When it spun them around in ascending corkscrews, they howled as if they were actually disoriented and dizzy. At one point, Davis reached over Britt's shoulder to ruffle Rachel's hair, and the little girl didn't even turn her head, for she was pirouetting through the air and could spare him no more than a thumbs-up for fear of missing something awesome.

Britt turned back to him, clearly impressed. "This is amazing," she whispered.

"Tell the kid," he whispered back. "It was her idea."

He thought he could read something on Britt's face. He hoped—prayed—that what he saw was the simple, effortless, pain-free joy of having their family complete again, her husband right behind her, her daughter right in front. She was pining for it just like he was, longing for that wholeness, just like on that spring day at the fair.

He yearned to touch her, to grip her shoulders, to make circles on her back with the palm of his hand. He wanted her to hear him say, *I'm sorry, Britt. I'm so sorry*, and to know how much he meant it.

But he held it all back. He sat there, swept away with these two precious women aboard the windblown wisps of a flying rug, content to just savor the ride.

CHAPTER 36

The bar McGuinn suggested was called Assassins & Cons. It had been open for business in the same location in the Hampden neighborhood since 1979. When Molly looked up the address and learned that its name was borrowed from a Steely Dan song, which in full referenced "assassins, cons, and rapers," it only heightened her unease. Why hadn't the proprietors chosen a more wholesome Steely Dan lyric, perhaps something about Rikki losing somebody's number, or Jack going back and doing it again?

Although McGuinn had given her fair warning that an invitation for a proper date might be forthcoming, she was still caught off guard when he actually called. It just seemed like a waste of everyone's time. When she reminded him that she was in a relationship, he told her he hadn't forgotten, he'd heard her the first time, moving on.

The fact that Zach was currently on his Vegas trip injected an air of illicitness into this get-together, and Molly was, to say the least, unaccustomed to illicit behavior.

She arrived early. She'd never been to this bar before and thought she might need a few minutes to find it. That was because Molly had yet to fully embrace blind faith in GPS, a technology that still took her breath away. One day everyone looked down, and in the palm of our hand was this machine that knew every single road in the world, and it knew exactly which one you were driving on, and it told you when to turn, and it found you the closest gas station or Subway, and it was the size of a candy bar, and you could take it wherever you went and it still knew exactly where you were, and everyone could have one, and if you plugged it into your car with a flimsy wire, it talked to you, a reassuringly tyrannical female robot who knew just what to do whether you were in Midtown Manhattan or Burnt Corn, Alabama. Everyone took her for granted, this officious know-it-all hiding inside the Twix-size machine, but damned if she didn't get everybody where they needed to be exactly when they needed to be there.

The front door of the place had a cartoon tongue painted on it. Pink, steamy, and glistening with spit, the organ salivated at Molly. She entered anyway, and found a quiet table against a wall of exposed brick. Industrial ductwork stretched out across the ceiling. Air-conditioning wafted overhead with the freshness of a flipped pillow.

She'd said nothing of this rendezvous to Davis, as he surely would not have lent it his blessing. But then the stereo was playing that old Creedence Clearwater Revival song "The Midnight Special," and Molly couldn't help but think that her brother was there in the bar with her, perhaps spying on her. Davis had been obsessed with classic rock practically since birth (never mind that by the time he was born, they'd stopped making it), and through his bedroom walls there'd always been a steady flow of music from a vast, impenetrable Milky Way in which Davis was a local and Molly a curious foreigner, fumbling around for her bearings, figuring out little by little that Stevie Wonder and Steve Winwood were different people, that Stevie Nicks was a woman, and that Van Morrison was the singer's full name. (He wasn't, like, Ludwig van Morrison; it wasn't an Eddie Van Halen situation.) This galaxy was exciting and dangerous and pretentious as hell, for it had routinely prompted Davis to say things like, "Man, what an exhilarating chord change!" or "Listen to the notes he *doesn't* play." He'd once declared that it was unarguable—you couldn't argue with it!—that "Down by the

Seaside," "Ten Years Gone," and "Night Flight" on *Physical Graffiti* were the greatest three consecutive songs on any album ever. It was a claim he would go on to make in regards to at least a dozen other albums.

In those days, the classic rock station held a competition each morning called "Sing for Your Song," and Davis would often dial in to participate while getting dressed for school. It was a dreadful contest in which listeners were invited to call in and belt out a few lines from their favorite song, of which there were apparently only three in those days, because pretty much everyone sang "American Woman" by The Guess Who, "Roxanne" by The Police, or "Aqualung" by Jethro Tull. On one such morning, Davis dialed in and launched into "The Midnight Special":

> Let the midnight special shine a light on me,
> Let the midnight special shine a ever-lovin' light on me.

The song brought Norman strutting down the hall, crooning along in that square, dad-like manner, and Molly watched from her doorway as father and son, both still only half-dressed, serenaded the rush hour traffic while Davis held the phone out between them.

Later, when Molly and Davis had assembled around the breakfast table, their father came downstairs, asking, "You know what that song is about, don't you?"

They didn't.

"It's about a train," Norman explained. He was standing over them, tying his tie while they consumed the waffles and oranges that Peti had set down on the table. "It's an old traditional folk song, so no one knows for sure, but legend has it that the singer was an inmate at a prison in Sugar Land, Texas. There was a train that ran past the prison in the middle of the night—this was probably 1920 or so—and the inmates believed that if the light from the locomotive shone into your cell, that was a sign that you were going to be set free come morning. The prisoners would all stay up late, praying that it would be their cell that night. So you see, kids, the Midnight Special is the train of redemption, and its headlight is salvation, a light that comes along in the dead of night to save you, no matter what your prison is, no matter how dark your night." At that, he dumped his coffee into the sink and kissed Peti on the mouth. "You, Petra Kovacs, are my Midnight Special," he said, and out the door he went.

———

Like a train running on schedule, McGuinn came through the door of Assassins & Cons at the top of the hour. He spied Molly, shined the light of his smile on her, and lumbered over to her table, his alpine shoulders rolling under his royal-blue polo.

"You showed up," he said.

"Did you expect me not to?"

"You think you'd have been the first to stand me up?"

A cocktail waitress instantly materialized. She was a forbidding pixie of a girl under a jagged rug of black hair, and Molly decided that she was either an art student or a petty criminal. Instead of greeting her new customers, the server merely raised her eyebrows. Molly ordered a Heineken, and McGuinn seemed happy about that. For some reason, men liked to learn that a woman had a taste for beer.

"Got any Knob Creek back there?" he asked the harsh creature with the pencil behind her ear.

"Neat? Rocks?"

"Nothing but the glass, ma'am." McGuinn spotted a tattoo on the woman's forearm. It was a rudimentary drawing of a sailboat, something Rachel might sketch, right down to the string of *u*'s representing the ocean. He looked up at her and said, "A smooth sea never made a skilled sailor."

Her burning mouselike eyes cooled. "Well then," she said, and they exchanged sly grins like members of a secret society long ago outlawed.

When she walked away, McGuinn gave Molly a modest shrug. "My buddy owns a tattoo parlor. It's a long story."

Molly couldn't help but find something appealing about this man. He was rugged, more so than outright handsome, and constitutionally physical, with an intriguing scar on his chin that reinforced her impression that he was a veteran of brawls, altercations, and accidents involving heavy machinery. This was someone who couldn't leave home without knowing his own blood type. McGuinn was precisely the opposite of Zacharias Klinefelter, a guy who didn't get hurt so much as he got his feelings hurt. Zach's physical injuries were reserved for cloddish accidents like bumping his head on the open trunk of his car. Or taking a tennis racquet to the nose.

"I'm dying to hear about your baseball career," she said. "If it's not a touchy subject."

"Now, that would be a *short* story," he said. "And a pretty boring one. Not nearly as interesting as the exploits of a nationally syndicated columnist. But you did ask me first, and fair is fair."

Throwing a fastball was one of the only things McGuinn was ever good at, but he was exceptionally good at it. It got him recruited by Arizona State and, four years later, drafted by the San Francisco Giants, who were keen on grooming him as their next fire-throwing starter, an anchor in their rotation for years to come. He moved briskly through the farm system, developing a formidable reputation for his filthy pitches. And also for feistiness. He dusted off many a batter, beaned plenty, too, and was often awarded an early shower by intolerant umpires.

When the coaches had deemed him ready, the organization shipped him to the majors, and in his very first big-league start, with two outs in the fourth inning, a runner on second, and Ramon Blanco at the plate, he threw a two-seam fastball right down the middle. Blanco was one of the league's best sluggers, but he was mired in an 0-for-18 slump at the time, and the arrogant rookie on the mound thought he could blow it past him. He didn't. Ramon got a big fat piece of it and cracked a comebacker that McGuinn never even saw. Like a flash of light in the corner of his eye, the ball struck him in the right temple.

"It was just—boom!—lights out," McGuinn said, smiling easily. "One minute I'm hurling a fastball toward the catcher's mitt, the next minute I'm flat on my back, some ugly old trainer telling me not to move. It was just a concussion, but I was never the same after that. It messed with my head. I was out of baseball within a year."

Molly was shaking her head. "That's terrible. I can't even imagine the disappointment."

"It certainly wasn't optimal. Look, do I wish like hell it hadn't gone down that way? Sure. But it did. And the thing is, if I had it to do all over again, I'd still throw that bastard the same damn pitch. Maybe I'd put it on the outside corner."

"Sounds like you've made peace with it," Molly said.

"If I hadn't by now, I'd be sleeping under a bridge somewhere. Things could be a lot worse. I don't mind working for my brother. He's a good kid, runs a fine construction business. And anyway, boo-hoo for me, right? I took the mound in a major league baseball game. Every kid's dream." He reclined into the beam of an overhead floodlight, and his face took on an air of reflection. "'A truck carves the valley of burning pine; there are old men in the branches.' Emily Dickinson, I think. Maybe Robert Frost. I don't remember."

"What's with you and poets?" Molly asked, her eyes tightening, a grin flowering. "You did that in my brother's apartment, the night I met you. You quoted Whitman."

"Was your brother serving me cheap beer? I tend to bust out Walt when I'm drinking cheap beer. Now, bourbon—that brings out Emily."

"I never would've figured you to be a closet poetry reader," she said.

"Who says I'm not out and proud?" he boasted. "But you're right. I'm very much closeted. You're not recording this, are you? I don't trust you journalists."

"We're off the record," she said, and raised her beer to her lips.

McGuinn suggested they order some food, so they perused the laminated bookmark of a menu, agreeing on a spinach-and-artichoke dip and a french fry concoction with Old Bay and jalapeños. McGuinn also took the liberty of getting them both another round. When the server with the sailboat tattoo listened and nodded but committed nothing to her pad, McGuinn grew concerned.

"You're not going to write any of this down?" he asked her.

"Nope," the server replied. "Does that make you nervous?"

"It's just about the only thing I can think of that does make me nervous."

"Sounds like a whole lot of your problem. I'm still not going to write it down." And she walked away.

It was McGuinn's turn to play journalist. He wanted to know everything about Maternity Leave and the sudden notoriety for which Molly felt so unprepared and undeserving. Because his interest seemed sincere, and because she'd had a drink, she shared with him every unlikely development. She told him what a surreal adventure it was to wake up every day and remember all over again that she had a story on the *Lotus* website, that photos of Kate Middleton and Chris Hemsworth were inches away from a link to her podcast, that she had a podcast! The amount of horsepower being brought to bear by Jamie Okoye and her staff was nothing less than heart-stopping. They seemed in a fever to rush this product to market, to get the articles up on the website and printed in the very next issue. Only two episodes of the podcast had been released when Molly's college friend Sara texted her, saying, Why is my phone recommending your podcast??? Who are you??? Such was the heavy roll of the *Lotus* promotional machine.

"I honestly don't get it," she told McGuinn, her laughter, like her voice, louder now than usual. "It literally makes no sense. I mean, have you read some of these pieces?"

"All of them," he replied.

"Wait—really?"

"How many celebs do you think I know?"

She stared at him. She was confounded by him. "You're not at all what I expected."

"And what exactly did you expect?"

"Less Emily Dickinson, more spitting into a cup."

McGuinn's fluency in Molly's output more than validated her decision to come out here tonight and sip not one but two drinks at a dangerously named watering hole with a former pitcher for the San Francisco Giants. Was this what "fame" wrought? How far a cry this was from an evening out with Zach, where she generally sat bored and restless, listening to him and his roommates overuse the word *dude* and watching them guffaw at unfunny faux pas they hyperbolically deemed *classic*.

Across the table, Molly detected a subtle shift in McGuinn's demeanor, something quietly undoing his composure. He looked, for the very first time since she'd met him, uncomfortable, as though there were some skirmish catching fire behind his eyes.

"Did I say something wrong?" she asked, his tenseness contagious. "You know I was just joking about the spitting thing."

He shook his head. "Actually, you raised a good point, something I should probably clear up."

Molly didn't realize she'd made any point at all.

"I have kind of a confession to make," he continued. "I don't know why, but I feel like I can be open and honest with you, even though you're a reporter, and showing honesty to a reporter goes against every rule in the book." He took a breath. "I'm just going to say this."

"You're making me nervous," Molly said.

"And you have the opposite effect on me," he told her. "The thing is, I might have lied before. That whole bit about 'a truck carves the valley of burning pine'—that ain't Emily Dickinson. And the Walt Whitman line I quoted at your brother's place the night we met—that ain't Walt Whitman. I don't quote Whitman when I drink beer, I don't quote Dickinson when I drink bourbon, and I don't know what kind of a pompous idiot would say such a thing."

She stared at him over their refills. A Hammond organ on Bob Dylan's "Like a Rolling Stone" bleated in the background.

McGuinn dipped his head. "Would you think any less of me if I told you I wrote poetry?"

She stared blankly at him, and he stared back. She wasn't getting it, until at last her jaw dropped. "You were quoting *you*?"

He nodded carefully. "That's kind of my covert way of letting my lines out of the barn and seeing how they run in broad daylight. I attribute them to the masters. I find fewer people laugh in my face that way."

Molly was dubious. "Are you messing with me?"

He held his palms open. "These are our truths, scratched from the dirt, hidden among the leaves."

"I think you're messing with me."

"Scout's honor." He leaned in so close she could make out another scar, a faint one carved above his left eye. "It's not something I throw around. Or more accurately, I've never told anyone. Ever. So I hope you're good with a secret."

Molly was flattered that he'd chosen her to receive his confession, but amazed that he'd never revealed to anyone else what was obviously a talent. "You don't strike me as the bashful type," she told him.

"Oh, I'm not shy, but I'm not stupid either, and I know when there's something I should be shy about."

Yet he'd fooled her, handily passing off his own verse as that of Walt Whitman. "I really don't think you have anything to be ashamed of," she said.

"Molly Winger, I've lived most of my life on or near baseball diamonds, locker rooms, and construction sites, and I have not found them to be poet-friendly environments. Being good at it wouldn't make it any less of a crime."

McGuinn proceeded to describe how he'd been deaf to his poetic inclinations until his undergraduate education forced his nose into it. Showing up at ASU on an athletic scholarship, he staked out as undemanding a course load as he could. That led him to the famously painless Writing and Reading Poetry, a class populated with students whose approach to academics might best be described as carefree. Literally— they didn't care. A month or so into the semester, after he'd submitted a handful of assignments, his professor, an edgy African American with a shaved head and a goatee, asked him to stay after class. McGuinn knew the drill: he would listen with humility and contrition as the prof took him to task for his insulting lack of engagement, and he would promise to do better next time. But instead, the professor asked a few questions, reminded him that plagiarism was an expellable offense, and then admitted that McGuinn's verse had blown him away.

"You've written poetry before, I take it," the professor had inquired.

"Fuck no, bro," McGuinn had replied with a derisive cackle.

"Never?"

"I know a few limericks, if you wanna hear one?"

The prof folded his arms and frowned. "But you've read a lot of poetry."

McGuinn adjusted his cap and blew a bubble with his Big League Chew. "Come on, Teach. Do I look like a guy who's read a lot of poetry?"

He had talent, the professor told him—talent that deserved to be nurtured, talent worthy of commitment. McGuinn didn't see it that way. He had pitching mechanics worthy of his commitment, a curveball that deserved to be nurtured.

But the more poetry he wrote for class, the more he took to it and found the unlikeliest joy in composing quatrains, sonnets, haiku, and stanzas in free form. He wrote poetry in the library stacks when he should've been studying. He wrote poetry late at night in his dorm. He wrote poetry on the bus after games to the snoring of his fellow players and coaches. He kept it all hidden from what would have been mercilessly mocking teammates, but he never stopped.

"It got me through the injury," he revealed to Molly. "I don't mean to go all cornball, but it kind of kept me sane when my career went down the tubes."

"Have you ever tried to get published, even anonymously?" she asked. "I might be able to help."

McGuinn shook his head. "Very kind of you, but that doesn't interest me. It's not why I told you either. I'm not after your Rolodex. I scribble my little poems in my trusty notebook, and I have no plans for anyone to read them except me. Maybe my wife gets to peek. My kids will find the notebook after I'm dead and go, 'Dad did this? That clown?'"

Molly wondered why anyone would want to be so unknown to his own children. She continued to deplete the contents of her second Heineken bottle, trying not to look as stunned by this man as she was.

"So why did you tell me?" she asked.

"I don't know," he drawled. His discomfort was gone now, blown off like a weather pattern. "I could lie and say it's because you're the only writer I know, so you were a safe bet not to make fun of me. But the truth is, you just seem like the kind of person you tell such a thing to. Maybe that's why your new column is so bangin'. The people of the world open up to Molly Winger. That's quite a cross you're bearing."

They drank their drinks and regarded each other with mutual fascination.

Eventually he asked, "Isn't your boyfriend displeased that you're out here with me tonight?"

"He doesn't know," Molly said, sinking guiltily. "He's in Las Vegas."

"Good golly, Miss Molly. Aren't you a scandal!"

"Am I? Isn't it more scandalous to go to Vegas than to stay behind?"

"I'm not much of a Vegas guy myself. All the gambling and artificial light. I know it doesn't fit the profile."

"Oh, there's no profile anymore," Molly said. "The profile has been smashed to pieces."

When the appetizers arrived, Molly bit into a fry, made a noise of intense gratification, and declared that she could eat french fries at every meal. McGuinn countered that he pretty much did eat french fries at every meal. Molly proceeded to tell him how, as a little girl, she would wait all year long for the family trips to Ocean City just for the Thrasher's, indisputably the best fries anywhere. On those summer vacations with her father and brother, they would go to the boardwalk in the evenings and Norman would buy strips of yellow tickets so that they could go on all the rides. Davis, of course, gravitated to the big white roller coaster that loomed over the pier, but Molly loved the Himalaya, that wheel of connected cars that spun them around and around at a speed that sucked the breath from her lungs. She remembered the way the three of them would get pressed together in a shrieking cluster while Def Leppard roared over them. Then, with the sigh of the waves somewhere out in the darkness, they'd consume their fries and chocolate fudge while sitting on the boardwalk, their legs dangling over the side of the splintery planks, their eyes on the green neon rings being tossed on the beach by unlit figures. One time, a gull swooped down and stole a fry right out of Molly's fingers, and she cried and cried until Davis fed one of his own fries to a hovering bird, just to show it was okay.

"There's something I have to know," Molly said, emboldened by two hours with this guy, time that had coursed by like no time at all. "Something I feel like I should know by now."

"I'll certainly try to help," he said.

"Is McGuinn your last name or your first?"

He chuckled a bit. "Well. A little of both."

It was all she got out of him.

Later, as he refused her money and paid the check, he said, "Tell me again why you wouldn't date someone like me."

"I don't know. We're just so different. Aren't we?"

"Isn't that what people say right before they hook up?"

"It's also what they say right before they shake hands and thank each other for a very nice evening."

"Fair enough," he said. "I did have a nice evening, and I thank you for that. But I'm probably going to ask you out again. You don't have to say yes, but be forewarned."

"Okay," she said, laughing at his forthrightness. "Thanks for the heads-up. I'll probably say yes."

Outside the bar, just as they were about to part, he put a finger over his lips. "You'll keep my secret, right?"

She said she would. "It is a really cool secret."

"Think so?" he said. "Most days it's a terrible secret. I think it's terrible to have secrets."

CHAPTER 37

Turned out, Heather Baskin was serious about Davis stopping into her office to meet with Brian Ong. She called him on her first day back from her Outer Banks vacation.

"We won't even call it an interview," she said. "It'll just be an informal chat."

"But I have to wear pants, right?" Davis asked. He was smudging sunscreen onto his nose just out of range of the obnoxious splashing of those Crockett-Johnson twins.

"How's tomorrow?" Heather asked. "I know that sounds kind of desperate, but Brian is free, and after that, things get a little hectic for me. My kids start school next week, and then there's Rosh Hashanah and Yom Kippur. I know—I just played the Jew card. Can you blame me? It's been so effective throughout history."

The following day, Davis slid into a pair of slacks and drove downtown. He brought along his laptop and a manila folder crammed with sketches of his summer project. He wasn't sure why.

IlluMind was like Pavelka's hotter sister, the one you had no shot with. The moment you stepped into the lobby and smelled the pumped-in aroma of moist tree bark and you experienced the leather furniture and took a gander at the receptionist, both of them more glossy and taut than what they had over at P&G, you fell victim to its promise.

It was clean and futuristic, like an Epcot exhibit, and the conference room into which Heather guided Davis shimmered with state-of-the-art phone and video technology. Anyone intent on structurally engineering anything would want to do it here. So why was Davis suddenly suffering an identity crisis? Why did he feel so out of place here? For all the distress and botheration of the past few months, Pavelka & Gates still smelled like home, not like forestry and orange peel. So much of his life had turned out different; would it be so wrong to just go back to his old office and indulge his hunger for familiar things?

Brian Ong greeted him in a crisp white shirt with the sleeves rolled up past his wrists. He had short hair, a meticulous tan, and a resting face that set his mouth at a perfectly level horizontal line. He was not much older than Davis, and possibly, inexcusably, younger.

As Heather and Brian sat down across from him at the table, Davis braced for a grilling on the flume accident. Naturally, a prospective employer would want to know his take on what had gone wrong and why he wouldn't be a liability. Davis had decided he would stand behind his work product, but do so with minimal defensiveness, defensiveness being an unattractive quality. He might point out that if there had been a problem with the design of the ride, all the regulators and their battery of inspections had missed it. The official report exonerating P&G—and Davis personally—hadn't yet been made public, so the furthest he could go on that front was to project quiet smugness.

The accident was, in fact, the first thing Brian brought up. "We know all about the incident at the High Seas property in Virginia, and quite candidly, from what I've read, I struggle to see how it was Pavelka's fault. If there's anything you feel we must know, we're happy to listen. Otherwise, I see no need to belabor it."

Davis shrugged. "I'm good."

And that was the end of it.

Brian then generally described the firm's current projects, which were numerous and diverse. Most were in the design stage, as that was the meat of any engineering firm's involvement, but some had progressed to the construction phase, which required the firm's consultation and oversight.

"If you were to start today, there would be three or four projects that could immediately use your help," Brian told him. "The industry is in an upswing right now, as I'm sure you know, and park owners are really investing in their properties. We need a set of hands, and yours would do quite nicely."

Davis glanced at Heather, then back at Brian. "Sorry—are you offering me a job?"

"You're a known quantity, Davis. Your record speaks for itself." Then Brian offered him a salary that was $35,000 more than he'd earned at Pavelka.

Davis was lost for words. An hour ago he was a poor man's Flamingo Kid.

"Forgive me," he said. "I just wasn't expecting this. Like, at all."

"Oh, bullshit," Heather said, pointing to Davis's manila folder, out of which some of his papers were peeking. "You brought a résumé. And what are those, diagrams? Aren't you adorable. Want to tell us your undergraduate GPA?"

Brian gave a mild smile. "Yeah, none of that will be necessary. Plus, we obviously can't look at anything you brought from your old firm."

"Oh no, these aren't Pavelka's," Davis was quick to say.

And all at once he knew exactly why he'd tossed these diagrams and renderings into the car with him. This was an interview, all right, but it was he who was interviewing them. The flying carpet ride meant more to him than any job ever could. It was one of the last threads connecting him to his family, his house, his dream—to the Davis Winger he'd pissed away. Building the Sultan wouldn't necessarily fix things, but letting it go would guarantee that he would remain broken.

"If you've got a minute," he said, "I can show you how I spent my summer vacation."

He opened up the folder and divulged the whole story. The book his daughter loved. Their vision for the ride. The simulation of magic carpet flight through magnetic levitation technology, smooth and frictionless, an airy glide through batwings and boomerangs, corkscrews and vertical rolls, riders slicing the wind at impossible inclines and four-G free fall.

Brian and Heather studied the sketches. They leafed through the pages with a skeptic's eye.

"You do know how expensive maglev is," Brian said to him. "It's a money pit. Just ask any of the countries that have tried to build a rail system with it."

"Yeah, I know," Davis said.

Amusement park owners could jack up their ticket prices only so high to recoup their construction costs, so maglev had basically been tossed out the window. But Davis had made the ride work. Figuring out how to make it profitable was someone else's concern.

"What about stability?" Heather asked. "Isn't that a problem when you're working with magnets?"

"Absolutely, Heather," Davis replied. "I gave that a lot of attention. Stability shouldn't be an issue with the way I've designed it. Take a look."

Brian made a face at the wealth of drawings and schematics splayed out on the table. "I don't know. Wouldn't this work better as a virtual reality ride? The ride you seem to be envisioning would lend itself well to VR, and it would be a lot easier."

Davis smiled politely, but shook his head. "That's actually not at all the ride I'm envisioning."

It was true that more and more rides were built around virtual reality. But they weren't rides. They were movie theaters in which your chair rocked and rattled and large fans blew air at you to simulate wind. You didn't actually go anywhere. That wasn't the Sultan. The Sultan of his daughter's dreams was not a glorified video game.

"I'll tell you what," Davis said, lifting his computer bag off the floor, a sly gleam in his eye. "Why don't you ride it?" He pointed to the enormous video screen at the far end of the conference table. "Can I access that on your Wi-Fi?"

He booted up the simulator and took the liberty of dimming the lights. He knew he was being a little theatrical, but screw it—the Sultan was entitled to grandiosity. It deserved a little overdoing.

While Brian and Heather watched the sim on the big screen, Davis chimed in like an excited sixth grader showing off his science fair volcano. He pointed out how he'd adjusted the radii of his clothoid loops, those inverted teardrops borrowed from Kepler, to reduce the electromagnetic force needed to carry passengers up the incline. He showed them the external braking mechanism on the cars, an added safety feature for a train that hovered over the track instead of gripping it wheel to steel.

One hundred sixty-three seconds later, the ride ended and the simulator file went to black. Brian and Heather each removed their glasses. They had a lot of questions. They wanted to know about materials, about on-site space requirements, about comparable engineering undertakings and the success or failure thereof, about areas in the budget where Davis could see flexibility. The barrage of challenges kept coming, and Davis met them, battling back against their skepticism not with the heat of emotion, but with the cool of science.

"Look, guys, only a park developer with a certain kind of vision is going to splurge on this," Davis acknowledged. "This is not a magic carpet–themed ride. This is a magic carpet ride. And I know it can work. If you look at the blueprints, you'll see that." Out came the winning Winger smile. "This is the kind of ride you put front and center on the park's brochure, on the home page of the website. This is the kind of ride that opens parks."

"You don't take pills for an ego deficiency, do you, Winger?" Heather said. She rolled her eyes at Brian. "He's always like this."

Brian then asked Heather to join him in his office for a minute, so they excused themselves and left Davis alone in the conference room. He perused the tea chest, each packet decorated with an ornate design, and helped himself to a cup of coffee from the stainless-steel kettle. Gazing out the window, he imagined the conversation taking place down the hall. *Who does this guy think he is? I know, right? Talk about delusions of grandeur. Let's rescind the job offer and get him out of the building. I hope he's not in there drinking the expensive tea.* They wouldn't be wrong to think those things. Davis had waltzed into the top engineering firm in the city and claimed to have rewritten the playbook. His reputation may have been solid, but it wasn't that solid, and in fact, in recent months, it was the opposite of solid. Anyway, on-the-spot job offers were too good to be true, the kind of thing that happened only in movies—like sex in restaurant bathrooms, or knockdown fistfights that ended in handshakes of mutual respect. And the truth was, Davis may have believed that the Sultan could work, but he didn't *know* it could work, and the fact that nothing like it had ever worked before was probably all these guys needed to know.

A few moments later, Brian and Heather strode back into the room and didn't sit down.

"Have you been to Turkey?" Brian asked him.

Davis blinked. "The country in Europe?"

"I think it's mostly in Asia," Heather said. "But I'll look that up."

"I have meetings there in a few weeks," Brian said. "A consortium is planning to build a slew of rides in parks across Asia and Europe, and they're convening a group of engineers in Izmir to discuss new projects and listen to pitches."

Davis nodded agreeably.

"Izmir is supposed to be quite beautiful," Brian went on. "It's a coastal city, on the Aegean Sea. Lots of Ottoman history. Clock towers and bazaars, great beaches."

"Cool," Davis said.

The even line of Brian's mouth curled gently. "Davis, I'm not gloating about my travel plans. I'm inviting you to join me."

"Oh." Davis paused. "Thank you." Another pause. "And why exactly?"

"Don't you think you should be in the room when your project gets pitched? Look, do I think it's a long shot? I do. But this is a well-capitalized, highly motivated client that seems to want to spend money. It wants to be dazzled, to be tantalized with ambitious ideas. I really want to impress these people, and having seen your designs, your schematics, your vision for this project, I think it's worth finding out if others are as enamored of it as you are."

Davis was momentarily too stunned to speak.

"Look, now that I've told you about these meetings, you could always take your blueprints to one of our competitors. I can't stop you," Brian said. "Go with your gut, Davis. I know you'll make the right decision."

Under the burden of four eager eyes, Davis felt besieged. He must've begun to look it too.

"Let's not put our friend on the spot," Heather suggested. "We've given you a lot to think about, so why don't you get the hell out of here and think about it?"

Brian extended his hand. "It was good of you to come in on such short notice. I hope you accept our offer, Davis. It would be great to work with you."

Heather escorted him through the glass double doors and out to the elevators. She pressed the button with the down arrow and they waited.

"So that was unexpected," Davis mused, as much to himself as to her.

"Ong didn't invite my ass to Turkey," Heather said.

With a ding, the elevator doors parted.

"Thank you, Heather," Davis said. "It was good of you to set this meeting up. No matter what happens, I really appreciate it."

"Oh, just shut up and say yes, Winger."

Later, he went for a run. He was running again these days—newly revitalized, shots of vigor and vitality surging through his body. As he jogged through the evening, past the dimming lawns and flagging trees, all living things tiring of summer, he peered into the windows of houses set back from the road and pondered how easily he could've been someone else. All it would've taken was falling in love with someone who lived in another city or accepting a job in another state, and that would've changed everything. He would've lived the length of his days among a completely different cast of characters and eventually died among them, buried in strange soil for all of time. So much of life was holding on to the people and the things that rooted you in the world, so that you didn't have to wake up each day and start anew.

CHAPTER 38

Zach's tie resembled a gray downward-pointing dagger drawing one's eye to his brown shorts. Molly wasn't clear as to why the shirt, immaculately pressed and chalk-white, needed to be tucked into the shorts, or why he was wearing a tie in the first place, since he'd spent the day in his home office servicing clients who couldn't see him. On top of that, the workday was over, and he was reclining in front of the TV with his girlfriend. The stupid tie should've been long gone. At a minimum, loosened.

As he squeezed and released a pink rubber ball and regaled Molly with his adventures in Las Vegas, Molly couldn't help but notice how scrupulously Zach was working the word *tame* into his account. It was as though he was baiting her, like the more he described the trip as tame, the less she would think it actually had been, and on would come her jealous cross-examination over whether he'd indulged in the seedy pleasures on offer in that desert Gomorrah. Had he helped himself to a strip-joint lap dance? Had he stuffed singles into the G-strings of pole dancers? Where was the girlfriend's third degree to which he was entitled? Of course, Molly couldn't have cared less what he and his coterie of friends had gotten into out there. Of all the emotions she felt about his Vegas trip, jealousy was at the bottom of the list.

A commercial for a frighteningly immersive video game struck Zach silent. A military helicopter crashes on some rocky landscape, and grotesque-looking enemy soldiers pop up to immolate you in bazooka fire. It looked like a commercial for an actual war. As Zach watched with rapture, Molly fought another type of battle, more intense than the video game: guilt over her date with McGuinn. She hadn't considered it a date at the time, but the facts spoke for themselves. While her boyfriend was a five-hour plane ride away, she'd put on one of her more form-fitting pairs of jeans and gone out for drinks with a man who seemed intent on getting to know her better. Said man had even confided in her, entrusted her with a secret about himself he'd kept from the rest of the world, which was surely an act of intimacy that, for the likes of McGuinn, exceeded sex.

Speaking of which—Molly had assumed that she'd disqualified herself from future outings by not going home with him. Why would a guy like him put up with that? But a few days later, he'd called her.

"I don't know," she'd said when he invited her out again.

"You didn't have fun with me? Impossible."

"I had a lot of fun. But you have to admit, I'm nowhere near your type."

"I thought opposites attract," he'd said.

"Yeah, but they also tend to stay away from each other."

"I'm not hearing a yes," he'd said, sounding disappointed.

"That's because I haven't said it."

"But I'm not hearing a no."

"I guess I haven't said that either."

She just couldn't see where all of this could lead. Closet poet or no, he was something of a layabout, something of a barfly, he was grizzled and hooked on chewing tobacco, and he was fluent in tattoo when speaking to scary cocktail waitresses. By the same token, her boyfriend had gone to Nevada and brought her back a snow globe of the MGM lion, an afterthought of a souvenir he'd surely snagged at the airport just before catching his flight home.

The front door opened and one of Zach's roommates came in. It was Duke or Duker or The Duker—Ethan when his mother called. She barely recognized him in the oxford shirt and charcoal slacks, both a size too big, that he had to wear having landed an internship at some stuffy investment firm downtown.

Before heading up to his room, a sport coat dangling over his shoulder on two fingers, Duker paused. "Yo." He meant Molly. "Seems you have a fan."

"Oh. Thank you. That's nice of you."

"No, not me," he said. "My sister in LA. She reads *Lotus* online. Checked out your podcast and really dug it."

"LA?" Out came the dumbstruck smile she still hadn't figured out how to suppress whenever someone demographically or geographically outlying claimed acquaintance with her work.

"She saw the Baltimore connection and asked if I'd heard of you, and I was like, I totally know that chick!" Duker bragged.

The wingspan of the *Lotus* publicity apparatus was an endlessly unfolding wonder. Deserted daughters from Bridgeport, Connecticut, were writing to her. From Terre Haute, Indiana, and Broken Arrow, Oklahoma.

By the time Zach trotted up to his room to change his shirt before they headed out to dinner, Molly had already made up her mind. She was certain this time. Today was the day. He probably wouldn't even feel bad about it. They would talk, they would hug, they might even still go out for sandwiches. The only disappointment she felt about it, which came upon her as she climbed the steps to his bedroom, was that this was going to be the first time in her life she'd ever broken up with someone. Had she really made it through high school and college and into her thirties without breaking one stupid heart?

Just as she entered the room, Zach's head burst through the collar of the black shirt he was changing into. "Almost ready," he sang, his arms swimming through the sleeves.

"Do you mind if we talk first?" Molly sidestepped the laundry basket in the center of his room. It contained a wreckage of unwashed clothes. "The thing is, Zach," she said, dropping onto his bed, "I don't think this is working."

"What's not working?" He was checking himself out in the mirror, admiring the snugness of his shirt against his non-musculature.

"Us?" she said, sounding tentative. "This relationship?"

He turned to her. "What do you mean?"

"I don't know. I guess I just don't see where this is going. I mean, you and I get along well and we have fun together, we really do. But do you see me as 'the one'?"

Zach held up his hands as if to shield himself from bodily harm. "Is this a conversation about things not progressing fast enough? Because, Mol, I'm totally into you, but I'm not at the point in my life where I'm thinking about rings or cohabitation or anything like that. You're awesome, really, but I'm just not there."

Molly smiled charitably and pointed to the framed photo of her boyfriend standing alongside a Wookiee. "Zach, you have more pictures of Muppets in your room than you have of me."

"Muppets?"

She pointed to another frame. "That's you and Princess Leia. Not Carrie Fisher—that would be different. It's just some woman in a costume."

A look of worry clouded Zach's face, as if he'd just been diagnosed with an untreatable and possibly disfiguring condition. "Are you saying we don't have a lot in common?"

"I'm saying that you have a Buck Rogers lunchbox. And you work from home, so you really don't even need a lunchbox."

"It's Battlestar Galactica, and sometimes when the weather's nice I eat down by the water."

"I'm not trying to attack you," she said.

And yet he looked wounded, pitiably so.

"I like you, Zach, I really do. You're a nice guy, a good guy, and I adore that you're a Big Brother. But I'm a lot older than you, and we just don't want the same things right now."

"But I want to be with you. Isn't that enough?"

"Well, no, actually, it's not." She watched him try to understand that. "Look, I don't want us to end on bad terms."

An ugly emotional scene just wasn't warranted here. They were casual daters who should've been able to walk away with a light parting quip. *Now get back out there, you big lug. Miss Right is just around the corner.* For a long time now Molly had suspected that they were wasting each other's time, and if you're not sure whether or not you're wasting time, then you probably are.

Then Zach went for an unfortunate Hail Mary. "Our sex life is fun, though." His throat undulated nervously. "Right?"

Hmm. Well. He still referred to physical contact as "nookie," and that was regrettable. She'd never quite gotten used to this thing where he talked to her in kind of a baby voice, like she was a little girl. Ditto his habit of greeting her breasts, literally saying hello to them. None of these proclivities were deal breakers per se. They were merely weird, and weird would've been tolerable if things weren't weird all the time.

She cringed. "I don't think either of us wants to talk about that, do we?"

That was not the reaction he was looking for. "You know what? You're mean, Molly. I've never seen this side of you."

"Zach."

"I'm sorry if I'm not boring like you. I have interests and hobbies. I'm actually a pretty interesting guy. I think you should go now."

"Zach, I'm sorry."

"Just go."

"You are an interesting guy. And a really nice guy too. Look, be patient with me. I've never broken up with anyone before. It's not my thing."

And yet she was handling it like a pro. So much of this felt like lip service, a vain attempt to let him down easy. The truth was, Zach wasn't a *really* nice guy. He was just a *sort of* nice guy. Sometimes not even that. And having interests didn't make you interesting. Everyone knew that.

"I'm not trying to hurt your feelings," she told him. "I'm doing you a favor."

"Yeah? Well, when you walk out of here, you're going to be sorry! Very sorry! You're going to miss me! You're going to miss us!"

Now that he'd moved on to whining, she figured it was safe for her to leave.

"You're probably right," she said, touching him gently on the shoulder. "I'll check in with you later, okay?"

Down the stairs she flew, dizzy with accomplishment. When she reached the front porch, she waited for the winds of regret to blow through her. Instead, there came a breeze of magnificent relief.

Not sorry yet, she thought to herself.

She bounded off the curb and sailed up the block, little white stars gathering before her eyes like frost on a winter's window.

"Nope, not sorry yet." This time it was out loud.

CHAPTER 39

Davis's suspicions intensified when Norman gave him his two Orioles tickets, and not only were both Molly and McGuinn unavailable to join him and take the extra seat, but both independently offered the same excuse: "lunch plans." In McGuinn's case, it was just an outright lie. It had to be. McGuinn wasn't the lunch plans type. Most days he slept through lunch entirely.

Eager to investigate, Davis rapped on his door. "I find it interesting that you can't go to the game with me today because you have, quote-unquote, lunch plans, and coincidentally, Molly can't go to the game with me today because she has, quote-unquote, lunch plans."

"I find it weird that you find that interesting," McGuinn replied. "Lunchtime shows up every day for everybody."

"Not for you it doesn't. For you, it's like leap year."

McGuinn yawned. He was shirtless and half-awake. "D, is this your pathetic way of asking me if I have a social engagement with your sister?"

"I suppose it is."

"Well, the answer is yes, I do."

"Nice." Davis glared at him and shook his head.

"Now, don't go all sad puppy on me," McGuinn said. "Look, I'm going to let you decide how we deal with this, okay? You can come inside and we can talk about it. You can take a swing at me. You can just drop it because we're talking about consenting adults here, people in their frickin' thirties, D. Whatever makes you happy, that's how we'll play it."

Davis stood there feeling crestfallen and weak for having been unable to protect his sister from this friendly neighborhood barbarian. McGuinn had so many repulsive attributes it was hard to keep track of them all. The dip, the ladies of the night, the murky employment status, the fact that he lived *here* and didn't seem to have a plan or even any interest in getting out.

At the same time, it was hard to deny the grit in the man's friendship. Davis had arrived here in his U-Haul at his absolute lowest point. Rock bottom. A day on which he'd never felt more ashamed, more alone, or more lost. And lo and behold, there was McGuinn, unloading crates, listening to Davis's hard-luck story, helping him work his way through a case of Yards.

Davis sighed. "I'm not going to take a swing at you."

McGuinn whistled. "Whew. Boy, is that a relief."

"Molly's a smart woman. She's an adult. She can take care of herself," Davis rhapsodized. "But more than that, McGuinn, you've earned my trust. It would be wrong of me to withhold my blessing. You kids go and have a good time. Have a wonderful lunch."

Davis's bare feet flopped back toward his door, but McGuinn stopped him. "Hang on there, D." The large man scoured the terrace for eavesdropping ears, then parked the midpoint of his bare back against his doorframe and folded his arms. "I know you're deeply troubled by these women who come over to my place, so I'm going to tell you a little something about them."

"You mean the prostitutes?" Davis asked.

"Do you know what I do with these women?"

"I'm sure a great many things, things far beyond my imagination, sometimes with props."

"I appreciate the compliment," McGuinn said, "and while I hate to shatter your illusions, the truth is, I don't have sex with them."

Davis waited for the large lout to crack up at his own joke. But he didn't. "Not even a little bit?" Davis asked.

"Well, sure, a little bit. But not every time, and not in groups, but yeah, sometimes with props. But that's not why I invite them over." McGuinn pitched a contemplative gaze into the sky and let it hang there a moment as if waiting for it to echo back with some kind of direction. "Let's just say these women provide me with inspiration. They're like—how shall I put this?—muses."

This was becoming one of those conversations Davis seemed to have only with McGuinn. "Do I want to know why you need a muse?" he asked.

"I write poetry, D."

"You do what?"

"I'm pretty sure you heard me. We're standing an inch away from each other."

"Is 'writing poetry' code for something?"

"Yeah—the search for truth and beauty."

Davis sniffed with irritation. "I know I say this every time we speak, but I have literally no idea what the hell you're talking about."

At which point Davis became the second member of the Winger family upon whom McGuinn dropped his dirty little secret. He explained how from the moment he'd discovered his knack for verse, he'd taken great pains to conceal it. Among the men's men in whose circles he traveled—the beer-chugging power hitters, the chain-smoking pitching coaches, the galloping centerfielders with blue eyes and John Hamm chins—McGuinn wouldn't be caught dead *reading* poetry, let alone writing it. He decided to permit the world to think him a man of lecherous ways and limited cogitation, and only roll back his poetic floodgates under cover of darkness or in the sanctity of his room. Even though it had been years since he had teammates to hide this from, he'd never gotten comfortable with the bard beneath the jock.

"Then your sister came along," McGuinn said. "In her, I sensed a companion, a kindred spirit struggling to come down from the vines and be her true self. She too was in search of her own voice."

Davis took it all in, even believed some of it, then said, "So why the hooker thing?"

"Not my idea," McGuinn replied. "Do I look like the kind of guy who has to pay for it?"

McGuinn explained that years ago, on his birthday, some of his more brutish friends sent a bouquet of international beauties to his door. A man of good manners, McGuinn invited them in and poured them a drink. They got to talking. He asked them about their lives. Instantly he was captivated by the events that had landed these women on American soil to become practitioners of the world's oldest profession. Some of them had spent their childhoods on the impoverished streets of Kiev and Minsk. Another was shipped off at a young age from her Krakow home to marry a stranger in New York, an older man who was dead of a heart attack within a year. As these foreign women recounted their utterly foreign experiences, McGuinn found himself aroused—but not in the usual way one gets in the company of prostitutes. Artistic inspiration deluged him. He couldn't put down his pen.

"My poems aren't even about these women or the worlds they come from or their struggles," McGuinn said. "Being around them just makes me want to write. And being around them *allows* me to write because I'm free in their presence. I can be the person no one else knows."

Davis wasn't quite over his cynicism. "This sounds like an elaborate excuse to hang out with a bunch of hot immigrants."

"Look, one can't help but be in a heightened state when a young lovely is straddling the arm of one's sofa. But it's mostly poetry that comes spurting out of me. Not exclusively, I confess, but mostly."

"That was uncalled for," Davis said, making a face. "Not a terrible use of imagery, but uncalled for."

"Look, man, I can't explain it," McGuinn said. "You go with what works—like Dali and his power naps, or Balzac and the aquariums of coffee he guzzled down. And you can stand there and smirk all you want, D. It makes no difference whether or not you believe me."

Davis did believe him. He certainly wanted to. When your neighbor has designs on dating your sister, it's always preferable that he not be a petri dish of STDs, or at least less of one than previously suspected. But now Davis was wondering which McGuinn was the true one. Was it the closet softie who scribbled odes to daffodils and seashells when no one was looking? Or was it the guy with whom Davis had passed an entire evening concocting porn titles for movies by subbing in the word *breast* for *beast?* (*Beauty and the Breast, Breasts of the Southern Wild, Breasts of No Nation, Fantastic Breasts and Where to Find Them*— although that too was poetry, was it not?) Davis had known McGuinn for exactly one season, and yet he'd come to believe that they were past the point of surprises. Then again, Britt had thought the same of Davis. We are never past the point of surprises.

Davis stared for a long moment at his shirtless friend. "Minsk, huh?"

"It's the capital of Belarus," McGuinn said. "Known for its fountains."

"Fountains, huh?"

"You can google that shit," McGuinn said.

Davis emitted a sigh of acceptance. "So do I have to pretend I want to read your stuff?"

"Why don't you just pretend to pretend, if that makes you feel any better?"

And with that, McGuinn clasped his meaty arms around Davis's waist and hoisted him up into a bear hug. Davis tried to writhe free of the humid woolen rug of the man's bosom, but it was no use. He closed his eyes and waited for it to be over.

CHAPTER 40

McGuinn wanted fries. Ever since Molly had waxed romantic about Thrasher's—that fresh-cut, double-fried, vinegar-drenched boardwalk confection—there'd been a rumble in his belly, he said when he picked her up, and that rumble spoke only one name.

"I think we need to have fries for lunch," he told Molly when she climbed into the cab of his truck.

"I'm game," Molly said, eyeing him from the passenger seat. "What's the closest place?"

"Ocean City, I think," said McGuinn.

"Isn't that, like, the farthest place?"

They went anyway. Equipped with coffees from the Morning Dew, they set out on the three-hour drive to the Eastern Shore. They stopped along the way at a roadside farmers market to comb through the overflowing displays of fruits and vegetables, all bursting electric with color. They sampled the berries and peaches and nectarines, and Molly laughed when McGuinn spit out a shockingly sour plum slice and wiped his fingers on his Ozzy Osbourne tee.

Back in the car, they rolled down the windows and blasted Garth Brooks while picking pre-sliced watermelon from the plastic container that Molly held in her lap. She noticed McGuinn's hands as he gripped the steering wheel. His fingers were an expo of cuts and bruises, newer ones showing deep reds and blues, others on their way out, fading into the landscape of his skin. She thought of the gash across his abdomen, that grisly laceration that looked as though it had been inflicted by some primitive Civil War–era instrument. How a man got hurt spoke volumes about how he lived. McGuinn got stress fractures and torn rotator cuffs; most of the other men in her life got carpal tunnel and paper cuts, injuries sustained at a desk. She couldn't stop stealing glances at him. He was an adventure.

They parked down by the boardwalk and moseyed through the crowds. The beach was thick with families savoring the last days of summer before the opening school bell pulled them home for the cold months. Vacationers were buying up the last of the key rings, kites, T-shirts with trendy sayings, all manner of trinkets and souvenirs. Their lips and chins were streaked with powdered sugar from their funnel cakes. Robotic video game music drifted out from the arcades.

When McGuinn went to find a bathroom, Molly spotted the ideal gift for him in one of the beach shops.

"For me?" he said when she presented him with the bag. "You shouldn't have." He pulled out the shirt and held it up. It was an iron-on of the Vegas strip with the words, I DON'T NEED LAS VEGAS. I AM LAS VEGAS.

He smiled. "You remembered."

Late afternoon found them on a bench, facing the waves with an oily bucket of Thrasher's fries between them. The sunbathers and bodysurfers were all in vivid color saturation as the orange sun dipped below the hotels. Molly bit into a fry and suddenly found herself telling McGuinn how the taste and smell of salt and vinegar stirred up images from when she was a little girl.

"Are those happy memories, those vacations with just your dad and brother?" McGuinn wanted to know.

She thought of the rides, the games, the cotton candy, the glow-in-the-dark Frisbees sailing over a dark beach late into the night. Molly had never forgotten the seagull that stole the french fry out of her fingers all those years ago. She used to think that she resembled one of these gulls—endlessly circling, least like itself when it landed. But less and less was she feeling that way. Immersing herself in other people's Kitty Wingers had not brought closure for her, but it had brought something else. Peace with the fact that closure might always be denied.

"Happy," she answered. Then she smiled at him. "Today is a good day."

When the bucket of fries was empty, they strolled down to the surf with their shoes in their hands. The Atlantic puffed a sand-specked breeze at them. The tide tugged at their ankles, and the water felt good over their feet and toes after a full season of being warmed by the fat summer sun.

Afterward McGuinn put his pitching arm to good use, felling milk bottles and heaving darts at balloons, winning Molly a half dozen stuffed animals from the top shelf.

"How many teddy bears do you think a thirty-two-year-old woman needs?" she asked. All the winning was getting ridiculous.

At that, he smirked. "Needs?"

They bought a box of fudge from Candy Kitchen and found another bench. As the lights of distant ships hovered in the darkness, they broke off wedges of cookies 'n' cream, and McGuinn complained about all the flavors of fudge that weren't chocolate. Fudge *is* chocolate, he reasoned. It was shameful to contaminate it with Oreos or garnish it with M&Ms. It had no business being white or pink or—God save us all—green.

"Now that you've told me that you write poetry, when do I get to actually read some of it?" she asked him.

"I think we're a ways away from that," he said, laughing low. "I'm still trying to get you to like me."

"What if I promised to like you no matter how awful your poems are?"

"I'd say that you don't know a whole lot about promises."

On the drive home, the roads were quiet and empty. Molly stared through the cracked window as they drove past the silent farms, the gas stations of small towns, the billboards advertising Bible verses. Rural America in its last hours of oblivious sleep before day broke.

She must have fallen asleep, because the next thing she knew they were idling in front of her house.

"Now that's what I call a leisurely lunch," she said. "Thank you."

McGuinn killed the engine. "I'll help you carry in your zoo."

Together they lugged the stiff, hefty creatures up the front path, Molly walking ahead with the bird, the bear, and the turtle, McGuinn trailing behind with the giraffe, the octopus, and the gorilla. She opened the door and set them all down. She asked McGuinn if he'd like to come in, but she did so in a yawning tone suggesting that it was late and perhaps tonight wasn't the night for him to accept.

"Rain check?" he said.

She swept a strand of hair off her eye, then hugged him and kissed him on the cheek, and he left.

Sliding off her sandals and setting down her purse, Molly lugged her new collection of fuzzy beasts from the foyer to the sofa, ordering them comfortably on the cushions for the night. Tomorrow she'd donate the whole multispecies wildlife family to Rachel.

A text arrived on her phone. She plucked the device from her purse, wondering who would be up at this hour. It was from McGuinn.

All right, don't laugh, he wrote. Here goes nothing: 'Where once she hummed from the mud, awaiting a distant tomorrow, now she's the tune, looking down from the moon, without a trace of sorrow.'

Molly did laugh—partially at it, partially because of it, and partially for the reason that no one had ever presented her with the opportunity to laugh at their poetry before.

She peered between the slats of her blinds. Seeing the monster Chevy still out there, she suddenly felt like a charged particle. She opened her door and trotted down the front walk. McGuinn saw her coming and rolled down the window.

"Hi," she said, standing on the curb in bare feet.

"Hi," he said. "So that was the cheesiest thing I've ever done in my life. You're welcome."

"Did you make that up just now?"

"Actually, I jotted it down in the bathroom that night at Assassins & Cons." He looked sheepish. "I just made it creepy, didn't I?"

"A little," she admitted. "But the good kind of creepy."

"That's not a thing," he said. "And I know you laughed when you read it. I can see it on your face."

She smiled. "I did. But it's good."

"No, it isn't."

"I like it," she said.

"I do, too, actually."

She rested her forearms on the car door, her head practically inside the cab. "What if I were to ask you one more time if you wanted to come inside?"

She'd scarcely led him through the door when she spun on her heels and pressed her mouth against his. Up close he was a patchwork of crude, hard-boiled smells. Tobacco, alcohol, motor oil, ancient baseball mitt—some attached to him, others, she suspected, to her imagination.

Her mouth was now in and on and all over his. His arms swam down the length of her back. The tips of his fingers breached the northernmost border of her ass, the North Dakota of her ass, and pined for all the territory that lay below. Gripping the underside of her thighs, he lifted her in one smooth maneuver and carried her up the stairs.

CHAPTER 41

The trail of cracked concrete that led to the pool was empty that night. It was as if all the other residents had been bused out to a party, only Davis left behind to sit in the dead quiet surrounded by dark apartment windows. Which was fine. Moments of serenity were few and far between at the Deluxe.

He groped for a chaise, then uncapped one of the two bottles of beer he'd brought down with him. Chugging liberally, he stretched out under the luminous moon. He missed the moon. So much of childhood was spent in contemplation of the sky, dreaming of flying saucers and little green men, relishing the foregone certainty that at some point in your life you'd visit space. *Sure, I'll go on a rocket ship one day. Why wouldn't I? We all will.* That was what youth was all about: gazing upward into your infinite, star-spangled imagination, daring to envisage all the wondrous thrusts and unknowable trajectories that awaited you.

He'd accepted the job at IlluMind. It was the only real option. When a gravedigger comes to exhume you, only a fool refuses his shovel. Brian Ong wanted him to work there, wanted to pay him a lot of money to do so, and most important, wanted to help get the Sultan built. He even wanted to see it built in Turkey, which had to be some kind of omen, since surely, once upon a time, magic carpets waved all across Ottoman skies. The problem with omens, though, is that you can't tell the good ones from the bad until the dust settles.

He'd called Britt before accepting.

"I think I'm going to take a new job," he'd told her.

"Oh." She'd been unable to conceal her surprise.

"What part of this astounds you? That anyone would hire me?"

"No. You're a good engineer, and you had nothing to do with that girl's injuries. I guess I just figured you'd go back to Hans."

"Why?" he'd wanted to know.

"I don't know. I've never pictured you anywhere else. But change is good—if that's what you want."

"I don't have any hard feelings toward Hans," he'd said. "I forgave him."

"My, that was big of you."

"No, I take some responsibility," he'd told her. "I could've handled it better. And that's the point, Britt. I know I fall short sometimes. I'm just like everyone else. I hurt people. But I'm learning to own up to it."

"I have to go," she'd said, sounding annoyed. Not every conversation needed to be about his personal growth, for God's sake, his magical transformation into A Better Person.

After speaking with Brian Ong, Davis had called Hans and told him he was moving on, that it was time for a fresh start and all. He thanked Hans for giving him all the experience, for being a true mentor all these years, for helping to make Davis the engineer that he now was. Also, he apologized for the way he'd behaved.

"I'm sorry I made things uglier than they needed to be just because I couldn't imagine that I was capable of a lapse," Davis had said. "I know better now."

And Hans wished him well. "If you ever need anything, you call me," he'd said.

Earlier in the evening, Davis had had a pour of rye, and now the amber ale was mixing nicely with it. If nothing else, this detour in life had reacquainted him with the virtues of hard drinking, and he had McGuinn to thank for that. It had been baptism by bourbon since day one. Davis had known better than to try to keep up with his neighbor, who claimed to have been desensitized to alcoholism by his hard-drinking Irish upbringing. But Davis didn't think that being raised by alcoholics made you a better drinker any more than being raised by a newscaster gave you a better smile.

Out of the night came a voice that nearly startled him into arrhythmia. "Boo!"

Davis jumped, then heard laughter. It was Charlie.

"Christ Jesus!"

"Sorry. Man, that never gets old." Charlie was still giggling, clearly not sorry. "I've been looking for you."

"I'm so pleased," Davis grumbled.

While Davis concentrated on regulating his heart rate, Charlie screeched a chair over the asphalt and sat down beside him. "I've got some news, and for the first time, like, in the history of me, it's good news."

"Oh yeah?"

"I'm finally moving out of this five-star resort."

He peered at her through the moonlight. "You're leaving?"

"I am. I'm moving to a little town you might've heard of called College Park."

"Maryland let you back in? You passed your exams, didn't you?"

She pumped her first. "I made those exams my bitch! Every last one of them."

"Damn, Charles. Congratulations."

"It's okay. You can be shocked."

"I'm really happy for you," he said.

"Can you believe I graduated high school?"

"Frankly—no."

"I owe you in a big way," Charlie said. "Seriously. I couldn't have done it without you."

"Yeah, probably not," Davis agreed.

"Sooooo, actually, there's something I want to give you. Just my little way of saying thank you." She bit her bottom lip. "I think you're going to like it."

With a low feline snicker, she lifted herself out of her chair and stood over him, pausing to muss up her hair, shaking it full of body. In the semidarkness, he caught a coy twinkle in her eye and all at once his heart pitched into another arrhythmic fit. When she leaned toward him, he ducked.

"Whoa!" he yelled. "Hold on there."

"What?"

"What do you mean, what? This is not going to happen. Charlie, I'm way too old for you. And I love my wife. Look, I'm flattered, but no. I'm sorry. Just—no."

Her silhouette withdrew and her hands dropped with shame onto her hips. He now felt guilty for embarrassing her. But what was she thinking? "Look, I didn't mean to hurt your feelings."

"Hurt my feelings?" she said. "I just threw up down the front of my shirt. Are you *joking*? You thought I was going to kiss you? Or worse?"

He didn't answer. *Worse?*

"That might literally be the most disgusting thing I've ever heard."

"Okay. Take it easy."

"You think that's my idea of a celebration?"

"It doesn't have to be the most disgusting thing you've ever heard."

"I'm seriously going to puke in your pool."

"So it would seem," he grunted. "The important thing is that we're both in agreement that it would be very, very bad—"

"Let's just pretend this never happened," she said. "That's what we're in agreement on. We're in agreement that this never happened."

She arched her spine, shuddered her limbs, and pitched a fit of horrible spasms and pained puffs. Davis could only look on impotently at this girl and her emasculating display of disgust. "Oh, my god, I'm so fucking nauseous," she yelped.

Davis lay there shaking his head. "Go ahead, take my dignity. I wasn't using it anyway."

Eventually—it took a while—she calmed down. "I was just going to give you this," she said.

She lifted something off her chair. It was a wrapped box. She held it out to him, and after regarding it with suspicion, he accepted and unwrapped it. It was a book. Raising it into the beam of a security spotlight, he read the title. *Crybaby: A Physiological and Cultural Study of Crying and What Moves Us to Tears.* She'd taped a little packet of tissues to the front cover.

He smiled.

"You might learn something. The guy's a PhD," Charlie said. "There's an inscription too."

He leafed to the title page and found a scribble of black ink. It read:

Dear Lifeguard,

Thank you for saving me.

Charlie

He looked up at her. "Thank you. It's generally not nice to make fun of other people's frailties, but I know you mean well."

She set herself down at the end of his chaise. "In recent months I have been accused by my father of being—and I quote—a young lady sorely in need of getting her act together, and by my mother of being— and I quote—an ungrateful little shit. Now, as a matter of policy, I don't give a giggleberry fuck what my parents say, but there were times this summer when you were pretty much all I had going for me. And if that doesn't make you cry like the emotional wreck we both know you are, nothing will."

He hoisted his beer in salute. "Again, I know you mean well."

At that, she slid closer to his chaise and dropped her hands into her lap. "Okay. So now that we've fixed me, it's your turn."

"Meaning?"

"Meaning we've gotta get you the fuck out of here. I don't feel good leaving you here. If I can change, you can change."

"You've had a high school diploma for, what, an hour, and already you're doling out graduation speeches?"

"If anyone could use one," she said.

Davis sucked back the last of his first bottle and chuckled without mirth. "It's funny. I actually remember my high school graduation speaker. It was some dude—the CEO of some company, or maybe he was the president of Grenada. Anyway, he assured us of all the glorious opportunities awaiting us beyond our school walls. We had promise! We were the future! Sure, there were some rules, but they were cheese-ball Mr. Rogers rules. 'Only do things that make you happy.' 'Don't be afraid of a little hard work.' 'Look forward, but always take some time to look back.' I got news for you, Charles, those aren't the rules. The rules—"

"Go home, Davis," Charlie interrupted. "Just shut up and go home to your wife and daughter. If you made a mistake, go make it better. You're going to die one of these days. You know that, right? Your wife wants things to be the way they were before you fucked everything up, and the only way to convince her that that's possible is to never stop trying to convince her."

"Wow. Okay. So I guess you just jumped right to the PhD."

"I'm right, Davis."

"You're a presumptuous little brat. That's what you are."

"And you're sitting here on your ass, doing nothing but waiting."

"I'm not waiting."

"No, you are waiting. You're just doing other shit while you're waiting."

"You don't seem to know how it works," he said. "I don't get to hurt my wife and then dictate the time frame for her recovery."

"You want to give her time? Fine, give her time," Charlie said. "But you should know—and trust me on this, because I've seen this movie before, had fucking front-row seats—time is not on your side."

Davis grunted and cracked open the second bottle.

"Or you could just drink another beer. That's always an option," Charlie said. "Look, you want to be an idiot? Go right ahead. Be an idiot."

An eighteen-year-old deigning to dispense relationship advice to a grown man—who did that? She really was a presumptuous little brat. But was she wrong? All summer, Davis had been clear with Britt about his feelings, but he hadn't been insistent. He'd been forceful, perhaps, but not urgent. His sales tactics had been low-pressure because he thought Britt deserved her space. But maybe Charlie was right that the only way to ensure that Britt never left him was to refuse to let her go. He too had had front-row seats. He'd watched Norman let go of Kitty, and what had that wrought? It had wrought Molly, a daughter who'd spent most of her life unsure of herself, wondering why she hadn't been enough of a reason for her mother to stay. Davis could never abide his own daughter thinking that way about him, not for a fraction of a second. But with Rachel, there was still time to make it right. Children learned to accept all the outrageous imperfections of their parents; they worked with what they had. Britt, on the other hand, could walk away. Her, he could lose forever.

"Maybe you're right," he said.

"That you're an idiot?" Charlie asked.

"That I'm going to die one day."

"Yeah, I think I'm onto something there."

"Unfortunately, I think you are," Davis said, his voice soft and full of pondering. He was too old now to view death as a mere punch line. He'd reached the age where he knew—truly understood—that one day he'd be pulled off into the unbroken nightfall, away from everyone, and he'd stay gone forever.

"You should go over there now," Charlie told him.

"That's not a good idea," he said. "It's late. It'll piss Britt off. It'll also freak Rachel out, which will piss Britt off even more."

"Excellent reasons to kiss your family goodbye," Charlie said.

As he stared at her, a thrum of urgency began to flood through him. A newly minted graduate like Charlie was either the least qualified person in the world to deliver a commencement address or the most qualified. But one way or the other, Davis needed to hear something stirring, and damned if she hadn't delivered. This should happen all the time, he decided. It should be a thing. Someone should knock on your door first thing every Monday morning and lead you in a renewal of your graduation vows. A weekly exhortation of those cap-and-gown imperatives, a reminder of all those ideals that had been reduced by the passage of time to vacuous poetry and empty movie lines.

"You know what?" Davis said. "I'm fucking doing it."

"All right," Charlie enthused.

"I'm going over there right now and putting it all on the line."

"Yeah, you are! You know why? Because you're the fucking cabana boy. That's why! But don't lead with that."

He jumped to his feet. The electricity of purpose coursed all through his limbs. He started bouncing on the balls of his feet, shaking out his hands. "By the way," he said. "At some point I might want to talk to you about Tweedy."

"What about him?" She was sliding back into her sandals.

"Well, I assume you can't have a pet in a freshman dorm, right?"

"You can't have one in these fleabag apartments either, but you know me. I'm a gangster."

Davis scratched his mane. "The thing is, gangster, you gave a dog to a guy with a six-year-old."

"Hmm. I see where you're going with this."

He shrugged plaintively. "They're soul mates, man. Soul mates."

"I see," she said. "Well, let's be on the side of love, shall we? We'll work something out."

As the gate trumpeted their exit with a rusty squeal, they stood at the edge of the parking lot, which glowed like alabaster and clicked with invisible bugs. Davis's eyes lifted hopefully over the trees in the direction of home.

"Any final words of motivation?" he asked.

Charlie gripped his shoulders and stared into his eyes. "You have promise! You are the future! Only do things that make you happy. Look forward and backward and sometimes even sideways. Yes! Never forget to look sideways! Also, your complexion is a little off."

"Thanks. That should do it."

"I'm not kidding. You're flushed." She was seeing him in the light for the first time tonight, and it apparently troubled her. "Are you having some sort of cardiac event?"

"Do I even have time to have a cardiac event?"

"Well, you're red. You're, like, really red."

"Don't worry," he told her. "That's because I'm an idiot, remember? Idiots are red."

———

The crimson in his cheeks was not on account of heart trouble or even idiocy but drunkenness, the extent of which only really hit him when he lost his balance sprinting up the steps to his unit and nearly hurtled through the door of his neighbor two doors down (Randall something-or-other, whom he'd met only once but often overheard laughing hysterically at dinner-hour sitcoms). Declaring himself unfit for driving,

Davis sniffed around his apartment for a clean pair of running shorts, laced up his sneakers, and barreled back into the hot night.

His ASICS slapped rhythmically against the concrete as he jogged. The alcohol weighed down his limbs into a syrupy drag, but dogged ambition flung him forward, and after fifteen minutes he stood, drenched in perspiration, in front of the single-family dwelling that housed his beloved wife and daughter.

The upstairs windows were dark; Rachel was surely long asleep. Downstairs, the spongy yellow light from the living room flared against the curtains. He crept up the walkway and knocked softly, leaving a sweat stain on the door with the imprint of his knuckles.

After some time, the door opened. Britt saw him and froze.

"Hi," he said.

"What are you doing here?"

"I came to talk."

"Do you know what time it is?"

"I don't care what time it is."

"We're not talking now," she said, standing in front of the door, barricading him from his own home.

"Britt, please. This can't wait."

"It's going to have to."

"I can't live apart from you anymore. I love you too much. I want to move back in and make things better. I accuse myself of failing you, Britt. I accuse myself, and I find myself guilty. But now what? That's the only question." He paused to evaluate his volume. He couldn't decide if he was shouting or whispering. "I can't tell you what to do, but know this: you are everything to me. Everything. We can get back to the way we were before, I swear it, but the only way I'll ever convince you of that is to never stop trying to convince you."

That's when he noticed that instead of her standard evening uniform—fluffy socks and that roomy blue sweatshirt she bought at the Gap before they even met—Britt was clad in heels and dark jeans.

"Were you out tonight?" he asked.

"I have a friend over," she replied stiffly. "And you've been drinking."

"No, I haven't. Who's over?"

"Go home, Davis."

"No. I refuse to let you go, Britt."

"You're making a scene."

"I refuse to care if I'm making a scene."

The sight of the man standing behind her threw a cinch around his throat. His blood ran cold, and he stared into his wife's face as if the most horrible secret of the universe were etched upon it.

Britt had no choice but to acknowledge the stranger. "This is my friend Gustavo. His son, Jake, is in Rachel's class."

Davis felt light-headed. "Okay. Yeah . . . well . . . I get it now."

"Davis," she said.

He started to back away, his steps spiraling into a stumble. "No, it's fine, I totally understand." The instant had arrived when everything changed. He'd misjudged her, misjudged himself.

"You can't come over here like this," Britt was saying.

"I won't bother you anymore." He staggered backward like a wounded soldier. "I promise."

The man shuffled up to Britt, hands stuffed inoffensively into his back pockets. He affected a perverse sort of neutrality, as if somehow hoping, however ridiculously, to play neither the villain nor the hero in this piece. Davis blinked back a tear of rage at the sight of a strange man side-by-side with his own wife, in the doorway to his own home, in the cocoon of his own front light, while he himself swayed on the lawn, limp as a marionette.

"I'm sorry, Britt. I'm sorry for everything. You won't ever have to listen to my apologies again. I give you my word."

"Davis," she said. "Just go home and sleep it off."

He attempted to snarl in Gustavo's direction, but he couldn't help but notice that Gustavo had an oddly appealing face, a nice-guy face, a face that didn't deserve to be snarled at. That was disappointing. All at once, an autobahn of images screamed through Davis's mind. Gustavo and Britt strolling hand-in-hand on a rocky coast, stopping to make love on a dune. Gustavo introducing Britt and Rachel to his world-famous churros-with-chocolate recipe. Gustavo and Rachel shrieking jubilantly as they rode the Sultan of the Indies.

A queasiness rose within him. It gained strength, as irrepressible as it was ill-timed. He made for the road and got as far as the mailbox before the nausea surged. He bent at the waist and splashed a funnel of vomit onto the curb.

———

The following morning was bright and clear with a crispness that gave one a false sense of autumn. Standing in sunglasses with an aching that could only partially be blamed on the rye and ale, Davis slowly ladled the previous night's insect casualties out of the pool. The air was thick with chlorine. Residents shuffled to their cars and headed off to work. Across the parking lot, the Crockett-Johnsons were loading up their minivan, the beefy twins firing water pistols at each other while their father stood at the opened rear door and grappled with the spatial-relations puzzle presented by suitcases, beach chairs, and buckets.

As Davis knelt to inspect a filter, a shadow shifted over him. He squinted up into the sunlight and saw Britt. She was suited for the office in that silk magenta blouse that he'd once called pink. She'd corrected him, informed him that, no, this was, in fact, magenta, and Davis had suffered a minor shock, having spent his whole life up to that point believing magenta to be a weak shade of blue.

Before he could say a word, before he could violate his own pro-hibition on apologies, Britt put her arms around him and drew him close. They stayed that way for a while, like slow dancers at the prom.

He rested his chin on her shoulder blade. The familiar sweetness of her cherry blossom shampoo devastated him.

When she pulled back and looked into his eyes, her every feature had settled into sad resolve. Then, without a word, she walked to the gate, closed it behind her, and got into her car.

"I wasn't ready to let you go," he said out loud as he watched her drive off.

Long after she was gone, he was still staring at that deserted parking space.

CHAPTER 42

She was spending a lot of time in that underground tech den. Her cup had runneth over with deserted daughters, each with a tale to tell, so she continued to record podcast episodes and let Jamie and her team worry about the pace at which to release them, whether to keep them in sync with the weekly articles or fire them off at will.

The moment each of her tapings wrapped, Molly made for the stairs. She saw no reason to subject herself any longer than necessary to Wyatt's snarky condescension about her audiovisual neophytism or, for that matter, the reek of apple juice, which brought to mind honeyed urine. At the end of each interview, she thanked Wyatt, made a minor fuss over how he made a difficult job look easy (even though he was clearly taking pains to make a relatively easy job look difficult), and fled the scene.

One morning, as she emerged from the basement, she ran headlong into a familiar face.

"Bo?"

"In the flesh, baby." The music critic flashed her punk-rock grin.

"What are you doing here?" Molly asked.

"I'm unfired."

"You're kidding."

"The boss called, said this place just wasn't the same without me."

"That's terrific," Molly said. "Welcome back."

"Turns out there's a little more cash lying around this joint, thanks to the Molly Winger multimedia blitz. So keep churning 'em out. I want to ask boss man for a raise." And she winked.

Molly flamed with overpowering relief.

"We'll catch up later," Bo said. "The Districts are playing The 8x10 tomorrow night, and I gotta chase them down for an interview." She turned to go, then spun back around. "Any interest in joining me for the show?"

"None whatsoever," said Molly.

Bo drew a finger pistol from the side of her vinyl pants. "I'll put you down as a yes."

Molly practically skipped back to her desk, high on a vintage of professional gratification she'd never before tasted. Bo's return may have meant that Molly would have to once again fend off invitations to late-night concerts and lunches at that falafel stand–cum–tattoo parlor, but that was a tiny price to pay for the satisfaction of seeing Bo's job restored. It was the first tangible reward of Molly's overappreciated column.

She slid into her chair to check her email. In addition to the communiqués from readers, listeners, and would-be interview subjects, awaiting Molly today was another missive from Zach. In this one, he asked how she was "surviving," reiterated his request to meet so they could "talk things through," and iced the cake with a terrifically manipulative (and rather unsportsmanlike) invocation of his Little Brothers. "By the way," he wrote, "Anthony and Gabe really miss you." It was the sad truth that Molly's estrangement from those boys had turned out to be the most regrettable part of the breakup.

She deleted the email in accordance with her policy of responding to only every third of Zach's messages. To reply more frequently would've sent the wrong signal; to reply less often would've been heartless.

The next email was sent by someone named Katherine Lowell.

Just the sight of that name robbed Molly of breath, and she pushed her chair away from her computer as though it were a tarantula.

It couldn't be. Her heart vaulted into her throat and pummeled her eardrums. *This is a cruel coincidence.* But the letters still spelled those two words.

Her fingers all but faltering, she clicked on the email, and it opened—along with a torrent of emotions, all rolling out like Pharaoh's plagues. Fear, hope, grief, longing, release, panic. Heavy on the panic.

It was from her.

Dear Molly,

I didn't know how to begin this note. I'm trembling as I write it. I can only imagine how much you hate me, or maybe you've put me out of your mind altogether. I know your father won't be pleased to learn that I've broken my promises and written to you. And maybe he's right. Maybe this email is an intrusion and I should keep my distance.

A few weeks ago, while perusing the New and Noteworthy tab on iTunes, I came across a podcast by someone with your name. You're a journalist! I screamed with joy when I saw that, and I cried. You were always writing me stories. Do you remember that? My god, you are such a wonderful writer. I've been devouring your articles and your podcasts. When I hear your voice now, I can still hear that sweet little girl with those watchful eyes. I remember her so well.

I suppose I'm the reason you write about these women. You'll never know how sorry I am for that, for having sent you down this path, for pushing you into this lifelong search. That was not my plan. I was so happy back in Columbus, when it was just your father and me and our two precious babies. Those were my best days. I never dreamed I'd leave my children and run off to California with my psychiatrist, an act that now sounds comically hideous. As I write this, I'm looking at your picture on the *Lotus* website. You are so beautiful, Molly. The only redemption I've been able to find is seeing you and Davis looking happy and safe in the world. I hope with the whole of my heart that that's true.

I take full responsibility for what I did, but as you surely know by now, it wasn't really a choice. My manic and depressive episodes, those horrible highs and lows, and what they much later started calling bipolar disorder, it was all so hard on your father, and he was right to let me go. Barry, however, paid for it in spades. He dealt with me, my mental illness, and my hospitalizations for many years after we ran off. I have been healthy and managing myself for a while now, and even had been at the time that Barry took his life, which will be two years ago this January. I can now say with a true mind that I am sorry. I'm sorry I left. I'm sorry I turned you away when you came to find me. I have so much to be sorry for, and believe me when I tell you that I'm sorry for all of it.

It took me a long time to get here. I didn't know how to come back, and I've been scared to do it. I thought maybe you and Davis deserved better, and your father. Peti deserves better, after all she's done for my family. It is, I know, more her family now.

But it's you, Molly, who showed me that all is never lost. Your stories about these women, your sweet voice on my speakers—that is what has given me the courage to write to you, to believe that there could be a way back for me, and that even if it leads nowhere, you and Davis are worth the risk. Maybe even I'm worth it too. I learned that from you.

One day soon, I'll break my promises to your father for a second time and I'll write to Davis. There are countless reasons for both of you to delete my notes and go on with what I hope are happy, full lives. I'm prepared for that. I'll understand. I really will. But even if you choose to dismiss me, at least do this: allow yourself to believe, as crazy as it sounds, that you are still loved. That's all I really wanted to tell you. And despite what you think of me, despite what I've done, and despite all the time that has gone by, I want you to know that I'm out here should you ever need someone. I really am, Molly.

Thank you for reading this.

Kitty

CHAPTER 43

On the ride across town Molly stared out the window, seeing and not seeing the rumbling city. Skyler was waiting for her at the curb, staring at the traffic when the taxi pulled up. When Molly got out of the cab, Skyler held her, right there on the sidewalk, then led her into the lobby of her office building.

They sat down in a pair of black leather chairs against a far wall, safe from the commotion of the elevator bank and the revolving doors. Molly felt like a can of soda that somebody kept shaking but refused to open.

"How much of this did you already know?" Skyler asked.

All Molly really knew was that the move to Baltimore had been the beginning of the end for Kitty Winger, the end of the woman who seemed so joyously immersed in motherhood just two states west. The distance from her friends and family, the isolation of a new town teeming with strangers, the sequestering of herself away in some suburb with two small children while her husband was off working long hours—it was supposed to be new and exciting, but it had brought her only misery and confinement. Misery led to therapy, therapy to Barry Lowell, and with the patient being gorgeous and charming and the shrink being weak and ethically flexible, Barry Lowell led to California. Comically hideous didn't do it justice.

This was what she'd been told and what had thus become cemented history. Had there been gusts of curiosity about those circumstances over the years? There had, but Molly had trained herself to wait them out whenever they blew in, especially after that devastating road trip rebuke. Davis had dealt with it differently. It was almost as if he lost interest in Kitty. Shit happened. Families combusted in all sorts of ways. Besides, each new day after Kitty left was another opportunity for her to return with apologies and explanations, and yet, day after day, week after week, year after year, it was an opportunity she continued to decline. So, as far as Davis was concerned, you know, fuck her.

Somewhere in the back of her mind, Molly had always suspected that Kitty suffered from depression or anxiety or some other mental or emotional plague. She was, after all, seeing a therapist. But that seemed an inadequate answer to the ultimate question of why she left, since, as many of her Maternity Leave subjects had testified, people in their right minds walked out on their kids all the time. You didn't need to be crazy to leave. Sometimes you had to be crazy to stay. Sometimes all you needed was a better offer. The whiff of mental illness had therefore offered little in the way of explaining why Kitty had run off with Barry—Barry, a therapist who surely knew that marrying your patient and running off with her to California was an epic ethical violation, if not an outright crime.

"I feel like maybe there are things that have been kept from me," Molly said. "Why would she say that she was breaking a promise by writing to me? What promise is she talking about?"

"I don't know," Skyler said. "Maybe your dad told her that if she left, she could never come back. Have you talked to him yet? Or your brother?"

Molly shook her head. She slunk back in the chair and raised her eyes to the disciplined formation of faux-wood drop tiles, that lifeless corporate ceiling that seemed to come standard in all office buildings.

"Talking to your dad might actually help," Skyler suggested. "You could just ask him, point blank, what happened. He can probably explain every confusing thing in that email."

Now that she thought about it, that night they'd met for dinner, hadn't Norman alluded to Kitty as having "lost it"? Turned out, it had been a slip of the tongue, an inadvertent reveal of a secret he'd kept from his children.

"You could also ignore this whole thing," Skyler told her. "You don't owe anybody anything."

But ignoring Kitty, who sounded so naked with regret, so honest about her sorrow, would be matching one cruelty with another, and not once in all these years had Molly ever wished pain upon this woman. Never could she stomach the notion that her mother was out there suffering. She was still the woman who'd cozied up on Molly's bed, playfully tapping her feet together on the comforter while reading *The Giving Tree* and *The Lorax*.

"I can't ignore it," Molly said. A gatherer of stories now, Molly couldn't well refuse her own.

"Of course you can't," Skyler said. "This was what you wanted all along."

Molly looked at her. "What's that supposed to mean?"

"You're a writer, Molly. Every week you push words into the world. I think there's a little part of you that hoped that your words—these words more than any of your others—would find their way to her, and that she would see them as an invitation, a sign that you're ready. Maybe somewhere deep in your skin you've known that."

Molly seriously doubted but couldn't truly dismiss the notion that her career, the area of study to which she'd gravitated in school, everything she'd ever done had been engineered for this moment. "So my entire life has been one big search?" she said.

"Isn't every life?" Skyler said.

Molly looked around the lobby at all the lives funneling in and out, coiling through the revolving doors, stepping onto elevators, stepping off elevators—gratuitous motion in every direction.

"Maybe you're right that I've been calling out to her all this time," she said. "But another part of me was hoping history would just stay history."

"History is never over, little chickie."

Unsure of her options, and overwhelmed by all of them, Molly looked at the one human being on the planet who seemed to truly know her. She was so grateful that Skyler Jones existed.

"What do you get out of being friends with me?" Molly asked her.

Skyler's sudden laugh ricocheted around the lobby. "Are you kidding?"

"No."

"That's like asking me what I get out of Craisins," Skyler said. "I've loved them for so long, how could I possibly remember? Look, it's going to be okay. You don't have anything to be afraid of."

"I'm not afraid," Molly decided.

"But if you are, that's okay too."

"But I'm not. Is that okay too?"

They followed each other out onto the sidewalk. Skyler raised her arm at the flow of cars, and they waited together for a taxi to pull over.

"Magnesium," Molly said.

"What?"

"That's what you get out of Craisins. Magnesium."

Skyler smiled. "My nephew slept over recently. He's three. In the morning I asked him if he wanted french toast for breakfast, and the kid goes, 'It's scary.' I wanted to tell him that that wasn't an appropriate answer to my question. Nobody is scared of french toast. But the therapist in me recognized that there's no emotion that isn't valid. You want to be afraid of breakfast? Knock yourself out."

Molly stared down the oncoming traffic. She took Skyler's point. It was okay to fear anything, even french toast. As long as you ate it anyway.

CHAPTER 44

Davis drew open his closet doors and looked upon the shirts, slacks, and suits dangling like artifacts amid the scent of sawdust. He proceeded to unsheathe pants from their hangers and fold them into the suitcase that lay open-mouthed on the bed. Once filled, the suitcase would be zipped, placed by the door, then driven to the airport tomorrow evening, where it would be checked and stowed in the cargo hold of a wide-body airliner en route to Istanbul.

He was glad to be starting a new job at a new firm with new people. Change was coming, like autumn, irrepressible and bittersweet, and it seemed healthier to start accepting things, like the irreversibility of his sins and Britt's resolution that there was no going back. Whatever was to be between them, Davis needed to set the right example for his daughter. Just as Norman had kept things together for his children, Davis needed to get his act together, to refuse to crumble, to be someone other than the clod who hid behind maternity dresses at big-box stores, who puked on the lawn in front of Gustavo, the well-hung Barcelonese matador.

For Davis, the first stage of grief would not be denial, but international travel. Over the course of a week he would breathe the air of another continent, meet fresh faces, and witness the vast unfolding of humanity that scurried about and got things done and even managed to be happy despite all of life's havoc. He surveyed the walls of his apartment. In a day he'd be on the shores of the Aegean, sucking into his lungs the olive-tinged breeze of the Mediterranean basin. This room, this furniture, this lighting—the whole operation—suddenly felt very temporary.

As he folded the sleeves of an oxford shirt, something drove him to his computer. Without any plan in mind, he started typing a letter to a girl in Williamsburg, Virginia, whom he'd never met.

Lilly Pennebaker
1575 Parkside Lane
Williamsburg, Virginia 23185

Dear Lilly,

You don't know me. My name is Davis Winger, and I was one of the engineers who worked on the Squall, the log flume at High Seas Adventure World where you got hurt last spring. I'm writing to say I'm sorry, and I say it on behalf of no one except me, because I'm the one who is sorry. I don't know about anyone else.

I don't know if anyone from the engineering firm where I worked, Pavelka & Gates, ever reached out to you. They should have, even if their lawyers told them not to. Because of what happened to you, I don't work at that engineering firm anymore, which is not to say that the accident was my fault. I honestly don't know whether it was or it wasn't, and I'm not sure it matters all that much. All I know is that this apology is long overdue. It got lost in the contentious, complicated discussion of responsibility. It got lost in hurt feelings and stupid grudges. It got lost in my self-centeredness, my summer of self-reflection. Very poor excuses, all of them.

I have a daughter who is and will always be the most precious thing in this life to me. If anything ever happened to her, the very idea that ego or legal considerations would be placed above an apology or a simple "get well soon" appalls me. It's flat-out unacceptable, and anyone who thinks otherwise is far worse off than you or I.

I understand that your injuries, while no doubt painful, inconvenient, and terrifying, were not life-threatening and that you've recovered. For that I'm really happy, because a young woman such as yourself has a long, exciting road ahead of her, with lots of strange turns and some pretty wild views along the way. I wish for you all of those things, and I hope this log flume accident is the worst thing the world has in store for you. Forgive me if all of that sounds weirdly overwrought, seeing as how, again, you don't know me. But I've decided that between saying too much in this letter and saying too little, the former is the lesser crime.

So—I say this from the bottom of my heart, Lilly: I'm sorry. And I'm glad you're okay.

Yours,

Davis Winger

P.S. I've designed what I think is a really cool ride that simulates flight on a magic carpet. If it ever gets built, I will see to it that you get a seat on its maiden voyage, wherever in the world it is, all expenses paid. (Then again, given your recent experience on rides of my creation, I'll understand if you take a pass.)

CHAPTER 45

Late afternoons in summer generally found Norman taking a dip out back, lulling the day to an end by gliding his silver-matted body through the water. After toweling off poolside, he slid into dry khaki shorts and one of his monochromatic polos, and fixed two vodka-and-grapefruit juices—one for himself, one for Peti—and together they sipped them while Peti readied dinner.

Tonight, however, Norman had been invited out to dine with some friends from the station. Molly learned this only after driving all the way out to their house unannounced.

"I should've called," Molly said when Peti answered the door and informed her that her dad wasn't home. Her success rate with parental ambushes was still zero. "God, I'm stupid."

"Yes," Peti said with a chuckle. "So terribly stupid."

But Molly was there, which meant Peti would attempt to feed her. Molly wasn't hungry, but since when was that relevant? So into the kitchen they headed, the older woman leading the way, ensconced in her ever-present shawl.

Once Molly and Davis went off to college, Norman and Peti decided it was time to turn the old house over to a younger family, one that would populate it with memories of their own and displace the ones that the Wingers had set like traps in the rooms and hallways and outside in the deep grass. It had been well over a decade since they'd bought their current house, a rather palatial bungalow in a woodsy Owings Mills neighborhood, and yet to this day, every time Molly stepped inside, she had to acclimate herself to the fact that this was her father's home. Even with the same old furniture on the floor and the same old pictures in the frames, it was still a shock to find her dad living in a place where neither she nor Davis nor Kitty ever had.

Molly sat down at the long butcher-block table and waited until Peti had poured lemonade and thrown together a plate of hummus with sliced vegetables and pita.

"So, Peti. I got an email from my mom today," she said.

Peti looked at her almost as if she hadn't quite heard.

"That's never happened before," Molly said. "I need to ask you something. Why did she leave?"

"Honey, isn't this a discussion you should be having with your father?"

"Well, he's not here, and he'd probably just tell me a story anyway. Please, Peti. I'm thirty-two years old and I need to know."

Peti turned her head to the sliding glass doors, a wide window to stare out of. Clouds of melancholia shadowed her face, and for the first time Molly noticed that while no one was looking, Petra Kovacs had become middle-aged. Everything Peti did was done while heads were turned.

"I know Barry was her psychiatrist, so I've always known she was in therapy," Molly said. "But it was more than that, wasn't it? A lot more."

"Kitty was . . . troubled," Peti ventured.

Troubled was the way the older generations neatly boxed up depression, psychosis, schizophrenia, and pretty much anything else that made one volatile or chronically blue.

"Troubled how?" Molly asked.

"She was going through a lot back then, when you and Davey were little." Peti looked at her glass of lemonade as if she were about to pick it up, but she didn't.

"Manic depression? Bipolar disorder? There was a lot in that email," Molly said. "Did Dad make her promise never to write to us?"

Peti looked down and scraped burgundy nail polish off her thumbnail. If it could be said that the Winger family spoke of Kitty almost never, Peti spoke of her exactly never. Maybe she felt it wasn't her place, maybe she had some lingering guilt over having so efficiently stepped into Kitty's shoes, or maybe it scared her how the rest of the family avoided the subject like a taboo, how in some perverse way the departed woman's stature had grown into a daunting shadow simply because of the silence that enshrouded her.

"Try the hummus, honey," Peti attempted. "I just made it today."

"If you don't want to help me, that's okay. I guess it's not fair of me to put this on you."

Peti sighed. "Things were different then. Nowadays, depression, anxiety—everybody talks about these things all the time. It's all out in the open. But even just a few decades ago, the average person didn't know much about them. What your father saw in Kitty was someone who had become very angry, and when she wasn't angry, she was sad and withdrawn. The real Kitty, the one he'd married, was around less and less. You remember that, don't you?"

Molly would never forget that awful sense of her mother becoming someone best left alone, a parent slipping farther and farther away, all in plain view.

"At first, your father just thought Kitty was having a difficult adjustment to a new city, that she missed home. Then things got worse. They found her a doctor, but therapy and medication weren't helping. She was becoming unpredictable, so much so that your father was afraid to leave you and Davey alone with her—not because she would hurt you or anything, but because she would disappear to her room or the basement or simply not come home for hours at a time. You may not remember, but the very first time you kids ever met me, I picked you up at school. Your mother had disappeared that day, and your father asked me to come get you. He gave me pictures from his wallet so that I could find you in the dismissal line. I was a total stranger to you, but I explained that I worked with your dad, and eventually, after some rather intense negotiating with Davey, you both got into my car and I brought you to the station. Nobody knew where your mother was that day."

The older woman eyed her glass again, this time raising it to her lips and taking a shallow sip.

"Then one day she came home and said that she and her doctor were in love, that Barry understood her in a way that your father never could. So she was leaving."

"No. I don't buy it," Molly said. "Dad's not stupid. He knew she was sick. Didn't he see that Barry was just preying on a vulnerable patient? That man was a criminal. He should've lost his license. He should've gone to jail."

"Your father confronted Barry. He assumed your mother had become delusional, that this was some sort of transference thing and that running away with her therapist was a figment of her imagination. Your dad went and barged into the man's office one day. But she hadn't made it up. Barry was in love with her, and he didn't care if it cost him his practice and his livelihood. You remember how beautiful your mother was. She was a stunning woman. Bright and charming too. It seems crazy and wrong now, I know, but at the time it wasn't at all far-fetched."

Molly stared searchingly across the table, her fingers worrying her blonde mane. "My mom needed help, and nobody was there for her. Not her doctor, not her husband. How could Dad have just given up on her?"

"That's not how it was, honey. Your father couldn't bear the thought of his children losing their mother, but Kitty had made your house a waking nightmare. She was miserable all the time, and dangerously unreliable as a parent and a wife. In the end, your father was willing to let her go because he truly believed that you were all better off without her. Maybe it would've been different had he known just how sick she was. Maybe he wouldn't have given up on her. Knowing your father, he probably wouldn't have." There was honest anguish on her face, having to say these things to Molly. "But you're wrong that no one was there for her. Barry truly loved her. It wasn't a fling. He stayed with her."

Molly gazed through the glass doors that opened onto the deck. Outside was a silent, swaying wilderness of greens and browns.

"He's dead, you know," Molly said. "Barry."

Peti nodded; she knew. How had she known?

"My dad and Kitty are in touch, aren't they?"

"Somewhat. Yes."

"How often?"

"On and off over the years. It depends a lot on her, on how she's doing." Peti sighed. "I'm sorry he kept that from you all this time. When she first wrote to him—and it was a long time ago—he asked her not to contact you kids. He was trying to protect you. Anything she wanted to know about you and Davey she would have to learn through him. And I give her credit. She respected his wishes."

"Until now," said Molly.

Peti shrugged. "And why not? You're an adult."

Molly got up from the table, walked over to the glass doors, and slid them open. She stepped out onto the deck and leaned against the rail, looking down on the pool. A yellow inner tube, a tricolored beach ball, and a semi-inflated pair of water wings were clustered idly on the pool deck. The toys looked lonely, waiting there for Rachel to come back and play with them.

Molly knew what a lonely toy felt like. She'd been one, waiting upstairs to play classroom with the parent who had gone out to the garage and for some reason wouldn't come back inside, leaving Molly to sit by herself on one of the undersized chairs she'd arranged just so, the words "Miss Winger" scrawled in chalk on her Toys "R" Us blackboard. It was always Norman who eventually showed up, shuffling in with his tie unloosened, a smile stretched over the weariness of a long day and an even longer evening, offering another excuse for his wife. "Mommy doesn't feel great tonight." Then a clap of the hands. "Now. What are we playing, Molly-bear?"

Peti appeared next to her on the deck and pulled her shawl tighter, as if the flimsy silk embroidery could keep the evening breeze off her shoulders and neck. Together they watched the setting sun ripple through the gently stirring branches.

"I didn't want your mother out of the picture," Peti said. "It would be easy for you to believe that I did, but it wasn't like that. I cared for your father a great deal, and for you kids too. I wanted what was best for you."

"You don't need to say that, Peti. I've never doubted that."

"And yet," Peti said, "I've often wondered what would've happened if I hadn't been in the picture, if my marriage hadn't just ended. I wonder if maybe your dad would have fought harder for her. I guess we were falling in love, and I was another reason for him to let her go. I'm sorry for that, Molly. Believe me when I say that I really am sorry."

Molly now thought of all the fear that Peti had reckoned with for so long, the fear that Kitty would one day return, healed and healthy and repentant. It could've happened at any time, and it would've brought everything to an end for her. She would've lost them all, this family that had never belonged to her in the first place.

"You have nothing to apologize for," Molly told her. "You saved us, all of us. It's my dad who's been lying to me all my life."

Peti placed a hand atop Molly's. "Don't be angry with your father. He told you that Kitty fell in love with another man because that was easier for you kids to process than a truth that was so much uglier and messier. If he'd told you what your mother really was—how unwell, how damaged—you would've spent your childhood wondering why no one had been able to fix her."

They stood there quietly, listening to the thirsty slurp of the pool, watching the last of the sunlight flicker across the water's surface.

"The last thing your dad wanted was for you to grow up feeling like these women you write about," Peti said, a flutter having crept into her voice. Her eyes were flooding. "It breaks my heart to think of you feeling that way. I'm so proud of you, honey, but it breaks my heart that after all this time, you're still searching."

Molly couldn't recall a single instance in which Peti had cried. It had been a house strangely free of crying. She put an arm around the older woman. "No tears for me, Peti. I'm not one of them." Hugging her felt like a soothing relic of childhood, so much so that it brought on a swell of homesickness. "I've never felt like a deserted daughter, because I always had you."

———

Molly sat in her car outside the house at the foot of the driveway, her forearms on the steering wheel, eyes fixed blindly ahead, straight through the windshield. The past was different now, as was this ghost whom Molly had spent her life remembering in foggy glimpses. Instead of moodiness and misery, she now saw someone clinically broken, unable to free herself of a dark force tugging at her ankle. Someone in dire need of repair who may not have fully understood what she was doing when she left. Someone unfought for, but not unloved. Someone not beyond fault, but not beyond redemption either. Suddenly, it no longer mattered who'd been hiding and who'd been seeking, who was the track and who was the derailment.

She lifted her phone off the passenger seat and found her mother's email. She hit the reply button and typed.

Mom,

I am, as it happens, really happy to get your email. I have a lot of questions. I'm not ready to ask them of you now, but I think one day I will be. Soon, I hope.
In the meantime, I am still your daughter and you are still my mother. Thank you for telling me you're out there. I'm out here too.

Molly

CHAPTER 46

All through the night the plane hummed, ten hours over the world, from New York to Istanbul. Davis sat wide awake with his low-grade fear of flying, an unfortunate byproduct of an aborted takeoff in which he'd participated a few years back. No thrill ride could've prepared him for that experience, and since then he was convinced that every plane he boarded was on a direct route to a crash site. His heart rate always hiked as the engines growled and the absurdly heavy thing skipped off the runway. He tensed when the pilot came on and warned of "light chop" (turbulence was a subjective thing, and one man's light chop was another man's death spiral), and tried to imagine he was on a nice, safe roller coaster instead.

He reclined his seat as far back as it would go, and to the balm of pleasant snores drifting about the cabin, he opened the first chapter of the treatise on crying that Charlie had given him. Somewhere inside lay a cure. Maybe he would learn how to heal himself of it, or maybe he would learn not to heal himself of it, that it served a purpose, that crying itself was a form of healing. Later, while reading a *New York Times* article about an obscure eighteenth-century British explorer who sailed the South Pacific gifting the natives with Christianity and the printing press (two things they obviously couldn't live without), something wonderful happened. Davis drifted off. Mostly he dozed, but sometimes he even slept, until the plane began its descent into Istanbul.

During the layover until his flight connection to Izmir, he perused the English section of the airport bookstore and picked up a copy of *The Wit and Wisdom of Mark Twain*. He'd never read any Twain, not even *The Adventures of Huckleberry Finn*, a ridiculous, unforgivable gap in his literary escapades for which Britt had always chided him. Standing nearby was an older man in a seersucker suit. He looked the very picture of bygone southern American courtliness. It was an omen too glaring to ignore.

"You know, I've never read any Twain," Davis blurted out to the stranger.

The man understood English. Spoke it too. "In fact, I did not know that," he said, "but you're missing out."

"I should read it, shouldn't I? I should read some Twain before I die."

"You should do that very thing," the man said. "Because who knows if you'll have the opportunity afterward."

Davis paid for the tome and boarded his southbound connection. Throughout the entirety of the hour-long flight, he stared out at the brilliant sea waters, the sun-bleached houses, and the headstrong highways beating their way through the crusted terrain.

When he landed in Izmir, reminders of Britt were everywhere. The bleary-eyed exhilaration of deboarding a plane in a strange land brought to mind all the vacations the two of them had taken together. He saw her in the airport café, in the taxi lines where travelers yammered at each other in foreign languages, in the hotel lobby that smelled of the old stone artifacts on display. He kept expecting her to materialize with a map in her hand, point down the street toward the minarets of a mosque, and say, "I think we should start walking in that direction." Was there enough miracle left in the world to transport her to his side?

Brian had flown over a few days earlier to meet with captains of industry and would-be colonialists about projects in the emerging amusement park markets. Davis was to let him know when he arrived, so when the cab deposited him at the hotel, he stood beside his suitcase and thumbed out a text.

Hey, Brian. This is Davis. I'm here. What's the plan?

Brian's response came quickly. Glad you made it. I'll be tied up all afternoon, so relax a bit and get your bearings. Plan on meeting up for dinner around 7:30.

Davis wheeled his bag across the grand foyer to the reception counter. There he was greeted by a round-faced man with an intrepid cop 'stache across his lip and thick Scorsese eyebrows. His name tag read **Murat**. Murat checked Davis in and instantly gauged that he was the sort of traveler who was receptive to informality and joshing. "Oh good, the Americans are here," he joked through distantly accented English.

Davis asked for sightseeing advice, and the man ran a red pen up and down a map, helpfully charting Davis's day. "Like all Americans, you are restless for discovery, hmm?" said Murat.

"We like to think of it as conquest," Davis quipped.

His room was beautiful and stately, the walls and furniture all dark tones, the linens a luscious cream, the color of cake frosting. His first thought was how happy this room would have made Britt, whose tolerance for subpar accommodations was waning with age. Before Rachel had come along, they'd given little thought to the quality of their lodging. The time they hiked the Rockies, they'd selected a hotel because of its proximity to a glacier, even though its sole review on TripAdvisor had read, "Housekeeping stole my glasses. One star." He and Britt were unfazed; they both had perfect vision. But Britt had grown fussy as the years wore on, less tolerant of carpet stains, blemishes in the sink, and lethal microbes on the light switches.

Immediately after unpacking, Davis was back outside, walking briskly along the avenues, absorbing as much of the city as he could in an afternoon. He didn't know how much downtime there would be during the balance of his stay, so he made sure to eat baklava at the Kemeralti Market, to sit under a palm tree at the Saat Kulesi clock tower, and stroll among the ruins of the Agora Open Air Museum. "I'm in Turkey," he kept reminding himself, as he often did when traveling abroad. It was important to drink up the differentness of where he was, to celebrate the fact that he was somewhere he'd never been before and might never be again.

Later in the afternoon, the jetlag weighing on him like a three-martini hangover, Davis returned to the hotel and asked Murat if he could suggest a beach, something quiet and secluded, heavy on the sand and water, light on the people. Murat's mustache frowned; then he recommended the ideal spot for a twilight recluse. It sat on the outskirts of the city, accessible by public transportation. With Twain and a towel cinched into his daypack, Davis hopped on a bus and rode it until the cars and buildings faded into the rearview and he was the last remaining passenger on the vehicle. He hopped off and found the beach just as Murat had advertised. Not a soul in sight. Only the warm sand and the calypso-blue waters of the Aegean Sea. As good a place as any to disappear.

He dropped his backpack on the grass and slid out of his flip-flops. The blades felt sharp under his feet, and he took ginger steps to the edge of the sand, where the grains swaddled his toes. The beach was smooth, unblemished by rocks or shells, and it blended into the mild tide like a french kiss. Other than the rustle of a faint breeze stirring the olive branches and the occasional breath of a car engine up on the road, all was still.

He walked forward, closed his eyes, and felt the warm lapping flow around his ankles. *I'm in Turkey,* he said to himself. *I'm going to be okay. Rachel is going to be okay. We're all going to be fine.*

The next few seconds were a surreal burst upon his senses. The skidding of tires. The sight of a car hurtling off the ridge. The thunderous splash. The tiny Hyundai had taken the turn too fast and shot off the road. After clipping a tree, it plunged into the water not fifty yards from the very spot on the beach where Davis stood.

A trained and seasoned lifeguard, he sprang into action. He swam after the sinking car and glided down to it in smooth winged strokes. Inside the Hyundai, trapped behind the steering wheel, was a young woman, her eyes ablaze with panic. She thrashed at the enveloping waters, tiny bubbles exploding from her tight lips. Davis reached in, unclasped the girl's seat belt, and yanked her out by her arms. As soon as she fluttered through the window, he summoned every pulse of strength within him and pushed her by the hips toward the surface, then watched her skinny legs and dark streak of hair as she scissor-kicked up to safety.

It was then, just as he was about to follow after her, that the car let out an awful underwater groan. It had come to rest not on the seabed, but on a ledge of rocks and stones, and though stable for those initial moments, the rocks were now shifting under the car's heft. The vehicle creaked and turned in the slow-motion drench, then rolled onto his legs. He knew instantly that he was trapped.

Here was where Davis Winger would die. This was to be his open grave. Buried under a hunk of metal for all of time. All that was left to do was wait—for the salt water to fill his chest, for the sky to shimmer to black, for whatever came next.

Davis was sorry.

He yearned for his wife. Britt would never know that, regardless of what he'd said that night at the house, he would've never given up. Never. He'd set out that night hell-bent on not taking no for an answer, and yet that's exactly what he did. She would've taken him back if she really understood. That's what you do with the one who refuses to be refused. You find a way because you are more to each other than the pain you've caused.

Molly would be fine. She'd finally found her footing. Her career had taken off, and while her taste in men was still sketchy, there were plenty of people left in the world to look out for her—Norman, Britt, Peti, eventually even Rachel. She'd be okay without her older brother.

I got one, sis. One more before I go. You ready? It's a beach, the most beautiful beach in the world, and while the bathers are relaxing and enjoying the quietude, cars are flung on top of them from a nearby road. Run with it, Mol. It's a can't-miss.

Norman. For him, this would be hard. He'd weather another loss bravely, but this would knock a little life out of the old man. Like every son, Davis had always wanted to know more about his father, and he now regretted that so much of the man was still a mystery.

"Dad, tell me something about you that I don't know," he'd asked long ago.

Norman had grinned in a way Davis had never seen before. The grin of a rascal. "I once spent two nights in jail."

"You what?!"

"Don't you dare tell your sister."

"What did you do?"

"As a teenager, I ran away from home to join some protests in Mississippi. I went to a march and got myself arrested."

"Are you kidding me? You were a hippie?" Davis couldn't have asked for a more wonderful scoop. The Dylan, the psychedelic sixties music—it all finally made sense.

"Oh no, son. I was no hippie. I was a political activist. And my activism lasted all of a week, because your grandfather was, shall we say, displeased to have a son with an incarceration and a criminal record." Then slowly, the grin crept back. "Well, maybe I was a little bit of a hippie, after all."

Davis wished he had one more secret to take with him into the next world. *What else don't I know about you, Dad? What else will I never learn?*

Then something his father had once said to him returned. *We're all terribly unsure of ourselves, son, each one of us tunneling toward something strange.*

The end being near, Davis soothed himself with thoughts of his daughter. He saw Rachel on that first day of kindergarten once again. Her pigtails, her fearless little legs swinging under the tiny chair, the look of irritation she flashed him as he loitered by the door and had to be physically removed from the premises by Britt. It would still be years before Rachel's innocence was obliterated by the horrible truth that everything ends. Everything. The summer when you're sixteen. The vibrancy of your parents. The way your kid burrows into bed with you at six o'clock on a Saturday morning and falls back to sleep with her nose in the cushion of your cheek. It all leaves you, and it doesn't ever come back.

Could a person cry underwater? Did tears come? He'd read in Charlie's book that the evolutionary purpose of tears was the signaling of distress to those closest to us, a sign to our intimates, those near enough to see our eyes watering and to offer a hand. But there were no intimates here, no one to receive his SOS.

The death of Norman's mother the year before had brought a tide of questions from Rachel.

"What does it feel like to die?" she'd asked.

"It doesn't feel like anything," Davis told her.

"Everything feels like something."

"Well, since I've never died before, I can only speculate, but I imagine it feels like going to sleep."

"Was Great-Grandma afraid of dying?"

"I don't think she was overjoyed with the idea, but she was very, very old."

"How old?"

"Ninety-six, ninety-seven. Nobody really knows. They don't have records that far back. But no, little face, she wasn't scared. She was ready."

Davis was not ready. He'd never get to see his little girl as a first grader. He'd never get to sit beside her on the Sultan of the Indies, raise his arms into the air next to her and shriek in unison with wild joy. She would grow up without him and spend her life thinking of her father as someone in photographs, an occasional trespasser into her dreams, a remote memory incrementally nudged away behind newer ones. That thought crushed him more than any sunken Hyundai ever could. It enraged him.

Now Davis was angry.

He could handle the dying. It was the being gone he could not accept.

He thrashed and flailed and pummeled the steel with his fists and shoulders. He wailed a flurry of bubbles. Then another. Then another.

High above him at the surface of the sea there was only silence, not so much as a hint of the struggle below. Having swallowed up a car and a human life, the Aegean had returned to its peaceful, bath-like gargling.

———

The driver of the car crawled up the beach. Crouched on all fours, desperate gasps sputtering from her lungs, she looked back. She didn't see her rescuer. She screamed for help at a volume and voltage that her voice had never before attempted. But the cove, the road, the olive trees, the lonesome bus stop, the deepening blue of the sky, even the breeze—the world entire was as deaf and unmoved as the sea.

CHAPTER 47

Molly could only be so irritated at her brother for not answering. There was the seven-hour time difference, the desire to give his new employer undivided attention, the potentially incompatible cell services way over in Asia (or was it Europe?), and the fact that she hadn't tipped him off about why she was contacting him. Fleetingly, she'd considered enlisting Britt's assistance in reaching him, but better impulses prevailed. The woman had endured enough Winger family drama for one lifetime. Besides, in the end, this was only an emergency because Molly had decided to treat it like one.

At the falafel stand, Molly barely needed to participate in the lunchtime conversation. Bo had it covered. The convenient thing about Bo was that at the beginning of each conversation, she helped you out with a brief summary of all the relevant plot points in her life, such as the music scene she was trying to document, or her plans to finally move out of her parents' house. She was like a television show that brought you up to speed before each episode. "Previously on *Grey's Anatomy . . .*" Molly often wished she had a voice that whispered little reminders into her ear whenever she encountered the people in her life. *Previously on* **ADAM FROM DOWN THE BLOCK:** *a tree fell and wrecked his garage door last week, and his wife is having her gallbladder removed.*

Bo was talking about her upcoming excursion to New York to try to convince her sister, a marginally employed actress, to move back to Baltimore.

"She's broke and unhappy, she just won't admit it," Bo said, as the two women leaned against a brick wall and took bites of their pitas. "I'm not even going to tell her I'm coming. I'm just going to show up at her pad and talk some sense into the kid."

"I don't know," Molly said. "Surprise visits to unsuspecting family members—they don't always go as planned."

Bo scoffed. "Fuck that. I've got something to say. I'm going to talk and she's going to listen." Molly envied the clarity of purpose with which Bo forged her missions. "I can't make her do what I say, but I can tell her how I feel. She can't stop me." She wiped a stream of tahini sauce off her lips. "I honestly don't know whether my sister's a frustrated actress or just a shitty one."

Molly guessed that if you were the latter, it was only a matter of time before you became the former.

Everyone at the *Weekly Ramble* now seemed to walk around with a restored sense of stability. All over the country, people were subscribing to her podcast and clicking on her articles in thrilling numbers, and if that hadn't made the paper flush with cash or altered its fortunes forever, it had at least staved off insolvency and layoffs for the time being. Maternity Leave was not a permanent fix; it was a popular series that was bringing in money but was ultimately incapable of transforming an industry. It was a treatment, not a cure, and one day it would stop working. Richard would then have to figure out what was next. Molly would have to figure out what was next, too, for the paper and for her.

"I want you to know that we're all very impressed with you," Jamie had told her on a recent call. "We couldn't be happier that this has taken off, but either way, you're very highly thought of here at *Lotus*."

"Thank you, Jamie," Molly had replied. "I know I acted like a basket case at first, but I have to admit, this does feel pretty good."

"Let's ride this out," Jamie had suggested. "Maybe this endures. Maybe Molly Winger's tales of deserted daughters will be an institution. But if not, when it runs its course, we would all love to work with you again."

"Really? You would?"

Jamie laughed. "I thought we talked about camouflaging our self-doubt."

"Yeah," Molly chuckled. "I guess I've got a ways to go."

"We'll keep talking, you and I," Jamie said, before hanging up.

That evening, on her walk home through the Inner Harbor, Molly stopped to watch the children in paddleboats, their pinwheeling feet on the pedals, their parents raising cameras at them from the pier. A van from one of the local TV stations had pulled up to capture some footage, and for some reason it reminded Molly of the time, early in her tenure at the *Ramble*, when she was dispatched to cover a story at a nuclear power plant way up at the Pennsylvania state line. The facility had abruptly shut down, and a slew of employees had been fired after it was discovered that they'd been engaging in, according to the press release, "horseplay." Molly, a shrinking violet who trembled at the sight of most things—certainly at the nightmarish, Chernobyl-chic cooling towers of a nuclear reactor—was literally shaking as she walked in for the interview. She knew she lacked the journalistic chops to grill the plant rep on the precise nature of *horseplay*, an absurd term that conjured up images of technicians chasing each other with water guns around machines marked CAUTION: EXTREMELY HAZARDOUS MATERIALS, or debating whether a Wiffle ball that hit the chemical tank was fair or foul. But Molly surprised herself, even if she hadn't surprised her boss.

"You asked that man some very pointed questions," Richard had said to her after reading the draft of her article.

"I did?" Molly said.

"You put him on the spot. You didn't let him hide behind his PR script. Let this be a lesson to you."

"I will," she replied, vaguely. "The lesson being . . . ?"

"That you are capable of asking hard questions," Richard said. "That you aren't rattled by uncomfortable situations."

"Ah, but you see, Richard, I'm totally rattled by uncomfortable situations."

"Ah, but you see, Ms. Winger, you have the potential *not* to be."

Ever since Molly's heart-to-heart with Peti, Norman had been calling. He'd returned home that night, heard the whole story about Molly's visit and the email she'd received from Kitty, and left his daughter an empathetic and duly parental voice mail. "Molly-bear. Sounds like you and I have some things to talk about. Call me when you can. And please don't be upset." He'd left one or two more messages, but for now Molly couldn't bring herself to do anything but avoid him.

A father had every right to protect his children, even from their own mother, if need be. But for a long time now the children had been capable of deciding on their own whether to welcome or to refuse Kitty, and in what measure. The whole thing had left Molly with a miserable pang that more time had been lost than there needed to have been. And God knows there wasn't much of it to begin with.

Molly went upstairs to throw in a load of laundry, and something strange happened. As she dropped her clothes into the washing machine in the hall closet, that memory returned again, the one of finding her mother in the laundry room of the old house, the same memory that had resurfaced after her interview with LaTonya, one of her first deserted daughters. Again it came pouring back, like water flushing into the drum, and again she saw herself, a little girl with a piece of paper pinched between her fingers, flitting from room to room. *Mommy! I wrote a story for you!* And then there was Kitty, slumped against the dryer, a mess of tears.

But now, through the mist of time, a new detail took shape. When Kitty raised her face out of her palms and looked her young daughter in the eye, she'd spoken. *I'm not well,* were the words the desolate woman had sobbed. *I want to be well for you kids.*

Numbness advanced throughout Molly's body. She slid down the closet door, coming to rest in very nearly the same position in which she'd found Kitty on that afternoon decades ago. Of all the memories that had crept up out of the past to haunt her, why had this piece of information remained stubbornly unremembered until now? *I'm not well. I want to be well.*

A great sense of grief overtook her. It was for all the things Molly had never known. She'd grown up believing that her mother had been unhappy when all along she'd been unwell, and the dust-covered history of it all was that once upon a time, Kitty had even told her so.

She booked an airline ticket, then called Skyler.

"I think my mom tried to tell me she was in trouble," Molly said. "Before she left, I mean."

Molly relayed the scene in the laundry room, how she now recalled her mother's desperate prayer. She'd uttered it to the eight-year-old daughter who hadn't given up on her yet, who perhaps never would.

"She was reaching out to me," Molly said. "She was asking for my help."

"Maybe," Skyler said. "That's an old memory. You were really young."

"I'm going back there," Molly told her. "I've decided to go see her."

"In California?"

"Yeah."

Skyler paused. "Yeah, we're going to need to talk about that."

"My flight's tomorrow morning."

"Oh come on, Mol. Let's have a conversation first."

"We are. This is a conversation."

"At least wait for Davis," Skyler counseled. "He might want to go with you."

"Davis has his hands full. And you know he'll only try to talk me out of it."

"Maybe you should listen to him when he tries to talk you out of it."

"No," Molly said. "I don't think I'm going to do that."

There was an extended drip of silence.

"Okay. Fuck it," Skyler said. "What flight are you on?"

"Why?"

"I'm coming with you."

"No, you're not."

"I can't let you go see Joe alone."

"Joe?" Molly said.

"Joe Mama. Look, I was there for the first disaster. I should have to sit through the sequel."

"But what if this is something I should do alone?"

"Just listen to me, little chickie. For once."

"I listen to you all the time and I always regret it."

Skyler drew a worried breath. "I'm not down with this."

"The little chickie can handle Joe," Molly said. "The little chickie is going to be fine."

CHAPTER 48

Over the august country Molly blazed, six miles above backyards, factories, and amber waves of grain. She drank orange juice. Molly only drank orange juice on airplanes.

She was as jittery as the plastic cup quivering on the tray table in front of her, but she was not afraid. She'd moved past fear. Having spent her whole life not knowing, she would welcome the end of the uncertainty, whatever that ending was to be.

Neither Davis nor Norman had any idea that Molly was currently traversing the continent to visit Kitty. Her brother had been completely out of touch since leaving for Turkey, so the decision about whether or not to clue him in had resolved itself. As for her father, Molly had decided not to call him back. She knew it would hurt him to be blown off, which was not her intention, but nor could she stomach his all-too-reasonable explanations, his genial way that would make her feel silly for labeling him the enemy. So she headed west still dismayed that Norman could let his adult children labor under a misimpression about something so essential to their past and future selves.

McGuinn—him she'd called. She'd phoned him last night to let him know she was leaving for a few days, and what she was up to.

"Do you have any lines of verse you want to rattle off for me before I go?" she'd joked. Half joked, actually.

He thought for a moment, then said, "I'll do you one better. You've heard of Carl Sandburg, the Chicago poet?"

She remembered having read something by him in high school English.

"Check your email in a few minutes," McGuinn said. "I've got this audio clip of Sandburg reciting a poem called 'Evening Waterfall.' It's old, it's scratchy, and don't worry—it's not even a minute long."

"Is this a poem that's near and dear to your heart?" Molly asked, wanting to know just how much to read into the words.

"Not especially," he said. "I mean, I like it, but that's not the point of this exercise. I'm sending you this recording because I think there's something cool about the fact that no one else in the world will be listening to it except us. If we both put it on when you land, then at the same time that Carl is reading 'Evening Waterfall' to pretty little Molly on the West Coast, he'll also be reading it to big ugly McGuinn on the East Coast. And since it ain't exactly 'Thriller' or 'Hotel California,' we could assume that we'll be alone with it, you and I, every other ear in the universe preoccupied with lesser things."

Molly found that sentiment electrifying. The two of them separated by thousands of miles, but united in the insulated cosmos of their headphones by a single voice speaking only to them.

"This is pretentious, isn't it?" McGuinn said.

"No."

"A little hokey, though."

"I'm okay with hokey."

"And definitely clichéd. This is like the worst cliché."

"Clichés get a bad rap," she told him. "There are worse things than being a cliché."

Later that night, she cheated and listened to the clip, despite his specific instructions not to do so until her feet were on California soil. The old poet's voice scratched into her ears: *What was the name you called me? And why did you go so soon?*

How did he know?

Sinking into her window seat, Molly now imagined that the airplane was peppered with deserted daughters. Abigail and Jodi in the row behind her, Harper and LaTonya across the aisle, Beth and Annette and other faceless voices whom Molly had never met. All of these unshakable souls were up here in the cabin with her, having her back.

The jet sliced through streaks of high clouds over Ohio, perhaps directly above that old split-level in Columbus. With her wispy locks snaking over her cheek as if playing connect-the-dots with her freckles, Molly centered her neck against the headrest, closed her eyes, and slipped from waking consciousness. She dreamed she was flying on this very plane, and that as she leaned into the window to spot something on the ground, the glass gave way and she fell through it, plunging toward earth like a bomb. It was one of those dreams where you know it's a dream and decide to play along because the danger isn't real. So she celebrated the fall and the onrush of implacable wind, the tumbling of her legs over her head, the freedom to swim through the air.

She heard Sandburg again, the voiceover of his midwestern milk wagon timbre. *The crows lift their caw on the wind, and the wind changed and was lonely.*

The shimmying of her cup in the tray table's circular depression awakened her. She silenced it with a finger on the rim.

"Don't think this is going to be easy," Skyler had warned her last night before they'd hung up. "I know she wrote to you and all, but don't expect a champagne toast and an afternoon of photo albums."

But Molly had no expectations. There were no speeches she needed to hear, none she needed to deliver. Kitty Winger was just a woman, another adult human being who had no answers, who'd made mistakes, who for a long time had not been herself, and who probably couldn't be fixed by her child's acceptance but was unlikely to be harmed by it.

"I'm not rattled by uncomfortable situations," Molly had told Skyler. "Or at least I have the potential not to be. My editor told me that once, and I'm going to choose to believe him."

What was the name you called me? And why did you go so soon?

Molly gazed with jet pilot eyes through the small square airplane window, her pupils constricting against the sun's glint upon the wing. She had to laugh at what a summer it had been, at how every single thing about her world had begun to feel made up, as if she were a character in a fictionalized account of her own life.

CHAPTER 49

Davis would always remember that on the afternoon he showed up, the house smelled of his favorite dinner, Thai basil chicken. It was pure coincidence. She surely hadn't been cooking it for him.

Britt pulled open the door expecting to see Rachel, due to be dropped off any minute from a playdate, and instead saw her husband.

"Davis?" She tugged on Tweedy's collar so as to thwart a jailbreak by the animal she'd agreed to house—for Rachel's sake—while Davis was abroad.

"Can I come in?" he asked.

She regarded the suitcase standing upright behind him on the porch. "I didn't know you were back."

"Yeah. I'm back." He squatted to massage the hanging folds on the dog's fleshy head. "Is Rach home?"

Britt allowed him in. "She's at Gaby's. She'll be back in a few minutes."

"Mind if I wait? I really need to see her."

Britt eyed him in this state, disheveled and almost frighteningly distracted. "Are you all right?" she asked.

Davis just looked at her as she stood there in the foyer, her face delicate and mellow. He thought of the moment they'd met, that collision in the Palo Alto coffee shop. She was everything he'd wanted then and everything he wanted now, and still he'd found a way to bankrupt himself of her.

"You should sit down," she told him. "You're not yourself."

He suddenly lurched forward and threw his arms around her, pulling her into a tight clasp, permitting no space between them.

"Davis?" she said.

"I was a goner," he whispered.

"You're scaring me a little."

"I thought it was all over. I was trapped underwater. I couldn't move. I was going to die so far away from you and Rachel, on some stupid beach, in some stupid country. And that would've been it. The end."

"Slow down," Britt said. "What are you talking about?"

"One or two seconds longer and my lungs would've exploded and I would've drowned. I came so close to giving up and just letting it happen too. But I couldn't, because I didn't feel peace. There's supposed to be peace." He shook his head. "It didn't come. I wasn't ready."

A look of alarm made an anxious oval of Britt's mouth as she gawked at her husband.

"I need you to hear this," he went on. "Since the day I met you, I have never thought about being with anyone else. Every man dreams of both loving his wife and lusting after her, of the inseparability of those two things in the person he wakes up to. And I have it. You want to know what makes me different from every guy I know? I have fantasies about my wife. No lie—the woman I've been with for ten years. When you're not around to be naked with, I think about being naked with you. You think I send you all those racy texts as a joke? I think about lying under our covers and gliding my hand up your leg, hearing the quickening of your breath—"

"I'm going to stop you there," Britt said.

"But you see my point."

"I'm not sure I do."

"I've always known that with you, I won the lottery. I slept with that woman in Virginia *one time*. It should've been no times, but it was once, and you know why it was only once? Because it wasn't you. Yes, I felt guilty. Yes, I knew I was doing something wrong. But the heart of it all, the absolute truth—the stone groove—is that the whole thing left me cold because she didn't measure up. Nobody's calling me a hero. I don't expect you to thank me for betraying you on only one occasion. But you need to know the truth right now because—Christ Jesus, Britt—I came *this* close to losing the chance to tell you."

"Davis, wait—"

"Let me get this out." He looked her square in the eye. "I fought my way out from under that Hyundai, and I'm not going to stop fighting now. You know how badly I want to undo what I did. I'm done apologizing. That time has passed. Now it's time for me to take back what's mine. You're mine, Britt. I know that sounds sexist, and it probably is, but fuck it. I don't care. You were born for me, you belong to me, and you know it. You are wonderful and beautiful and good, and there are armies of men who would jump at the chance to gather what I've spilled, to spend every waking second of their short lives with you. But they'll never feel the way I do. They just won't. Not one of them. I deserve a second chance. I won't deserve a third, but it'll never come to that. I refuse to let you go."

Britt was a wreckage of incredulity. She stared at him, gripping both of his shoulders, not knowing what to make of any of this. "How in the world did you end up under a Hyundai?"

"My decision-making has been spotty of late, if you haven't noticed. But the driver survived, so I suppose I can finally call myself a lifeguard." He shook his head and groaned. "Waterlogged young women. They're going to be the death of me."

She reached for his hand and braided her fingers into his. "My god, Davis."

They stared at each other a long time. Then he sniffed at the air like a bloodhound. "You're making Thai basil chicken, aren't you?"

"I am," Britt said.

"That just hurts, man." It was the holiest of gastronomic holies.

"I have to admit, right after you moved out, I made it all the time, hoping you were close enough to smell it," she said.

"Spite cooking. I deserve that."

"As it happens, revenge is a dish occasionally served hot," Britt said.

"That reminds me," Davis said. "I finally read that Mark Twain guy you've been wanting me to read. Checked it out on the plane home. He's not bad."

"No, he's not."

"He taught me this little nugget: 'Forgiveness is the fragrance that the violet sheds on the heel that has crushed it.'"

He raised an eyebrow and waited for her to be impressed, but she raised an eyebrow of her own, and hers meant business. "And what do you suppose that means, Davis?"

"I don't know, but I think I'm the heel." He hugged her again. "I'm so sorry I was the heel," he whispered.

He pondered the comfort of her cheek against his sleeve. He saw the tears that slipped from the corners of her eyes.

"I'm glad you didn't drown," she said.

"I was hoping you'd feel that way."

"I don't want you gone, Davis. You know that, right?"

"I can't say I was sure of it, but thank you for saying that." Then he pulled back. "However, I am leaving again. I have to go to San Francisco tomorrow."

"San Francisco? Another work trip?"

"Actually, Molly's out there, and I kind of need to join her."

"Hold on. Your sister is in San Francisco? As of when?"

"This morning."

"Why?"

"Well, it's super trippy to be saying this, but"—his eyes went wide at the insanity of it—"she's visiting my mother."

"Your mother?" Britt was apparently running out of means to absorb the blitzkrieg of calamities that had come barging through her door.

"Don't ask," Davis said.

"I'm asking."

Between the long flights and the fiasco on that beach in Izmir, Davis hadn't gotten around to returning his sister's call until landing in the States little more than an hour ago. When he and Molly finally spoke, each of them hovering around a baggage carousel, he at Dulles, she at SFO, Davis had listened, slack-jawed, speechless, head spinning, as Molly brought him up to speed on all the family madness he'd missed. Kitty's email. Molly's confab with Tom Petty. Severely belated epiphanies regarding their mom's psychological erratica.

"I still don't understand," Davis had complained to his sister, staggering away from the baggage claim crowd, leaving his lonely little piece of luggage on the carousel. "Why did you race out there like a crazy person?"

"Because I want to talk to her, and she wants to talk to us, and suddenly the past twenty years aren't what we thought they were."

"My question stands."

Molly huffed with irritation. "This is why I came without you. I knew you wouldn't be able to handle it."

In point of fact, he'd handled quite a bit in recent hours. Quite a bit. He saw his bedraggled self in the reflection of a window. What was it about long flights that made people look like shit? You just sat there.

"I guess you want me to come out there with you," said Davis.

"No, I don't," said Molly.

Davis sighed. "Okay, fine. I'm coming. Sit tight for one more day."

"Wait. Why?"

"Because you want me to be there."

"No, *you* want you to be there."

"We'll sort this out when I arrive."

But nothing anyone could throw at him today—not even that—could diminish the impossible gratitude he felt at being home, being on dry land, being nearer to his wife and daughter. It was a thrill to be alive, even if being alive meant that sometimes you found yourself trudging up the shores of an unknown continent in leaden boots. Battling the winds of some tempest hell-bent on knocking you on your ass.

Tweedy suddenly charged at the front door in response to a knock. Davis pulled it open, and there was Rachel, looking startled. "What are you doing here?" It was an extraordinary thing she beheld, her father in the house without her there to supervise.

"Get on up in here!" he crowed, opening his arms and letting her charge into him like a pint-size linebacker.

"You came back from Turkey?" This was somehow a question. "Mommy, look! Daddy came home!"

"I noticed," said Britt.

"Did you see Tweedy?" Rachel asked him. "Isn't he adorable beyond words?"

"Hmm," Davis mused. "Is he?"

"He's the sexiest dog in the land!" she declared.

"A conversation for another day."

With the three of them standing there in the foyer, Davis found himself imagining another Wondrous Life of the Fabulous Rachel Winger, another future, one without Vespas or Nepal or Soho smoke dens. In this one, Rachel lived in a house just like theirs, in a neighborhood just like theirs—not too far, in fact, a twenty-minute drive at most—and on Sundays in December, Davis and Britt came over with wine, red velvet cupcakes, and some of Britt's delectables, and they noised up the house playing games with Rachel's children while the embers of the fireplace danced over the street. Oh, how wondrous! Oh, how fabulous!

Davis knelt down, reaching eye level with his daughter. "Listen, little face, you and I have a lot to talk about."

"We do?"

"We do. You know those people in Turkey I went to meet?"

"The Turkeys?"

"Yes, the Turkeys. The Turkeys want to build our magic carpet ride. They absolutely loved it, and they wanted to know all about the little girl who came up with the idea."

"Are you literally serious?" she asked.

"Literally."

"So it's going to happen? Like, for real?"

"It's going to happen. Like, for real," he said. "The Sultan of the Indies is going to be a ride, and it's all because of you."

"Well, you helped, Daddy."

"I guess maybe a little bit. Listen, I'm not saying you're going to be famous, but I'm not saying you're not going to be famous either."

They high-fived.

"But first I have to go away again," he told her. "Just a quick trip this time. To California with Aunt Molly. I'll only be gone a few days."

"Will you be back for my first day of school? It's on Tuesday."

"Girlfriend, please. Would I miss that?"

Then the geography of Rachel's face scrambled. "Wait. Why are you going to California with Aunt Molly?"

For a moment Davis couldn't find his voice. The words he wanted to form felt utterly foreign on his own tongue, a sentence he'd never expected to say in the whole of his life.

"Because," he said, through a mangled smile, "my mommy needs me. Now—where's me hug? Where's me kiss?"

CHAPTER 50

Molly arrived at the airport in a Dodge Neon, the cheapest rental available, just as Davis emerged from the terminal. He tossed his overnight bag into the trunk, and they eyed each other guardedly in the cool San Francisco air.

"Hi, sister," Davis said.

"Hi, brother."

They hugged; Molly got behind the wheel; they drove off.

"I want you to know that I'm okay with the whole McGuinn thing," he announced as they headed north in the scabrous lanes of Highway 101. "I give you my blessing."

"You do?" she said. "Gee, thanks. That's awfully important to me."

"I disapproved initially because—well, for a number of reasons we don't need to go into. But I see things differently now. Want to hear why?"

"I can't physically stop you from talking, but I'm already tuning you out."

Her brother had tried to keep McGuinn away from her; her father had tried to keep Kitty away from her. How nice to always believe you knew better. Couldn't people just mind their own business?

"I felt better about him after he told me he writes poems," Davis said. "You know about the poems, right?"

"I do."

"I don't know why I take comfort in that. Poets are fucking bananas. They're alcoholics, they go through women like it earns them miles, and they all end up depressed and suicidal. But since I figure McGuinn is probably a crappy poet, mediocre at best, the risk seems lower that he behaves like one."

Molly nodded at the windshield. "As I said, I'm not really paying attention."

In truth, she had no clue as to the literary merit of McGuinn's work, but unless his poems sucked spectacularly—undeniably, hilariously—it never would've occurred to her to critique them. That was hardly the miracle.

"I told Dad about this little expedition of ours," Davis volunteered. "He said you're not speaking to him."

"I'm not," she replied, a wedge of petulance in her voice that struck even her as unbecoming. "I'm angry with him." She looked across the seat. "Aren't you?"

It hadn't occurred to Davis to find fault with his father's protective impulses. "I guess I'm not," he said.

"Why? He withheld a lot from us, Davis. He withheld *her* from us, our own mother. I know he thought he was doing the right thing, but he wasn't. We're adults, and we have been for a long time. Everything could've been different."

"Not everything would've been different," he said.

"But everything *is* different now. Don't you see?"

"I understand you're upset, Mol, but you can't be angry at the old man. He's the parent who stayed, remember? He gave us normalcy, and under those circumstances normal was extraordinary. You and I had kickass childhoods, and it was because of him."

She rolled her eyes. Davis was going to have a kickass childhood regardless; he would've always made it so. She, on the other hand, had a good childhood. She was cared for and loved. But it was not a childhood free from wondering or doubt.

"Dad doesn't get a free pass for every deed or decision for the rest of his life just because he was a good father," she said.

"Look. You want to be mad for a while? Be mad," Davis said. "But you have to forgive him, Molly. He made a judgment call. You might think it was the wrong one, you might even be right that it was the wrong one, but the guy vowed never to let that woman hurt us again, and he's been working ever since to keep that promise."

"She was sick, Davis," Molly said. "The woman was sick, and Dad gave her a life sentence."

Davis threw up his hands and cracked the window as though he might climb out. Molly looked over at him, this brother of hers who had never before expressed a single thought about Kitty and had suddenly become a champion for amnesty. This wasn't like him. He looked truly distressed, which also wasn't like him. It startled her.

"Relax, Davis," she said. "Of course I'm going to forgive him. I just need a little time."

He looked relieved. Clearly, he'd needed to hear her acknowledge that Norman's crimes were pardonable, that her grudges were too great a burden to carry around for very long. That, in the end, this was a family that forgives.

Davis reached out and pressed down on the loudly twitching dashboard. This rental had all the roadworthiness of a Big Wheel, its meager tin frame knocked around by the light wind, jerking in and out of neighboring lanes as though they were plowing through the gusts of a category-five hurricane. He wished it had been a Neon that had landed on him back in the Aegean. He could've swatted it away with one hand.

"Hey, Davis?"

"Yeah?" He was shifting around in the passenger seat like he was being born. The stiffness and pent-up restlessness of so many long flights evidently clung to his back and legs and neck, making it impossible for him to get comfortable.

"Do you remember the night Mom left?"

"No." He kneaded the shadowy stubble on his chin. "Do you?"

"I think so," she said. "There was a lot of arguing, which got you and me out of bed. We went down to the kitchen, and it was quite an ugly scene. Dad was yelling at Mom, and Mom was crying. But I also remember thinking that something just wasn't right, like this wasn't really her."

Davis shrugged. "I don't remember that."

"I was so petrified, shaking," Molly went on. "You know what else I remember? I remember that you weren't. Even back then, you were so strong. You were eleven years old, your world was falling apart, and you were taking care of your little sister. You lay in bed next to me, you held my hand until I fell asleep. You don't realize how lucky you are to go through life with your circuitry. Because my circuitry has done me no favors."

Davis said nothing. He stared out in contemplation of the highway.

After a while, Molly asked him if he ever thought about Peti.

"I think about how she's an 'American Girl,'" Davis replied.

"I've been thinking about her a lot since my conversation with her that day at their house," Molly said. "I think about what that poor woman went through."

"Yeah, that whole situation was a heartbreaker, no doubt about it," Davis said. "But she's a tough old girl. She was like, 'I Won't Back Down.'"

"Our house was a monumental mess," Molly continued, ignoring him, "and she just waltzed in and started cleaning it up, very quietly, without anyone asking her to."

"Well, she was 'Runnin' Down a Dream,'" Davis said.

"Can you be serious? For a minute?"

"And she was 'A Woman in Love.'"

"Just for a minute?"

He looked over at her. "Can't you see how hard I'm trying not to be?"

After they passed through the Financial District, I-80 led them out over the water and into the East Bay. With the chiseled city behind them, Davis felt the rush of salt air all over his face and in the tight knots of his hair.

"I went to see her, you know," Molly said. "Back in college."

"Who?" He looked at her. "Mom?"

Molly nodded. "I found her online and drove all the way out here. Skyler came with me."

"You never told me that."

"No, I didn't. I never told Dad either."

Davis stared at his sister's profile. "What happened?"

Her lips twisted into a bitter smile. "She told me to get lost."

"She did not."

"She opened the door, looked at me, and literally told me to leave and never come back. And I never did."

A vector of wind sliced through her window. She rolled it up, reducing the roar to a whistle.

For Davis, the thought of his sister being chased off her own mother's front porch after driving through three time zones—the picture of her so hopeful and defenseless—was almost unbearable. "That actually makes me a little sick," he said.

How different he was from her, he thought. He'd spent two years at Stanford, and even though he'd known that Kitty had run off to California, not once had he thought to look her up.

And then, quietly, in her timid little Molly voice, Molly did something she rarely did. She began to sing. The song was "Don't Come Around Here No More." She looked over at her brother. "Aren't you impressed? That's Tom Petty, isn't it?"

"You should've told me," Davis said.

"I wanted to forget it." He could see the vapor of hurt clinging to her.

"Now that I know, I wish I could forget it too," he said.

A muscle spasm flared in Molly's left quadriceps, and she reached down to massage the top of her leg. Such was the fallout of all the miles she'd hoofed yesterday on the steep streets of the city, a deliberate attempt to tire herself out, to zap her mind of the energy to worry while awaiting her brother's arrival.

"Are you and Britt okay?" she asked.

Davis puffed his cheeks up with air and slowly let it out. "Yeah. I actually think we might be."

Britt had let him stick around yesterday, allowed him to partake of her Thai basil chicken after all, to toe a soccer ball with Rachel out on the front lawn, and to watch the impromptu fashion show staged by the rising first grader, who'd wanted to model her new school clothes. Britt had even let him tuck Rachel into bed and read her a story. She'd chosen a new one, one that had nothing to do with flying carpets, nothing that might involve homework.

"She still loves you," Molly told him.

"She said that when I get back, we could talk about me moving back in."

Molly was warmed by this, the promise of another broken fragment of her world locking back into place. "I'm happy for you," she said. "I'm happy for all of us."

Davis smiled weakly. "I was beginning to think it was too late."

As if on cue, they passed a road sign warning them that their Walnut Creek exit was a mile away.

Molly threw her brother a direful look. "Until further notice, it's never too late."

CHAPTER 51

No sooner had Molly steered the feisty Dodge onto the exit ramp than she was stricken with déjà vu. She'd been here only once before, a long time ago, yet she vaguely recognized the sequence of shopping centers and gas stations along the main thoroughfare, the way the road descended steeply down a hill into an intersection. Street names—Ygnacio Valley, Las Lomas—rang distantly familiar. The turns and stop signs that guided them farther from town and into the winding streets where Kitty Winger lived, where she'd been living her life all this time while her children were living theirs three thousand miles away, came flooding back in a way that churned Molly's stomach.

At the sight of the house, her foot came down heavy on the brake. Slowly she looped around and parked on the opposite curb, a safe, anonymous distance. She killed the engine, and the two of them stared up the driveway.

The house seemed to have shed years, as opposed to having collected them. It looked cared for, attended to, perhaps a hopeful reflection of the woman living there. The wood siding, a drab beige in Molly's memory, was now an almost inviting firepit brown. The shrubs, which she remembered as having been neglected to a state of wildness, looked loyally manicured. Even the wide rectangle of the garage door was free of scratches and weather stains. Then again, this was California. What weather was there to speak of?

Molly thought of the Sandburg poem. *What was the name you called me? And why did you go so soon?*

She looked at her brother. "Are you ready?"

Davis was holding the house in a confrontational gaze, as though it were a wild animal. "What if she's not home?" he asked.

"We wait," she replied.

He nodded, but didn't move.

"Let's go," she said.

"Hey, Mol?"

"What?" She wanted to get on with it before she lost her nerve. When he didn't speak, she repeated herself. "What?"

"I do remember that night—the night she left," he said, not taking his eyes off the house. "I don't know why I said I didn't. I remember it like it was yesterday. And I was just as scared as you were. I slept in your bed that night because it made *me* feel better. *You* were holding *my* hand."

"Okay," she said, looking at the side of his face. "It doesn't matter."

"Of course it matters. I want to set the record straight with regards to my circuitry. And yours."

Little streams were spilling out of his eyes. His lips were moving, syllables being mouthed under his breath as though he were praying.

"Davis? Are you crying?"

"No," he said, his voice warbling through a sniffle. He was groping for the roster of ballplayers of yore. But this meltdown felt unlike the others. He wasn't convulsing over widowed brothers in Seattle, cancer-stricken fathers in Michigan, or condemned killers in Texas. This episode was about him. Davis was a character in his own conniption.

"I don't think I've ever seen you cry," Molly marveled.

"Well," he said, wiping his face with the palm of his hand. "I cry all the time. Happy?"

The confession brought an unbefitting smile to his sister's face. His fear and vulnerability, so imperfect, so pardonable, was a hundred times more reassuring than all that enigmatic strength.

"It's going to be okay," she told him. "You've had a rough summer, Davis. But summer is over."

He looked at her nakedly. "I'm not the person everyone thinks I am."

"You're close enough. And that will have to do." Then she smiled. "It could be worse. You could be me. I'm exactly the person everyone thinks I am."

He sniffed. "Some of us are grateful for that every day."

She reached over and squeezed his arm, then gripped the door handle. "Let's do this."

"Wait," he said. "Hold on. How about one for the road?" She was giving him a blank stare. "You know what I mean."

"Really?" she groaned. "Now?"

"Really. Now."

"Fine. Go. Don't think I don't know you're stalling."

"Don't think I don't know you know that," he retorted. "Okay. Ready?"

"Yes."

"Hold on tight, this is going to get ugly."

"Just go!"

"Okay. It's a used-underwear store. Pre-owned undies. That's all we sell."

She gasped. "That's so out of bounds I can't even."

"And not just women's. That would almost be okay," he said. "We're selling men's too."

"Now you've gone too far." And she tried to laugh. Laughing at these ridiculous ventures would feel normal, like she and her brother weren't about to cross an unremarkable street on an ordinary day, knock on the door of the most typical-looking American house, and watch everything change in a way that could never change back.

"Now you go," he said, trying to bury a note of desperation.

Molly stared into the diffused afternoon sunlight, hunting for inspiration on front lawns, mailbox posts, and uncollected newspapers.

"Okay. How about an adventure tour company that you don't know is an adventure tour company?"

"Go on," said Davis.

"It's like a travel agency with a secret and possibly dangerous agenda. You book your vacation, but when you show up, all kinds of crazy happens. They drop you in the middle of the wilderness with a backpack and a canteen, or they take you out in a boat and force you onto a raft in the middle of the ocean. You didn't want an adventure, you certainly didn't plan for one, but there you are."

"Huh. So, like, they put you in the penthouse of a hotel, then set the motherfucker on fire."

"Exactly. Or they take you to the top of a mountain—you might have a baby with you—and they just let you out and wish you luck. This is something you pay for, by the way. It doesn't come cheap."

Davis was frowning. "I have to be honest. This one deeply concerns me. Sometimes you just want things to go smoothly."

"Yeah, but that's the point. They never do."

"A surprise adventure company," Davis said, slow and pensive. "Isn't that just what happens when you step out of the house every day?"

"And that's why it's a bad business idea, not a good one," Molly said. "Nobody will want any part of it."

"Of course not. It's atrocious."

"The worst," she said.

They looked at each other one last time, then pushed open their car doors and headed up the walkway. It was the second time Molly Winger was making this journey, her second trek over this trail of concrete carrying only the hope that a missing piece, the shape of which she couldn't possibly know, lay at the end of it.

Molly's was the first fist to rise. She knocked.

As they waited, her mind flashed to something her father had said. Words of wisdom, or perhaps just a comforting turn of phrase, offered to her that night they'd gone out to dinner. *We're all terribly unsure of ourselves,* he'd said, *each one of us tunneling toward something strange.*

There were signs of life deep inside the house now. Then footsteps in the foyer. On the other side of the door, a woman's eye peered into the peephole. There was a pause, then a hand on the knob, and then Kitty Winger opened the door and found her children, their faces echoing with so many yesterdays gone and the promise of all the good tomorrows to come. She stepped onto the porch, and together they stood there, all three of them trying to breathe, not one of them knowing what in the world was coming next.

ACKNOWLEDGMENTS

This book doesn't happen without the support, encouragement, and sweat of so many:

My agent, Caryn Karmatz Rudy of DeFiore and Company, who is evidently capable of miracles, who suffers through all my drafts without firing me (thus far), and who has an endless supply of ideas I wish I'd thought of. Thank you. To put it mildly, I'm eternally grateful.

Chris Werner at Lake Union, to whom I am deeply indebted for his commitment and enthusiasm, for not only making this book happen, but for making it so much better. Heartfelt thanks to Chris, Megan Mulder, Nicole Pomeroy, Kristin King, and all the terrific, hardworking folks at Lake Union.

Kimberly Glyder, for *another* perfect cover design. Here's hoping people judge this book by its cover!

Tiffany Yates Martin, my editor, whose insights and suggestions, both large and small, improved this book exponentially, who deepened this story in countless places, who was always generous with ideas and overflowing with passion, and who, on top of everything else, is an absolute joy to work with. Thank you, Tiffany.

Ferne and Les Abramowitz, my parents, two wonderful people who taught me literally everything and, perhaps most importantly, to care about the right things. I couldn't have written about a family in such need of repair without being raised in one so overflowing with warmth, love, and all the best kinds of chaos.

It's not much of a challenge to write about siblings who get along so well when you've lived it your entire life, and I have my sister, Michelle Clay, and brother, Jon Abramowitz, whose friendship I truly cherish, to thank for that. This book wouldn't be possible without them. To boot, both have sweetened the deal by marrying so well. Thanks for bringing Mitch Clay and Stacy Abramowitz home to meet the fam.

Terry and Elliott Langbaum, for all the love and support. I won the lottery when it comes to in-laws.

David Small, whose trusted, insightful, and ever eloquent voice has been a tremendous source of inspiration and has guided my writing since I first put "pen" to "paper." I am lucky to call one of my very favorite authors a friend.

And then there are those whose encouragement and friendship have helped push this book along. Some of you know you who are, others may not, so heartfelt thanks goes out to Melissa April, Jonathan Palmatier, Gregg Marsano, Amy Montemarano, Rich Coughlin, Jamie and Michael Cohen (#notthatMichaelCohen), Marc Greenberg, Andy and Kelly Goldenberg, Sally Kim, Kim Roosevelt, and many others.

Chloe and Chelsea. Girls, my favorite thing in the world is being your dad. This book about siblings who stand by each other and behind each other through life is for you. (Incidentally, I've noticed that you keep getting older. I thought we talked about that.)

And Caryn, my wife, beautiful in all respects, especially the ones that matter most. We hold each other together, but you do most of the heavy lifting. I've said it before, I'll say it again: our stories are my favorites. But I didn't have to say that again, because you know.

ABOUT THE AUTHOR

Photo © 2018 Jonathan Palmatier

Andy Abramowitz is the author of one previous novel, *Thank You, Goodnight*. A native of Baltimore, he lives with his wife, two daughters, and their bichon poodle in Philadelphia, where he enjoys classic rock, pitchers' duels, birthday cake, the sound of a Fender Rhodes piano, and the month of October. He could never build a roller coaster, not even if his daughters begged him to, because he's terrible at math and he can't draw.